DOMINION

THE ENERGUMEN CHRONICLES
BOOK ONE

T.J. FALCO

QUO VADIS PRESS

Copyright © 2024 by T. J. Falco

Published in the United States by Quo Vadis Press.

T. J. Falco

Dominion: a novel / T. J. Falco

p. cm.

ISBN 978-09862438-6-8

Paranormal—Fiction. 2. Apocalypse—Fiction.
3. Vatican—Fiction. 4. Astronomy—Fiction. 5. Alchemy—Fiction.

Exorcism language courtesy of the Roman Ritual
(*Rituale Romanum*), one of the books commonly used during the
official rites of the Holy Roman Catholic Church.

Excerpt from the alleged third secret of Fatima courtesy of the
official translation revealed to the public by
Cardinal Joseph Ratzinger.

Book design by Phil Rinaldi
Printed in the United States of America on acid-free paper

First Edition

To My Steve
For Everything

*"The greatest evil is not now done in those sordid
'dens of crime' that Dickens loved to paint.
It is not done even in concentration camps and labour camps.
In those we see its final result. But it is conceived and ordered
(moved, seconded, carried, and minuted)
in clean, carpeted, warmed, and well-lighted offices,
by quiet men with white collars and cut fingernails
and smooth-shaven cheeks who do not need to raise their
voices."*

C. S. Lewis

*"The individual is handicapped by coming face to face
with a conspiracy so monstrous he cannot believe it exists."*

J. Edgar Hoover

ASHES

SEPTEMBER, 1958

Coimbra, Portugal

At precisely three-ten on a clear, moonless night, two shrouded figures waited beneath a tall wrought-iron gate. The man wore a cassock and Roman collar, his stout companion, the long woolen habit of a Carmelite. In the absence of the light welcoming travelers seeking shelter, they remained invisible, blending seamlessly into the shadows while crickets chirped their last summer songs and distant voices rose in chant. Both muffled the approach of the old woman who unlocked the gate and beckoned them within.

The couple followed the prioress through the small courtyard and into the convent silently. They hurried along the empty corridors with their heads down, while their guide cast furtive glances, her mouth reduced to a thin, white line. She halted before a padlocked door, conspicuous and forbidding in a line of otherwise open cells inviting scrutiny, undid the latch, followed the newcomers inside and bolted it.

Free at last from prying eyes, they allowed theirs to adjust to the candle-lit room and studied the emaciated woman on the narrow cot curiously. Her suffering was evident; the haggard lines, the sunken cheeks of one whose weight loss was neither slow nor intended; the fine sweat beading her brow. Nevertheless she raised a feeble arm.

The prioress rewarded her with a quivering smile.

"Are you sure she won't feel any pain?"

From a concealed pocket in the lining of his cassock, the priest drew out a small bottle and syringe, filled it and tapped it twice. "Quite sure but if it makes you feel better, pretend we're putting down a dog. I have a better question. Why is she still awake?"

"I assure you I put the sedative in her last meal myself."

"Don't tie your wimple in a knot; would've been easier is all."

The sick woman moaned. Despite her weakened state, her watery eyes traveled from the old nun to the priest and back again as if hoping to glimpse a fragment of compassion. She was met with revulsion in the one, indifference in the other.

"Now then, Sister, no need to fret."

"Enough with the small talk. The others will be returning soon. They must never know I was here."

Syringe firmly in hand, the priest approached the woman, ignoring the accusations hurled at him through her steady gaze. Still, he hesitated, studied the shrunken form, and brushed a strand of dark matted hair from her eyes.

"Tell me...would you do it all again? Would you still be so passionate? So resolute? Or would you have renounced everything if you knew it would end like this?"

A frail voice caught him off guard. He leaned in, straining to hear the barely-audible words.

"Warn them...you must warn them before it is too late."

"Who is there to warn, Sister? Surely you don't mean the scourge of useless eaters calling itself humanity? At least their deaths will be a tribute to their otherwise insignificant lives."

"Not just them. I speak of your brethren...the ones you serve. He is coming to feed on them too." In a feat of surprising strength, she clutched the front of his cassock and forced his ear to her lips.

"And on you."

The priest wrenched from her grasp. For a moment, the prioress glimpsed doubt behind his eyes, but it faded with his next words.

"It seems we have our answer; delusional to the very end. You...hold her feet!"

Shaken free of her trance, the nun obeyed, flinching as he ripped open the woman's sleeve, exposing skin that had grown too soft and flabby in the wake of her illness. With one hand, he jerked her arm up and over her head, pinning it in the unlikely event she resisted. With the other, he drove the needle into her armpit, ignoring the shudders that ripped through her body. Impatient, he pumped the golden liquid all at once, nearly broke off the tip as he yanked it out, and studied her closely for a reaction, the labored movement of her chest.

It was too late. Lips that had mouthed their plea stiffened in some premature form of rigor mortis, while a filmy sheen glazed over the eyes that had probed his only seconds before. Refusing to be silenced even in death, a single tear trickled down her cheek, more eloquent than any words she could have spoken in life.

A strange silence enveloped the tiny room, made more profound by the knowledge of what had just been accomplished. Powerless to look away from the body, the old nun drew in a sharp breath and crossed herself.

The priest smirked. "A little late for attacks of conscience." He turned as the third observer to these events emerged from the shadows, all the more pale due to what she'd witnessed. "My orders were to eliminate a pebble before it grew into something irritating. Mission accomplished. I trust you can handle it from here. If there's one thing I hate it's having to fix others' mistakes."

"You have my word," the prioress mumbled, watching as he shrouded the bed linens over the dead woman and lifted her easily, the wasting away she'd done for months making his load unquestionably lighter. Eager to be rid of him, she cracked open the door and peered into the dim light as he receded down the corridor with what appeared to be only a rag-tag pile of blankets in his arms then eased it shut.

Reassured by the lingering voices of her sisters finishing their nightly ritual, she turned her attention to the silent figure behind her reluctantly, unable to reconcile the silhouetted form still clinging to the darkness with the enormity of this moment.

"You received your instructions."

"Of course. For more than a year I have prepared for this assignment. Ask me anything. I am certain I know the most intimate..."

"Quiet. Listen to me carefully. You will remain locked in this cell until further notice. If anyone attempts to communicate with you, you will not respond. Come into the light," she motioned, studying the face before her; the higher cheek bones, the decisively

Anglo features and of course, most conspicuously, the nose, teeth and jaw line. Too late to do anything about those but, all in all, not a bad imitation. Over time perhaps, as she aged...

She let the thought die. A sudden overwhelming weariness made her want to be done with this business.

"I will bring your meals and empty your bed pan myself. Again I repeat, there will be no outside contact. Is that clear?"

Satisfied the woman would follow her orders to the letter, she crossed the room, then paused to deliver her parting shot.

"One more thing," she said, deliberately not looking at her. "I know nothing of you, of your past. It was one of my requirements. It is no concern of mine whether you were once a wife, a mother, or an assassin. Your life begins now. From this point forward, you will live the remainder of it within the spirit of this order, showing the utmost respect to the habit you wear. And when you die someday, even then, your gravestone will simply bear the epitaph of a bride of Christ and no other. On that note, sleep well...Sister Lucia. I trust you will have a peaceful night."

The prioress didn't linger to see how her words were received. She left quickly, locking the door behind her as she imagined her own heart to be now and turned down the hall as the other sisters filed back to their cells.

Though they nodded their greetings, the old nun barely noticed them, preferring to run the events of the last few minutes over and over in her head like a broken record.

She finally remembered why she'd made the decision to conspire against one of her very own: the suspicion—or rather the near certainty—that if she hadn't agreed to their plan, there would be two bodies taken from here this night.

ONE

Today—Wednesday, March 5
Los Angeles, California

*I*n *the grand scheme of things, did you actually believe their gilded promises? Fame, money, an everlasting blitz of exhilarating ecstasy? You? The girl voted most likely to join the realms of the celebrity undead before she reached her twenty-seventh birthday? Well hey...you did make it past that milestone. Way past! Do you hear that clock ticking? No? What's wrong with you then? Oh, I remember now. You're not even a single tick in the tock, the bang in the buck, the tit for the tat. You're not even a complete...*

I shot back a couple of pain pills then became still. An idea suddenly took hold, so right, so ripe and so complete, it seemed as if it had always existed somewhere just beyond conscious thought. I stopped crying long enough to find what I was looking for in the medicine cabinet, my fingers closing on it in a daze. Turning to the tub, I flipped on both faucets, tested the temperature, wondered why, then stripped to my underwear, folded my clothes neatly on a chair, and slid into the warmth up to my neck.   I didn't give much thought to not having removed the last bits of fabric, but it seemed perfectly logical that neither Eddy, his band mates, nor later the paramedics, should find me a floating, bloated mess *and* completely naked to boot.

Should I really be thinking about dignity at such a time?

How odd.   Actually, I didn't think I was capable of any thought at all.   The lethargic stupor and migraine torturing me all week had only gotten worse.   Now, my body felt mysteriously disconnected as if I were watching myself from just below the ceiling.   I wasn't desperate or depressed—just empty. How had I gotten into this fix? Hadn't I gone to the clinic yesterday thinking I'd be simplifying my life, not ending it?   Right.   So why couldn't I stop the waterworks?

Stabbing pain in the back of my head screamed for me to refocus.

I held up the item still clutched in my hand and studied it through shimmering tears. The razor was sleek, stainless; a high-end variety one didn't throw away after a single use and that had a name more suited to NASCAR than toiletries. I fiddled with the replacement mechanism, popped out the tiny blade and hoped it was as sharp as it appeared. Then again, in my present state, when the time came, I probably wouldn't feel much anyway.

Sudden inspiration insisted it was time. A moment's hesitation as I deliberated—above the water or beneath—and quickly decided on beneath. The sight of blood often made me sick to my stomach.

I slid both hands under, my left open and pliant, my right gripping the razor as I imagined had to be gripped to get the job done and felt it cold against my wrist, like I'd fished it out of a cryogenic tank. All that remained was the cut itself, deep and horizontal across my artery, so there was no chance of stemming the flow once it began. I closed my eyes, took a deep breath and pressed it into my skin.

The sob was unexpected, plaintive. The message it delivered, terrifying because the image it evoked didn't have a chance to evolve. It materialized fully formed; what I was about to do, exposed in all its raw ugliness, blowing away the dull film numbing my brain with the force of a hurricane.

The blade froze and my eyes jolted open. Had I cried out? An unconscious survival reflex?

I scanned the room but I was alone. Eddy had not found me nor cried out in horror at my attempt to annihilate myself. In fact, other than the drippy faucet, the house was complacently quiet, with no hint of the five men still roaming in search of food or fun.

When the second cry broke the silence and what was left of my resolve, I sat up straight and allowed the blade to sink. This one had sounded muffled, as if it had come from *beneath* the surface. Unable to avoid it any longer, I looked down at the crimson threads weaving their way through the water before blooming into a cloudy mass and came back to life feeling sure I had ended it.

Seconds later I stood at the foot of the tub, oblivious to how I got out. The pathetic sobbing had thankfully come to an end, but it was time to assess damages and if the bloody water was a clue, it was bad.

In the blink of an eye, I constructed the likely chain of events: I'd scream, Eddy would come rushing in, call 911, and by tomorrow, Trina Langford's attempt at self-extermination would be all over the news. I supposed bad publicity was better than none.

Expecting carnage, I examined my wrist but saw nothing.

Confusion deepened then cleared when my cervix spasmed. Something trickled down my leg and I understood, the relief so profound, even the pain was welcome since it proved I was still kicking.

Perched on the edge of the tub, hyper aware I'd been snatched from the brink of some abyss, I tried making sense of the urge that had nearly lulled me into slicing my wrists.

Was it really that easy to kill oneself? How had it taken me that far when I'd never had a single self-destructive bone in my body—that is, if you didn't count my addiction to Eddy.

Before the crash that took them from me the day after my eighteenth birthday, mom had taught music theory at the local community college, while my disillusioned dad had finally traded his artist's brush for an accountant's ledger to make ends meet. Contrary to the trend of shooting up the local burger joint over the wrong kind of fries, my family had been only run-of-the-mill neurotic. I was inanely, boringly normal.

Wasn't I?

Worse, since I obviously had no control over my compulsions, wasn't it reasonable to think this one could come back without warning? If it did, would that cry bring me out of it again? I sat still, trying to recall the particular timber, the inflection of the voice. There had been something familiar about it. I'd *known* it.

Exhaustion made any thought, rational or otherwise, impossible.

I powered off for now, slipped my shivering self into a bathrobe, threw the razor in the trash, and shuffled back to the bedroom.

Neither Carmen nor Eddy had bothered making the bed this morning but I slid beneath the rumpled sheets anyway and took a whiff.

A cloyingly-sweet perfume drifted off my pillow proving what

I already suspected.

Through the gloom, the long strand of black hair stood out like a neon sign and I finally understood why the housekeeper Eddy had been so keen on hiring hadn't bothered with chores.

I'd been away less than a day—surely not long enough for him to get into trouble. I was wrong. A pile of unopened mail, empty bottles and leftover pizza welcomed me home.

Scowls swept over the band as I flung open the door to the studio interrupting their session. Eddy exchanged some silent, private joke with his mates before his thick arms and heavy chest smothered me in a hug.

"Hey love, didn't know you'd be back so soon." He made a point of pawing my breast while the others looked on.

"Or what? You would've cleaned up after yourselves? Must've been quite the party last night," I said, taking a deliberate step back while resisting the urge to knee him in the groin. "Where's Carmen anyway?"

"Gave her the day off. So what's with you? Me and my guys can't have a few laughs while you're gone?"

"You know it was more than a few laughs," I said, feeling the sudden need for privacy when his *guys* snickered. "Was it too hard to pick up the phone and ask how it went?"

"I don't have time for this right now. You know what though? They were right. They all said to watch out for those killer mood swings as soon as it's over. So before you go into all-out bitch mode, why don't you just march yourself outta here like a good little girl and let us get back to work."

Tears soaked into the pillow, marking the territory Carmen had usurped last night. My last coherent thought before I drifted off was somehow consoling and in some ways a relief. At least I didn't have to wonder if I knew this one. But damn you, Eddy— don't you even have the decency to change the sheets?

TWO

D ark-thirty. I opened my eyes without moving my limbs, surprised I had slept through the evening hours, and took stock. My mouth was dry and I was thirsty but I didn't have to pee and the pills were still doing their thing. Although I'd slept soundly, my weariness had somehow intensified and I ignored Carmen's stink still wafting off the pillow.

Behind the bedroom door, Eddy's voice rose, slurred and angry, spilling into the phone at whomever held the line.

"I tell you I don't care anymore...I'm not responsible for her so why should I...no, but I don't see why it matters...then do it yourself. I've had all I can take of her tantrums...well I can't bloody force her, can I!"

"Give it a rest, Eddy," I whispered to the darkness. "We all know you're Detroit born and bred."

The mock Liverpool twang he and his crew sometimes affected as if it added a touch of international glamour, usually made me laugh. Now it only depressed me; further evidence of the lie I'd been living for two years.

There was silence for a good thirty seconds, but even through the closed door, I heard him pacing, sensed his frustration with the caller on the other end. When Eddy spoke again, he'd dropped the phony accent and his voice quivered slightly.

"No! Listen, I didn't mean it that way, okay? I'll try to get her to come. Of course you don't have to worry about me. You know I've always...yeah, yeah, alright. I'll talk to you tomorrow."

Goose bumps rose against my skin and I shivered. There was no longer any doubt who he'd been talking to. A faint beep ended the call before footsteps approached our room. I shut my eyes as the door opened, willed myself to breathe deeply and a moment later, felt the bed sag under his weight.

"Trina sweetheart, you awake?" he whispered, his breath reeking of expensive whiskey. I grunted, hoping he would take the hint, which he didn't.

"Hey, no hard feelings about this afternoon, right? You just took me by surprise, babe. You know, with the guys being here and all. Anyway, I just wanted to make sure you're okay after the...um...the thing yesterday."

One hand caressed my arm and it took everything I had to not flinch. Had he used the same technique to seduce Carmen the night before?

"Besides, it's not like you didn't know what to expect. Remember Bruce's gal? How she said it was like a fancy spa? Gourmet buffet, pedicure, and a massage while you wait. One-stop shopping, eh?"

An unpleasant thought tickled my memory; an annoying, fake-friendly and nosy staff.

Eddy chuckled softly at his moronic joke and I knew that he'd done more than just taste that whiskey. He'd been doing a lot of that lately.

"Look...if you really wanted, we could try again sometime; when we're both ready that is. You've got the deadline for the new songs, I've got the tour. It's not the end of the world, right?"

Betrayed by silent tears, I kept my eyes tightly shut and hoped he couldn't see my face.

As the twenty-seven year old lead for *The Screaming Eagles*, a thrash-metal band conceived in his parents' garage during his senior year at Southfield High, Eddy Pindar was a breathing, walking tribute to his icons. A couple inches shorter than I, he'd somehow made the accent, vintage tea shade glasses and eighties' hair trendy again, first on stage and then off, as he grew more image obsessed. I'd never said much about it, grateful I suppose, that at least the Kabuki-style face paint hadn't found its way into our bedroom.

According to the tabloids, he and I had been an item for the past two years. What they didn't report was that the honeymoon was over—how could they, when even I hadn't admitted it to myself?

Nearly two months ago I found myself pregnant. I kept it secret for a while, the idea of having a baby growing on me even as my body changed and shifted in a hundred-and-one ways obvious only to me. In my most delusional moments, I had hoped parenthood might even change everything and put an end to Eddy's roving eye. And then two things happened almost simultaneously.

I told him diaper duty was in his future and he introduced me to his new producer, Gregory Kadzik, who swore he could resuscitate a career already on life support. Though Eddy took the news in his usual immature manner—storming around the house for days, slamming doors, punishing me with the silent treatment—I could still handle him; but Gregory's reaction to the news was different—strangely cold and hostile.

"Go ahead," he'd threatened in the quiet, restrained way he has about him. "Keep the baby. But remember, the media already thinks of you as a has-been."

Which wasn't precisely true; can't be a *has-been* if you've never been a *somebody* in the first place. I ignored them both, refused to discuss it and, over time, found myself hashing out fewer tunes and lingering longer before store fronts featuring the latest baby ware.

That is, until about a week ago when something changed and Gregory's words began clanging around in my head, muffling all other thoughts to the point of exclusion. Here at last was my chance to prove I wasn't just a one-song wonder and I was throwing it away. Gregory and Eddy were right. Timing was everything and mine was off. I called the clinic the next day and made an appointment.

Eddy was quiet for some time and I knew he was trying to gauge if I was really asleep. "I know what you need," he said finally. "Stop moping around and have a little fun. Gregory's having a few friends over Saturday night. We should go."

I recalled Eddy's strange words to him over the phone and tried to curb my growing dread. There was something he wasn't saying. I could feel him holding it back. "Is *she* going to be there?" I mumbled into my pillow—stench or no stench.

"Don't know. Does it make a difference?"

"It does to me. Seems like wherever I go these days she's there."

"Do I detect a note of jealousy?"

"Once, maybe," I admitted truthfully. "Now I'm just tired. Besides, I don't think I'll be up to it yet."

"Well, right now you're not. But you'll see, you'll feel better by Saturday. Just don't make up your mind until then, okay?"

Eddy undressed and crawled under the sheets, his left arm snaking around my waist. I wondered if he still picked up Carmen's perfume on the linens then decided it didn't matter anymore.

A silent scream welled up inside as he touched me. Despite the sudden decision to end my pregnancy—why was that again—I'd still welcomed the closeness. The recollection wasn't so much a memory from a lifetime ago but of someone else's life altogether.

"Too hot," I murmured, wriggling my way to the edge of the bed; my best option considering I didn't think my legs would get me very far.

He turned abruptly, his breath eventually settling into a quiet snore.

Keyed up despite my continued exhaustion and finally having cried myself out, I gazed into the darkness, my insomnia due neither to our housekeeper's betrayal nor Eddy's cruelty. Two sets of eyes flickered in and out of my head; one greedy, mercenary, framed by a mass of platinum blond hair; the other, simply empty and dead.

I knew what I had to do.

THREE

Saturday, March 8
West Hollywood, California

Paparazzo, Logan O'Neill, decided he felt good about himself today. Despite the early hour, a little reward was in order.

He found the good stuff on the top shelf and went to work. Old-fashioned bourbon would definitely perk up his morning coffee. He unscrewed the top, added a couple fingers of the juice to the java, and then had a second thought and added a third. Might as well save himself a trip. Prize in hand, he grabbed a stack of magazines from off the counter, headed for the living room and, as was his daily ritual, pored over the latest scandals and hook-ups and smiled. Despite the provocative headlines, most were rehashes attempting to bleed news broken weeks ago. Good thing, considering last night's unexpected bonus.

He'd gotten the call as he'd waited behind a rope barrier for the newest next-sweet-thing to hit the red carpet and nearly hung up on the high-pitched falsetto.

His Aunt Louise wasn't really his aunt but one of those family friends parents insist kids treat as kin out of a misguided sense of respecting their elders; even if the elder was a vicious old biddy who'd pinched his cheek too hard at every reunion. But right then she was talking breathlessly at him, the name and medical procedure she let slip accidentally on purpose, enough for him to hightail it back to his ancient Buick for details and maybe even forgive his childhood bruisings.

Minutes later, he'd resisted the temptation to do a little tap number around the parking lot and called his editor instead. Louise had thrown him a lifeline. Far be it for him to throw it back since things had been a little shaky in that department lately.

And since when had things *not* been shaky?

He squelched the uncomfortable thought with another sip of corrosive coffee.

What he couldn't understand was why Louise had broken her silence and the nondisclosure she'd signed at that fancy clinic of hers. Not that it mattered. By the time he got through finessing the story, nobody would ever connect his *aunt* with her famous patient.

O'Neill timed his last gulp with the last page of his magazine. Time to punch in. He quickly made a mental list of Trina Langford facts. If he recalled, she'd shown promise about ten years before, swiped a major recording contract, did some touring; she'd even had a solid single that had risen to number two on the boards. Her songwriting at the time had seemed autobiographical, personal; her performing style, honest and genuine without the need for gimmicky theatrics and she'd had her loyal following—probably still did, somewhere. And then she'd fallen strangely out of grace and the limelight. There were rumors of a major disagreement with her producer at the time, a hint of scandal, but ultimately never anything concrete. When she'd reappeared on the radar a couple of years ago, it had primarily been due to her budding relationship with Eddy Pindar—a   hard-living, coke-snorting rocker who'd fast-tracked his way to stardom and suddenly, Trina Langford was front-page news again. Who knew she'd be the type to go for the beauty-and-the-beast routine? Just went to show you never knew about women.

He scowled, wondered how he'd get close enough to make the tip pay for itself, then remembered the rumor and made a few calls. There would be a gathering of the glitterati tonight and Trina and Eddy were on the guest list.

A distant but familiar flash of interest caught him off guard. He quickly stifled it. What was so special about Trina Langford anyway? Just another dime-a-dozen wannabe with a pretty face, decent voice, and rotten taste in guys.

Deciding analysis wasn't his strong suit, O'Neill stood and forced his mind back to more important matters. How exactly was he going to weasel an invitation to this shindig? He headed back to the kitchen knowing it would come to him eventually. Until then, couldn't hurt to celebrate just a tad longer.

FOUR

Benedict Canyon, California

It was nearly ten before we drove through the main gate of Kadzik's estate. I brooded silently as I brought Eddy's Cobra around the circular drive, handed the keys to a valet and looked at it one last time. I planned on taking an Uber home tonight, have the driver wait while I packed my belongings, and then have him drop me off at the nearest motel where I would plan the rest of my life.

From the moment we'd gotten in the car—with me behind the wheel since Eddy was already crocked—we'd argued. It was partly my fault. I was feeling jubilant, maybe even a little rash; dropping clues to a confused Eddy that our days together were numbered, perhaps even over; that tonight should be an interesting evening all around. And whatever Eddy didn't understand—which was considerable—made him crabby and short tempered.

I turned towards the sound of music, knew we were unfashionably late, and smiled.

Gregory Kadzik's manse had been built in the late 1890s for one of Southern California's early land barons and had stayed in the family until a famous silent-movie diva offered an obscene amount of cash for it some thirty years later. It stood imposing on twenty acres of prime real estate; a towering hodge podge of different styles that had been added onto over the years.

I hated it but thought it suited its present owner to perfection. I'd always thought Eddy's producer, and now mine as well, was a little weird; or maybe *intense* was a better word for it. Although he'd dragged the house into the twenty-first century with a major overhaul, it still retained its gloomy core and the reputation for being haunted by that same diva who, having been jilted by her lover, decided she could no longer face life.

Would the house I'd lived in for two years be part of a ghost tour if I'd finished the job the other night? Eddy squeezed my hand sharply as we walked up the front steps, precluding an answer.

"You're in rare form tonight. Not planning to cause any problems, are you?" he slurred. Despite his tanked-up state, he obviously remembered some of our earlier chat.

"Whatever do you mean?"

"You know what it takes for Gregory to take on a new client. Do you realize how many would kill to take your place?"

"I'm thinking that might be the going price."

"What was that?"

"Nothing. What a prince among men. Remind me to swoon like the others."

He grumbled, clearly irritated with me, but it was too late for a rebuttal as he led me up the formal entry and into a marbled foyer.

So much for Gregory having a *few* friends over. The place crawled with partygoers flushed with too much free booze, the anticipation of nailing a new deal, or someone new for the night. While most of the faces were unfamiliar, I did recognize a couple of his clients and though I wasn't here to work the room, I was suddenly grateful I'd put a little effort into my appearance after all. I'd nixed Eddy's earlier recommendation of short and sexy, but thought my choice of a black silk dress and matching high-heeled sandals appropriate given my mood. I'd gathered my chestnut hair in a loose chignon, relied on dangling diamond earrings to provide the only sparkle, and knew I'd hit a nerve when more than a few heads turned.

I took a deep breath, reminded myself to focus, and recognized Gregory sitting at a massive antique bar at the far end of the room. He had his back to us, whispering something to a siliconed starlet with adoring eyes. He hesitated for an instant then turned fluidly and fixed his gaze on me. Not for the first time, I wondered if the man had a sixth sense. Ignoring the now-pouting woman, he swiped a glass off the counter and headed straight for us.

Eddy once told me Gregory was nearing seventy. I thought he looked at least twenty years younger but that wasn't surprising, given his reputation for sheep-testicle injections in Switzerland and other, over-the-top health crazes. Distinguished looking, tall, and perpetually tanned, he wore his gray-at-the-temples hair slicked back, while his silk Italian suit shimmered in the ambient light. Now as they stood beside one another, the difference was stark: compared to our producer, Eddy looked as scruffy as a shaggy dog.

"Edward," he said with a nod to Eddy who hated it when any-one used the name on his birth certificate.

He returned the greeting stiffly and I noticed he'd slipped back into his U.K. persona.

"Trina...stunning as usual," Gregory continued, handing me the glass of wine. "I trust there were no ill effects from your procedure the other day."

I mumbled something and flushed red at the casual mention— as if he'd been the maître'd at Spago's inquiring after the quality of my slow-braised, short-rib tortellini. The village drums had certainly been busy. If he knew, I'd bet the rest of the room did as well. I imagined every brow arched in my direction, every ear cocked for the latest update. But it was more than this too; it spoke volumes about the power he wielded in this kingdom, in which I now belonged.

"Got a minute?" I blurted with a little too much gusto.

Gregory studied me through veiled eyes. "Of course. You must have read my mind. I was about to suggest we settle some preliminaries before enjoying the rest of the evening. Edward, would you care to join us?"

Edward looked as if he were about to refuse, caught the unspoken mandate in Gregory's voice, and seemed to think better of it. He nodded silently and we both followed like good little soldiers, exchanging speculative glances behind our emperor's back. It occurred to me that as surely as we were adversaries in other aspects of our lives, we were also allies as far as Kadzik was concerned.

If others felt the same, they hid it well beneath a lot of fawning. He stopped to shake hands, offer friendly hugs and words of encouragement, then led us into the dining room with its intricately-carved table and vintage chandelier. Beneath it, caviar, smoked salmon, powdered smack, and other nameless gourmet fare would've outed me as the hick at the Hilton if Eddy hadn't explained their benefits at similar soirees.

I nibbled on a prawn while he drooled over the candy bowls brimming with colorful pills and trailed after Gregory into the huge bustling kitchen.

Eddy frowned before a door squeezed between two sub-zero refrigerators. "No office?"

"Tonight is special," Gregory said, the skin around his mouth remaining abnormally smooth as he grinned. "We're celebrating Trina's well-deserved inauguration."

What inauguration?

He punctuated the compliment by grazing his fingers over my bare arm, opened the door and motioned for us to lead the way down a steep, winding staircase.

I swallowed my last bite of shrimp, shuddered, and hurried down the steps so he couldn't touch me again. It disturbed me as his flirting had grown to something more over these last few weeks. The more I resisted, the more insistent he'd become—and more dangerous. The idea refused to go away and only strengthened my resolve as I wound my way down into the basement.

Since he'd demanded no structural changes be made to this part of the house, this was where Gregory's penchant for the theatrical became obvious. The steps were narrow, hewn from the original rock foundation. They bottomed out abruptly, opening on to an enormous cavern that ran the length of the house, stocked with more wine than a body could drink in three lifetimes. A tasting room with a long oaken table and throne chairs dominated the rest of the space.

The first time Gregory had invited me down here I'd been impressed. The sophisticated setting was the perfect place to celebrate our business relationship and my new beginning—the reinvention of Trina Langford. I soon learned that wasn't quite what he had in mind as he'd guided us deeper through the maze; the claustrophobic sensation competing with the dank, moldy smell that permeated everything and clung to my clothes.

We stopped along one of the winding corridors, an exact replica of the other dozen or so we'd passed. Still amazed at the ingenuity of the whole thing, I watched Gregory lean against the edge of a certain rack and heard the predictable click. The wall of wine sprang forward, revealing a twenty-foot walkway lit by a single, naked bulb. Unimpressed with the secret passageway beneath his house, he motioned us towards the arched, wooden door at the other end. I glanced at Eddy and tried to read him through the shades he refused to take off, but he purposely ignored me. It could have been the lighting, but his face had taken on a waxy pallor I hadn't noticed before.

Gregory paused before a keypad—his only nod to modern tech—and punched in a complicated-sounding code. Under his touch, the lever twisted without protest while hinges swung in silently, the enveloping darkness nearly throwing me off balance.

He flipped a switch and I shut my eyes, as much to steady my knees as to give my brain time to adjust to my new surroundings; and when I opened them, I reluctantly followed him into the strangest room I'd ever had the misfortune to see.

FIVE

Though not as large as the wine cellar, much of the chamber lay shrouded in the usual gloom, making it difficult to get a true sense.

Hacked from the same foundation rock and windowless, the only way in or out of the medieval carnival fun-house—as I affectionately called it—was through the door through which we'd entered. My nose twitched and I realized something had been added. The stone floor had been painted since I'd been here last; a dull, flat black that reeked of formaldehyde and brought a funerary stillness to everything. Focusing on this minor detail and the other points of interest silhouetted against the outer darkness required too much effort. I turned to the grouping of four armchairs in the center of the room, stunned, when a burst of color flashed across my vision.

A woman sat draped over one of the two chairs facing us,

arms and legs extended, a portrait of ease and arrogance. Other than a small smile framing her red lips and the bird-like flicker of her heavily-made-up eyes following mine, she appeared to be a permanent fixture. The contrast between the monochrome walls and the bright plumage of her clothes, the stark paleness of skin and hair were dazzling, blindingly brilliant. She temporarily silenced all other sensory detail.

Gregory eagerly made his way towards her, while Eddy, hot on his heels, appeared more disturbed than ever. I followed cautiously.

"So good of you to join us, Chloe," Gregory murmured, unimpressed by her presence. "I believe you know everyone."

Although she'd been waiting for us in the dark, I suspected her vision could rival a night owl's.

Appropriate greetings were traded all around as we sat in the remaining three chairs with Gregory seated alongside Chloe so they appeared united. *Against us?* I dismissed the notion, ignored the obligatory small talk, and studied the caricature before me.

Her six-inch heels were Lucite, chunky. I imagined their serious clatter announcing her arrival from a mile away, adding to the stature she craved, then moved up to her stockinged legs, sausaged in holey white nylon resembling spider silk.

Concealing most of her body-builder thighs that could double as nutcrackers—and had, according to rumors—her main ensemble sprang directly from an old mummy movie. The rags were a fiery blend of primary Crayola colors and then the designer of this creation had gone mad.

Instead of the usual arm holes and waistline, the garment hung over her anorexic shoulders like a sniper in a ghillie suit; one moving stealthily across a Picasso canvas rather than through brush or field marsh.

Afraid I'd suffer a bout of lazy eye if I lingered on one spot for too long, I continued my upward trek.

The neckline of Chloe's dress actually came up to her chin, giving way to the nearly cadaverous skin alongside her cheeks; and then to the nose, slightly beaky but having the potential of appearing mildly aristocratic under more normal circumstances.

The whole effect was framed by a pouf of neon blond hair that gave off a mild glow, much like a halo in the dim light. The result would've been comical if it hadn't been accompanied by icy purpose.

I heard my name and decided I'd better start paying attention.

"...help with the planning of the first show," Gregory finished. He reached inside his jacket, pulled out some papers and threw them on the coffee table between us. "I think it will surpass anything we've done in the past. The effect will be remarkable: the changing of the guard...Chloe Six, the queen, handing the reigns over to the newly initiated while she herself, enters the realm of myth, the stuff of legend."

Gregory's eyes were on fire, living some vision only he and Chloe Six—previously Anna-Beth Bartram of Omaha, but presently the reigning queen—were plugged into. Perhaps her name would change again once she was transformed into the *stuff of legend* and then she would be known as Chloe Five. I wasn't sure I wanted to know what would happen if she ever reached Chloe One status.

"I don't follow."

Chloe looked at me as if it were obvious I'd need to have something so simple explained while Gregory smirked. "You've been through the fire, cleansed. All that is needed now is for the world to know and they will worship at your feet. The contract we will sign tonight is just a formality. The true offering has already been delivered."

I almost laughed, then changed my mind as sweat wound its way down my back and puddled in the folds of my dress. These people were serious—or seriously disillusioned—and I knew this was where I'd have to proceed with extreme caution.

After Eddy had first introduced me to Gregory, I'd realized it was all an act—albeit one everyone else took for gospel; bad theater designed to create an aura of mystique and self-importance, complete with some made-up occult touches for added drama.

So I made a decision. I stubbornly ignored it, going through the motions for the sake of having my career jumpstarted back to life; a small price, I thought, for actually getting paid to write my songs and sing them. In the end, I told myself whatever he and his cronies did down here—be it illusion or insanity—was none of my business. But it was never my plan to be a circus sideshow freak or its main attraction, and if I was hearing Gregory correctly, my metamorphosis into something akin to Chloe Six was close. He was making it way too easy for me.

"Gregory, I want you to know how much all this has meant to me. The opportunity's been awesome and it's not that I don't appreciate it, but..."

I glanced at my audience.

Chloe appeared hungry, but I couldn't tell if it was because she'd thrown up her last two meals or she was fondly dreaming of her latest power grab.

Gregory, on the other hand, didn't so much as stare *at* me as *down* me—no mean feat since we were both seated; while Eddy—dear God, what was wrong with him—seemed unusually preoccupied with his hands.

"...but I've changed my mind."

"You wish to renegotiate."

Damn. He was going to make me work for it after all.

"No, I want to be let out of our agreement."

"That won't be possible."

"But like you said, nothing's been set in stone," I reminded. It was my turn to feel confused and—something else—an irritating niggling at the back of my neck, gathering steam.

"The real contract has already been signed...and is unbreakable."

"You say that, but how? Your lawyer can call me first thing Monday morning to discuss a reasonable settlement. I assure you, it was never my intention to take advantage of your generosity. It's just that I don't think we'd be a good fit."

The only sense I had of Gregory's increasing anger was the unnatural dilation of his pupils nearly obscuring any white left in his eyes; unnatural—because what looked out at me was as flat and black as the room and as incapable of producing a reflection.

"This isn't a game, Trina. You can't merely change your mind on a whim. You sought me out, remember?"

"Yes...but only because Eddy spoke so highly of you." I glanced at my significant other, hoping he would back me up, but he was obsessively rubbing his hands now, presumably alleviating pain in some arthritic limb.

"He's impressed with what you're doing with his career so naturally, we both thought you could do the same with mine. I just didn't think I'd have to stop being who I am."

"And who are you really? Are you satisfied with who you see in the mirror each morning? Don't you wonder what could've happened if you'd allowed your career to develop before you cut it short out of some naïve notion of staying true to yourself...your art?"

I tried not to linger on the fact that he knew the details to this primitive piece of history. But of course he'd know. "Changing who I am, my music, my entire image, seems a little too steep a price. There has to be another way."

"Success has its price. Isn't that right, Chloe?"

She peered at me from under heavy eyelids garnished by long, glittery lashes.

"I told you she'd never be ready." Her eyes glazed over me, picking me apart one atom at a time. "It could've been fun," she purred, still not moving a fraction.

I ignored her and turned back to Gregory. "Let's be clear about this. I'm prepared to pay a reasonable sum but quite frankly, there isn't a single court in this state that wouldn't side with me. Without a contract, you don't have a case."

"There are many different types of courts and contracts, Trina. I would advise you to think carefully before making a rash decision."

"Or you'll sue?"

"It's possible...although I can think of a few more interesting options."

I reached for some conventional meaning to his words— couldn't find one, and came crashing through an invisible barrier, realizing too late it had been my only shield.

"Something to do with the good-old-boys network you run down here?"

"Now Trina...you know very well we're an equal-opportunity coven. We exclude no one and in return the only thing we ask for is loyalty."

"Because I went to a few meetings? That doesn't automatically grant me membership. Technically, I haven't even been initiated yet."

"Quite right. But you forget it is our actions that ultimately provide the most powerful proof of our commitments. Wouldn't you agree, Chloe, that as our newest acolyte, Trina has mastered each successive level remarkably quickly?"

I reddened, wondering what I could have done to possibly give them that impression.

Chloe shrugged. "I guess...but does she have any real talent?"

"Only time can give us that answer."

"Let me make it easy for you. Since I've wasted too much of mine already, this arrangement is over. And by the way," I said, facing Eddy still slumped in his chair, "so is ours."

I looked for a reaction. Either too drunk to realize he'd been dumped or simply not giving a rip, Eddy didn't stir. I rose and moved towards the door with as much dignity as I could muster.

"Did I ever tell you the history of this place?"

"Your *church*?"

"A little less heavy on the sarcasm please. More of a chapel really. A grotto. I would have liked a real church, of course. An old one with a past. All those souls still resonating within its walls. I shouldn't complain though, as this has served our purposes nicely."

"Save it for the congregation."

"Do you know I chose the house for this very chamber? Oh yes...this is the focal point. Everything else is window dressing. The man who built it insisted on having a chapel on the premises; a throwback to his ancient European roots, no doubt, when landowners could worship on their own schedules without mixing with the unwashed masses."

I could see how that would appeal to Gregory.

"There was a rumor of activities touching on the unorthodox. Certain sacrifices for fortunes made, shall we say? History records seven children born to the lord of the manor, yet two simply disappeared only days after their births. While this prompted speculation as you can imagine, no accusations were made. Not surprising, since he was rumored to have most city officials in his back pocket.

"And let's not forget that great tragic talent; a rising star in a brand-new industry and one of the first of her kind; bright, driven. Imagine the heights she could've reached if only she hadn't checked out early. You know the claw foot tub upstairs is the very one she used to breathe her last? I can almost feel her sometimes as I bathe...her essence..."

"Is your twisted history lesson supposed to change my mind?"

"Not at all. Just helping you understand the importance of sacrifice; how nothing can be achieved in this world without it and consequently, how there's nothing that can't be achieved when its power is exploited. We're all witnesses to that, aren't we?" he asked Chloe and Eddy. "It only hurts the first time."

He whipped around to face me suddenly, his gaze calculated. "It's no use. I know you can feel it. The pull of this chamber, its power."

"You've been at this too long, Gregory. You're starting to believe your own delusions."

"Prove it then. Take it all in. Understand what you're giving up. If it fails to impress you, you're free to leave."

"Alright. Where do you suggest I start?" I said, forcing the bile down. "How about the Halloween masks against the walls?" I resisted the urge to touch one and pointed to the cowled robe hung beside it. "Or maybe you'd like me to model the latest in ritual fashion one last time? Have to admit...drab brown doesn't do much for my complexion, but then again, it does give the chanting and flailing around a bit more credibility. As do your other props, I might add."

I turned to the raised platform with the massive stone slab in the center and climbed it for the first time.

"I see what you mean. Things do look different from this angle. I feel more important already."

I ran my fingers over the rough rock, took in the ancient volume propped open on a stand, its large, illuminated letters, spelling unfamiliar words that were somehow familiar. I was about to touch the crinkled pages when a sharp gasp signaled I'd gone too far.

"Sacrilege!" Chloe shrieked. "Come down at once! How dare you defile the sacred altar?"

"But Gregory said I've been anointed and part of the club now. And since I'm clearly part of the club, I should have the right to know certain things. For instance, what's so important, you have to keep it hidden in there?" I motioned towards the ornate gold tabernacle behind me, its brilliance dancing in defiance of the dull, oppressive quality in the rest of the chamber. Above it, something else tickled the edge of my vision; the fact I'd chosen to ignore it I told myself—a testament to the chaos that was Chloe.

About to cry, she shot Gregory a petulant scowl. "Make her stop!"

"All in good time. After all, it's her indomitable spirit that makes her so valuable. Even now, after everything she's been through."

"Enough with the psychobabble! Just so you know, I won't be satisfying any more of your cravings for sacrifices."

"But that's the point. You already have. It would simply be a shame to allow all that work to go to waste."

"When? When have I ever agreed to sacrifice anything?"

"Surely you know. The sacrifice has never changed, Trina. From time immemorial it has always remained the same. The fact that you went for the blood of the innocent without even much prompting, shows me you're destined to be one of the great ones. Don't throw it all away."

I hadn't looked above the locker yet but I did so now. Despite the promise of madness it offered, it was a safer haven than my thoughts. It was also the only thing left to see; the highpoint of the tour.

My eyes made the lethargic crawl up the wall. It only took an instant for my vision to adjust to the shape in the shadows, and though I expected it, for a moment it still didn't register.

A towering crucifix hung suspended from the dark ceiling by thick, black rope. The figure in the center, arms outstretched as if to embrace—hung upside down in cruel mockery—yet another sacrifice to some carrion god.

SIX

Gregory's words accomplished what bravado never could. I floated off the platform and sank back in my chair.

Silence, muffled and oppressive, sharpened my senses. Blood thrummed through my body and I visualized the tediousness of the whole process. Heart pumping blood into my vessels—vessels channeling it into ever-smaller capillaries—arteries laboring against the natural current of things—repeated ad nauseam.

Despite my best efforts, the chamber's finer details surrendered to the excited southern drawl in my head...

"There we are, Ms. Langford. We're all done and we'll feel better real soon, won't we?" I arch an eyebrow at the continued reference to *we*. The woman who stares is in her late fifties, more than pleasantly plump, with frosty gray hair coiffed into a rigid helmet. A name tag on her nurse's smock identifies her as

Louise in large, flowing cursive and harmonizes with her cheerful surroundings designed to reassure.

"I know this isn't the right time and all, but I just had to tell you how much me and my daughter love your music. Why, she even had them play one of your songs at her wedding. Ooh, what was that...somethin' about a bird and a fire and everlastin' love..."

"*Rise of the Phoenix.*"

"That's right! Chose it for their very first dance as husband and wife. The two of 'em waltzin' around that floor like they'd been doin' it for years. Oh, listen to me ramblin' on. I just wanted to say you are such an inspiration. Most women your age...they're thinkin' about family and kids. And look at you, hon...still livin' the kind of life others only dream of."

She runs out of the room, tears streaming down her pudgy cheeks because I snap, coming back at her with something crude and offensive...

"That was never a sacrifice. It was..."

"Yes?"

"Look...all I know is my decision had nothing to do with you."

"Whatever helps you sleep dear. Edward was supposed to fill you in on the specifics. Isn't that right, Edward? That was one of your responsibilities, was it not, to prepare her for the final sacrament?"

The compulsion driving Eddy to rub his skin raw still held sway. Even now, he refused to look into his inquisitor's eyes. "I didn't have time."

"What was that, Edward?"

"You heard me. We've been practicing hard for the tour. Just didn't find the right moment that's all. Anyway, she did it, didn't she? I never even had to say anything."

"Oh my, someone's in trouble," Chloe chirped.

"Eddy, you knew about this...what did he call it...a sacrament? And you still let me go through with it?"

He remained silent in his haste to expose his metacarpals. I changed tactics and turned to Big Bird and her handler.

"Let's say you're serious and you really think my procedure was a sacrifice to some pagan god. I'm sure there are others like me who think it was a mistake and want to forget about it. There has to be a formula, some ritual that can reverse everything, right?"

It was the sanest solution I could come up with. Anything else and I'd be joining Eddy.

Gregory and Chloe snickered, exchanging a look. Roughly translated, it was a reminder to persevere when dealing with dim-wits.

"I assure you, Trina, everything that happens here is taken with the utmost seriousness," Gregory said. "Whether or not you still think this is some kind of joke is really of no consequence. We deal with eternal matters here; with a future so far advanced, most in our society will never understand. Think of teaching physics to a chimp. Of course, we thought you were different, enlightened." He shook his head sadly. "It pains me to know you will never ascend to that level of consciousness; that you don't want the gift offered."

"So we're good then? You won't sue?"

"Of course not, Trina. You're free to go," he said, waving a hand towards the only door. "What did you expect? That we tie you to the altar? I'm sure all that talk about sacrifice has given you the wrong idea."

"And you'll find a way to reverse my *offering*?"

"Consider the matter dealt with."

"Liar!"

Eddy wobbled to his feet and removed his glasses, fingers trembling. "He's lying. He just wants you to think it's going to be okay but it never is. I've seen it before."

"It's just for show, Eddy. It's not real."

"You don't know anything. There've been others who've wanted out but it's always too late. Once you've been chosen, there's nowhere to go."

From the corner of my eye I watched Gregory and Chloe rise in unison. Though neither of them approached us, I found the move threatening and joined them.

"That's what he wants you to believe."

"Wrong! Trina, ask yourself why no one talks, at least not for long. Ask yourself why they had to paint the floor. What were they hiding?"

My mind reeled. *Was* it more than theater? And if it was, *what* was it?

Gregory's soothing voice interrupted this new path. "Come now. When I spoke of sacrifices, I meant symbolically. Spiritually. What you're implying is not only ludicrous, it's offensive."

Eddy cringed, quickly reverting to inertia and I knew once he'd wrapped himself in his cocoon, I'd never get my answers.

"Let him finish. Tell me about the floor, Eddy. Were you here before they painted it?" I tried to think of the last time he'd been away all night, his mood the next day. "What did you see?" I coaxed, moving slowly towards him until we stood side by side, my eyes never leaving Gregory or Chloe. We were two for two now, the line in the dirt clearly drawn.

He whimpered, the pathetic mewling a far cry from his image plastered across the cover of last month's *Rolling Stone*.

"It's alright, honey...just tell me."

He pointed to the altar. "They had a girl up there. She couldn't have been much older than thirteen."

"How dare you! To think...the exemplar trusted you!"

"Not now, Chloe," Gregory said.

"They cut her and...and most of her blood was poured into a cup. A sacramental chalice, they called it. But something was wrong. There was too much of it. It spilled over the steps and pooled down here, right where I'm standing. I didn't know...okay! I didn't know someone so young could bleed so hard."

"What happened to the girl, Eddy?"

He didn't answer, still wrapped up in some memory that I, thankfully, could never share, while in the background, Chloe began chanting gibberish.

"Eddy, what happened to her? Was she in pain?"

"I don't think she felt anything. She was out of it. Her eyes were open but it's like she didn't know what was going on; like maybe they drugged or hypnotized her."

The one shrimp I'd consumed earlier was coming back up and I tried to focus on something else. Anything else. Chloe seemed like a safe bet. She'd stretched out her arms, her rhythmic chanting gathering force. Maybe it was my rising hysteria—still, I had to squelch the urge to laugh. Her high priestess act didn't go well with my impression of a flightless bird clucking away.

Gregory glared at her, his control fraying around the edges. "Did I not make myself absolutely clear?"

She halted in the middle of a Latin phrase, her plumage and ego now properly deflated.

"My son...your words wound me," he continued, facing Eddy. "How could you lie to Trina like this? And after everything I've done for you? Admit it. You know what you saw was simply the blessed wine poured out for believers."

He walked towards us, his steps measured, calculated. Beside me, Eddy's body convulsed as if he'd stuck his finger in a socket.

"Could it have been wine, Eddy?"

"Of course it was," Gregory said. "Think about it, Trina. You know Edward better than anyone in this room. You know his appetite for certain mood enhancers. Quite honestly, I'm surprised he remembers anything of the other night since he was out of it before we even began. It was a matter of time before I spoke to both of you about this as his habit is getting out of control."

"And the girl?"

"I don't have to tell you about Edward's proclivity towards sweet, young things. Again, he's projecting his own passions and desires. I can assure you what he imagined to be a thirteen year old was nowhere close to jail bait."

"Eddy, think back. Did you take anything the other night?"

"So what if I did? I wasn't the only one. You know everyone's expected to partake. I wasn't that stoned," he insisted. "I saw what happened to her."

"Exactly what did you see, Edward? A knife plunged into a heart? A dead body?"

"No one could survive that much blood loss."

"Are you sure it was blood?"

"That's what it tasted like!"

My ears began to ring, a sure sign passing out couldn't be far behind. Certain threads wove themselves together almost randomly. The disturbing changes I'd seen in Eddy. His nights spent with Gregory when he didn't come home until the following afternoon; his face drawn, lethargic, much like tonight. The sudden secrecy; his growing insistence that he now served a higher purpose, seesawing between flamboyant bouts of euphoria and manic depression; and finally and most recently, his palpable fear. The same fear I'd heard in his voice the other night on the phone.

"Truly there are none so blind as those who will not see, none so deaf as those who will not hear. I can tell you exactly what happened to her," Gregory said, now standing within arm's reach of us. "When our ceremony was over, she simply put her clothes back on, went upstairs with the others for some refreshments, then got in her Beamer and drove off."

"It didn't happen that way."

"More hallucinations, Edward. You saw what you wanted to see. I have the number of a good specialist. I'll call him next week and ask him to get in touch with you since you refuse to take that crucial first step."

"Trina, you believe me, right?"

"Dear boy...how long have you been on the junk? Don't you think after all this time the effects change, perhaps even cause psychosis?"

It was a reasonable argument and I clung to it stubbornly— until Eddy pushed his way forward.

"I can prove it. There's an old coal incinerator at the back of the house. I think that's where they took her. I think that's where they take everyone when they don't want proof they were here."

"Don't be ridiculous," Gregory poo-poohed. "So I'm burning bodies now? In front of God and all the neighbors?"

"What God? What neighbors?"

"Be careful, Edward. Slander is a punitive offence. Wouldn't it be a shame to lose everything you've worked for? I can't tell you how difficult that would make my life and yours; or the damage control necessary to repair it."

"Are you threatening him?"

"In a manner of speaking. If Edward insists on this garbage, I'm afraid I can't work with either of you any longer. There must be trust between artists and their producer."

"Then you probably won't mind the police paying you a visit. Since the sacrifices are purely *spiritual*...you shouldn't have anything to worry about."

Gregory opened his mouth then snapped it shut. A new sound broke through the tension: Chloe hissing at me, her face contorted into something I was sure her fans would never be allowed to see.

"I always knew you were wrong for Gregory. Too bad all he could see was fresh meat. A lot of good it did him! You're not the type, are you? Too busy trying to live up to Trina Langford's personal code of honor. We'll see how far it gets you when the labyrinth is complete and the sacred triad unsealed!"

I expected Chloe to end her declaration of doom with the requisite evil cackle when Gregory exploded.

"Enough!"

His voice echoed through the stagnant chamber I had thought too lifeless to produce one, and I knew that at last the charade was over.

Something bubbled up from within him, taking command of muscle and bone and only hinted at before. The skeletal aspects of Gregory's face darkened as he moved more deeply into the shadows. I was looking at a negative, the peaks and valleys of his features reversed, so what jumped out was the shape of his skull, only slightly cloaked by skin. I was seeing Gregory for the first time; foreign, enigmatic, and stark-raving mad.

As if this profound change and Eddy's wild accusations weren't enough, his next words proved beyond doubt that I was in deep trouble—possibly the deepest I'd ever been in.

"Chloe, didn't anyone tell you to use a filter when you get the urge to spew your venom? All that work...out the window in a single moment of carelessness."

"Maybe it wasn't carelessness. Besides, you know it was too late when moron here spilled the beans."

A frown creased Gregory's forehead as he pondered her comment. "I suppose you're right. Though I must say," he said, turning to me, "I did have grand hopes for you, regardless of how crudely Chloe put it." He took a step towards us and I grabbed Eddy's hand out of some primeval sense of survival.

"As you've probably guessed by now, I can't allow either of you to leave."

The mechanics of exactly how Gregory planned on pulling this off remained a mystery until I watched him reach inside his pocket for his phone and punch in a single digit.

"Too much information, you see. Things you weren't meant to know and that should've never been revealed. Yes, I know it's not your fault," he quickly interjected. "But as we all know, loose lips sink ships and that can't be allowed to happen. Not at this time." The frown deepened as if the idea caused him pain.

I took a step back, then another, urging Eddy to do the same, while Gregory and Chloe moved apart like a single cancer cell, dividing and multiplying in order to conquer, and saw my immediate future with crystal clarity. Any sudden moves from us and the dynamic duo would pounce, effectively blocking our escape until the cavalry arrived, at which point, all bets were off. Our only option—a blind backwards shuffle towards the door; agonizingly slow, since I wasn't about to take my eyes off of the pair just yet.

Behind me, my hand groped air but reached for something solid, preferably with a lever attached to it. I touched cold brass, wrenched it and felt a ridiculous swelling in my chest.

Fingers tightened around Eddy's as we flew into the narrow tunnel towards the secret portal separating us from the wine cellar. I'd never watched Gregory open it from this angle, tried to gauge how much force it might take to bust the lock and—in the moment before we rammed our shoulders against the bogus rack—decided too much was better than not enough. Momentum ejected us into the outer basement and on a collision course with thousands of bottles. Since death by impalement didn't sound tempting, I stumbled, bringing Eddy down with me. He sprawled, crushing my chest but rather than resist, I pushed him to the side and rolled with the motion. Dazed and sweaty, he blinked repeatedly as I got to my feet and hauled him up with strength I shouldn't have had.

"You okay?"

"Can't do this anymore. Go ahead without me. You'll have a better chance that way."

"And leave you here when I have so many burning questions?"

I grabbed the front of his shirt, bolted between the aisles and rounded the corner. Where were we? Was I leading us in circles? Heading back to Gregory's lair? Wrong questions. Where the hell was that hit squad?

I glimpsed stairs peeking out from between bottles of Cabernet and temporarily shelved the nasty notion as we took them two at a time, fell into the kitchen, and slammed the door on the madness below. The kitchen crew glanced at us but continued about their business. If they recognized hysteria, they chose to ignore it. Did they know? Did anyone here know? Then again—how could they not know?

Never mind, it's over. You're safe now. Breathe.

I had just bought into the lie when I saw the two approach—dressed to the nines, elegant and deadly.

We hadn't escaped the evil. We'd run headlong into it.

SEVEN

Sunday, March 9

About damned time. Hours earlier O'Neill had watched Langford and Pindar disappear behind a door he'd learned led to a private cellar. He'd settled in for the long haul, blending in with the culinary confusion and downing martinis. Now he focused on the drama unfolding before him as the couple reappeared pale, wide eyed and hounded by two, over-grown gorillas clearly uncomfortable in their tuxes. Too noisy to hear what was said, he nevertheless picked up on their overbearing attitude and wondered what could have happened to turn Kadzik against the pair. It wasn't as if they were trying to loot his wine reserves. Well—maybe Eddy was. Trina just didn't seem like the type. So why the ruckus?

The taller of the two placed his hands on Trina's shoulders. She swatted him away and with Eddy in tow, marched straight for O'Neill and veered right.

He could hear bits and pieces now: how badly they'd been

treated—how everyone around them was a witness—how she'd be calling the police. Strange thing—the farther they moved away, the louder her voice carried. O'Neill felt an unfamiliar burst of pride. Whatever this was about, the lady had spunk.

He shifted his attention to the two thugs, speculating on their job description and recognized the type; bullies who spent their free time increasing muscle mass rather than brain density and whose early history of petty crime had bloomed under careful guidance to include torturing puppies and who-the-hell-knew what else. Compared to what they were used to, they probably thought they'd hit the jackpot running interference for the likes of Gregory Kadzik, which made them all the more dangerous since they'd want to prove themselves. A moment later, the men resumed the chase, vetting his theory. Time to see how it played out.

O'Neill trailed casually, keeping enough distance to avoid suspicion; through a hallway, still packed with guests at this late hour, then into the dining room overflowing with more food than he'd eaten all year. Resisting the temptation to grab a plate, he followed everyone into the main salon and nearly piled into the two men who seemed unsure of their next move.

A few feet of the wide open door, Trina halted. Eddy prodded her on but she shook her head and turned, despair stamped across her face as the hunters resumed the hunt. Annoyed at their cocky swagger now that they were assured of conquest, O'Neill swept past them and reached the couple first.

"There you two are," he said loudly, wrapping his arms round their shoulders. "Not trying to avoid me, are you?"

"Take your hands off us," Trina whispered. "Who do you think..."

"Look, I don't know what you did to piss off Tweedle Dee and

Tweedle Dumber, but for now I'd just assume I was your new best friend."

Trina searched his face. Behind the vivid green of her eyes—a green reminding him of spring rains and rolling hills and, that he realized, photos had never done justice—her expression was ripe with fear.

"How do we know you're not with them?"

"You don't. But I think we can both agree this isn't the time for resumes or background checks. Which way?"

"The front," she answered, taking an uncertain step. O'Neill glanced back. For now, his stunt had slowed the duo but one was already on his phone, no doubt receiving new orders from Kadzik.

"We don't have much time. Did they bring your car around yet?"

She shook her head.

"Of course...and you don't want to wait for it in the dark. Be right back." He hurried towards the obliging staff, made his request and beat it back before the count of two. "Car's on its way. I'll wait with you provided you let me stop your shivering."

He took off his jacket and draped it around her shoulders, surprised when she slipped her arms inside gratefully. Determined not to stare, he turned to Eddy and studied him for the first time since the three had begun their dubious partnership. If there had been a contest of who was worse for wear, Eddy would've won. The man looked positively ashen—and why was he rubbing his hands that way? O'Neill doubted he was capable of more than a few grunts and realized what he wanted would have to come from Trina. Reassured their pursuers still hung back, he faced her, willing her to look at him.

"Mind telling me what happened in that cellar?"

"What would you know about that?"

"I followed you. Logan O'Neill. *Celebrity Weekly.*"

She patently refused his proffered hand but if looks could kill...

"You helped us, so now we're supposed to spill our guts? Is that how it works?"

"I wouldn't put it quite that way but one good turn does deserve another."

She scoured the empty driveway before looking at him pointedly. "Trust me, Mr. O'Neill, you don't want to know."

"Come on, give me something to work with here."

"Eddy and I appreciate your help. Can't you leave it at that?"

"It's in my blood, sweetheart. I have to ask myself why those gentlemen behind us don't want you to leave and what Kadzik has to do with it."

A red Cobra appeared in the driveway, its engine idling—the only prompting Trina and Eddy needed to fly out the door.

Certain she was about to bolt with what was left of his tip, O'Neill went after them and leapt around the grill, the term vehicular homicide stuck in his head as she slid behind the wheel and shifted gears. Lucky for him, she hesitated, panic in her eyes prompting him to follow her line of sight.

The goons were gone, replaced by Kadzik silhouetted against his mansion lights, eyeing them intently. It was now or never.

"I know about your abortion."

"You and the rest of the tribe in there. You want me to throw you a bone? I don't really care who knows. Go ahead, plaster it all over media, rip me to shreds."

He searched her face for an explanation. Sorrow gave way to nameless horror then a blank stare that gave nothing away. The mystery surrounding this woman deepened by the minute reigniting the morning's temporary thrill.

"Why would you willingly do that to yourself?"

"Because whatever my critics do...it can't compare to what's already been done."

She floored it and O'Neill jumped back as a cloud of exhaust swallowed him. The bone Trina Langford had thrown hadn't dug up any answers—only more questions.

Without a glance at the man whose stare bore into the back of his head, O'Neill strolled casually down the drive towards the parking lot and his 1969 Wildcat, in various stages of a complete overhaul. Whistling some half-remembered tune about roving the high hills for the sake of the Irish green, he thrust his hands deep into his trouser pockets to ward off the night's chill, not even remotely regretting the absence of his jacket.

EIGHT

Benedict Canyon

As it usually did in this neighborhood, morning dawned graciously. Not yet seven, a team of gardeners plucked, mowed, and pruned Gregory Kadzik's twenty acres to their usual pastoral perfection, while a secondary clean-up crew helped the live-ins erase every trace of last night's bacchanal. Hard to believe partygoers had swarmed over the property little more than two hours ago. The estate was nearly back to its pristine glory—just as he always insisted.

Indifferent to all this activity, Kadzik sat in the armchair he'd occupied hours earlier. Though still dressed in the Armani, his tie now hung limply around his neck. Despite a crippling exhaustion, sleep was the farthest thing from his mind. In his fertile imagination, he still smelled the delicate floral perfume of the woman who'd fled his inner sanctum; the delicious fragrance of her skin, the remnant of fear that came with her acceptance of her sacrifice; the realization that what had been done could not be undone.

Reluctantly, he admitted he might have erred with her. Perhaps he'd even been a little careless, a little too arrogant for his own good. Certainly he'd craved her acceptance since she possessed that rarest of qualities: a combination of beauty, talent and brains he found charming and unusual in this day and age. He hadn't exaggerated when he told her she could have been one of the great ones. What a gift she would have made The Old One. Yet she'd refused and now, thanks to the spewing black hole in Chloe's face and Pindar's confession, she also knew more than she should. They both did.

He quickly dismissed a wisp of carefully-contained dread. He was known for his stellar service and obedience. He had no reason to worry.

To ease his conscience, he turned his attention to the other breathing entity in the room, rousing her from her noxious snoring with a not-too-gentle nudge to her feet, still encased in those preposterous shoes.

Chloe woke with a snort and a profanity. "I'll kill the bitch! Please let me perform a summoning, Gregory," she pleaded. "I have been practicing. I'm sure if I remote viewed first, I wouldn't have a problem pinpointing her exact location."

"And so you shall, my dove. Your turn is coming," he placated in an effort to render her mute. Chloe had her place in the world— particularly as a cash cow—but most of the time, he would have rather listened to her talons screeching across a black board than to her insipid crowing.

"But remember...this time we deal with two...not one," he continued. "Trina is as much of a liability now as that drunken idiot she calls her boyfriend. She proved it early this morning when she went to the police."

"Pffft...like that would turn up anything. Thanks to you they'll be too busy counting their Cayman cash."

"Still, we'll have to do something about both of them soon. And that, as you know, takes a tremendous amount of planning and effort. It wouldn't hurt us to call in another master."

A delighted grunt told him Chloe was properly impressed. "Will I be taking part in the invocation?"

"I wouldn't have it any other way."

"And you'll introduce me to the exemplar?"

A vein in his left temple began throbbing. "Of course. Now... why don't you run upstairs, find a bed and take a nice long nap. We'll discuss it further this afternoon."

She hesitated, then slid off the chair and curled her arms around her mentor's neck.

"Not still angry with me, are you?" Taking his stony silence for proof she'd been forgiven, she droned on. "If it makes you feel better, you're doing the right thing. Even the coven doesn't trust her completely. Too snooty, if you ask me. Thinks everyone's too good for her. Besides, she's not right for you. No sense of adventure. I bet she can't even begin to scratch that certain itch of yours, at least not like I can. If you need proof, I'll be waiting upstairs. Don't be long," she added, punctuating her invitation by nipping his earlobe hard enough to draw blood.

Gregory watched her lick her reddened lips as she moved sensuously towards the door, a blur of color temporarily marring the near perfect darkness in which he'd always felt most comfortable.

"Chloe..." he said, catching her with her hand on the lever. "If I ever hear you mention labyrinths and triads in the presence of an outsider again, I will rip your throat out with my bare hands, cut you in a million little pieces and feed you to that incinerator Pindar made the mistake of remembering. It really makes no difference to me if you are the reigning queen of pop. I created you. Just think what I can do with real talent. Are we clear?"

Satisfied with the shudder that rocked her bony frame head to toe, he looked away, sighing only once he'd heard the lock click into place.

Rather than be consoled, Chloe's words only made him more irritable. He had the peculiar feeling that he'd missed something important—and Gregory Kadzik never missed anything.

Alone in the remote and Stygian silence of his chamber, Kadzik roared in fury, a resonance that tortured his features into something both less and more than the successful image he so carefully cultivated.

When his breathing returned to normal moments later, he felt calmer and more in control. He was unaccustomed to such outbursts, considering them beneath his dignity. He was simply overreacting, feeding the annoying nagging which insisted that by allowing Trina Langford to leave, he had set certain events in motion; that somehow, this was a direct threat to plans carefully laid out ages ago. Could she have discovered the truth?

Nonsense. Chloe was the only one in the coven to whom he'd fed even a crumb of truth; something he'd chalked up to a moment of reckless abandon after a particularly energetic session with a riding crop. He'd regretted it ever since.

As it had been grilled into him from a very young age, you must mix the reality with the lie. Accord each member just one or two pieces of the puzzle and keep its key to yourself. The rule had served him well through the years.

There was only one other in his region who, through his power and audacity, understood the chronicle of events unfolding; and even he was limited by a need-to-know basis: his grand master; the exemplar under whose guidance he had trained. In turn, he alone knew the identities of the ones above him with each tier out-ranking the previous by station, power and knowledge but linked by their age-old quest.

Very few were privy to who held the top wrung—the one known only as The Caretaker—but speculation ran rampant and Kadzik always enjoyed a good guessing game. He looked forward to the day he'd be considered worthy of meeting him and the others, finally proclaiming their allegiance as one. Their number would indeed be legion.

"May it be soon," he appealed, astounded, as usual, at the scope of his goals.

Before reaching them, however, he needed to rid himself of some obstacles, and for this he needed power; loads of it.

He dialed a number, pleased when he heard the familiar voice after only the second ring.

"Sinistrus, my old friend...how are things in the music business?"

Using an avatar of a demon was the standard practice when coven members addressed each other. To address one another by any other, especially at a formal convocation, would invite censure.

"You know the only things that change are the faces."

"Too right. So to what do I owe this pleasure at...good lord... don't tell me it's nearly time for my morning latté?"

"Doesn't sound like I woke you from your beauty sleep."

"Well, this is crunch time for us. Gotta get that budget signed and delivered before the session's over. I'm glad you called. Quite honestly, I think I dozed off. After the first eight-hundred mill, all the numbers start running together."

Gregory chuckled. "How else are you going to pay for all those perks?"

"I'll try to hold on to that thought. What can I do for you, bro?"

"Can you make it down here tonight?"

"Tonight...that's awfully-short notice. What have you got that can't wait?"

"Just a small problem that needs containing."

"A problem you say? The Quickening?"

"No...no...nothing like that. More like damage control before the damage," Gregory quickly amended, thankful no one could see him flush.

"How many?"

"Two."

"Well known?

"Relatively. One of them is a live wire...on his way up but unpredictable and a general pain in the ass. The other, I think we brought her in too early. I believe she may be the greater threat."

He heard a disapproving *tsk-tsk*. "You've been a bad boy. Still, why can't you handle it?"

"They're becoming increasingly annoying. I want to make them pay."

Laughter boomed in his ear. "Ahh, you want revenge. Why didn't you say so in the first place? What do you have in mind?"

"Energy manipulation perhaps? A special invocation with a dual effect?"

"Huh...I see what you mean...a complicated ritual at best. Haven't tried one for years. Might be interesting at that though

I'll have to scrounge around to see who's available on such short notice. Everyone's so busy these days but it never hurts to go into these things fully loaded."

Gregory breathed a quiet sigh of relief. "I won't ask who," he remarked, thinking about Chloe's reaction to being in the presence of not two but three masters.

"That's always best but don't worry, you'll recognize him as he practically lives on the five o'clock news. So we're on the same page, what's the preferred outcome? Temporary or permanent?"

"Permanence, preceded by pain," Gregory said. He recalled Trina's disloyalty; the way she'd thrown his offer in his face. And then Edward, foolishly divulging the mysteries of the sacred rite. By all accounts, they should have never left and then he wouldn't have had to make this call. But it was as if at the very last minute, The Enemy had intervened, sending in that third-rate hack he'd vaguely recognized. His face darkened at the memory.

"Anything in particular?"

"Something to remind them of their betrayal, I think."

"Creativity...what would we do for entertainment without it! You know, if I didn't consider myself purely evil, I think I'd feel some sympathy for what's coming at them. Consider it done."

An abrupt click signaled their chat was over and Gregory turned off his own phone considerably cheered. As usual, his master's parting words had hit all the right notes. Surely his earlier doubt was due to an over-active imagination. Amazing how The Old One took over once the wheels were set in motion. Now it was just a matter of timing since, with the added influence, a single deadly blow would rid him of both his problems. What they would achieve tonight was very close to pure genius and, after all, The Old One always rewarded genius.

No longer wearied by his endless night, buoyed by the certainty of tonight's grand success, Kadzik rose. He crossed the short distance to the altar, stepped behind it and with a small key that never left him, unlocked the door to the gleaming tabernacle.

He pushed aside a small, round tin containing a consecrated Host and reached for the dagger behind it; an instrument so ancient and timeless, it had long since relinquished its luster to its grizzly past—the most recent being the episode Pindar had so boorishly described to Trina earlier. For a moment, he brought it up to his face, studied the barely-perceptible filaments of its Damascus steel and imagined them weaving about, undulating like snakes recalled through a charmer's flute. His teacher's words returned effortlessly.

Welcome pain; learn to crave it, rather than fear it; seek physical, spiritual and emotional agony at every opportunity and, over time, you will gain strength over your enemies. They will crumple before you, defeated and powerless against your skill, your daring. Do not waste your sentiments on them but rather, use them as they should be used; as a means to an end, propelling you ever forward towards the path of true destiny...

With one fluid motion, he tore open his dress shirt and dragged the point of the blade down over his skin until he drew blood. Pain seared but was already being replaced by arousal as his body gave itself up to the visceral response. He allowed it to trickle down his chest without stemming the flow; a scarlet stream veining its way over both older and newer scars and mutilations.

The dim lights flickered and Kadzik's eyes filled with tears. Waves of gratitude poured over him; for his brilliance at engineering the demise of his enemies; for his ability to react instantaneously to the challenges of the moment and reap the benefits; for The

Old One who had cared and nurtured him when his own mother had abandoned him to the streets; that other who'd shown him the wonders of the universe and on whom he'd called upon in his darkest hour.

He turned his eyes to the inverted crucifix above him and smiled in triumph.

NINE

Monday, March 10
Los Angeles

I woke with a start, still clothed in the little black dress I'd donned more than twenty-four hours ago. Rumpled, reeking of sweat and fear, it had lost its allure.

I glanced at the clock in time to see the glowing digital display three-thirty-three; in my condition, an omen I presumed meant all was definitely *not* right with my universe.

The house was as silent as a tomb but I knew I was no longer alone. The big question: was it Eddy returning from whatever sanctuary he'd fled to as soon as we'd driven home, or act two of last night's nightmare?

I grabbed the bottle of pepper spray I'd shoved under my pillow and tip-toed to the door. Hyper aware it wouldn't do much against brutes with guns, I kept my finger on the nozzle, pressed an ear against the wood and listened.

Several moments passed. Impatient with the stubborn silence,

I cracked open the door, emboldened when I detected neither shadow nor movement and poked my head and shoulders out. A rush of air blew across my face before something hard threw me against the jamb.

I gulped a lungful of air, sprayed blindly through the darkness, and hoped some of it reached its mark. A familiar cough told me it had but that I'd misjudged the threat as it had misjudged me.

"What the hell are you doing?" Eddy gasped as I flipped on the light.

"Same thing you are," I said, rubbing my head while trying not to breathe the toxic air. "Ever think of yelling *honey I'm home*?"

"I didn't think you'd still be here," he answered, wobbling to his feet, giving me the chance to truly see him for the first time. In the time he'd been away, Eddy Pindar had aged a decade. Yesterday's pale countenance had metastasized. His eyes had sunk into his skull and appeared jaundiced around the irises, the skin beneath, bruised and sagging, as if he'd been in a bar fight. Last night's clothes, now stained and filthy, drooped over his body that had somehow lost much of its substance over twenty-four hours. Even his hair had undergone a dramatic change—stringy, oily, matted against his face.

"Come on, let's get you in the shower," I mumbled, urging him to follow, but also eager to look away from the ravaging that had taken place.

"There's no time. We have to leave." He followed me as far as the closet and flung it open, the pungent stench of whiskey leaving a wake as he moved. Not hard to figure out where he'd been after all.

He lifted an empty suitcase off the shelf, threw it on the bed, and emptied the contents of a drawer into it.

I stood still, following him with my eyes. "There is no *we* anymore, Eddy. After you left last night, I went down to the police station and filed a report. It's the only reason I'm still here. They want to talk with both of us when you got back."

"You did what?"

"It's our protection against what happened. Gregory would never risk hurting us now. Not with an impending investigation."

"Who'd you talk with?"

"Some detective on duty. I have his card here somewhere. Does it matter? He said we should hear back from him later today. The point is, Gregory is helpless to do anything. If he's guilty of the things you accused him of, it's going to come out sooner or later. Only there was no way not to bring you into it since you were a witness."

He halted and I waited for his temper to kick in—the accusations of betrayal. Instead, he sank onto the bed and covered his face with his hands. "We might have had a chance before, but not now. Don't you see what you've done?"

"Why don't you explain it to me. One of us had to take responsibility and since you were busy drinking yourself into oblivion...you do the math!"

"There will never be an investigation."

"Because Gregory is so rich and famous, shit doesn't stick to him?"

"Damn right it doesn't. Not when he's paid others to keep him smelling like a rose."

"Everyone can't be on his payroll. The conspiracy has to end somewhere, Eddy."

"So where does it end? I saw the way you looked at everyone last night when we were cornered. You wanted to ask for help but didn't know who has a standing invite to Gregory's midnight services. Kinda hard to tell the good guys from the bad when their faces are shrouded by masks and cowls, ain't it?"

I shook my head and tried to forget the pervading helplessness Eddy's words brought to mind.

"But someone did help us and we are safe."

"Some two-bit reporter desperate for dirt? Yeah...really selfless, Trina. And we're not safe. Thanks to you, we'll never be safe again."

"Are you telling me I have to grow eyes at the back of my head? That maybe five...ten years from now, some lunatic with a vendetta will still be coming after me?"

"I doubt you'll have that long to wait. We'll probably both be dead by the end of the week."

"I don't believe you. He and his mafia coven can't be everywhere at once."

"They don't need to be," he shrugged. "Gregory has certain gifts. He can make things happen, influence people certain ways. I've seen it. The stuff Chloe was chanting...it *means* something, Trina."

"Now what? Gregory is some sort of psychic?"

"It's more than that but yes, he's got a natural gift; only it's grown because he's tapped into something more. Something not human. Chloe knows; that's why she's in it so deep; why she's so thirsty for knowledge. She's on a power quest."

I searched my memory for a clue that what Eddy was telling me was true. How many times had I been invited to Gregory's basement rituals? Three, four times max? Other than the robes and silly words, intoned with a solemnity more appropriate to a funeral, nothing woo-woo had ever happened. But there was another possibility.

"What about those mood enhancers Gregory was talking about? Those bowls passed around like Halloween candy? What's in them? Coke? Heroin? LSD? Some special cocktail Gregory dreamed up to make you believe you're seeing the Easter Bunny sprouting horns?"

"Now you sound like him!"

"He has a point. Look, I have no more illusions about who Gregory and Chloe are, what they choose to believe or who they use and hurt as a result. They *are* evil. You've convinced me, okay? But it's a human evil, Eddy, using every psychological trick written to control you."

His unruly mane whipped side to side. "You weren't there. Gregory didn't think you were ready for the more advanced rituals. He was right I think. I've seen things, Trina. I've even done some things." He looked away, a spot of color returning to his wasted face. "Stuff I didn't know I could do. Not like Gregory, of course. He's the exemplar. He makes it look easy, effortless."

His eyes suddenly probed mine. "I know I've lied to you a lot but I swear to you I'm telling the truth now. If you want to survive this, you're gonna have to make yourself believe. It's the only way and reading some shrink manual won't cut it."

I know I've lied to you a lot. An apology? Probably the closest Eddy would ever come to one.

Though last night had only postponed the inevitable, nothing had changed between us. He and I were through and his pleas fell on deaf ears. But now, despite the lies, betrayals, drunken bouts, and temper tantrums, I also saw a broken man tied to a strange delusion.   If I drew him out, gave him time to regain his composure, perhaps I'd learn something that might help the police.

"Alright," I complied, sitting across from him. "Tell me about those sacrifices Gregory was talking about. He made it sound like you and Chloe had already passed some test."

"Part of the process," he said, avoiding my eyes. "Everyone is continually tested. That's how they move up the ladder. It's different for each member, of course. It's one of the ways Gregory uses his second sight. Somehow, he can tell how far someone's willing to go and he exploits it."

"So with me..."

"Like I said, he didn't think you were fully committed yet. He was being careful. Any suggestions or influencing had to be done in a roundabout way so it felt like it was coming from you. Perception is reality."

"And I played right into it. But does it count when I wasn't fully aware of what I was doing?"

"It doesn't depend on just you. It's the magnitude of the sacrifice. An unborn child is considered the most powerful of all... its purity...its innocence..."

"I get it! What about Chloe?"

His grin could've been mistaken for a nervous tick. "Chloe was different. She's been with Gregory for almost three years and from what I've heard, he never really had to work hard to get her to do anything. Whore that she is, from the start, she took it all in hook, line, and sinker."

"You mean she sold herself to Gregory, to the industry?"

"And to The Old One."

"That mythical entity we're all supposed to worship?

Eddy glared at me, his disappointment only second to his urgency and impatience. I quickly changed the subject.

"What did Chloe sacrifice?"

"Remember how she got started?"

"Only what I've read. Midwestern upbringing; her parents are farmers, I think. She even sang some gospel back home. I've seen some of her early videos. She seems almost normal," I said, comparing her to last night's shrieking banshee.

"But she wasn't getting anywhere until she hooked up with Gregory," he reminded. "She was sharing a place with another girl at the time. A wannabe with lots of ambition and a pretty good head. In fact, she was the one who introduced her to Gregory. As you can guess, under his guidance this chick was about to hit the jackpot. You should look her up. Kinda spooky when you see how she dressed...how she did her hair. You'd think you were looking at Chloe."

"She stole her image?"

"Seems obvious, but not until after she ended up in the morgue juiced up to the hilt on an eight-ball cocktail of coke and heroin; not a combo a light-weight like her would've tried. She'd take a hit when it was offered but always knew when to stop. Rumor has it there was so much junk percolating inside her, it's unlikely she self-medicated."

"You're saying Chloe had something to do with it?"

"Evidence points that way. They were both in the right place at the right time. Chloe certainly had a motive. She was even brought in for questioning before the whole thing was dropped."

"But how? If they suspected murder, why didn't they go after her?"

"Because it wasn't to the coven's advantage. Still think you can bring down Gregory?"

Bits and pieces of an earlier conversation: my impression of a seasoned detective jotting down notes; the certainty I was doing the right thing, the sincere promise that this very morning, an investigation would be opened, questions answered. Was Eddy right? Was I wrong? Was Chloe a murderous lunatic? Was the earth round and did we really go to the moon? I needed time to process.

"What about you? You never told me what your sacrifice was. Then again, after hearing about Chloe, maybe I don't want to know."

"We have more important things to think about right now," he insisted. "You need to hear what I'm telling you, Trina. I know I've never given you a reason to trust me but I'm asking just this once. Get away. Okay, maybe not with me but go. Now."

"Not until I know more. Chloe said something about labyrinths and triangles; triads, she called them. How it was too late for everyone but the anointed."

"Gregory doesn't tell me everything but I've heard some of the others talking about something that's about to happen. Something big. It's supposed to change the world; bring it to its knees."

"And you believe it?"

"I don't know anymore. Sometimes it makes perfect sense, like when I see what he can do, his power. If he can work that kind of magic, who's to say the other stuff's not real?"

"But that's my point. How do you know any of it is real? Think about the science. A hundred years ago, our movies, cell phones, cars, everything we use today would've been mistaken for witchcraft. We'd have been burned at the stake. How easy would it be for him to manipulate some new gadget that's probably not even on the market yet? And he's rich enough to do it too."

"You're wrong."

"Prove it."

"I've done it too, Trina. I've summoned spirits. I've made them do my bidding. Look...you wanted to know what my sacrifice was. If I tell you, will you go then?"

I shrugged, refusing to give him a real answer.

He closed his eyes for a moment but when he opened them, he'd lost some of the panic and focused on me clearly. "What do you remember from the other night? The night you came home from the clinic?"

"I drove up, went into the studio. You were a first-class jerk and then I took a bath and went to bed."

"Something else happened; something that took place while you were in the tub."

The way he said it—it wasn't a question but hard fact. I saw myself as I had been days earlier, holding the razor over my wrist with the sudden conviction that I *had* to do this thing.

"You weren't there. How could you know what happened?"

"Gregory suggested it over a month ago. It was to be my final test before moving up. I thought he was kidding at first. Why would he want to get rid of you when he'd invested so much? I didn't realize at the time it was a way of testing both of us at once; me for my aptitude and courage; you for your willingness to offer a worthy sacrifice to The Old One but also your ability to resist."

"Courage...is that what he calls it?"

"I didn't know what I was hoping for. I liked what I could do, the feeling it gave me. I went along, but somehow I didn't really think Gregory would make me go through with it. Then a couple of weeks ago, he called everyone in for a special session."

"The one with the thirteen-year-old girl?"

He nodded. "For the first time, I was in charge. I led the

invocation, performed the summoning. You have no idea what The Old One is capable of. The power that surged through me was phenomenal. At that moment, I knew anything I asked for would be mine."

"So of course the first thing you asked for was my death and the death of your child."

"Doesn't work like that," he answered, oblivious to my sarcasm. "The only thing the invocation does is set up the event. The actual execution comes later, at my own discretion. I started by feeding you suggestions, closing doors to certain thoughts while opening others. At first it worked but then you kept talking about keeping the baby. I had to do something fast despite the physical toll I knew it would have on your body."

"You caused it? The lethargy? The migraine that kept pounding me, like my brain was stuffed with cotton?"

"Unavoidable side effect of the Scopolamine."

"...the hell is that?"

"The ultimate roofie. Comes from a tree found only in Colombia. It bends your will, makes you helpless to resist. That was the hardest part...compelling you to go through with the abortion, making you see it was the right thing to do."

"You son-of-a-bitch. You drugged me into killing our baby?"

"You have to understand. I had to prove myself to Gregory. The next part was easy. I chose the day after your procedure, knowing you'd be at your weakest and most susceptible."

I tried to peel myself off the chair but my legs were not responding.

"You failed."

"Yes and no. You can blame the drugs for going to the clinic but the razor in the tub...that was all me. Gregory says it means I have some natural talent like he does. He figures the only reason you're still alive is you're strong willed. You're able to withstand attacks better than most. He needs members with that ability."

But did I really possess the will he accused me of having? Even now, the memory of that cry hurling me back to life almost against my will, staggered. Here was something not even Gregory or Eddy would ever know. If it hadn't shaken me to the core, I'd simply have been labeled as the latest victim in an industry that eats it own.

"So when he congratulated me on how well I'd performed..."

"It was both for your sacrifice and your shielding abilities."

"Nobody can possibly have that much influence on another human being."

Eddy smiled; a certain smugness that negated his earlier despair. "Happens all the time, Trina. Welcome to my world. Ready to believe now?"

"Only that you and Gregory deserve each other. The girl on the altar...the one sacrificed...did you have anything to do with her death?"

A blanket of silence hung over us. Outside, night gave way to encroaching dawn reluctantly, bathing the world in dreary gray tones. Here in the room, Eddy hung his head. The anxiety was back, and with it, his hand fetish; returning with vengeance as he stared at his fingers, no longer seeing me.

"I don't remember. I woke up at the bathroom sink. I wasn't alone. One of the others came with me. He was helping me wash the blood off my fingers only it wasn't working. No matter how much I scrubbed damned stuff wouldn't come out."

In my mind's eye I saw a pendulum. The earth shook and it swung in one direction; then a connecting but divergent fault line shifted and its course altered. I was the pendulum and now it trembled and shuddered then fell; irresistible to the forces that jolted it with impunity.

TEN

A slideshow ran through my head. Eddy's hands caressing me, touching me, holding mine. Eddy making love to me. Had that been before or after—had that been the first time—the only time? Did it really matter anymore?

His cheerless laughter cut through the shock as he eyed me through wisps of scraggly hair. "You're starting to think about it. Good. You need to believe before you can act. Just don't take all day...and while you're at it, open a goddamn window," he said, fanning himself."

I reeled at the abrupt switch and looked up. He'd lost his earlier pallor and his face glowed feverishly as bright red spots appeared beneath his cheeks.

"What are you talking about?"

"It's like a furnace in here!"

"Eddy, did you hear what you just said? What you admitted? I don't care how powerful you think Gregory is. Even he won't be able to prevent an inquiry now. And you're right. I do need to leave. I can't be around you anymore. Not after this."

Some long-suppressed voice screamed for me to move. I jerked to my feet, while in another world, Eddy droned on about how I needed him, how there were more things I had to know to survive. I ignored him, now preoccupied with completing the packing he'd begun.

"Don't leave me, Trina!"

The raw emotion caught my attention but it was the movement behind him—the wrongness of it—that held me transfixed.

No more than ten feet away, Eddy remained seated on the edge of our bed, his face buried in those hands that had, at the very least, made him an accessory to murder.

At first, I thought my eyes were deceiving me. I caught a wisp of something transparent ghosting its way towards the ceiling behind him. Why not? Thanks to his revelations, it wouldn't have been much of a stretch. But after a moment, the haze shifted then thickened and I gasped.

"What?"

"There's...there's smoke behind you," I explained, quickly checking off potential threats. Our bedroom was on the opposite end from the kitchen and backed up against the yard. It had been two years since Eddy had put in the studio with all its electronics, and neither one of us smoked. It didn't make sense.

Confused, Eddy turned his head left, right and shrugged.

That's when I knew; the smoke wasn't originating from *behind* Eddy but *from* him—from the top of his furiously-rumpled head.

For a moment I watched, fascinated. The smoke flared, rose up above him, not black and sooty, but nearly white—a specter without a body beginning its last journey to some ephemeral land unknown to those still earth bound. But no—spirits didn't reek of singed hair, burned oil, and something else; something I'd never smelled before but imagined: the stench of human flesh as it seared out of control. I stared, spellbound; felt the earth sliding, shifting beneath me; sensed the new rift being formed, a gaping chasm calling from the depths.

"Oh God, Eddy..."

I moved closer, my mind refusing to process what I was seeing. Twin tendrils appeared, one at his left elbow, the other just above his right shoulder; tiny at first but gathering force, as if some invisible bellows were giving them life and substance.

Thinking I'd gone mad, Eddy looked at me blankly, oblivious to what was occurring around him, in him. Then his eyes followed mine and I noted the change—the pivotal moment of understanding that preceded the panic.

He shot off the bed with a cry, hugging and slapping himself in a crazy dance of survival as he ripped off his clothes; his shirt first, where the heat had already seared a hole, then his pants—tripping over them. He wasn't nearly fast enough. By now, several more threads materialized on his skin and each time he tried to erase one, two more appeared as if the genetic composition of his body had altered into something resembling a volcano, igniting it from the inside out, the pressure points too volatile to yield to mere human touch. The more he fanned, slapped and rubbed, the more the smoke intensified until we were surrounded by a cloud and breathing suddenly became a problem.

He stared at me helplessly. Why wasn't the fire alarm blaring by now?

"On the floor!" I shouted over his screams. I swiped the blanket off the bed and hurled it over him as he fell to the ground, his cries beneath, muffled.

Coughing, I knelt beside him, felt my hands burn through the cloth and ripped it off his face. The top of his head was charred, most of his hair gone. Eddy's mouth was deformed into a rictus of pain, his eyes open but glazed over by some inexpressible sensation defying any known language.

I stripped the blanket back even farther and understood what could not be spoken.

The cloth had not doused the inferno that had erupted over his body—but rather sparked a new horror.

Wherever the smoke had done its damage, burn marks appeared; some no larger than a dime, others the size of silver dollars, eating into his flesh, peeling back his skin like paper. And in each glowing center, a tiny flame sizzled brightly; dozens of little beacons pulsing, announcing their monstrous presence.

I tore my eyes away from the wounds of his body with effort and focused on his face. The damage there wasn't quite as severe, yet his skin continued to smolder and if the previous timeline of his suffering was any indication, I knew he had only seconds before it reached the same level of virulence that consumed his chest and shoulders, arms and legs, feet. Had a full minute actually passed since I'd seen that first wisp of smoke? Hard to tell. Time had ceased.

"Waa...daa..." he gurgled, the wet whisper nearly obliterated by my cry of revulsion because I hadn't *heard* it as much as *seen* it—the jaw, in various stages of decomposition, working up and down to form the sound.

"Waa...daa..." The plea was stronger this time, breaking through my defenses and I sprang to my feet.

Water!

I sprinted towards the bathroom and the slim promise it offered, looked at the tub, and considered it for a moment. Did I have the strength to drag him in here and haul him over the side? Disregarded the notion for fear I'd do more damage than good and turned towards the sink, caught a glimpse of the madness reflected above it and blinked it away; flung open the cupboard beneath—fingers probing, searching—grasping the bucket—too small but I'd take it. Rushed back to the tub—flipped on the tap—watched it fill up quickly but not quickly enough.

"Come on!   COME ON!"

I was stunned to silence by an ominous *woomph* and ran back into the bedroom with Eddy's name stuck in my throat and the sloshing bucket of water.

What was left of him had somehow managed to slide to his knees facing me, his arms extended at his sides, palms out in silent petition.

Engulfed by the fire that licked every part of his flesh, his head and face were no longer visible. What little remained was reduced to a fueling device for the flames as they continued their obliteration.

At some point, I threw the meager water at the blaze, but it simply countered by expanding for a moment, burning brighter and hotter, resisting any effort to destroy it before it consumed its victim.

I stared at it mutely, its silence so deafening and abnormal, it forced me to become aware of other, even stranger anomalies: the flames, no longer orange, but nearly white and contained; tempted by neither the wooden floor, the furniture, nor me, the beast unwilling to stray too far from its feast. The smoke—still white as well; swirling into the ceiling, leaving a large greasy circle above but no charring, no blackness anywhere.

Then there was Eddy—still kneeling, absolutely as silent as the fire that consumed him. He neither writhed, squirmed nor thrashed in agony, but remained perfectly motionless and unmoving. *Taking it*—for God's sake; the white flames obliterating him to the point where I could no longer see any sign of skin, charred or otherwise; to the point where there was just the fire—curling itself around the shape of a man—but really no more man.

Half aware of what I was doing, I extended a hand towards the pyre—not brave, just morbidly curious. What would happen if I dared reach within and touch him? Was he still in there? Or would the flames jump now that they had nearly finished feeding off their host and the nightmare begin anew with me?

Only part of me cared and then only in theory as I drew near. I thought of all the times I'd been warned as a child not to play with matches. Sound advice, yet I still needed to know.

A stab of irrational anger cut through me when the blaze blinked out as if it had never existed.

Snow fell soundlessly, without flourish; a scattering of white ash as if someone had ripped open a feather pillow, its contents spilling over, making a mess, showering me. I was in the midst of a storm, unable to see through or past it as it littered me with the fine particles I knew were Eddy's only remains.

I shuddered and covered my nose and mouth with an elbow, the idea of breathing at the moment too obscene to contemplate. Instead, I fought, gagged, and coughed my way towards the spot where he'd suffered; the floor where he should have been, cool and unspoiled beneath my feet. I turned on a dime and called for him, then fell to my hands and knees and felt—nothing; nothing human anyway or that had once been.

Slowly, other things began to sink in; one of Eddy's sneakers, lying on its side; a tee shirt with his band's name embossed beneath an image of the quintet, a burn hole where Eddy should've been. A sock here—a belt there—a chain with a gold charm of an eagle—my Christmas present to him last year. Cool to the touch, I picked it up absently and wrapped it around my wrist, then listened for other sounds.

The fire alarm had still not interrupted the deathly pall. Outside, the world was coming to life; a lark sang, insects buzzed, and somewhere, a child laughed; all oblivious to the destruction of one human being and the abrupt transformation of another.

I leaned over to vomit and dry heaved. Denied the small consolation, a sob ripped from my throat.

"I'm sorry, Eddy. I'm so very sorry..."

The irony wasn't lost on me. I thought of the insistent voice taunting, drumming inside my head, posing as my own; Eddy's psychic suggestion that I should slice my wrists although, technically, I was five years too late to take my rightful place beside Kurt Cobain, Janis Joplin, and Jimi Hendrix of the 27 Club; its dues, Eddy had told me more than once, to be paid only with the blood of rockers meeting their untimely ends. Strange that he was now part of that exclusive circle forever.

"I'm so sorry..."

My lips were repeating one thing, my thoughts another.

Kinda hard to tell the good guys from the bad when their faces are shrouded by masks and cowls, ain't it? We'll never be safe again. Who did you talk to down at the station?

The words echoed faintly but gained strength until my head pounded. Until somewhere, a clock once again resumed its journey around the dial reminding me that even now, time stopped for no one and that mine had run out.

I stood, turning towards the suitcase still half empty. When I finished dumping the contents of my life into it moments later, the memory of it no longer existed in any clear, meaningful way. I left the room without a backwards glance and hurried through the house, avoiding the hall mirror. Would I even recognize my own face? Or would the last week be forever etched across it, each new line and wrinkle a permanent landmark on a map leading to hell? Better not. That would require acceptance; certain truths that had barely begun to wriggle their way to the surface. They would come in time but I would not force them.

Instead I walked into a day designed more for family picnics than the malice I now knew lurked on the edge of polite society— its presence cloaked in a wavelength visible only through the lenses of the initiated.

A man stood at the bottom of the driveway, leaning against a faded, battered car; his casual stance a challenge to the coiled, barely-suppressed energy he radiated. He smiled broadly—a gesture I recognized that reached some part of me even the sunshine couldn't thaw.

Gratitude, unexpectedly sweet and strong, struck a chord. I tried returning his smile, failed, slammed the door shut, and made my way to him. Perhaps one day that expression would again come naturally. Right now I'd have to be satisfied that even this fragile hope—delicate and brittle as it was—hadn't gone up in smoke with Eddy.

SCRUTINY

ELEVEN

The unusual heat blistered, too unforgiving for the time of year. What might have been sufficient to a camel—didn't come close to replenishing vital fluids while we drove through the desert without AC. I grabbed the water bottle anyway, dribbled half of it over my head before chugging down the rest and pitched it in back with the others.

"Remind me again why we took your ride," I shouted over road noise.

Logan O'Neill grinned without taking his eyes off the road shimmering like a mirage. "Let's see...we had our choice between a fiery-red Cobra or your silver Mercedes SLK350 Roadster, neither of which are exactly low profile."

"The Roadster isn't mine. After Eddy signed on with Gregory, he went on a spree and bought his-and-hers. I told him I'd only take it when I had enough money saved up to buy it off him. Same with the house. Everything I own is in the trunk of this Buick."

"Nevertheless, discreet and unremarkable is good when you're trying to outrun a cabal of devil worshipers armed with guns and curses. Besides, where we're going they chop-shop cars like yours for lunch."

"I'm not arguing. Just wondering if it's worth it, that's all."

"Got any better ideas?" Logan asked, mopping his face with a sweat-drenched shirt.

"You know I don't. But if this doesn't work, then what? If I can't convince anyone..."

"You convinced me. Don't underestimate yourself."

"Yeah, but you're a reporter and the worst kind at that. You'd print anything as long as it's remotely feasible."

"Ouch! I'll pretend you didn't say that."

"I've dealt with the paparazzi before, remember? You all prefer to jump to any conclusion, however illogical, rather than dig deeper."

"Like you just did? Haven't you heard? Perception is reality. But don't worry," he continued, clueless to the memory he'd triggered. "The fact I showed up on your doorstep should tell you digging around is my specialty. I have to admit, though, I've got my work cut out. If I don't come up with something, I might have to find another way to pay the bills."

"You're not even on the clock?"

Logan shrugged.

"But your editor..."

"Haven't taken a vacation in three years. She owes me."

I turned to him, knowing my eyes betrayed the emotion behind them. "Even after I gave you the go ahead?"

"Don't go soft on me. I'll make up for it on the next one. Why settle for fish and chips when you can have lobster, right?

Anyway, it's been a long time since I've worked on a story that actually means something."

His expression shifted from wistful to excited. I wanted to ask what he meant but screaming to one another over the howling blast furnace masquerading as a 1960's muscle car took too much effort. By unspoken agreement, we both fell silent, each lost in our own silent worries and regrets. Unable to dissect his, I fixated on mine. Sorrow over my now-barren womb competed with dread of seeing the first wisp of smoke rising off my skin any moment. I knew the fact I hadn't slept in thirty-six hours wasn't helping but that was a feat I hadn't dared attempt since we'd begun our cross-country trip, stopping only when necessary.

I glanced sideways at Logan and studied his calm profile. As usual, my fears abated a little and I wondered at the strange effect he seemed to have on me.

He was unflappable, I decided. As cool and composed as the tar beneath us was corrosive and caustic. Simply put, he just didn't react the way I expected; not even when I showed him the white flecks that had once been a man, revealed Gregory and Chloe's fondness for human blood, or admitted to nearly slicing my wrists after unknowingly offering my unborn child to seal a covenant I never knew I'd made. The man was either brilliant at hiding his true feelings, a sociopath missing a few of the more vital emotions, or had a past so grizzly, mine didn't raise an eyebrow.

Logan O'Neill had taken it all in stride, the inquisitive reporter dealing rather well, I thought, with a strange woman's tale of secret cabals and satanic murder.

The insight led me to one even more startling: with him here, beside me, I felt safe.

I leaned back against my seat, felt the heat lash across my face, and took another stab at closing my eyes, waiting for the familiar images to appear.

For the first time since we'd left L.A., the darkness didn't immediately evolve into mutant snowflakes.

TWELVE

Outside El Paso, Texas

I woke to cooler temperatures and the crunch of gravel beneath the tires; a marked improvement over the odor of melting tar. Purple twilight softened the shabby neighborhood and its uniform pre-fabs that spoke volumes of their uninspired builder. Despite the sprouting patches of green and kids playing in their yards, most of the homes were a tribute to the harshness of their environment.

To our right, a large, brick building took up an entire block; the name *St. Joseph the Worker* stenciled on a marquee in both English and Spanish.

"Must have made good time. We're here already."

"Just what I'd expect someone to say after she slept across a state line and five counties."

"You should've woken me. I would've switched places with you."

"After the week you've had, wasn't about to try."

I mumbled my thanks as we drove around the side of the church, gravel giving way to compact dirt. Two other structures stood hidden behind it, more modest but clearly part of the compound. Logan parked beside one of the smaller buildings and we got out, stretched our cramped legs, and headed towards the man bent over two sawhorses, measuring a piece of plywood. When we were a few feet of him, he finally looked up, recognition and a hint of mischief flooding his bronze face.

"I was wondering when you'd get here. Any later and I would've been tempted to send in the cavalry, seein' you're still driving that old rust bucket."

"It got us here, didn't it?"

"But at what cost? You look like one of those drowned rats the dog drags in every night."

"Just as long as you don't decide to feed me to him. I've seen what the beast looks like," Logan countered, then clasped his arm before stepping back. "I want you to meet someone. Trina, this is Pearce Rhomer. Pearce...Trina Langford."

Logan told me what to expect. Still, I blinked a couple of times before taking the outstretched hand—hard and callused, but warm; the pressure of his fingers firm but not crushing.

"Welcome to El Paso," he greeted, his voice deep and resonant. "It's a pleasure to meet you, Trina. I know it must get old hearing it, but I've gotta confess, I'm a real fan. Your *Phoenix* album...one of my favorites."

I flushed a bit but doubted anyone could tell it was due to any-thing but heat. "I hate to break it to you, but that's all she wrote. Besides, aren't we supposed to confess to you?"

He smiled crookedly. "Give me a moment to go back to looking like a priest and we'll talk."

He was right—he didn't look much like a priest. The man who

faced me had a full head of dark hair and a trim beard tinged with a bit of gray. Bare to the waist, sporting a tan that would turn Angelinos pea-green with envy, Father Pearce looked like he'd be more proficient with a nail gun than behind a pulpit.

He noticed me staring but rather than appear self-conscious, raised his brown eyes to mine in understanding. "Adapt and overcome. Basic carpentry in full uniform isn't very practical around these parts," he explained. "It's also why I come out at night with the cockroaches. At least right now it's tolerable. Only way this lumber is going to resemble buffet tables by the end of the week."

"Pearce was Marine Force Recon which is why he can't break himself of the lingo," Logan explained."

The priest laughed easily. "Since we're reminiscing about past lives, don't let that paparazzi routine fool you. Have him take you down to the gulch tomorrow and show you what he can do with a decent rifle and scope at a thousand yards. Coyotes are running amok again. Wouldn't mind a hand with them."

Logan glared oddly at the priest; a look I could've sworn meant zip it.

"You too?" I asked. "But I thought..."

"Yeah well, after our stint in the Corp, Pearce found his calling and I found mine," he said quickly. "Speaking of which, am I going to have to shoot one of those coyotes to get some dinner around here?"

"Only if you decide mangy mutt is tastier than that great big pot of chili I've had simmering all day."

"By all means then...lead on!"

The men bantered back and forth as we made our way past the shed and towards the priest's *residence*—as Pearce called it tongue in cheek; his overinflated name for the four walls and tin roof that didn't have much in the way of character but made up in its nearly-austere spotlessness.

I only half listened to their good-natured ribbing and remembered the two men who had led me through the dark, winding corridors of a wine cellar only days before, and how even the cool air had seemed stifling; a stark contrast to the vast purity of this desert with which I now filled my lungs.

Indoors, my stomach rumbled in response to the smells from Pearce's kitchen. I temporarily put away those other memories, my recent history and the reason I was here at all, in this tiny, unremarkable house, with a man I barely knew and another I didn't know at all. I sat down and let the darkness outside reduce my world to the steaming bowl of chili set before me.

THIRTEEN

A coyote howled in some distant gorge and the *beast* spoken of earlier staggered to all fours from under the table, passed judgment on his cousin with a single bark, and settled back down to resume his nap.

I turned towards Pearce. Although now fully clothed and respectable, I still had a hard time prefixing his title to his name. With dinner devoured hours ago and Logan succumbing to weariness shortly after, he'd kept up a steady stream of chatter—most likely to put me at ease. At some point, I'd have to ask Logan exactly what he had told him about the last week of my existence. For now, I was content as he regaled me with stories of the community he served.

I learned he'd lived on the fringes of El Paso for nearly six years; that aside from a deacon, an elderly nun showed up for basic admin and housekeeping twice a week, and that the buffet tables were for the wedding of a couple expecting their first baby in a couple of weeks. Most surprisingly, I learned I could feel a measure of peace at a stranger's table in the back of beyond.

"You don't smile much, do you?" he prompted during a comfortable lull.

"Is that your way of letting me know it's time to get down to brass tacks?"

"Only if you have a thing for sharp objects that get stuck to the bottom of your feet. I'd rather you just tell me what's making it so hard for you to smile."

He was sneaky. He'd almost had me. "How much did Logan tell you?" I asked, glancing at the slumbering body on the couch who'd be oblivious to a semi crashing through the wall.

"Let me see if I've got the gist of it. You're stuck with the producer from hell who thinks you've already sold your soul. Your boyfriend drugs you into aborting your baby, curses you into nearly killing yourself, and then spontaneously combusts in front of your eyes. If that weren't enough, you suspect you're next on the hit list. Did I leave anything out?"

"Those are the highlights," I murmured. The soft lighting might as well have been a five-hundred watter shoved in my face.

"And now you're wondering if you did the right thing coming here and how I could possibly make any of it go away."

"That's part of it. Although I also wonder why you would believe any of this. I know you're a priest, but even so, I'm sure it doesn't come up every day."

Slouched comfortably, his long legs extended casually, Pearce appeared steeped in thought. "You've already learned a lot, Trina. Too much, most would say, even if you have been led kicking and screaming. What if I were to tell you what you know now is just a drop in the ocean?"

"What are you hinting at? That there's something worse than human sacrifice and watching someone burn through some remote form of hocus-pocus? Bring it!"

"I'm not so sure. So far, you've adapted. You haven't gone on some memory-suppressing binge, you haven't checked into an asylum."

I thought of Eddy; the excessive rubbing. "Is that where most end up when they've had their *third eye* opened?"

"More than you think. But the fact is, there's a point of no return. Once you're past it, there's no going back. You need to ask yourself what that knowledge is worth."

"If I decide I don't want it?"

"I know some people who can help. You may have to go underground for a while. How do you feel about anonymity? Starting your life over without the limelight?"

"You make it sound like witness protection," I protested. The implications were staggering.

He cocked his head to the side. "Normally, I wouldn't even suggest it. But from what I'm hearing, these folks are serious, well connected and powerful. They would've never been able to pull off such a stunt otherwise. The fact there hasn't been a peep in the news about Kadzik, Pindar, his band or you proves it and well...there's something wrong with the whole picture. I need to do some digging first, find out who and what we're dealing with. But meanwhile, living quietly may help you to keep both eyes closed at night. That's only part of it, of course. There's the spiritual. I can make it nearly impossible for them to curse you. I can show you how to protect yourself. It shouldn't be that hard. Looks like you may already have a lead on it," he said, placing a callused hand over Eddy's chain still wrapped around my wrist before removing it quickly.

"Why would you say that?"

"You're alive."

"Doesn't make sense, does it? I was in the room with him. Why should I be handed a special dispensation?"

"One of the mysteries of good and evil. You'll know when the time's right. Important thing right now is to gain strength so when you do come face to face with Kadzik, his curses slip off like axle grease."

"That's if I go face to face. What happens if I do decide to take the blinders off?"

"You go back and open up the can of worms but...knowledge is power," he said simply.

"Enough to destroy Gregory? To take down his empire and everyone in it?"

"I'll let you know in a few days. If you do though, you may be risking everything; your career, maybe even your own life."

"I doubt I have much of a career left and consequently, not much of a life. So when do I take the red pill and go down the rabbit hole?" I persisted.

"After you've had a chance to..."

"...think about the cost."

"...try my famous homemade waffles with raspberry butter. Don't be in such a hurry to jump down that hole, Trina. You already know where it leads."

He stood, crossed to the couch and tossed a pillow at Logan who groaned. "Things never change. The man's been known to sleep through mortar fire. What do you say we let the lady get some real rest?" he said loudly, forcing the reporter to his feet and out the door. before grabbing a couple bedrolls and a shotgun and shells out of a closet.

"Sheets are clean. Barbara Walters and I will be right outside in case you need us, but make sure you lock up anyway. Those coyotes aren't the most dangerous things out here by far," he warned, shucking a couple shells in the double chambers to make his point.

"Gregory doesn't need a door, remember?"

"Either way we've got him covered," he said as he locked the lever action into place in a practiced, familiar way. "Teufel..." Pearce called out, watching as the midnight-black Dane immediately perked up and lumbered to him. "Sleep by the door tonight," he commanded. The enormous hound grunted, looking up at him with intelligent eyes.

"Teufel?" I echoed, astonished at how easily the dog seemed to understand. "That's an odd name."

"Short for *Teufelhunden*. It means Devil Hound; the name the Germans gave the Marines during World War I. Apparently, our fierce tenacity and courage reminded them of their legends and in his case," he added, pondering Teufel in appreciation, "it fits."

"Father, you never did tell me why Logan decided to bring me here or why you took me at my word."

He hesitated, looked at the floor for a moment, then brought his eyes up to mine.

"Before St. Jo's, I spent several years as an envoy to the Vatican. Among my other duties, I was also the assistant to the chief exorcist of Rome."

He watched me carefully, gauging my reaction as I struggled to understand.

"But how did you get all the way from Rome to El Paso?"

"That's a story for another night and you've got enough things to think about."

The latch clicked gently behind him as if he couldn't risk jarring me again; as if this last bit of trivia was all I needed to push me over the edge and into that asylum.

"Don't forget the door," he reminded from behind it as I stood rooted to one spot.

I turned the lock and got ready for bed, my head reeling. Where had Logan O'Neill brought me? Who was Father Pearce, really? And why was a priest keeping company with a dog named after his eternal nemesis—who, as I watched, yawned and stretched his massive form across the entry obediently. I had the feeling I could peel back the layers till kingdom come and still not come up with a satisfying answer.

FOURTEEN

Thursday, March 13
New York City

C hloe couldn't remember the last time she'd felt this uncomfortable. Not because she was shooting up to the thirty-third floor of a high rise at tremendous speed; nor even because of the two, stone-faced droids assigned to make sure she didn't get *lost*. It was the cream-colored silk blouse, tanned woolen skirt and matching jacket that did it; too tight, suffocating and common; pinching and squeezing in all the wrong places and— she was sure—doing nothing for her bland complexion bereft of makeup. But the directions had been explicit. She was to ban the bling on this official visit, appear demure and blend in. A part of her bristled in outrage, the urge to argue great, but not as great as her curiosity. Still, they were helpless to do anything about the leather stilettos laced to mid-calf, dripping with baubles that chimed as the elevator slid open, ushering her and her welcoming committee into a reception area.

A sign to their right heralded their arrival at the Havana Club.

She was led in the opposite direction, towards an unremarkable set of double doors she could have mistaken for a broom closet. Chloe clamped her legs together as her escorts pulled them open; a last-ditch effort to control her suddenly traitorous bladder.

No stranger to entertaining hordes at huge auditoriums, she stared numbly into the faces of the thirteen gathered before her, knew she faced her toughest audience yet, and hoped her flimsy underwear absorbed the trace leakage taking place.

Clearly she was in a boardroom; an unremarkable match to most others around the country but for one distinguishing feature; the conference table—round and wooden, with a series of runic symbols carved along the edge and an enormous goat's head in the center. Chloe's unusual anxiety receded a fraction. There was no doubt of this group's allegiance. They might be higher up on the totem pole but they *were* her own kind.

Seated with her back against the door, the honor guard by her side and the thirteen clustered together facing her, she was dissected with the intensity of a microscope laying bare the secrets of microbial fungus. She returned the favor with voracity.

It was an interesting assembly; seven men, six women, with the youngest around fifty and the oldest in his mid-eighties, she guessed; their standard-issue business suits so dull, they might have been mid-level executives discussing their company's benefits' program. She knew better as most of their faces were familiar. Three corporate heads who practically lived on CNN; a couple movie producers whose combined net worth would rival that of a small nation. The others comprised a wide variety of the power elite with a dash of royalty here—a dollop of science and technology there—and a smidgen of the financial, communications, military, and political crowd thrown in for flavor. She recognized Gregory's exemplar in that category. Quite the witch's brew, she thought, settling back in her chair slightly mollified. Chloe Six had made the next rung; Gregory—the old bastard—had not. Karma was such a bitch.

"We have a celebrity in our midst," his exemplar—or Hael as he'd been introduced to her only days ago—announced. "We will dispense with introductions as I'm sure we all recognize a rising star whose popularity multiplies daily. Welcome, Canicula."

Moving as a single organism, each member raised his left hand. Chloe felt a surge of power, primitive and raw, slam through her solar plexus and spread into each living cell as they intoned the ancient salutation upon her. She gasped involuntarily, trying to funnel the near-orgasmic shudders into something manageable. So this was what true power felt like. The supremacy of this group made a joke of the ritual Gregory had attempted the other night. Small wonder they'd only half succeeded, even with three masters.

A wild craving interrupted the pulses of energy still coursing through her veins. A day ago, who would've thought she'd be sitting here, in this monument to the unseen powers ruling the world and in the presence of greatness? And if she'd made it this far, was it a stretch to hope she could rise higher? After all, compared to the nameless one above them known only as The Caretaker, even these privileged old fossils would be considered rubes.

"I take it you had no problem coming up with a suitable excuse for your sudden absence?" Hael asked.

"Too wrapped up in his own pity party to give a shit. Thinks I was called away due to family illness."

"Wonderful!" he said, clapping his hands. "Let me be honest. Sinistrus has always been one of our most dedicated allies. With the work he's done over the years, he's truly propelled us into our final phase. But...I'm concerned. He's showing signs of stress. Instability. You understand how this might endanger our enterprise. We can't afford glitches. Now that I've had the opportunity to witness this first hand, it pains me to admit this poses a problem. Sinistrus has become a weak link."

Despite the friendly tone, Chloe watched as Hael's pleasant, earnest features that had won him five reelections, twisted into a menacing scowl and felt her bladder quiver in response. Gregory *had* lost it the other night. Bad enough he threw a tantrum and tossed the place but did he have to do it in full view of his coven and two exemplars? She couldn't think of a greater show of weakness.

Worse yet, as his student and protégé, was she guilty by association? Had he incriminated her, letting on how irrational envy towards one woman made her blurt out certain proprietary secrets? She didn't think so or she'd be dead by now. Justice carried out by this crowd was sure to be more swift and fierce than any of her exemplar's threats.

Nostrils flared at the memory. Although the urge to twist a knife into his back had grown as painful as an abscessed tooth, a suggestion by her inner muse offered a hint of relief.

"You know...it wouldn't be so bad if he wasn't constantly harping on how failure to complete the ritual was all your fault."

Hael's eyes lit up briefly before resuming their usual ennui. "A mite uncharitable, since there was a third master present."

"Apparently, bringing him in was your first mistake. He said if he'd known you'd turn the whole thing into a circus, he wouldn't have bothered calling. Next time he's flying solo since he claims his skills now surpass even yours."

"We appreciate your candor, Canicula, but your remarks only prove his mental state is worse than previously thought. Perhaps in view of your special relationship you could do us a favor. We would be in your debt if you would be our sentinel. Nothing elaborate, you understand. Do what you do, just keep an eye out for unusual behavior; proof that maybe he should be relieved of some of his responsibilities."

Chloe simultaneously sighed and cringed. Never a good idea to get too personal about how they *relieved* members. Better to just align oneself with the winning team. After all, they did say they would be in her debt.

"Who do I speak to when I make a report?"

Hael slid a piece of paper across the table. "Memorize the number then burn it."

"And if you're satisfied?"

"You'll be rewarded accordingly. What do you want? Another Grammy? Your own production company?"

She leaned forward eagerly. "The chance to be an acolyte in this coven, to learn the ancient ways. And to be present at The Summoning."

Hael appeared amused as he studied her through veiled eyes. "There are no acolytes in this coven, Canicula. But then, you knew that. We'll see what we can arrange."

Mollified she hadn't fallen out of favor but rather was asked for one, Chloe sank back in her chair, eager to voice her next question.

"What about the other half of Sinistrus' problem? The one who's still alive?"

She watched Hael turn towards one of the oldest members in the room. The media mogul shook his head just once; a nearly-imperceptible tweak that never disturbed his leathered face.

"She'll be dealt with in our own way," he said, now refocused on Chloe. "We've already sent someone to assess the situation and to see if she's allied."

"But I've studied her. I could help."

"Rule number one; a very important one if you have serious ambitions. Never challenge a verdict given by an elder. Besides... Scaevus' superior track record practically guarantees a favorable outcome." He turned to address his fellow members. "If we're done here, shall we go on to the next item on our agenda?"

Chloe flushed amid the ayes; a reaction to hearing the name of the legendary assassin as well as her abrupt dismissal. That was it? She'd been flown twenty-five hundred miles to be scrutinized for five minutes?

Her escorts placed firm hands under her elbows, forcing her to stand. She resisted the urge to swat them away and thought better. Maybe this was just another test; a way to see how she handled herself; essential if she wanted them to offer her a seat at The Council's table. After all, contrary to Gregory's rebuke, she wasn't some two-bit pop star with the shelf life of road kill left to rot. She was a well-oiled machine, an industry unto herself, with the power to influence millions.

Fuming, she retraced her steps down the hall and into the elevator, her silent babysitters proof she was still not to be trusted on her own.

Something else bothered her; a sense that what was being done to Gregory could, conceivably, be done to her one day. She shrugged off the pesky notion. The trick, she told herself, was not to remain stagnant like Gregory. Upward mobility was vital to surviving these twists and turns.

An illuminated dial announced the basement level, and as her escorts ejected her into the restricted underground garage, Chloe gave in to the storm percolating within. "I don't see why I'm being forced to skulk around like a rat. Is this how they treat VIPs?"

"Protocol ma'am," came the monotone reply. "It's for your privacy and protection."

"Well...they need to rethink their protocols. Some of us might believe we're not even respected enough to walk through the front doors."

She quickened her pace, eager to put some distance between her and the nannies, reach the limo that would take her back to the private air field and nurse her wounded pride. Truth be known, there was another reason why she'd have liked to parade through the main lobby in full view of all those boobs on vacation from the potato belt. How often would they have the privilege of touring the United Nations Building *and* catching a glimpse of Chloe Six—all on the same day?

Fifteen feet back, her escorts lagged, purposely allowing the diva her distance.

"Greedy little animal, isn't she?" the one commented, voicing his opinion without any fear of reprisal; the cow bells on her feet assured him of that.

"Aren't we all?" his partner countered, prompting some bored laughter. "You think we ought to tell her?"

"Nah! It's more fun this way."

They enjoyed the remainder of the show with relish; Chloe Six sashaying provocatively—the mushrooming damp spot on her behind a stark contrast to the air of superiority with which she carried herself.

FIFTEEN

Friday, March 14
Outside El Paso

Gotta say, I'm stunned," Pearce announced, halting in his tracks.

We'd walked a few hundred feet from the church compound to give the homemade waffles, as delicious as he'd promised, time to settle.

"Do I appear that vengeful and bloodthirsty to you?" I asked.

"More eager for justice is all. A couple nights ago, you seemed ready to join the crusade, rid the world of its scourge of evil."

"I thought you'd be pleased. Isn't that what all the warnings were about?"

"Don't get me wrong. I think you made the right decision. Those touched by this think they can learn a few tricks, waltz in, stir up the hive and not get stung. I just wondered what caused the one-eighty?"

I looked across the lowlands towards the Rio Grande in the distance, the barren landscape broken only by brush, tumbleweed, and a few dilapidated shacks. Behind one of them, Logan waited patiently, rifle in hand, for a scraggly coyote to appear; a fitting addition to this far-flung section of El Paso ignored most of the time by its more prestigious citizens.

"Would you understand if I told you I was tired and just want it to end?" I asked, turning to Pearce and thinking I couldn't get used to the split personality.

This morning he wore a wide-brimmed hat, plaid shirt and well-worn jeans over equally-worn western boots. If I hadn't walked in on him in church earlier—standing at the foot of the altar in his vestments, facing the parishioners filling the pews to near capacity—I'd have suspected I'd been had.

More than the clothes and props though, had been the unexpected ardor flooding his face: a strange radiance that found each individual personally, recognized his dignity—and settled on me. I'd looked away uncomfortably; a naughty child who didn't deserve that level of compassion.

"I mean...is it wrong for me to want that? Does it make me a coward?"

"Not at all. It's the normal response, Trina. Even by today's standards, most people shy away from the type of evil that makes pacts with the devil. If you ask me, we're hard-wired for it."

"Didn't know there was another kind."

"Right as rain. Packaged up all nice and pretty with a bow, begging to be unwrapped. Sin's a funny thing. It beguiles. It tells us what we're doing is for our own good; that it won't hurt anyone. And most of the time, it's far more effective than cheap parlor tricks."

I stared at him dubiously. "I knew sooner or later you'd start sounding like a priest."

"Should've stuck long enough to hear my spiel this morning. Sounds archaic to you, doesn't it? The concept of a moral good and evil in our enlightened world?"

"I take it you don't think we're very enlightened?"

"Look around you, Trina. Do enlightened people allow this type of poverty to exist?"

"Okay, I get it. But what happened to me...to Eddy...that was different. It seems worse somehow."

"An illusion. It's exactly the same brand of evil, just the flip side of the coin. The only difference is when most of us do bad things, it's out of human weakness. We're only half aware of what we're doing and usually ignorant of the consequences.

"When Kadzik and his breed go to town, it's with their full knowledge and complete consent. You might say they're the *energumens perfecte,* the perfectly possessed. They're not interested in salvation, just damnation, running headlong into it like moths to a flame."

A distant gunshot tweaked his memory. Pearce spun towards the buildings behind us. "Walk with me. I need to finish those tables before it gets too hot and windy. I sense a storm coming on."

Though the sky appeared as cloudless as ever, the air around us felt charged, the breeze already a steady moan.

I hurried after him, trying to keep up with his long strides. "So which breed am I?" I asked. Sensing I was about to be condemned to an eternity of hellfire, I wasn't sure I really wanted to know, but his next words surprised me.

"Are you here of your own free will?" he asked, glancing at me sideways. I nodded and he continued.

"With your knowledge, did you at any time swear allegiance to a demon or other entity?"

"Of course not!"

I was aware of how ludicrous those words would sound to a casual observer, but also how comfortable I'd become with my new vocabulary. Nevertheless, the question nagged.

"How would I know though, since it was in Latin?"

"Doesn't work that way. You need to buy into it. There needs to be a willingness, an openness. Call it a conscious decision. Under those circumstances, the effects would be mitigated. In any case, a minor exorcism should erase any lingering influences."

I blinked a couple of times and halted in mid track, forcing him to face me. "You're kidding, right?"

"I never kid around about evil, Trina," he said, dark eyes penetrating mine like lasers. He smiled. "Let me guess...another archaic notion that scientific, modern man could do without?"

"No offense, Padre, but that's where I come from. Both my parents were down to earth. When they died, their words and deeds were supposed to live through me. There was never any talk about committing their eternal souls to some unknown paradise. Up until a week ago, I would've laughed at such a thing."

"But you believe in the existence of the supernatural now?"

"I don't want to, but there doesn't seem to be room for any of my old thoughts anymore. Not after what happened to Eddy."

"Good. That part's necessary. Can't do a damn thing unless you believe; even more important since you've never been baptized...am I right?"

"Yes...no, I haven't...but what does that mean? Are you saying I need to get dunked for this to work?"

"I won't lie to you. It would certainly give you an edge since the only real way to combat supernatural evil is through the supernatural."

"Not sure I'm ready for that."

"Have it your way but remember, it's never a good idea to bring a knife to a gun fight," he explained, heading towards his work shed while I hurried after him. "Truth is, the spiritual realm will always be more powerful than the material."

"An exorcism though..."

"What are you seeing, Trina? Visions of sadistic monks using the instruments of the Inquisition to torture helpless victims? The Rite is simply a collection of Church-sanctioned prayers and blessings."

"But that's just it," I argued. "They're words. How are they supposed to make a difference? How are *words* going to protect me from burning?"

He didn't answer immediately. With practiced ease, Pearce dragged the necessary boards and tools from the shed and made a cut. His actions were slow and thoughtful; much like his voice when he spoke again.

"Everything begins with words, or rather the thoughts behind them. No single war, not a single man-made tragedy or triumph has ever occurred without someone, somewhere, having a thought, putting it into words, and breathing life into it; or in some cases, death.

"If you have no trouble believing entire civilizations have crumbled because of the authority behind the words, why do you doubt their ability to heal and cleanse when they're spoken in the name of the very highest authority?"

I couldn't help it. I'd seen too much—my excuse for playing devil's advocate. "How can you be so sure this authority you speak of is stronger? The Yin and the Yang, remember? For every force, there is an equal and opposite force?"

"A common misconception when it comes to the spiritual," he countered, placing a couple pieces of wood to the side and prepping a new one. "And one the crowd you ran with takes enormous pleasure spreading, I might add." Amused, he looked up, searching my face. "Do you know anything at all about angels?"

"Only the kind wearing skimpy lace on fashion runways."

"Lucifer...the Prince of Darkness...Beelzebub...Old Scratch... Satan; different names for the same entity. The Deceiver."

"Gregory calls him The Old One."

"His titles are many and vary from culture to culture," Pearce agreed. "But what he is and will always remain is a fallen angel; nothing less, nothing more. One of many in the angelic realm created by God and, tradition has it, the most beautiful and exalted of all...but with one fatal flaw. He would not serve; neither God nor man, considering it beneath his dignity to minister to a race so inferior to his own. Word has it he took a third of the angels with him when he fell."

"Angels have free will? I thought we were the only ones cursed with it."

Pearce threw the sander to the ground and grabbed my arm. He led me to the relative shelter of the shed, away from the increasing winds and faced me squarely.

"Would you want someone to love and accept you for who you are, or because he was pre-programmed to do so? All angels have free will but since they exist outside of time, their choice and the resulting damnation of the fallen was instantaneous and absolute. The important thing to take away from this is that although they're powerful, there's a limit to their power. They're not all seeing and all knowing. They rely on us to feed them."

"Through our actions?"

"Through our choices that either choke the life out of us or give us the means to soak it up. Take your pick. That's the true beauty of power and the funny thing is...it's always been ours."

His words hung in the air like a stubborn perfume refusing to dissipate while beyond our make-shift shelter, dust rose, twisted, and whined into a thousand tiny cyclones. I stared at Pearce in silence, trying to understand how what he said could fix the mess I was in, but it was too new to me; a foreign language never before spoken whose translation eluded.

Minutes passed. I was getting a headache and was about to give up on the whole concept when I sensed his words forming into an idea; one that existed free from time and all restraints.

The notion of possibilities—unlimited and without borders—poked its head out, played hide-and-seek with me for a moment, then darted out of my grasp before I could drag it to the surface for good. Though maddening, the brief glimpse left me something the storm seemed to have already understood.

I recognized the tempest for what it was: no longer a death knell insisting I was bound to my choices as surely as Gregory's victims were bound to his altar waiting to be ripped apart; but a fury—a frustration crying out to those who didn't realize possibilities even existed.

The strength of Pearce's gaze drew me back to him. Though his eyes still shown with concern, his lips pulled back into a cautious smile; a response to my own tentative one. The movement felt odd, as if I were exercising muscles that had wasted away through years of neglect.

I staggered, allowing the gale to force me back, and felt

another drawing me close, giving human voice to what I had only perceived on some mystical realm. I sank against Pearce, grateful for the strength and purity being offered and looked out into the arid wilderness.

A solitary, wind-swept figure stood watching us from a distance. With his rifle slung over his shoulder, he could have easily passed for the ghost of some soldier destined to roam his killing fields forever. As silent as a ghost, Logan didn't make his presence known, but merely nodded and smiled before moving away.

The notion of possibilities suddenly gained momentum.

SIXTEEN

Benedict Canyon

Do you hear me, Sinistrus? The Council has requested you leave the woman to us," his exemplar advised softly.

Kadzik wandered through the vast, empty rooms, an all-too familiar claustrophobic anxiety returning with vengeance. Far from calming, Hael's quiet tone irritated and chafed like a cheap razor against nubile skin.

"If this is about the other night, I assure you, it won't happen again. Most of my acolytes have never attempted anything so complicated before, that's all. We'll get it right next time."

"There won't be a next time. The situation has escalated. We've been forced to take more direct measures. Don't worry, it will all be over in a few days. In the meantime, it wouldn't hurt to take some time off; maybe even a much-deserved vacation. Your hard work and dedication haven't gone unnoticed."

Gregory grimaced. The compliment sounded more like a reproach. Despite his exemplar's tone, he was sure he detected a certain coldness that hadn't existed a week ago.

"Of course. You know The Council's wishes are my own," he said, hoping he'd infused his voice with the appropriate amount of enthusiasm.

"It's settled then. Someone will call you before the week is out. Until then...take my advice. Relax."

Mute silence followed the click. Gregory glanced at his phone, trying to quiet the tremor in his hand. Relax? Not likely in light of the royal decree. Behind his exemplar's friendly, chatty tone was an unmistakable warning. His weakness in failing to deal with Langford adequately was perceived as a threat to The Quickening.

He nearly laughed at his predicament. He'd always wondered how long it took for justice to be dispensed and now he knew. He was being shunned; his wings clipped just enough so he understood exactly where he stood in the pecking order.

Gregory groaned. Wasn't he allowed a single slip up in a career spanning more than fifty years? Apparently not, as he remembered the greedy expressions of his coven the night of the invocation; a strange mixture of embarrassment, condemnation, and amusement.

He shook off his unease as best he could. At least he was suffering his present humiliation alone. Chloe was gone on family business; something about her father and a stroke. Funny, he'd never imagined her having human parents as he'd always harbored the suspicion she'd been raised by a pack of hyenas.

The pride he felt as he wandered the opulent rooms seemed tainted. The masterpieces of art few were privileged to own were testaments to his wealth bought in service to The Old One; a good-faith reward for his loyalty and skill. Was he still deserving? Had he ever been?

The thought rankled. Perfection slipped a notch as the room contracted.

Impossible!

Beside his grotto—in need of serious TLC after he'd tossed it the other night—he'd chosen this house precisely for its expansive rooms, its fifteen-foot ceilings. He'd waited for it as he'd imagined it had waited for him; house and owner, both larger than life, both misunderstood, complimenting one another, belonging to one another. The walls seemed to agree as he caught the wisp of an asthmatic sigh.

Gregory shuddered and turned to the bureau that usually stood beneath the window but now jutted out at an odd angle. It taunted him, as did the coffee table and the Louis XV chaise beyond it. Had the crew forgotten his number one rule about the furniture? He scanned the perimeter. It was off! Everything was off!

A twitch grew into a tremor. He fell to his knees and covered his eyes, certain that witnessing any other abnormalities would drag him back to that ancient place of suffocating agony. He was right.

Darkness behind his lids gave way to other images even more vivid than those viewed in the physical world. In that life, he hadn't yet learned about The Old One; didn't know—much less care—how to harness the weakness of others and wield it in his favor.

But he was well versed in shame and fear, so acrid, it was only right he be punished, locked in unblemished darkness and solitude for days with nothing for company but his grievous sins; a space so tiny, even the thin, small boy he had been could barely turn without brushing against the smooth, cold walls of the tomb.

Years faded into a singular reality. Reduced to repeating

the past once more, Gregory cried out, his plea no longer for a mother who never came, but for The Old One. The response was immediate, dissolving the bitterness as a stronger force clawed its way to the surface.

He opened his eyes, now black as coal, and looked down at his hand. The tremor was gone, replaced by a surge of current running down the length of his arm and into his fingertips like liquid iron. He flexed his fingers, then coiled them into a fist.

Rage—already fully formed but quiet, focused and, as a result, more deadly—reared up with a single name emblazoned in red.

Trina Langford.

SEVENTEEN

Saturday, March 15
Outside El Paso

Yesterday's dust storm left the air fresh and clean for the wedding feast. The break from muggy heat worked wonders for me. My appetite returned along with my smile.

Father Pearce fell in step as I headed back to my seat balancing a second helping of Carne Asada, stewed lamb and fresh tortillas. I was getting used to his quiet, no-nonsense authority and realized why Logan had brought me here.

At nearly midnight, the party was still going strong. The bride and groom—a tired, faded girl and a boy, just past his teens— looked dazed at being launched into married life and soon-to-be parenthood. Their faces were strained despite their best efforts to keep the party alive and reality at bay.

Logan helped, kicking up his heels with the locals; proof that his recent subdued mood had only been temporary. I suspected I was to blame for this change since Pearce had asked him to assist at my so-called exorcism yesterday afternoon.

The deliverance took place in church. I had been seated with the altar as my backdrop, the two men hovering as if they expected me to speak in tongues. Luckily, I disappointed, and Father Pearce completed the ritual without any embarrassing special effects from me. I was grateful; the thought of giving Logan extra proof of my raving lunacy, abhorrent somehow.

Still, as the priest transitioned between the prayers chanted in Latin, the idea that had first bloomed in the shed, defined itself more clearly. I could no longer deny what he'd said about the creative power of words, yet I sensed I'd only scratched the surface and that this mystery would never completely give up its secrets. I ran with it, taking it one step further. Gregory and his minions didn't know a damned thing about second chances. In their ignorance, they had tied themselves to a belief that was limited, stunted; a tiny cube with a capacity of one—their own egos.

In between all this, school came into session. Pearce filled my head with all sorts of useful and surprising tools against the war Gregory had waged; surprising—because none of them entailed garlic and stakes to the heart but rather, a shift in attitude he insisted led to a union with this new world of possibilities. My acceptance was rocky, peppered with an ever-growing list of questions he answered without contempt for my ignorance.

I realized he was about to speak when a shadow blocked the ambient light of the lanterns strung around the perimeter.

A figure loomed over us, breathing heavily; Logan, stretching out his hand in silent invitation. I reached for him automatically—linking our fingers together for the first time. His touch felt warm and natural, helping me forge the lie that we were simply two people who had met under normal circumstances and whose conversations would never gravitate towards anything as vile as human sacrifice.

I glanced back at Pearce and caught him smiling like he'd received proof of a foregone conclusion. Blushing, I turned towards the mass of bodies swaying to the slower beat, thankful when the crowd swallowed us.

As my dance partner, Logan O'Neill was a perfect fit. A head taller than I, we complimented each other, avoiding those first awkward moments when couples struggle to come together gracefully.

He danced me through the throng, to the far corner of the floor, as far from the others as the square on which we stood allowed.

"I didn't have a chance to tell you how beautiful you look tonight," he murmured over the softer strains of a solo guitar.

"You can thank the ladies of St. Jo's sewing league," I said, pirouetting so my new peasant skirt and off-the-shoulder blouse could be seen to their best advantage. I was flirting a little—still stubbornly entrenched in that lie. The woman who'd slammed the door on her life only days earlier was still there with all her problems. I was just giving her permission to take the night off. "Nice to know I can support the local cottage industry."

"You should be their poster child," he said as his eyes swept lazily over my body and lingered over my bare shoulders. I quickly changed the subject.

"I may be joining them if Pearce has his way. He says Gregory would never dream of looking for me here since he'd have to come down off his throne to the real world."

"He's probably right. On the other hand, this might not be the best venue for a singer and songwriter."

"The whole performing gig's a little overrated these days."

"You're selling yourself short again."

"Just trying to think of it as penance. God's little joke for getting caught up in Eddy's twisted, drug-induced fantasies."

"What about Eddy? Why him, when you could have had anyone?"

I'd been expecting the question, but didn't know if my answer would satisfy either one of us.

Focused on the words we danced around, we were barely moving to the music anymore, yet Logan continued to hold both my hands in his.

"Desperation," I said finally. "About ten years ago, my producer at the time decided our contract should also include some sessions on the proverbial casting couch. I rebelled, threatened to take him to court. He retaliated by making sure word got out I was toxic and a bad risk. The message was clear. I was on my own. No one wanted to touch me or my career after that.

"Years passed and I wasn't getting any younger. I got tired of all the doors slammed in my face. It got to the point I was barely hanging on, playing local bars, opening for second-string headliners. I began doubting myself, my decision.

"You might not understand, but by the time I met Eddy, I'd had enough. I was alone in the world and my ideals hadn't gotten me anywhere so maybe it was time for drastic change. Eddy fit the bill. I got lost in him, in his ambitions, and temporarily forgot about mine. I know...sounds lame, but that's it in a nutshell. Oldest story in the book."

Despite my reluctance to see the verdict plastered all over his face, I looked up. His eyes were clear, serious; reflecting empathy rather than pity or mockery. Self-judgment receded a fraction.

"More human than lame, actually. And you're wrong. I understand better than you think."

"So magazine editors pimp out their writers too? And if you refuse to pay your way to a byline, what happens then? You get thrown out of the paparazzi union?"

"Something like that. Why did Gregory decide to take you on if you were such a risk?"

"I wondered about that in the beginning. Desperation does funny things to people. I told myself he could see my potential, my talent. The truth, as you know, was far uglier. He wasn't just after my body..."

"He wanted your soul," Logan finished. "It's over now. He can't get to either one from here. Pearce and I won't let him."

"But you won't always be here and if I do what Pearce wants, I'll have to have plastic surgery and move to a cave in Afghanistan for the next fifty years.

"That's another thing. Do I have to pretend to be someone else for the rest of my life or does Trina Langford make a miraculous comeback someday?"

"Whoa! Slow down a bit. It doesn't have to be that dramatic. In any case, I don't think I'd like it if they made you hide those eyes," he said, coaxing my chin up with his fingers. "You do realize that color is extraordinary?"

"Dime a dozen."

"Beg to differ," he argued, but dropped his hand anyway.

Unsettled by the strange current flowing between us, I took a step back and studied his face. Separately, each feature seemed slightly odd, irregular: the nose too sharp, the cleft chin too dominant, the hollow cheekbones and bushy eyebrows nearly obscured by that mass of unruly black hair. Even the mouth, usually curled up as if he were on the verge of revealing a secret joke but now uncharacteristically serious, seemed too thin. But taken as a whole, his angular face was strangely appealing and unconventionally handsome; interesting.   It was a face one wouldn't tire of easily.

"It doesn't have to be that way, you know," he said, wrenching me away from my accounting.

"What doesn't?"

"I could be here for you. If you wanted me to."

"My life's a mess. I can't ask you to do that, Logan. I don't even know where I'm going to be a week from now, let alone a month, a year. It wouldn't be fair."

"I didn't ask you to be fair. I asked you what you wanted."

"It's too soon."

"Because you're still in love with a ghost?"

"I'm not sure I was ever in love with Eddy."

"Your grief, then? Guilt?"

"Trust. I don't know if I can trust you...Pearce...his God."

"Hate to break it to you, but there's only one way to find out," he murmured.

Indecision cleared. He touched my elbows with agonizing lightness, then moved higher, stroking my arms and shoulders as he drew me to him.

"If you knew me better, you'd know leaps of faith aren't my strong suit."

Warmth radiated through me even before his body pressed against mine, making it impossible to think beyond this moment. I allowed myself to breathe in the lingering trace of sandalwood mixed with his own clean scent, closed my eyes and heard him whisper...

"Then we'll jump together."

He brought his lips down to mine, his mouth deliberately slow and tender. I sensed him holding back, struggling against a private, one-man war that somehow fueled my own longing.

I groaned when he pulled away, clueless that the war had just become very real and that I stood right smack on its front lines.

EIGHTEEN

A sharp crack sliced the air and my world froze. The trance broke with the rapport of a second shot whizzing by my head. Understanding turned to dread, then chaos.

Logan dragged me to the ground; his transition from lover to soldier, effortless, fluid, the training kicking in as if there had been no lapse.

"Stay down but be ready to move!"

I nodded, tried to make sense of the turmoil, and recognized the same confusion plastered across every face. A blur of white stumbled past me; the bride propping up her belly as she ran awkwardly with her husband, their eyes stark, frightened. Pity their wedding day would now be memorable for all the wrong reasons.

Twenty feet out, Pearce shielded a young girl until her mother whisked her away. Free to act, he turned towards the dance floor, locking eyes with Logan as he signaled his directive.

"We're heading to the house on the count of three," Logan translated. "Keep your head down all the way."

"The house? Why not the church?"

"Too exposed and we need weapons."

He hoisted me to my feet and spun me towards the priest's lodging. A horde of bodies, moving with the commotion of a frantic beehive, blocked our way. I added the fear of being trampled to that of a bullet penetrating the back of my head. Someone elbowed me in the gut and I doubled over, my lungs frighteningly inadequate against the force of the blow.

I felt other hands pummeling and pawing, pressing me down, using me as leverage to vault over the masses stampeding to save themselves. Logan's grip was my last line of defense, buoying me up against the undertow. If I went down, I knew I wasn't coming back up.

A third shot cut through the mayhem and the human wave dispersed, leaving us alone but exposed.

Logan's eyes skimmed the horizon. "Stay close and follow my lead."

He pressed me to his side as we zig-zagged through the dust kicked up from countless feet. I wondered about the priest since I could no longer see him. Was he lying alone on the desert floor, unable to call for help and bleeding to death? Or had he managed to reach the safety of his four walls and retrieve his weapons? Then again, just how many weapons did a man of the cloth need and for what purpose?

The door flew open and I exchanged old questions for new.

Pearce Rhomer appeared, legs planted solidly across the threshold. Always the chameleon, he'd shed the skin to which I'd grown accustomed for one of a stranger. Face dark with the effort of keeping his temper in check, the priest's eyes narrowed, devoid of the warmth I'd come to expect. This was the first time I'd seen him flush with anger and it was unnerving. I was getting a glimpse of the Marine he'd been: precise, determined to finish the mission at all costs, and dangerous. The man who stared into the night with the unmistakable silhouette of an assault rifle in each hand would kill readily.

He tossed Logan one of the weapons, crouched low and leaned into the doorway while Logan worked the muzzle of his own rifle into the darkness. Using his body as a shield, he rounded me towards the door while the priest scanned the perimeter through his scope.

I was on the last step when something blurred past me with a ferocious snarl and bounded towards the river.

"Is that a good idea?" Logan murmured.

"Let him go. If anyone's still out there, Teufel will find him before we do."

The words were barely out of the priest's mouth when a fourth shot echoed into the night. It coincided with the fierce growl obliterating the cries of the few remaining guests still running for cover. The dog's fury, unleashed at last, only intensified; his rage articulated in snapping, crunching howls that would curdle cream and explained Pearce's decision to name his pet.

A new sound competed with Teufel's savage rumble; an inhuman screech proving the hound's fangs had found their mark in something all too human.

"That's our cue," Pearce remarked as he and Logan dragged me to the foot of the door with strict instructions to barricade myself behind it until their return.

"You're not seriously thinking about going out there!"

"Teufel's done most of the work for us. It's time to find the bastard and finish this thing."

"Assuming there's only one!"

"The shots are from the river bank and identical. Odds are, we're dealing with a lone sniper. Counting down the time since the last bullet, we should be good to go."

They turned, two figures blending into the night, their weapons natural extensions of their bodies, poised for battle. Despite their warning, I lingered, watching their swift, nimble movements until they were swallowed by darkness, then locked the door and slid to the floor, shuddering when Teufel the Devil Dog's ragged snarls changed into a long, lamenting wail.

The woman I'd been was at the threshold of that other door again—but this time it had blown wide open. How silly to have thought she could turn her back and simply walk away.

NINETEEN

Sunday, March 16

Gregory's never going to stop until I'm dead, is he?"

The two men exchanged a look then turned to me with as much optimism as they could muster. It wasn't nearly enough to make me feel better.

For most on the block, the night's ordeal had come to an end. For the three of us, too keyed up to sleep, it was just beginning. Huddled around Pearce's table with Teufel at our heels, the world beyond remained hidden behind blinds drawn resolutely against the encroaching dawn and any lingering danger.

Outside, the rumbling of an engine signaled the departure of a squad car; the last in a fleet that had arrived hours earlier, ushering in a slew of cops and agents. The shooter might have long-since disappeared, leaving behind a community dazed, suspicious and miraculously unhurt, but he'd also left traces of blood and plenty of evidence lodged in the walls of the church compound.

Pearce and Logan were first to recognize the .338 Lapua slugs;

the sufficiently-rare caliber making it unlikely they belonged to a local. Even without DNA, the sniper had left his calling card.

Immersed in thought, the priest leaned forward, elbows propped over his knees. "Maybe we've been looking at this the wrong way and we should ask ourselves why he's working so hard to kill you."

"You mean us," Logan chimed. "Each one of those bullets had one of our names on it. My guess is our shooter got more than he bargained for. You might've been his main target, Trina, but when he saw he'd have to go through us to get to you, he shifted gears. If it wasn't for the beast, once he got his bearings, he might've pulled it off."

"Our secret weapon," I whispered, reaching under the table to pat Teufel's head.

"Which leads me back to why he wants you dead," Pearce resumed. "We already know we're dealing with wounded pride. You refused Gregory's advances and his invitation into his cult so you're fair game. Revenge, vengeance. Not unusual when you're dealing with monstrous egos, but...something's missing."

"Kadzik's head on a platter?"

"Maybe. But I've come up against the likes of him before. He's an actor playing a part. A showman, conjuring up all sorts of flashy tricks to amaze his impressionable coven."

"I'd say having the ability to incinerate someone from across town makes him a bit more talented than a two-bit magician at a kid's party."

"Don't get me wrong, Kadzik's as evil as they get. Talented too, when you consider the complexity of his curses, though I'm sure he had help."

"Human or non-human?" I moaned as Logan pulled his chair

closer to rub my back; proof the intimacy we'd shared hours ago still simmered.

"Both," he said, not missing a beat. "And that's just it. This last stunt doesn't seem like him. It's too ordinary and prosaic. Why use something as dull as a gun when you can torture your victims and prolong their pain in a thousand-and-one novel ways like Pindar?"

"Remember when I said I needed to do some digging? I called a friend of mine. A priest and exorcist in L.A. I asked him to get back to me if he finds anything that might give us answers. He called last night before the wedding. I was about to tell you when things got out of hand."

"I'm not going to like this, am I?"

"He validated what I'd already guessed. Kadzik's not alone in this."

"And he knows this how?"

"When you're in that line of work, you make connections. The word on the street is that despite his wealth and influence, Kadzik is only the low rung of a very tall and powerful ladder. You've met Gregory's coven. Were you ever introduced to someone new? A guest perhaps? A VIP?"

"I wouldn't know. We all wore masks and cowls. Anyway, I doubt it. From what Eddy said, Gregory never trusted me completely."

"Then I'd wager Gregory brought in reinforcements to ensure both Eddy *and* you died that night."

"How disappointing for him!"

"Precisely. According to their code...yes, believe it or not, they have one...failure isn't just unacceptable, it's a sign of weakness. Your refusal might've been a slap in Gregory's face, since I doubt he considered it a possibility, but now you're also a threat since, thanks to Eddy, you found out where the bodies are buried. It's one thing for club members to divulge their bloody secrets among themselves. Quite another when you've made it clear you don't want any part of them and threatened exposure. Apparently, it was serious enough to warrant the higher ups getting their fingers dirty."

A memory, elusive and slippery, played catch-me-if-you-can with me.

"Not just thanks to him," I said, working to clear the cobwebs.

"You said Eddy and I were a threat because, thanks to him, we found out Gregory likes sacrificing virgins. But he's not the only one who spoke out of turn that night. Chloe got really angry at us. It bothered her I wanted out and that Eddy had broken his vow of secrecy. She said some really crazy things that didn't make sense to me at the time. I asked Eddy about it before he died. He said they were waiting for an event that would change everything. Something about a sealed labyrinth and a...a triad."

Pearce sprang out of his chair, nearly knocking it over. "You sure those were her exact words?"

"Positive," I murmured as Logan and I watched him pace the room, his face vacillating wildly between disbelief and bewilderment.

"All this time...it's been there all this time, and I never even thought...

"Trina, you asked me once how I ended up in El Paso."

"You said I wasn't ready to hear about it."

"That's right. You're still not ready, but I don't think you have a choice any more. I don't think any of us do."

He sat down heavily and Logan and I drew in our chairs,

exhaustion now forgotten.

"Bear with me," he continued. "What I'm about to tell you, I haven't spoken about for a very long time and then only to one other, but first you need to know I've only had two passions in my life; two things I believed I could be really good at: waging war and the priesthood. Not compatible, most would say, but each appeared when I was in a different place.

"By the time I'd finished with my tours, I was ready to commit to something more. That I did, with a hunger and enthusiasm even I couldn't explain. Everyone thought I was trying to make up for all the carnage I'd inflicted earlier. They were right I think, up to a point, but it wasn't all of it."

He turned to me without warning, his eyes burning brightly.

"Maybe it's too early for you to understand, but I yearned for what I knew existed invisible to the human eye, though not out of human reach.

"I entered seminary a month after I was discharged and took it all in, excelled in all my classes, and in particular, those dealing with Eschatology, the study of last things; Death, Judgment, Heaven and Hell.

"Eventually, my professors told me I was a good candidate for becoming an exorcist; a topic most of the other seminarians avoided like the plague and over time the idea grew on me. It seemed like a good fit. Weren't exorcists the special forces of the Church, trained to do what so few others could?

"And so despite my history...or maybe because of it...they were certain I also possessed the necessary traits to do battle with Satan; courage, humility, single-mindedness, and a simplicity and zeal that were rare.

"But they forgot to mention that this zeal could be read as a threat by some. And that the price I would have to pay would literally change my life overnight..."

TWENTY

Rome, Italy—Six Years Ago

Father Pearce Rhomer hurried along the Via del Falco, ignoring a group of noisy tourists stumbling back to their hotel at two in the morning. Following the directions he'd been given, he turned onto Borgo Vittorio, a narrow, quiet, one-way road and a stark contrast to the bustle of the main artery, only a stone's throw from Vatican City. Here the neighborhood gave way to the more traditional cobbled streets and quaint arched doorways visitors expected; Rome's answer to the Left Bank.

Anxiety gripped him—more to do with the strange call he'd received an hour earlier than walking alone at this late hour. Despite the vague details, there was an urgency about the directive. He was told to come at once without telling anyone and to bring his purple stole; the priestly scarf worn over the alb when dispensing certain sacraments. The question wasn't which rite he'd be assisting with tonight, but why there was such need for secrecy and haste—to the point the usual preconditions of

Confession and Mass had been dismissed.

He paused, squinting to read a house number in the dark, relieved it matched the one he'd jotted down earlier. It was a three-story building, an exact replica of the others on the street, and unremarkable in everything but its yellow stucco exterior. Though all of its windows were shrouded in darkness, a single light glowed dimly behind drawn curtains on the top floor; further proof he was expected. He rang a bell, waited for the buzzer to usher him in, and bounded up the steep stairs, ignoring the dilapidated-looking lift.

A familiar but tired face greeted him at the entry, wearied either by the late hour, old age, or that same, nameless anxiety Pearce felt. Father Aberto Gandini dispensed with his usual greeting and dragged him into the small, drab living area. In a gesture oddly out of character, he glanced down the hall both ways before quickly locking the door behind them.

"What's this all about, Father?" Pearce asked in fluent Italian. "What's so important, you couldn't tell me over the phone?"

The priest bid him to be silent and led him down a short hall.

"What we must do tonight, you can never speak of to anyone, Pearce," the old man cautioned.

"By this, I take it you mean the exorcism we're about to perform. You and I both know the Rite doesn't carry the same inviolability as the seal of Confession."

"Perhaps. Nevertheless you will understand soon enough," he continued, leading them towards a closed door. He paused, looking at Pearce with obvious regret.

"You must also steel yourself, Father. Most likely, you will hear things tonight that will come as a great shock. I fear for what it might do. Prepare yourself for the unexpected or the enemy may use it against you."

Pearce couldn't help but smile a little. "More shocking than the blasphemous filth usually spewed on such occasions?"

"Yes! And much more dangerous," he warned, watching the younger priest carefully for some time before motioning him to follow.

Pearce recognized the three men in the room immediately. Of the two standing, one was a doctor, the other, a bouncer whose day job at a popular nightclub made him the natural choice to restrain the *patient* in the event it became necessary. Pearce had worked with both of them before and felt great respect for their professional demeanor and courage.

Tonight, their unusually-tense faces were turned towards the third man. Pearce followed their gaze grudgingly, unwilling to accept what his mind insisted was true: Cardinal Vincent Mallory's corpulent form resting silently in bed with his eyes closed and his hands folded across his massive chest.

He swallowed hard and tried to contain his dread. Though he'd never been formally introduced to the Cardinal, how could he not know the man hailed as the champion of the poor; his image plastered throughout the western world and *Newsweek's* current Man of the Year?

He turned to Father Aberto, silently imploring him to explain what didn't make sense but the exorcist merely shook his head and motioned for the men to form a circle around the bed. He traced the sign of the cross over those present, anointed them with holy water then knelt and waited for the others to follow suit before opening a tattered volume worn with time.

"Lord have mercy...Christ have mercy...Lord have mercy."

Pearce willed his unspoken questions aside and focused on the sacred prayers and their necessary responses. If the Cardinal had indeed come under the influence of the Evil One, only the faith and purity with which those prayers were offered would help.

Five minutes turned to fifteen then twenty as Father Aberto chanted the Litany of the Saints.

Gradually, Pearce felt a nearly imperceptible change in the air. Experience taught him there was another presence in the room with them now—and that it wasn't remotely human or benign.

He lifted his head and gazed at the energumen. Although the Cardinal remained as still as a corpse, there was a brief flutter behind his eyelids like the erratic tapping of Morse code.

Pearce exchanged warning glances with the other men, the fervor in their voices intensifying in response to the threat that stirred.

"...almighty Father, everlasting God and Father of our Lord Jesus Christ, Who once and for all consigned that fallen and apostate tyrant to the flames of hell, Who sent Your only-begotten Son into the world to crush that roaring lion; hasten to our call for help and snatch from ruination and from the clutches of the noonday devil this human being made in Your image and likeness."

Cardinal Mallory's eyes snapped open, piercing each of the four men in turn with a cunning glare. "What have we here?" he intoned in a voice harsh and metallic; a tinny facsimile of something human transmitted over dimensional frequencies unknown to this world. It had found its mouthpiece in the unfortunate prelate. He studied the exorcist in silence before continuing conversationally.

"You do know you're too late, Priest, don't you? We've seen to that."

Ignoring both the look and the words accompanying it, Father Aberto continued to pray without breaking rhythm. To do so now would be to invite disaster.

"Strike terror, Lord, into the beast now laying waste Your vineyard. Fill Your servants with courage to fight manfully against that reprobate dragon, lest he despise those who put their trust in You..."

"Did you not hear us or are you simply deaf? How about addled...muddled...rancid...fetid...decayed. Useless! Your vomiting gibberish is useless! Like the nursery rhymes your harlot mother forced you to gush again and again to get over that annoying, embarrassing *lithp. Utheleth utheleth utheleth.* Didn't quite get there, did you? Poor...poor pitiful Aberto, trying not to *lithp* even while reciting his vows. How did those go again?

"*Ithy bithy thpider* climbing up the *thpout...*"

"Let Your mighty hand cast him out of Your servant, Vincent Mallory, so he may no longer hold captive this person whom it pleased You to make in Your image..."

"*Goothey goothey* gander where *thall* I wander?"

"...who, despite his sinfulness, was born for Your glory and to give light to Your everlasting mercy and to redeem through Your Son; who lives and reigns with You, in the unity of the Holy Spirit..."

"...little *Mith* Muffet, *that* on a tuffet...don't you get it, Priest? HE WANTS TO BE WITH US!"

"...one God, forever and ever, Amen."

Cloying stillness pervaded the room as Father Aberto completed the first part of the ritual and faced Mallory.

Legs splayed, arms stretched wide, fingers clasped around the corroded railings of his headboard, the Cardinal followed the old priest's gestures without moving a muscle then grinned.

Father Aberto motioned for the other men to be ready for

anything and continued.

"I command you, unclean spirit, along with all your minions now attacking this servant of God, by the mysteries of the incarnation, passion, resurrection, and ascension of our Lord Jesus Christ, by the descent of the Holy Spirit, by the coming of our Lord for judgment, that you tell me by some sign your name, and the day and hour of your departure."

A dreary chuckle filled the air, taking the exorcist and his assistants by surprise. They looked at one another nervously, sharing the same thought. In the years since they'd formed their alliance, taking part in a ritual most would consider insane, Father Aberto's words had never before elicited such a reaction.

"I command you, moreover, to obey me to the letter, I who am a minister of God despite my unworthiness; nor shall you be emboldened to harm in any way this creature of God, or the bystanders, or any of their possessions."

"*Utheleth...*"

The old priest stood and approached the Cardinal, then placed a hand on his forehead, ignoring the violent tremors jolting him.

"They shall lay their hands upon the sick and all will be well with them. May Jesus, Son of Mary, Lord and Savior of the world, through the merits and intercession of His holy apostles Peter and Paul and all His saints, show you favor and mercy..."

"You will fail Priest..."

"Not if I command you through the authority of the Most High; the Lord Jesus Christ, Alpha and Omega, the Word Incarnate."

"Burn as they may, even those vile names can no longer help that rotten mass of quivering flesh we now call our own," Mallory bellowed in obvious pain, his voice shifting unnaturally between a distant shrill and a low, guttural rasping.

"He'll be down there with us soon enough and...oooh...what fun we'll all have as we poke and prod that tender meat, doing to him what he's done to others...dreams of still doing...even now. Why, he'll feel every little jab and stab and thrust and he'll LIKE it. He'll more than like it. He'll grow to love it, and beg for it, every instant of an everlasting night of an endless existence."

Hollow laughter echoed and faded.

A flicker of doubt appeared in Father Aberto's eyes as he studied the writhing form. "In the name of our Lord Jesus Christ...I command you to tell me your name."

"We are Legion..."

"And by whose authority do you refuse to leave?"

As suddenly as they had begun, the Cardinal's convulsions ceased. He whipped his head, staring at the old priest intently.

"Only one way. By our host's of course," the disembodied voice proclaimed with flawless composure. "You waaant it, you gottt it...damnaaation," it sang, distorting the once-popular jingle. "We told you; he wants to be with us. And we aim to pleeease," it continued, shifting to a long southern drawl.

"In the name of The Most High...you must tell me immediately... what brought him under your influence?"

The command seemed to incite pain. Mallory winced, his face crumpling into a disfiguring mask. "Um...it might have something to do with those nocturnal activities of his."

"Earlier...before he took Holy Orders...or more recently? Speak!"

"Earlier...later...it's all the same. Only now, the opportunities are better. He's gained their trust, you see...with a schtup schtup here and a schtup schtup there...here a schtup...there a schtup... everywhere a schtup schtup."

They heard the remnant of tittering; a comedy routine designed, no doubt, for the discriminating tastes of the damned.

"Our Lord is, above all, compassionate and merciful. As black as this man's soul may be, it can be wiped clean by a contrite heart within the Sacrament of Penance. Explain yourself then, since you are still under the command of the Host of Hosts, why you will not leave!"

"*Thtuupid lithping* cancerous leech on a hog's ass! You know as well as we do, there is only one reason why we won't leave... CAN'T leave. He invited us in when he consecrated himself to the dark father. *Utheleth...*"

Beads of sweat appeared across Father Aberto's forehead. "When did he consecrate himself? How?"

"Five years ago. In a church that has long since thrown out the Infernal Resident. Across the pond in the land that once belonged to The Enemy and is now nearly ours."

"In a ceremony...?"

"The blackest of the black."

"A Black Mass?"

"What do you think, sweetums?"

"Who was there with him?"

"Other diddlers of the defenseless...cohorts in cranial intercourse...saying one thing, doing another, leading their flocks astray...as they creep closer to their doom."

Pearce shot Aberto a quick glance. The man appeared to shrink before his eyes.

"You're suggesting he's already perfectly possessed but you lie. Clearly, he is still undecided or he wouldn't be struggling so."

"A trifle longer then."

"You're lying again!"

"Can't lie under oath."

"He can still choose."

"Won't lie."

"He will make the right decision once he understands."

"No need to lie. It's too late. He's ours."

"By Christ's name...you must leave him be so that he may answer for himself!"

"It's your funeral."

There was a sudden and definite shift in Mallory. Like the coiling waters before a tsunami, the cold, hostile presence pervading the room receded a little; and like an impending flood, the four men surrounding the Cardinal knew it was temporary and that only moments remained before the deluge was upon them once more.

"Your Eminence...Vincent...if you can hear me, you must hurry and answer me now," Father Aberto implored. "Once and for all and by all that is holy...do you renounce Satan and all his demons?"

Disoriented as if he'd woken from a deep coma, the famous prelate looked up from his bed. Understanding flooded his face as he took in the somber scene before him—the presence of the priests—attired for battle."

"We don't have much time, Vincent," Aberto continued. "Do you understand the decision awaiting you? The importance of what must happen now? There is still a part of you that hesitates. It will not be too late if you resist. Turn towards that light, Father; give it permission to grow within you. Do it now!"

He turned to the others. "Pray brothers. Pray without ceasing."

Pearce had never stopped and doubted the other two needed reminding. This was no time to ponder the who, what, or why of this absurd moment. There would be plenty of time to dissect his shock and repugnance when it was over.

"Find your will, Father," the old priest persisted, "and you will find your way. Surely you know you have only one choice. That is all any of us truly has; the other is not a choice but a travesty. A lie that contains within itself all the pain the world has ever or could ever know!"

The Cardinal smiled; an expression familiar to millions around the world, tinged with surrender.

"Oh, but Father...you forget one thing," he conceded, now sounding very much like himself. "I would gladly suffer an eternity of it as long as the master throws me a few crumbs occasionally. You see, as true as it is that this pain exists...there is much pleasure to be found in pain. Better to rule in hell than serve in heaven, eh?"

Aberto moaned and something rushed back into the room, tickling the edge of Pearce's thoughts. He slammed the door on it, locking it firmly before it could gain a foothold.

From the looks of disgust on the other men's faces, they too were undergoing this mind rape and he quickly sent a blessing their way.

Contempt twisted Cardinal Mallory's face once more. "What say you now...*Preeetht*?"

The guttural, disjointed voice had returned. Despite his courage in such things, Father Aberto hesitated, the indecision on his wasted face so profound, Pearce placed a steadying hand on his shoulder. Aberto nodded once, flipped a large, intricately-carved silver crucifix from around his neck and held it resolutely over the squirming man.

"Prædicta omnia, quatenus opus sit, repeti possunt, donec obsessus sit omnino liberatus. Canticum Magnificat, ut supra; in

fine Glória Patri..."

The ancient, enduring words echoed through the room. Mallory's stiff body jerked in response, arching unnaturally. Heartened at the suffering prelate's response, Aberto pressed the crucifix into his hands without warning. Ignoring his screech of pain and the string of expletives that followed, he ground the icon into his adversary's flesh.

"He has reached the crisis point, brothers. Redouble your efforts. The moment of expulsion is nearly at hand."

"Is that what you really believe you withered old sack of bones?" the Cardinal taunted in between grunts of misery. "The only one expelled is our Tormentor...forever and ever...Aaamen! But you are right; something is nearly at hand and it comes for you...

"...and you...

"...and you..."

He twitched his head around, addressed each of the men personally, then fixed on Pearce with pure malice. "As for *you* brother! Something extra special comes just for you.

"Woe to the righteous priest who hunts the elusive worm;
His quest will be aborted before it comes to term.
Beneath the triad's spire, within the bitch's womb,
Bones knit with virgin blood, a labyrinth of doom.
Hidden, waiting, incubating; great its mighty yield.
Called forth at the holy hour,
when your own fate shall be sealed!"

There was no time to respond. Father Aberto screamed and lurched back, holding out his right hand. An angry, bright-red welt appeared in the center of his palm—in the vague but unmistakable shape of a crucifix.

"See...we can make up stupid little rhymes too."

Rather than hurl the icon, Mallory clasped it tightly, his body convulsing in pain while sweat poured down his face. For an endless moment, the four stared mutely at the writhing figure until, by subtle degrees, the torture contorting his features ebbed. When he released his death-grip on the icon, a similar wound scarred the hand that held it.

The men sensed a change in the air. There was a release of pressure that made it easier to breathe and lightened the mood in the room. Even the dull walls seemed brighter, cleaner. They exchanged fleeting looks; hopeful optimism cloaked in caution.

"Father, can you describe to us how you are feeling?" Aberto asked, wiping away sweat.

"As well as one can," The Cardinal admitted, sounding tired and listless but human. The answer prompted a collective sigh.

"Dottore, would you be so good as to check his vitals?" Aberto requested, waiting for the physician to diagnose the weak but stabilized condition of his patient.

"Father...Your Eminence, as you are aware, protocol must be followed. The Rite must be completed to ensure there are no lingering effects."

"Of course," the Cardinal agreed, meeting Aberto's gaze steadily.

The three gathered once more and Aberto resumed praying, transitioning smoothly into the crucial phase of the exorcism while Pearce found himself staring at Mallory. Calm and at peace, he murmured the petitions with eyes closed, fingering reverently the crucifix still in his hands.

"I cast you out, unclean spirit, along with every Satanic power of the enemy, every specter from hell, and all your fellow companions in the name of our Lord Jesus Christ. May we no longer fear any evil since the Lord is with us; Who lives and reigns with You, in the unity of the Holy Ghost, God, forever and ever. Amen."

The creases in the Cardinal's face faded as Aberto made the sign of the cross and anointed him with holy water. Mallory opened his eyes, wonder mixing with tears as he gazed upon each of the men in turn.

"Words cannot express the grace I have received this night."

Pearce's anxiety drained while the two men beside him slumped, muscles stretching as if they too had been released from some narrow, confined cage. With the worst over, he would get an explanation of all he'd heard tonight and he'd finally understand. Above all—he *had* to understand.

Seeking the exorcist's wisdom, Pearce glanced at him. An odd glint still shown in Aberto's eyes filling him with an anomalous dread. The priest seemed on edge and experience had taught him never to ignore his superior's moods.

"Beg your pardon, Your Eminence, but there is one more thing," Aberto murmured. "A small favor, to put an old man's mind at rest. Would you take that most holy of symbols and the sign of our redemption...the crucifix you still hold in your hand... and press it to your lips, merely as the last proof and seal of your deliverance?"

Pearce watched as the famous prelate, overcome with obvious devotion, slowly raised the icon to his lips. He exhaled gratefully—then gagged, unable to breathe at all.

Holding the sacred image with utmost reverence, his

expression beatific, Mallory rotated the crucifix one-hundred-and-eighty degrees, raised his eyes to Father Aberto, then winked—confirmation that he now had the old man's full attention. An appendage, too membranous and pink, slithered eagerly from between his parted lips like a tentacle; testing, probing the air—before it delivered its toxin with fatal accuracy, corrupting whatever it touched. Still fixed upon the exorcist, Cardinal Vincent Mallory—darling of the media, hero of the people—traced his tongue over the curves and contours of the icon—with an enthusiasm second only to the rapacious hunger that rivaled it.

It took Pearce only a moment to reach the point of wretchedness. He turned towards Father Aberto, saw him reel, then fall, and recognized in the old priest what was etched forever in his own soul.

It was the haunted look of a man who had lost.

TWENTY-ONE

Sunday, March 16
Outside El Paso

S ensing his master's turmoil at what his storytelling must have cost him, even Teufel remained quiet.

"I can see why you couldn't talk about that one, bro. Not even to me," Logan said finally.

Pearce ignored him, his earlier desolation replaced by nervous energy, while my own problems suddenly took on an all new perspective. I tried ridding myself of the suspicion that his tale had something to do with me.

"Where's Mallory now? Is he still alive?"

Like most, I'd heard of the Cardinal, of course, and tried to reconcile the vague, newsstand image with the demonic entity he'd described.

"Oh, yes...he's around," Pearce said. "He's been defrocked and excommunicated. Locked up in some cushy private sanatorium for the mentally insane in upstate New York; maximum security masquerading as Club Med. Other than a priest who visits once a month to check on the state of his soul, he's not allowed visitors. The powers-that-be thought it was the safest solution considering he was quite vocal about what he wanted to do if he ever got out."

"That wasn't the official story. I heard he was suffering from some chronic, debilitating disease. Some disease! So he's still... he hasn't shown signs of improving?"

"You can say it. Cardinal Vincent Mallory has joined the exclusive club of the damned. He's now one of the perfectly possessed; the *energumens perfecte*."

"But I don't understand how it failed. What about the Rite? You yourself said that words were powerful and when they were spoken in the name of the highest..."

"Yes! Of course they are, Trina. But you forget about free will. Mallory had a choice and he chose badly. God won't go against our free will."

"Did you ever find out why he made that choice?" Logan asked, clearly as curious as I. "And what about the others he mentioned? I assume they were priests. Tell me they're not still around, doing those things!"

Bitterness clouded Pearce's face.

"There isn't a day goes by I don't ask myself those same questions. The truth is...I don't know. It's not every day a cardinal undergoes an exorcism. As the only witnesses to what happened in that room, the four of us were immediately sequestered by Vatican authorities and drilled like terrorists.

"I soon learned quid pro quo wasn't in their vocabulary. If they had names, they weren't talking. Their attitudes rankled. I made it known to my superiors this type of travesty couldn't...shouldn't remain hidden. I threatened to go public if they didn't clean house, get rid of the vermin. They assured me proper measures would be taken, but countered with a threat of their own.

"If I made it public, I'd not only be defrocked, they'd make sure I was excommunicated like Mallory. I finally decided there was only one thing to do.

"Knowing I couldn't stay after what I'd learned, I asked to be reassigned. In exchange for promising to clean house and allowing me to leave on my own terms, I'd keep my mouth shut. Still wondering how I ended up at St. Jo's?"

"You're a better man than me," Logan muttered. "I'd trust them as much as a pack of hungry wolves."

"The thought occurred. I made it known before I left I had insurance. You see, the rules associated with the Rite are very precise. For the protection of the possessed as well as those presiding, all exorcisms are recorded.

Generally, an audio recording is considered sufficient, but when Father Aberto was instructed that under no circumstances should he record the event, he got suspicious and hid a video camera in the room instead. It was the only way he could think of to keep his vow of obedience and skirt around it at the same time. The recording is in a private vault, accessible only by him."

My head was spinning. "Are you suggesting they were so desperate, they would have actually considered..."

"Murder? If the wrong people thought I was a threat, maybe. Trouble is, their kind don't tattoo their intent across their foreheads.

"The blinders have long since come off, Trina. I'm no longer the priest I once was; but if it's any consolation, I believe I'm a better one."

"I'm surprised you stuck with it. I wouldn't want anything more to do with that lot."

"I almost didn't but in the end, only one thing mattered. Bottom line, I had to play my part in rebalancing the scales and there are too few of us to do the job right as it is. They did wet their pants when they learned of my reassignment. Out of sight, out of mind. Case closed."

"And Father Aberto...the other men?"

"Those assisting moved to Spain soon after. Despite my poking around, I haven't found either of them. I suspect that's by design. As for Aberto, they made sure he wouldn't be a threat either. He's retired now. It was a little easier with him since they figured he was too old to stir up trouble."

"Why did the crucifix burn him as well when Mallory was the one possessed?"

Pearce nodded. "He still has the scar, as does Mallory. Why it also manifested in him I don't know for sure but I have a theory. Our decision to either accept or reject God affects each of us differently.

"For Mallory, the mark of the crucifix is an everlasting condemnation of his betrayal; for Aberto...an everlasting reminder that as a priest, he must pick up the cross and ultimately be willing to die with Him.

"But I had more important reasons for breaking my silence after so many years," he said.

"When you spoke of the triad and labyrinth, you helped me remember Mallory's words. In the years since, I had never put much stock in them, believing them to be the usual lies spewed on such occasions. But now, I realize that what he said under possession was true and it complicates things more than I originally thought."

Slow to understand, Logan and I looked at one another. "How?" we asked together.

"Woe to the righteous priest who hunts the elusive worm;
        His quest will be aborted before it comes to term.
    Beneath the triad's spire, within the bitch's womb,
    Bones knit with virgin blood, a labyrinth of doom.
    Hidden, waiting, incubating; great its mighty yield.
            Called forth at the holy hour,
        when your own fate shall be sealed.

"Chloe and Eddy's words have been validated. The entity in that room that night somehow knew we would meet. It had foreknowledge of it. With some unimaginable, unholy intellect, it knew we were linked together in a way I would've said was impossible an hour ago."

"Go on," Logan prompted.

"Don't you see? Our connection is important. So important that hell itself was compelled to threaten me. Maybe because our alliance is a threat to it. And to Gregory Kadzik."

"This isn't just your problem anymore, Trina. If we want to stay alive, we'll need to understand those words before those who ordered the hit come back with reinforcements to finish the job."

"But you said Gregory's probably covered his tracks by now. How is marching up to his front door and accusing him of murder going to help us when there's no one we can trust?"

I swallowed dryly, trying to get my mind around coming face to face with him again.

"That might not be necessary. I know someone who might help us solve our riddle. In fact, he may be the only one who can."

"Well don't keep us in suspense. Who is he?" Logan urged.

"The keeper of the key. We need to go to Rome."

The announcement elicited a wide range of reactions. Logan

tensed, muscles flexing at the prospect of action, while Teufel scrambled to all fours and barked his resounding approval.

As for me, I merely stared at both men in mute silence, wondering if I'd ever be able to pinpoint the exact moment my life spiraled out of control.

TWENTY-TWO

Is our songbird's neck properly wrung?"

"She's getting help," Scaevus The Slayer announced during his courtesy call to his boss.

"I take it something went wrong?"

"She's outside El Paso. Hitched a ride with some guy who fancies himself a reporter for a celebrity rag."

"Ahh yes, Sinistrus mentioned him the other night. Regretted not taking care of him there and then. More evidence he's losing his edge."

"There's another one. A priest," Scaevus added, his voice as melodic as a prepubescent girl. "Does the name Pearce Rhomer ring any bells?"

"So he's reappeared. Amazing what crawls out when you kick over a few rocks. What happened? Did they see you?"

"No worries. The cloaking wore off just minutes ago."

What a rush that had been, and what a colossal waste of his

exemplar's gift. He'd been the unexpected wedding crasher; mingling with guests, toasting the bride and groom. Unfortunately, the moment of bliss was contaminated with the memory of what followed.

A single, vile creature had rendered all his preparations and his cloaking useless. The hateful thought turned his already black eyes into bottomless voids.

"It turns out the men have a history that includes considerable military training. If I didn't know better, I'd have said they were ready for the attack. I didn't expect the semi-autos. Even so, it would've been over if it wasn't for some damned mutt coming to their rescue."

Hael laughed, clearly enjoying a moment at his assassin's expense. "Careful, Scaevus. Wouldn't want it getting around that The Slayer got bested by a dog since reputations are so difficult to reestablish."

The Slayer's eyes narrowed. If it had been anyone but his exemplar insulting him, the dial counting down his last twenty-four hours would've begun ticking seconds ago. "It gets better. They're headed for Rome tonight."

"Are they now?"

"I could finish things before they have a chance to leave."

"I have a better idea. It's time to show Sinistrus how forgiving The Council can be. Having everyone together under the banner of the Eternal City may work to our advantage at this stage. Stay clear of them for now but follow. Find out what they're up to and why. We'll meet as soon as you know more. Until then, try not to grapple with any more dogs. It's so unbecoming."

The Slayer clicked off, resisting the urge to throw his phone into the weeds and stomp it into oblivion. Hael's remark resurrected his pain in more ways than one.

Thanks to the hound that had nearly severed his radial nerve, he now sported permanent fang marks that left his trigger finger useless. Strange how the mutt had no problem seeing him when the humans couldn't. He tuned out the throbbing in his hand for more amusing thoughts. He'd been with his exemplar long enough to know his patience would be rewarded. Sooner or later, here or in Rome, today, tomorrow, or next week, the woman and her two allies would die, and as payback for his troubles, he'd make sure it was creative, long, and painful. Then as an encore, he would return to this shit hole and nail the priest's mongrel to the altar of his church. After all, weren't the faithful beasts supposed to follow their masters everywhere, imitation being the sincerest form of flattery?

The morning's reconnaissance had reduced The Slayer's black, ankle-length duster to bronze. Though not as effective as Hael's cloaking, the result was similar to the gecko a few feet of him, blending into the Texan soil. It allowed him to remain virtually invisible as he sat down among the tall brush and turned up the volume to the directional listening device in his ear.

Shuddering with pent-up rage, he focused on the little house in the distance until his eyelids drooped and he swapped his twisted yearnings for the deviant dreams plaguing most of his nights; dark fantasies that would compel most of humanity to prop up their eyelids with bamboo skewers just to stay awake.

TWENTY-THREE

Benedict Canyon

I ntent on the larger-than-life figure on screen, Chloe back-arrowed to her favorite part of the routine for the third time in as many minutes. Absorbed in critiquing one of her earlier performances—a favorite pastime—she jumped when Gregory swept into the screening room, lacerated arms and calves still bleeding. Though seeing her exemplar torn and bloodied was nothing new, the self-inflicted damage produced by his barb-wire flogger seemed excessive, even for him.

"Everything go okay?"

"Pack your bags. We're leaving for Rome tonight," he muttered, heading for the adjoining private office.

"Rome? What's in Rome?"

"The chance to finish what we started."

"Have you forgotten I've got a concert in two days?"

"Have you forgotten I set it up? Consider it canceled. I have an overdue appointment with a certain bitch."

Chloe's eyes narrowed. "Who told you Langford's in Rome?"

"Need I remind you, yours is to obey," he said, strolling towards her. "Not that it's any of your business, but The Council just handed me a bonus. You're going to help me turn it into a dividend."

Despite what had to be painful wounds, Chloe detected a thrill of victory in his tone, coupled with a trace of erotic suggestion.

"So you're back in their good graces. What do you have in mind?"

"Still working out the details, though when you get tired of staring at yourself, we could channel our energies into some new, provocative ways guaranteed to inspire and get the juices flowing."

She pointed to his mangled legs. "Are you sure you'll be able to feel anything after your little session?"

"Foreplay, that's all. Designed to help me think but also remarkable in its ability to heighten certain sensory pleasures. But what am I saying? I'm preaching to the choir. You're just as talented in eliciting that elusive response, that exquisitely-sensitive balance."

"I should be, since you taught me everything I know," Chloe countered, grazing her nails down his tattered leg hard enough for his eyes to roll back into his head. "I'll see what I can do," she promised, watching him stagger into his office in a zombie-like stupor and close the door.

She waited to make sure he wasn't coming out, reached for her phone, dialed the number she'd memorized, and waited for the beep prompting her to reveal Gregory Kadzik's daily doings. At this rate, she could expect an invitation from The Council before her next performance.

She allowed her mind to wonder in this direction until her

on-screen image became too mesmerizing to resist. Cranking up the volume, she lost herself in the writhing, gyrating body on the screen and wished she'd made popcorn to enhance the awe-inspiring spectacle before her.

WISDOM

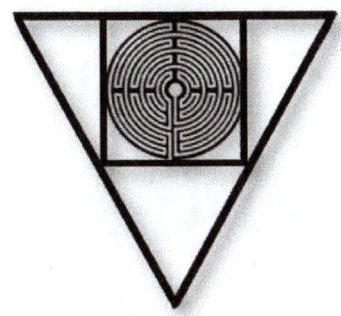

TWENTY-FOUR

Monday, March 17
Rome, Italy

Not knowing how long we'd be away, Pearce left the day-to-day handling of the parish and Teufel—indignant at being left behind—in the capable hands of his deacon and the elderly Sister Elise. Skeptical of his plan to traipse half way around the world with a couple of strangers, one of them a woman no less, they accepted his vague explanations grudgingly. Pearce reasoned it was better that way.

"Without us around, the shooter won't be tempted to come back. Everyone should be a lot safer."

"But will we?" Logan reminded. "They've been one step ahead of us all along. Seems reasonable they're already planning their next visit."

I ignored the comment. If they wanted to finish the job, I could think of countless ways to take advantage of our helplessness as we sat in a metal tube for several hours. Fear at this point, was pointless and by the time the jumbo 747 touched down, El Paso and its violence already seemed like a distant nightmare.

Despite our jet lag, we taxied directly to Father Gandini's flat where the driver dumped us before a building whose two-storied walls were literally crumbling before our eyes. Pearce's face darkened as he studied the shabby neighborhood, explaining we were just blocks from where they'd held the exorcism nearly six years ago.

The old man who greeted us at the door appeared shrunken and weak; a far cry from what I expected of an exorcist. He embraced Pearce with genuine affection and took a step back to study him more carefully.

"The American Southwest has been good to you, Pearce," he said, with just a slight tremor added to his thick English. "You look healthy. Perhaps this means some of the wounds have healed and you've managed to forget?"

Pearce winced as if he knew what he was about to say could only bring grief to the elderly priest.

"That's actually why we're here, Father. We need your help. Things are happening I couldn't explain over the phone. You may be the only one able to shed some light."

The old man seemed taken aback. He nodded absently and I was sure he'd been reminded of things best left buried.

"These are the friends I brought to meet you," Pearce continued. "They're part of this too now...somehow."

Father Aberto offered me his hand and I took it, feeling the strange, puckered skin of the scar on his palm. It was still there, as promised. Could it really be a symbol of love, to the point of death?

Reminiscent of Pearce my first night in El Paso, he focused on the eagle charm dangling from my wrist, his eyes bottomless blue pools that had seen too much but kept their secrets well.

"I will try to help you the best I can, despite my misgivings," he admitted, inviting us inside.

Unlike Pearce's home, the flat was littered with artifacts, mementos, and books jammed into every nook. We sat on a faded couch that looked original to the building, while Father Aberto poured out hot cups of tea and we took turns describing the events of the past two weeks. Pearce ended with how he thought the separate references to the triad and labyrinth connected our stories and were key to our staying alive.

For the longest time, the old priest remained silent and I wondered if he was passing judgment on me. Then he stood and drew open the heavy drapes behind us, the late afternoon sun filtering the dust into beams of hazy light.

"Forgive me. You will understand if I tell you I no longer find the darkness tolerable," he explained before sitting and becoming quiet again.

After a while, he sighed, saying, "I don't hear much these days, as you can well imagine. They keep things from me and perhaps that is for the best. Somehow, I have lost my appetite for the more exotic elements of my profession. But I can at least try to make sense of what burdens you. Maybe even point you in the right direction. I feel I owe you that much, Pearce.

"I must also warn all of you...these forces you are dealing with...they are not to be taken lightly. If you persist down this road, rest assured, there will be a price to pay."

"I don't think it's up to us anymore," Pearce said.

"Make of it what you will then. Both the triad and labyrinth have long histories dating back to antiquity. The legendary Minotaur, half man, half bull, devouring young children within his labyrinthine corridors, is one such example. And yet a labyrinth can also symbolize the path of initiation. A spiritual journey of the soul that leads to *gnosis*...hidden knowledge."

"Sort of like a maze?" Logan asked.

"That is what most people think, but no. Unlike a maze, a labyrinth has one unbroken path that leads towards its center. Those who adhere to this path have already made their choice. They know precisely where they are headed and how to get there."

"Like the *energumens perfecte*?"

"Possibly," Aberto agreed. "It does imply transformation in certain cases; life, death, rebirth. The soul's descent into the underworld. It would depend on the intent."

"But that's just it. How do you tell the difference?" I argued. "Can't it also represent the good...the benign?"

"You shall know them by their fruits," he said simply. "Remember, those you are running from take great pleasure in distorting everything. A lamb becomes a goat; the circle of life, chaos. The very stars in the solar system, designed to help humanity find its way, now reinvented as the inverted pentagram compelling it to stumble.

"It is the same with the triad or triangle," he murmured, lost in thought. "For many it is a symbol of hope; the Holy Trinity... Father, Son, and Holy Ghost. For others, it is the means for casting spells and can either denote ascension into a spiritual realm or a descent into the material world. Even the geometry itself, with its tri-folds, is highly symbolic and sacred."

"How so?"

"Numerology assigns certain properties to each number. While the number one signifies masculine force and strength, two is considered feminine and represents an opening. Add both together and you have the sum of their parts. That is to say, the union of one and two gives birth to three and, tradition has it, wisdom and *gnosis*."

Our questioning had exhausted the old priest. He sank back in his chair and closed his eyes while we exchanged uneasy glances.

"So Chloe was telling the truth. The path of initiation will soon be open for business," Pearce said. "Question is...why? What do they hope to accomplish unless this *gnosis* is intended to usher in a new age...one yielding more power."

Logan's mouth twisted into a smirk. "Well I'm feeling better knowing the club of the damned will be too busy with their Ouija boards to pay attention to us!"

"I wish I could share your optimism. Whatever they're waiting for, they believe it's happening soon. Their desperate attempt to tie up any loose ends threatening their little enterprise screams of it."

I took a wild stab. "As in *I'm* the loose end."

"I think we can assume we've been added to the list. It would explain the warning I received six years ago."

"Maybe you're reading too much into it. Aren't illusions of grandeur and delusion the lunatic fringe's usual stock in trade?"

"As old as the devil himself," Pearce admitted. "People like Gregory waste their entire lives in pursuit of shifting the dark powers to their side; harnessing them to their advantage. There's nothing new about that."

"Perhaps we should shift our attention to what has changed then," Aberto broke in suddenly. He opened his eyes, now bright with new-found excitement.

"Maybe there is something else I can offer, although you may say it is simply the ramblings of an old fool who has lived too long with one foot entrenched in the diabolical. But there may be a benefit in that, and now..." he said, holding up a withered finger, "...it may also be one way to understand these events and how they relate to you. You speak of evil struggling to breech our world. What occurs to you when you read the headlines? When you watch our news?"

"I know where you're headed, Father," Pearce said, shaking his head. "But it's always been that way. If it bleeds, it leads. Exploitation at its best."

"Certainly. But for the last several years, I have seen something more. The random chaos of the world is arranging itself in strange new patterns. Instances of evil have not only multiplied and gained momentum like a monstrous storm swirling over our heads. Evil itself, its genetic composition, if there could be such a thing, is mutating, changing; absorbing humanity's foul deeds to the point it has infected it; to the point evil is now called good and good, evil."

"Isn't that just perception? What of technology, better communication? The seven billion you call humanity?" I reasoned.

"Yes, but there are other elements that cannot be so quickly dismissed. We are not only flesh and bone, but spirit. Whatever happens in the human heart always has its counterpart in culture and society. One act of selfish cruelty or violence may not have much impact, but when it is repeated over and over and combined, it will, eventually, take its toll upon a civilization. It is no longer just psychopaths or renegade dictatorships that are responsible, but every faction of our planet."

"For instance?" Logan challenged.

Aberto threw him an old newspaper. "You don't have to know the language to understand the headlines, since I am certain they mirror yours. Wars and rumors of wars. Torture, genocide, profiteering from the blood of the people. Violence for the sake of violence. Dishonesty, greed, lust, and thievery so rampant, it has become the new normal. And perhaps most frightening, the disturbing insistence that these things are good and are to be celebrated. No, my friends. There is only one who can befuddle humanity's natural sense of right and wrong to this extent. You know him well, Pearce."

He paused, regret clouding his worn face.

"Ahh...I was hoping never to see this day. Strange, the folly of old men's dreams. Your questions have forced me to face truths I have avoided for too long, but now I see the futility of such a thing. As much as I would have liked to spare you, clearly there are other forces at work here. I think you are right, Pearce. Your enemies may indeed be waiting for a certain event."

"Won't matter if we don't know what it is."

"I may have an idea."

"If you have real evidence, Father, tell us."

The older priest laughed weakly. "I would be doing you a great disservice, my friend. Besides, I have said too much already. What you learn must come directly from those who know of such things. I will say only this: if humanity is deathly ill and on the path to self-destruction as I believe it is, then this illness will not only be limited to our small world and the poor creatures destined to walk upon it. There will be signs elsewhere in our universe. That is where you must seek to find your ultimate proof."

"You're suggesting I should look to the stars? What next? Astrology?"

"Not astrology, Pearce. Cosmology. I have a friend; someone I've known from my seminary days. He will give you the proof you seek. I will make the arrangements. Then after he has told you what you want to know, come back and we will speak again."

"How can anything going on in the cosmos have to do with what's happened to Trina? To us? You're asking me to believe the impossible."

"I seem to remember you made a profession of the impossible once and you were not so difficult to convince six years ago," Aberto said. "I must confess...I thought this is why you came; that you had heard about Vincent Mallory."

Pearce leaned forward. "Has there been a change? A sign perhaps, that he's seeking redemption?"

Aberto looked away, sorrow competing with disgust. "Then you don't know. Mallory went missing. He disappeared from the facility in New York a week ago and has not been heard from since. While no one knows where he went, I think it is safe to assume it has something to do with this."

The old priest reached into his pocket, drew out a folded sheet of paper and placed it on the table. "This is only a copy as the original was found on the wall of his room, scrawled in his own feces."

Unable to hide my own disgust, I looked down at the cryptic words separated by a crude, tightly-drawn spiral within a triangle, a strange symbol in each corner, and heard the door to that asylum creak open another inch.

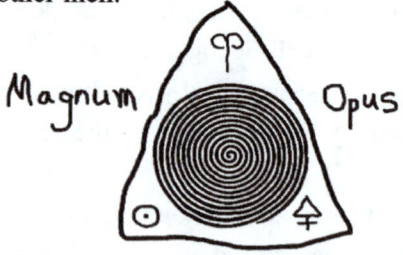

TWENTY-FIVE

Tuesday, March 18

"Which part of *I don't want to know more* did no one understand back in El Paso?"

"Snipers with laser crosshairs change things," Pearce reminded as we moved through the lobby of the Hotel Valencia.

After we'd retrieved the exorcism video hidden in a strong box in the back of Father Gandini's closet last night, we'd declined his offer to stay and instead opted for the modest lodgings off the beaten path.

Pearce continued. "The similarities between Mallory's symbol and Chloe's triads and labyrinths are uncanny. We ignore them at our own risk."

"So explain what it's doing alongside a Latin term meaning Great Work. If he was right about Kadzik's crowd ushering in this Magnum Opus, Mallory's just another piece of the puzzle. And while we're at it, how does he walk out of a maximum-level facility without raising alarms unless he had inside help? Surely he wouldn't leave his luxury digs and three square unless he was a man with a mission."

"Maybe he's decided to join Gregory's coven," Logan said. "Just think of the prestige of having a defrocked priest on his membership roster."

A month ago I would've called him crazy but crammed into a taxi after a fitful night tossing, my mind churned at the idea of the former cardinal decked out in ceremonial cloak and cowl, dagger hovering over some poor runaway who'd had the misfortune of running into one of Gregory's toadies.

With no easy answers, I forced my attention to the ever-changing vista out the window. Eventually, bustling Roman streets gave way to winding countryside and finally, to a long cypress-lined driveway leading to a classic-looking villa that had once been the summer residence of popes. A thin, anemic-looking priest waited beneath its elaborate doors.

"Welcome to The Vatican Observatory, better known in this part of the world as La Specola," greeted Luca Bertolucci in flawless English seasoned with a hint of Boston drawl. He ushered us into the fifteenth century mansion now turned into the museum behind the observatory, then led us through a series of exhibits to an office towards the back of the building.

"What a pleasure to hear from Aberto," he continued. "Haven't seen the old boy in ages. How's he doing? He sounded tired over the phone."

Logan and I exchanged raised eyebrows while Pearce updated the priest on Aberto's condition. Old was a bit ironic considering Bertolucci looked like he could've given a first-hand account of the Inquisition.

We followed him into a cramped, windowless room that reeked

of mothballs and the ancient volumes alongside one wall though he may have also had something to do with the odor. He motioned for us to be seated and being on the short side, nearly disappeared behind mounds of paperwork on his desk.

"Now, what can I do for you young people? I admit I'm a little puzzled at Aberto's request. He said something about unusual events? Cosmic signs? Did he mention anything specific?"

"Only one," Pearce said, handing him a copy of Mallory's symbol.

Bertolucci's eyes narrowed as he mouthed the words silently. "Where did he get this, if I may ask?"

"A friend."

"I take it you already know what it means?"

"The words...yes; the symbols...no. Aberto's never seen anything like it and wasn't sure if this Great Work has to do with the spiritual realm or the scientific. He thought you may have a clue since it resembles technical notation."

Bertolucci shrugged. "There are certain similarities to the coding used in physics. Other than that, nothing definite," he said, handing it back.

"So it doesn't mean anything to you? Anything...different?" Pearce suggested.

"Afraid not. While I can see how with Aberto's background, any sign, be it on paper or celestial, would be interpreted as mysterious and esoteric, my own field has led me in a completely different direction. If you would permit me to be blunt, Father, the observatory does not dabble in superstitious hocus-pocus. To do so now would be to crawl back into that black hole the Church has labored so hard to escape since the unfortunate misstep with Galileo."

He paused, eyeing us curiously. "But are you sure that's what he had in mind? Perhaps what he meant is that we're delving farther and deeper into the universe and seeing things science will undoubtedly explain in the near future. In which case, he would be absolutely correct. The observatory is on the cutting edge. Whatever it is you seek, maybe our research can help."

"Research into what?" Pearce asked.

"For one, whether we're alone in the universe...and you can put your eyes back in your heads. It's not what you think. Just a natural extension of studying the planetary sciences along with quantum gravity, meteorites, extrasolar planets."

"Quantum gravity...tasked with providing the link between quantum mechanics and the theory of relativity. Aren't you spinning your wheels since there's no way to observe their unification?"

Bertolucci laughed. "You've been holding out on us, Mr. O'Neill. Seems like you have more than a passing interest in physics."

"Information overload; one of the curses of being a journalist."

"Hey, if you'd given me a heads up, I would've cleaned up my office for the interview."

"Logan isn't here in a professional capacity," Pearce said. "He's simply a friend, nothing more. Please go on. Those things you mentioned...any recent breakthroughs? The discovery of a new planet? A huge meteor hurtling towards earth?"

"In a way I wish there were. The media blitz would certainly help our funding. I know this isn't what you're looking for but what we do here is more subtle; research that takes years, decades really, but nonetheless crucial in our understanding of the cosmos. Exciting to physics nerds maybe but of little interest to the public.

If I'm to point you in the right direction, I'll need more. Go back. Ask Aberto to elaborate. If he can think of anything else, my door's always open."

Bertolucci stood, indicating our meeting was over. We shook his proffered hand, as brittle as tissue paper, and headed out into the hallway.

"And Mr. O'Neill," Bertolucci called out. "Next time give me a little warning and I'll make sure you get the VIP tour."

Logan waved his thanks as we rounded the corner. "You heard the man. We're barking up the wrong tree. So what was Father Gandini getting at with the whole mysterious universe spiel?"

"Doesn't add up, does it?" Pearce agreed. "I know Aberto. He wouldn't have gone to all the trouble of setting this up if it wasn't important."

"Maybe the padre was just reading too much into it."

"Trina has a point. And since he also knows Bertolucci, he must've guessed we'd be wasting our time. There's something we're not getting," Logan added.

"Speaking of which, aren't you full of surprises," I said, nudging his elbow. "Where did you learn all that science stuff?"

"Later. Right now let's focus on making this goose chase pay for itself."

A blurry figure crossed our path; a man, dressed in the traditional brown robes of a monk, his face concealed by a cowl reminding me at once of other, more sinister memories. Immersed in a book, he collided headlong into Pearce, the force pushing him back against the wall.

"*Scuzi,*" the man apologized. Rather than step away, he grasped both of Pearce's hands in his and brought his lips to his ear, whispered something, then stepped around us lightly and disappeared behind a closed door. The exchange was over in seconds.

"Whoa! What was that all about?"

"Don't know yet," Pearce murmured. "But I think our luck might've just changed."

He uncurled the fingers of his left hand. Nestled in his palm was a folded piece of paper so tiny, it could have easily found its way into a fortune cookie.

TWENTY-SIX

Compliments of Roman smog drifting above the Alban Hills, the Vatican Observatory looked more like a haunted relic conjured through sleight of hand than the prestigious institution bragged about by Luca Bertolucci.

I ignored the evening chill and looked to the dark silhouette beside me. Logan grinned, his teeth the only white in a sea of looming darkness. "You're doing great," he whispered, taking both my clammy hands in his to squeeze them reassuringly. "This will be over before you know it."

"Easy for you. I don't think I was cut out for this commando crap," I wheezed, still winded from leaping over a six-foot rock wall and sprinting furtively through the meticulous grounds, trying to avoid detection from the array of cameras. I winced when I put my weight down on my ankle; a reminder I had twisted it on the uneven landscape.

"You're hurt," Logan murmured.

"It'll keep until I can soak it back at the hotel."

"I can do better. How about I pick up some rubbing alcohol, come over later and massage the kinks out of it?"

"Save the kinky stuff for when we get through this without getting thrown in an Italian jail," Pearce's disembodied voice interrupted from somewhere to my left.

Dressed entirely in black and one with the night, I'd temporarily forgotten about him and blushed, thankful for my own invisibility.

"Did he say exactly where we're supposed to meet him? Maybe we're in the wrong spot," Logan speculated.

"I got the impression he'll find us when he's ready. Why else would he have slipped us the location of all the cameras?"

Behind us, the rustling of brush preempted further talk. A shadow emerged, a blob of black defining itself more clearly as it approached.

I took a step back as something skeletal moved towards me. The monk from earlier in the day extended an arm clad in a long sleeve.

"Glad to meet you all finally. Brother Joe McCullough at your service," he said with no trace of a foreign accent. "Sorry for all the cloak and dagger nonsense but it's probably safer that way. Come with me and we'll get started," he continued, actions negating his previous claims as he led us confidently up the steps of the building behind the villa and pressed a buzzer.

A security guard unlocked the door, greeted him familiarly and ushered us into the reception area without a second glance.

"Tony, these are the friends I told you about earlier. As we discussed, there won't be a need to sign them in or out."

The guard smiled complicitly and I thought I saw him wink.

"Any problem with the motion detector at the front?"

McCullough asked, sweeping the hood off his head to expose a friendly face, clearly not over thirty, and a thick head of orange, curly hair.

"Not at all, Fratello," the man answered, returning to his post behind the security monitors. "As far as anyone knows, this is just another uneventful night at La Specola. You will let me know when you are ready to leave...yes?"

"Of course. And be sure to tell Elena I've got the upcoming blessed event covered at Sunday's Mass. What's that going to make...five?"

"Six, Fratello. But she told me to tell you her next intention will surely be for separate bedrooms."

Amid laughter, McCullough motioned for us to follow him to a metal door, took a key card from his pocket and swiped it, then faced us and clapped his hands together as if entertaining strangers at midnight was a regular pastime.

"So hey! Can I interest any of you in a cup of coffee since this is going to be a long night?"

TWENTY-SEVEN

Nursing our mugs, we padded across the catwalk to the Vatican telescope. Above us, a metal dome stood ready to reveal the secrets of the cosmos at the push of a button.

Seated at the observation post directly below the enormous instrument, Brother McCullough enjoyed our sense of awe and spun his seat 350 degrees like a five year old who couldn't wait to show off his shiny toy.

"I love to watch people's faces when I bring them here," he admitted, a smile lighting his like a beacon. "It's amazing when you think of it. This place, existing at the edge of the city like it does. I'd open it up and let you take a peek if I thought it would do any good but there's too much goop up there tonight to see anything," he said.

"Alright, you got us here. What's all this about?" Pearce asked.

"Following Father A's instructions is all. He said you were doing some research. Thought our stories might connect."

"Yeah, from someone he'd known in seminary."

"Oh...you thought you'd be meeting a colleague." McCullough shook his head. "You've got it wrong. I wasn't a colleague. I was a student. Father A was one of my guest professors while I was doing graduate work at St. Charles. Thanks to similar interests, we got to know each other fairly well."

"What about Bertolucci?" I asked.

McCullough grinned. "Far as I know he and Father A weren't so much friends as acquaintances. Quite the character, ain't he? Sorry you had to put up with him as long as you did but it really couldn't be helped."

"Let me get this straight. When Aberto said we needed to get answers about unseen forces in our universe, he meant you?"

"That's about it. I couldn't think of another way to get close enough to give you the message. And let me guess...Father A didn't clue you in."

We shook our heads and he continued. "Probably a good thing, considering what we'll be talking about."

"Right. Cloaks and daggers. Are you under some sort of gag order?"

"Not the kind you'd expect. It's just that after Father A explained the reason you're here, we thought it best not to call attention to ourselves. You'll understood more soon."

"Did he also tell you about this?" Pearce asked, handing him the copy of Mallory's malodorous graffiti.

"He explained its origins. Quite the nasty piece," McCullough said, examining the note from all angles. "Interesting...question is, what Great Work? My guess is, we find the meaning of the symbol, we'll have our answer."

"Any ideas?"

"Lots of 'em, but that's all they are right now. It feels familiar, though. Like I've seen it before. Could be part of the runic alphabet, a medieval cypher. Then again, it vaguely resembles an Egyptian tetractys."

"Then you don't think it's technical shorthand? Scientific notation?"

"Possible, though nothing stands out at first glance."

"That's what Bertolucci said when we showed it to him."

"He's probably right since it doesn't fit any of the standard abbreviations. I'd know. I'm as intimate with them as the back of my hand."

He saw our blank expressions and elaborated. "After my grad work at Caltech, I went to Palomar until they could bring me on at Mount Graham where I'm at now."

We expressed our surprise in silence. How many advanced degrees did this baby-faced genius hold and was he out of diapers by the time he'd earned his first?

"Mount Graham...?" I echoed.

"The other Vatican observatory in Arizona," Logan said. "They're affiliated with the university over there, if I'm not mistaken."

"Very good!" McCullough exclaimed, delighted with Logan's mysterious scope of knowledge. "Glad I won't have to start at the beginning."

"So what are you doing in Rome?"

"Trying not to butcher the local lingo. Actually, I come up to collaborate as needed. Guess they've decided I'm of some use after all."

"Not trying to be rude, but what do you know that Bertolucci doesn't? Despite his collar, I got the impression mentioning anything remotely fringe would send him into hysterical laughter."

The scientist snorted and rolled his eyes. "I'm not surprised. It's his standard spiel and the pervading attitude in the Church these days. In their eagerness to erase any embarrassing history and appear kinder, more politically correct, they've forgotten the Church has a supernatural core."

"An old-fashioned concept to be sure," Pearce admitted. "You don't buy into this new, improved version?"

"I, my friend, am a dinosaur along with Father A. And you, apparently, from what he said. One reason he and I got along so famously. We've both seen too much, each in our own way, proving we live in a world far more mysterious than any of us dreamed. I think that's why he thought I could help. Looks like we're all searching for the truth, just from different angles. By the way, you guys might be able to return the favor since a couple things he said really intrigued."

"As in...?"

He turned to face me. "Spontaneous human combustion. I've heard of it, of course, but never as a result of remote psychic influence. If it's proven, they'll have to give more credence to how mental processes affect the material world and I'll have to tweak my methane theory."

"Uhh...methane?"

"Sure. Why not? It's one of the few combustible gases humans produce. Mixed with intestinal enzymes, it could viably create the necessary chemical reaction. Bam! The perfect storm! By any chance, Ms. Langford, do you recall if your boyfriend ate any beans in the hours before his unfortunate demise?"

Somewhere behind me, Pearce and Logan were making strange gurgling noises I ignored deliberately. Not ready to tackle the earnest young friar's topic, I changed it. "What did you mean by seeing too much?"

"Focus McCullough...focus! *Mea culpa.* As I was saying, most of the time, they've got me working on the polarization induced by cataclysmic variables, star systems giving off sudden bursts of energy, that sort of thing. But about a year ago, my research revealed something puzzling. A glitch in the math that didn't jive with previous calculations. Every time I tried to get a straight answer, I hit a virtual brick wall. After months of error messages and system malfunctions, I figured someone didn't want me snooping so I changed tactics. Without telling anyone and on my own time, I went looking for proof in the morgue."

"Among the dead?"

"Nah...just the pet name for the old CIA archives. Every doodle, memo, or scrap of paper the agency has collected since before they changed their name from the OSS."

"How would you even..." I broke off when he cracked a shrewd grin.

"Encryption is sort of a hobby on my days off. Anyway, it's not like I was searching for the location of our nuclear missile silos. I just wanted to confirm my findings."

"And?"

"Bingo! It's simple as long as you remain intellectually honest and know where to look," he said, tapping his head. "Ever hear of *The Adam and Eve Story*?"

Pearce rolled his eyes.

"No listen...not Genesis but a mysterious book written in the 1960s and classified by the CIA. Know anything about the Carrington Event?"

"Back in 1859," Logan said. "The most wicked solar storm

in recorded history, probably due to the sun spewing a river of plasma that collided with our magnetosphere. The only thing saving planet Earth from the CME was our lack of technology and electronics. If the same thing were to happen now, it would be a different story and a cluster mess the modern world has never seen."

"So you know it blew out the telegraph system across a big part of the globe facing the sun at the time causing the operators to receive electrical shocks."

"That's right, and another like it would push our communications back to the early 1900s as it would fry our satellites and the grid *if and only if* safeguards weren't already in place."

McCullough studied him with an astute gleam. "True, but what if that's just half the equation?"

Without waiting for a response, he slid off his seat and headed towards a computer terminal on the west side of the room.

"What's a CME?" I whispered, leaning into Logan.

"Coronal Mass Ejection; a magnetic blob of plasma that erupts from the sun's outer atmosphere and travels through space at high speed."

By the time I'd wrapped my head around this factoid, the monk had keyed in a web address, waited a moment for the monitor to reveal the desired image, and stood back, inviting us to take a look.

"Vatican City. So what?" said Pearce.

"Maybe if I zoomed in," he replied, clicking a couple of keys.

All at once, the expansive courtyard surrounded by a cluster of buildings contracted until only one object filled the screen: a massive bronze globe, or rather, a globe within a globe; the outer one exposing the inner workings of the other—but both equally jagged, cracked and fragmented—as if some unfathomable force had impacted them with such blind intensity, it had peeled back every layer of strata all the way to the core.

I shuddered, knowing the distress behind my eyes was palpable.

"Why would the Vatican prominently display a sculpture depicting what I assume is Earth, totally annihilated?"

"My thought exactly, although they'd be the first ones to deny it," McCullough said. "The thing actually does have a name: *Sphere Within Sphere*. The official explanation is it's supposed to represent man's struggle to save his soul in an ever-changing world relying more and more on technology."

"But you're not buying it."

"Logic, remember? The first rule of science is observation. If it walks like a duck and talks like a duck...besides, this is only the first in a series. Another five are scattered around the world, including D.C. and the United Nations."

"The power centers," Logan mused. "So if they're not the usual existential garbage being rammed down our throats as high art these days, what are they?"

"Messages."

"To whom? By whom?"

"Still working that out, though talking to Father A about your producer problem gives us a clue. But what about the most basic question of all?" he blurted, ruddy complexion deepening. "What are the spheres trying to tell us? And what is my math telling me... over and over?"

"That we should expect another Carrington Event? How could that possibly relate to what's happened to me?"

Without answering, he motioned for us to follow him to a

chart hanging against a far wall depicting various stones; some no bigger than marbles, others uneven but translucent and strangely prism-like, reflecting reds and greens; an odd choice, I thought, considering the young genius was supposed to channel Stephen Hawking and not a rock hound.

"Anyone know what we're looking at?" he asked. While the question was open to all, his eyes sought Logan's.

"Lunar rock.   Mostly Amorthosite and Regolith with some Breccia and Basalt mixed in."

"And I bet you even know why some of them resemble glass."

"As does every sixth grader," Logan rejoined.   "Frequent volcanic eruptions and meteoric impacts over millennia.   It's what gives Breccia its unique look.   It's been vitrified.   The heat from the meteor liquefies the rock before cooling quickly essentially turning it into glass."

Tonight...I vowed.   Tonight I would get answers to his sudden scientific expertise.

The monk's eyes narrowed.   "What if I told you you're only partly right?"

"Meaning there's another mechanism at play for vitrification."

"Correct," McCullough said, pacing like an absent-minded professor.   "When tested, most moon rocks were shown to have identical chemical compounds. But some, like Breccia here, contained several extra ingredients including Aluminum 26 and Barium 10; radioactive elements formed only one way: through a nova event.

"The sun? That's impossible."

"The evidence doesn't lie my friend," McCullough insisted.

"Wait...why is that important and what's a *nova event* anyway?" I asked. Logan's serious tone annoyed like there was something I just wasn't getting while Pearce's frown hinted at similar doubts.

"Another type of solar explosion like Carrington, only bigger," Logan explained. "Think of it this way: if a flare equals a muzzle flash and a coronal mass ejection, a missile, a nova is a thermonuclear blast. Can't happen. Not even in a couple billion years. Our sun doesn't possess enough mass to cause a supernova. At best, it runs out of gas, bloats into a red giant, vaporizes earth, and cools into a white dwarf."

"Who said anything about supernova? We're talking micronova, not a planet killer. It won't be pleasant but we can survive this. In fact, we already have, over and over."

"Excuse me! Can the rest of us please get the astronomy-for-dummies version?"

"They knew, okay? Our government and all the major science players of the time knew. It's why the CIA classified *The Adam and Eve Story*. Despite its overly dramatic rendering of the event, it contained one basic truth:

"Our planet goes through a periodic catastrophe cycle. As early as the 1700s, astronomers saw the changes in our solar system, read the signs on prehistoric cave walls, studied the dust shelves around the world and the Polar Regions. Fast forward two hundred years and they began recording gradual changes on Earth. There was one problem though: they just couldn't come up with the right mechanism. Even Einstein never thought to look above the Earth. He had no clue how our crust could unzip from its mantle until someone thought to send up an Apollo team for moon rocks; the smoking gun that once every several thousands of years, death and destruction rain from above."

Despite my inability to conjure up anything of value from high-school science class, I understood only too well what the monk was getting at and knew the others did too. Suddenly of one mind, Logan, Pearce and I stepped closer to McCullough, laboring to give birth to something so ludicrous, it might as well have been conceived in some far-off galaxy.

"Are you saying we're due for one of these nova events within our lifetimes?" Logan whispered.

"Overdue actually, if my math is right. But yes, without question, people of Earth are about to get a front-row seat to a show that only comes around once every 12,000 years."

Grinning at us with the joy of discovery, McCullough paused for dramatic effect. "Hold on to your hats, boys and girls. It's going to be a bumpy ride!"

TWENTY-EIGHT

L ogan's arms shot out as I slumped against him. I pushed him away before I could get too comfortable. As much as I would have liked to crawl into them for a day or two, other more immediate matters demanded my attention.

"Is this what the spheres mean? The Church has known about this *micro* thing all along but isn't breathing a word to the public?"

"If I had to guess, I'd say only a handful in the upper ranks know anything. But you're missing the point. You see, what makes a micronova different from your run-of-the-mill solar flare is that it comes with a bunch of junk and a pole reversal."

McCullough saw my blank look and pointed behind us, to a large chart depicting the solar system. "Just like Earth, the Sun has its own rotating magnetic field. Over time, this field interacts with the stream of charged particles released from the Sun known as plasma and forms what we call a galactic current sheet...a gaseous cosmic bully that extends throughout the Sun's equatorial plane and keeps shoving and pushing its way across the cosmos causing a planet's magnetic fields to shift and wane. After thousands of years of stability, our magnetic field is weakening and our north and south poles drifting; ten percent in 2000; fifteen only ten years later and it's picking up steam. Our main solar event occurs when the sheet finally squares off with our planet's own magnetic field. Not only is it dragging a bunch of asteroids and meteors along, it's going to flip us like a grilled burger at the local greasy spoon."

"When?" Pearce asked, pushing past us.

"The uptick in asteroids, torrential rains, droughts, earthquakes and volcanic eruptions throughout the world should tell you it's already begun. I bet this heat's part of it too since drastic temperature fluctuations are the norm with this sort of thing. If you're asking about the main event though...the pole flip...that's still up for grabs, but ten, maybe fifteen years, if we're lucky."

"What is that even supposed to look like?"

"C'mon Father, I'm surprised you haven't figured it out. It is required reading in our line of work. Signs in sun, moon, and stars; roaring of the sea and waves; people fainting with fear and foreboding for the powers of the heavens will be shaken. Ring a bell?"

"So climate change isn't due to arctic displacement," Logan mused, quickly changing the subject.

"It is in a way but then you should ask what's causing it. The trouble is, the anomalies are neither slight nor are they restricted to this planet."

"Like the perturbations on Uranus and Neptune?"

"Negative. Their violent forty to fifty-degree pole shifts are just the tip."

The monk made his way back to the terminal and typed in his

query. Before long, the exploded globe was replaced by a long list of numbers we studied before he explained the highlights.

"More than 200-percent increases in the strength of Jupiter's and the sun's magnetic fields; a 300-percent increase in the amount of severe solar activity and a 200-percent increase in the density of Mars' atmosphere. A 400-percent increase in the speed with which solar particle emissions travel through interplanetary space; the significant melting of Martian polar icecaps. In fact, our entire solar system is undergoing dramatic change."

"And we should expect the same here."

"Sure. The earthquakes and volcanoes will keep coming, but they won't resemble anything we've seen so far. Think of mega seismic thrusts and tsunamis; a dramatic rise in sea levels and tides, violent magnetic lightning storms, crop failures, meteoric displays never before seen by modern man...all leading up to the moment our world is literally pitched upside down."

I reached blindly for Logan's hand. "How can you sound so cavalier about the end of the human race?"

"Oh, there will be survivors. Always has been, always will be. Most governments and elites probably already have their luxury shelters though those of us lower on the food chain will have to rely on the grace of God and our own ingenuity. Either way, ragged pockets of humanity will remain, although I can't say I'll envy them."

He flinched, turning uncharacteristically serious. "Despite what you think, I really do care deeply about what's going to happen. I know the suffering will be at an unimaginable scale. But don't forget the only reason I study the heavens is to discover the work of The Creator. Ultimately, I have to believe that somewhere, a better place awaits us all. Then again," he added, the sadness sloughing off his face as if he simply couldn't waste any more time on it, "in my line of work, I can't think of a better way to go. We'll probably learn more in the next five to ten years than we have since, well, since the last time this thing came around."

A strange new buzzing in my ears muffled Logan's next point. "You said geological proof exists everywhere on the planet; archaeological accounts from the survivors of ancient civilizations."

"Of course! The only dilemma is where to begin," the friar enthused. "Practically every ancient culture has recorded the mysterious winged lobe, the cloud of plasma that appears in the skies as the harbinger of the devastation; South American, Toltec, Aztec, Mayan, Babylonian, Egyptian, Iranian. Even the Hindu Vishnu and the Native American folklore of the Thunderbird speak of it. And you're right, our geological footprint proves it without question."

He jumped out of his seat and ran back to the chart he'd shown us earlier. With a flick of his wrist, it sprang back into its roller, revealing a whiteboard on which he began scribbling furiously.

"The easiest way to understand is to have it all laid out chronologically," he said, pointing to a crude diagram.

"Science proves our last magnetic excursion occurred around 12,000 years ago with the extinction of several species of mammals and megafauna, the extinction of the Siberian Mastodon, and a 1,200-meter rise of sea floor in the Indian Ocean.

"Count back another 12,000 years and we come to the Lake Mungo disaster in Australia. The LaChamp excursion is next at 41,000 to 43,000 years with the Vostok Core Event preceding it about 60,000 years ago. After that, the physical evidence gets a little harder to plow through..."

"We get the picture," Pearce said. "If the proof is that pronounced, why aren't you all shouting it from the roof tops?"

McCullough shifted his weight. "Right...the whole gag order thing. Truth is, the intel's already out there guys. It's the perfect open secret since you can't really hide the effects of something this huge. All you have to do is add two and two, though I admit there are forces who don't want anyone adding anything together. It didn't take too much digging to get that point across."

"The mysterious glitches on your computer."

"Amateur hour. Do you know how many scientists we've lost working in related fields due to suicides or accidents all within the last ten years? Those folks all had one thing in common: they were shouting from the rooftops."

"If you're saying what I think you're saying, that's quite the leap, Brother."

"Then explain how a left-handed professor of astrophysics killed herself by putting two bullet holes in the right side of her head. Or the environmental science guy investigating the melting of weather anomalies in the Arctic, *accidentally* falling down a flight of stairs after receiving multiple threats weeks earlier. They're just two out of hundreds. You'll understand why these days most of my work is done anonymously."

A familiar dread wormed its way to the surface as I digested his words. Was the monk an overworked genius with a paranoid streak or were there entities truly bent on suppressing the biggest story in 12,000 years? And then for what purpose? Given my recent history and Pearce's diabolical past, accepting his conspiracy theories wasn't the hardest thing I'd been forced to do recently, but it was Logan with his puzzling expertise who gave voice to my unease.

"Let's say you're right about everything...and at this point you haven't given me reason to doubt...where does it leave Trina? Where does it leave us?"

"Don't know but I'll keep working it; gathering intel. Covertly of course. Your story is helping me fill in the blanks."

"And yours still doesn't explain why triangles and labyrinths send them into murderous fits or why a cardinal would write cryptic messages in his own feces," I blurted.

McCullough looked wounded. "It's a puzzle alright but if Kadzik and his evil elves have anything to do with our micronova, we'll get to the bottom of it. There's no use getting ahead of ourselves before I find what Mallory's symbol means. It shouldn't take too long provided we don't get sideways of the wrong guys."

The door to Pearce's asylum was nearly wide open now, beckoning me inside. Maybe Eddy had it right all along. Hooded cowls were nothing. I finally understood there were other ways to remain anonymous.

"Can Bertolucci help?" Pearce asked.

"If you like wasting time. He used to be a scientist once, a damned good one, from what I've heard, but he gave it up for the more glamorous, public-relations' side of the biz several years ago. Guess he's so old, he figures he's paid his dues and likes his rubber-chicken dinners."

"And the man upstairs? Or did our pontiff buy into that whole sphere-representing-technology-overload crap?"

"Funny you should mention it. In the early '80s, German reporters asked Pope John Paul II about the contents of a secret given to a cloistered nun in Portugal. According to them, he answered that due to the seriousness of its contents, his predecessors in the Chair of Peter had diplomatically decided to withhold its publication. When asked why, he said that if there is a message informing us that the oceans will flood large sections of the earth, and that, from one moment to the other, millions of people will perish...there's no longer any point in troubling humanity."

This time I didn't resist as Logan folded me in his arms, hiding my eyes from the others. Past any point of caring, I pressed my body against the warmth of his and sobbed.

TWENTY-NINE

Wednesday, March 19

I t is said that in the midst of life we are in death. I would have bet mine—or what was left of it—that the early-morning stragglers on the Via Lazio, surrounded by the pulse of a restless city, would have found the idea morbidly inconceivable.

To the occupants huddled in the back seat of the taxi blurring towards the genteel but faded Valencia, the idea had not only taken root but would now be an unwelcome and constant companion. Still, no one bothered saying as much, our stony silence masked by our cabbie's non-stop chatter.

I wondered how we appeared to him and then later to the doorman, concierge, and other guests. Did we still look the same? Why weren't they shrinking from my clammy, pale skin, the bug eyes, stark and somber? Couldn't they hear the jack hammering of my heart? Didn't they know it was simply marking time, counting down the beats that would most likely end my life and theirs?

At my door, I fumbled with the key as if I had just staggered in from an all-night bender.

Across the hall outside their room, Logan and Pearce discussed my safety with the hushed tones reserved for funerals. "I don't think Trina should be alone tonight," Pearce declared.

"Still, she needs her sleep. She must be running on fumes by now. Can you remember the last time any of us slept a full eight hours?"

Easy. The night before the ill-fated wedding in El Paso. The odds of ever closing my eyes tonight suddenly went from slim to none.

"We could set up watch and take turns while she gets some shut eye."

"Good! I'll take the first three-hour shift."

"Come on now," Pearce chuckled. "Don't force me to twist your arm."

"Wouldn't happen. You know I've always..."

"Hey guys, I'm standing right here," I reminded, turning to face them. "Besides, who said anything about being able to sleep?"

Logan eyed me sheepishly. "You're right. I'm not much in the mood either, come to think of it. Does your ankle still hurt?"

"Not as much as my head."

Another minute of squabbling led to the decision that I would spend whatever remained of the night lodging with the men; something about defendable locations considering the monk's tales and our own recent past.

Would Sister Elise be shocked at our new sleeping arrangements? Would the hotel management and guests, since Pearce had done nothing to hide his priesthood? I decided propriety just wasn't that high on my list anymore. Logan came with me as I packed a few things for my journey across the hall while Pearce shifted things around to accommodate my privacy.

A few minutes later however, as Logan watched me gather my meager belongings, an uneasy silence enveloped us. Although I knew part of it was our reluctance to mention our imminent destruction, I also blamed it on being alone with him in a small room dominated by a huge bed.

"Never knew becoming a celebrity gossip monger required passing the entrance exam to MIT," I prompted, filling the uncomfortable quiet while trying to satisfy my curiosity. Despite Brother Joe's cheerful declaration of doom, there were still some things I needed to clarify.

"Would it surprise you to learn stalking the rich and famous wasn't my first career choice?"

"Not after my crash course in astronomy today," I admitted.

He nodded, smiling. "Some things you never forget. Especially if they're to blame for the complete and total destruction of every-thing you've worked for."

He came and stood beside me, and though he kept his hands to himself, I still felt that strange, coiled energy of his radiating through me.

"After my tours I decided to go back to school for my masters in communication. It wasn't long before I was writing for a national science journal. Almost immediately, my editor recognized my potential for increasing revenue and so, for a time, I was assigned some of the juiciest topics, interviewed the most renowned names. I seemed to have a gift for explaining technical material without talking down to the average reader while still maintaining the integrity of the research. Astronomy...astrophysics...those were my favorites."

"Explains why you understood McCullough's lecture."

"There's more. One day I received a call from an anonymous source; a mid-level government scientist refusing to give me his name but claiming to have made a breakthrough; the discovery of a huge super wave headed our way."

"The galactic current sheet spoken of by McCullough."

"That's right. Mind you, he hadn't made the leap to micronova yet but he was eager to share his discovery and didn't trust his superiors. He was also foolish enough to think his breakthrough would eventually take him up the ranks. Regardless, his theories peaked my curiosity. I told him to send me his research notes and that I'd look into it but that wasn't good enough for him. Obsessed and distrustful, he insisted on meeting with me in private with the caveat that I write the piece on my own time and without my editor's knowledge. Over a period of a couple weeks, he spoon-fed me the data bit by bit claiming it was for my safety and his. It was grueling; a crash course in advanced theoretical astrophysics I waded through night after night. At first I was skeptical but everything he'd lined out seemed to make sense. I was getting caught up in his excitement; the possibility that this massive cloud was real and what it could mean for humanity.

"Then one afternoon, it all went away. Someone broke into my apartment, stole all his research along with the laptop containing my notes. The next day, my editor fired me on the trumped-up charge I'd been drinking on the job. And that wasn't the worst of it. Over a period of forty-eight hours, I was blacklisted, my name dragged through the mud. I went from being a successful science writer with a solid reputation to one who couldn't even get a foot in the door at *The National Enquirer*. Somehow, someone made sure I'd never work in the field again."

"Didn't their actions scream cover up?"

"Of course. First thing I did was try to find my whistleblower but he'd covered his tracks well. I spent as much time and money as I could researching who was behind it and why, but after several months, I got tired of all the door slamming and, for the sake of being able to eat, laid it aside. You can probably guess the rest."

"You never thought to pursue it again?"

"For the sake of my sanity, I turned my back and walked away. In time, with no news, I lost interest until an article and photograph in *The New York Times* caught my eye nine months after the whole thing blew up. The death of a thirty-eight year old cosmologist whose work on dark energy and black holes heralded him as the next Carl Sagan. It was my guy. He was found poisoned by a deadly mushroom that found its way into his pasta primavera. Despite the odd circumstances, authorities were hesitant to label it as anything but an accident. The case was never solved."

"So much for coincidence."

"No such thing in my book anymore. Still wonder why I believe our young friar so readily? Anyway, in time I set my sights lower. Way lower. I jumped into celebrity gossip mongering with both feet. It was easy. I didn't have to think too hard and it satisfied my one requirement: it was mind numbing and the perfect drug." He paused, staring at his feet. "It wasn't the only one either. I'm not proud of it, but I figured since I'd been convicted of the crime, might as well be guilty. My new job description went down a lot easier with several daily doses of Kentucky bourbon."

"Even now?" I reached up to touch his face, forcing him to look at me. I hoped my eyes conveyed what words never could: he didn't need to medicate—not then, not ever. He was too good for that.

"No," he whispered. Covering my fingers with his own, he

turned my palm over and kissed it softly. "Not for a while now."

"What did Pearce say when you told him?"

"What you would expect from a priest: when God closes a door, He opens a window. Everything happens for a reason..."

"It's one of the mysteries of good and evil."

"So you've heard it too?"

"Uh-huh, but that doesn't mean he's wrong."

"I've been thinking about that," he murmured. "Sounds nuts, but if I hadn't shifted gears, I would've never run into you."

"Kismet? Pearce certainly seems to think the three of us are connected and that our combined experience can fix all this. His knowledge of the spiritual and the supernatural..."

"My background in science and astronomy..."

"Your combined history in the Corp."

"And then there's Trina Langford," he said, looking puzzled.

I busied myself stuffing my makeup case into my PJs, rolled them up, and stuck the whole lot under my arm. "Doesn't add up, does it? I'm not exactly an expert on anything, unless you can call getting in over my head a talent."

"Don't put yourself down," he said, wrapping his arms around my waist before I could resist. "Seems to me you're the glue holding this thing together. If it wasn't for you, we wouldn't even know what we're looking at a few years from now."

"But will it even matter? I thought the whole point of this trip was to find out why Gregory wants us dead and now I'm actually considering his way out may be less painful!" I stopped before the meltdown bearing down on me left a crumpled heap in its wake and decided we'd been right to avoid the subject.

"What I'm trying to say is, so what? Yeah, I know. It's defeatist, but what are the three of us supposed to do, Logan?"

The storm building all night finally broke over my head. I buried my face in his neck, guilty I'd unleashed the burden on him, but selfish enough to know I couldn't deny myself his comfort. He absorbed it all without complaint, pulling me ever closer, his arms vice grips proclaiming he too felt my urgency and that time was short.

His mouth pressed against the top of my head, my brow and the tip of my nose, then moved down to my chin and throat, his breath becoming shallower as desperation turned to desire.

This time when he brought his mouth up to mine, there was no hesitation as there had been that first night, but only a fierce determination to fulfill what had been interrupted so cruelly in El Paso—when time hadn't been marked by the approach of the next end of the world.

THIRTY

A discreet knock reminded us that our so-called privacy was just an illusion. Pearce, no doubt, letting us know even now, this was no time to be rubbing kinks out of anything.

"Give us a minute," Logan called out, setting me back on my feet reluctantly. "It's hard being his friend sometimes," he whispered. "Never know if you're dealing with your captain or your confessor."

I played along, crammed my things in a tote and followed him. "Which do you think it is now?"

"Probably a combo. The military side coming to my rescue so I don't lose my immortal soul," he teased, opening the door.

I stared into Gregory and Chloe's frozen scowls—more eloquent than any choice expletive—sensed faded wallpaper morphing into the torture chamber on the other side of the world, and fought to remain upright. In this timeline, Chloe grabbed a fistful of hair and yanked, her pointy talons digging into my scalp as she struggled to drag me across the threshold. I gave up trying to pry her off and countered with an open palm to her Botoxed lips, glimpsed blood oozing down her chin and murder in her eyes, and felt Logan pulling me back.

"Help me!" he shouted, ramming his body into the ancient panels. The move was met with brute force. I slammed my full weight against the door, heard the wood splinter, and yelled for Pearce. Enraged we might be gaining the upper hand, the pair grunted like rutting beasts. The door jerked in one inch, then another, the gap just wide enough for a metallic, open-toed shoe to wedge itself between it and the frame.

Chloe! Who else would attempt assault and battery in designer heels! A wave of doubt left me weak. My next shout-out didn't seem to carry nearly the force as my first. Didn't the dynamic duo have their unrelenting bloodlust to fuel their adrenaline? Wasn't Gregory maniacally obsessed with maintaining his youth and vigor? The list of attributes took a back seat as Logan wrenched the door wide open, hurling them both past us and careening into a free-standing armoire that had, up till now, been an antique.

"Get Pearce! Run," he cried, reaching the confused pair staggering to their feet, more stunned than hurt. Determined not to let them recover, Logan delivered a precise kick above Chloe's kneecap then followed up with a fist to Gregory's nose. Both blows were followed by groans of anguish and, in Gregory's case, a satisfying crunch I enjoyed more than I should have.

"Trina..."

"Going!" I dashed across the hall, saw the door ajar and pushed it open.

Pearce sprawled face down across bare, wooden planks, the widening pool of blood surrounding his head garish in the overhead light.

My cry shifted Logan's focus. He turned on the couple, his next words too muffled to hear.

Reassured by the priest's shallow breaths, I sprinted back across the hall. Logan had Gregory pinned against the wall. Crouched beside him, struggling to disappear into the wallpaper, Chloe moaned, then uttered something that sounded suspiciously like an incantation.

"You're next!" Logan promised, effectively shutting her up as his hands tightened around Gregory's throat.

"No Logan...don't!"

Muscles flexed, refusing to budge.

Gregory's pinched face drained from purple to white. "That's right, Logan," he wheezed, his voice still carrying the polish he'd worked so hard to perfect. "I don't think Italian authorities would see this as self-defense. Don't they still hang murderers in this country?"

Logan swore, refusing to let up on his chokehold. Rather than fill me with sympathy, Gregory's attempt at bargaining only made me think Logan should finish what he started—though he did have a point.

"Dammit, Logan! He's not worth it!" I cried, watching Gregory's face shift to a dangerous gray.

"Don't you see? It's over. They can't hurt us anymore but if you kill him, we'll never learn anything. You want to know, don't you?"

Had he even heard me?

"Logan, I...I love you!" I cried, the truth of it lost in more urgent needs. "I can't lose you to this. Not now."

His groan echoed frustration. Something in him shuddered

then died as he released his grip and Gregory crumpled to the floor, coughing.

"Pearce..."

"He's alive but he's lost a lot of blood," I said, already making a beeline for the phone.

He nodded, addressing the duo without a glance. "Either of you move a muscle, you die. Try any of that voodoo hocus-pocus, you die. And just so we're all on the same page," he warned softly, "If our friend dies...you die."

He squatted suddenly, now eye level with them. "Because you see, you were wrong on a couple points. Hanging might've gone out a long time ago, but I still figure rotting in prison is a small price to pay knowing both of you are rotting in hell."

PRAYERS

FOR THE DEAD

THIRTY-ONE

Friday, March 21

Streetlamps flickered then grew brighter. The last burst of sunlight soon fizzled into dusk. In a fifth-story window overlooking the entrance to a hospital, blinds were drawn, lamps turned on, illuminating two silhouetted figures, pacing.

From his table at a café across the street, The Slayer noted these changes patiently, filing them away with all the other innumerable details he absorbed as easily as parched desert welcomes the rainy season.

Minutes ticked by. An hour passed, then another, and still he waited. Time held no meaning for him. A waiter appeared at his side, took one look at the face that somehow repelled—though if pressed, he wouldn't have been able to say why since it resembled that of a dimpled, golden-haired cherub—and left without the proverbial warning to order something or get out.

All at once, he felt the presence of another; an unnerving sense that he, Scaevus The Slayer, was being watched.

A man materialized beside him, using the cover of twilight in much the same way as the painter who hid Sioux warriors and their steeds among dense, monochromatic forests.

He wondered how long Hael had been observing him and waited as his exemplar pulled up a chair without invitation.

"Anything new?" his superior asked, nodding towards the now-bare, dimly-lit window.

"Devotion is so touching. They're still waiting, worried Rhomer hasn't come out of it yet. The longer it takes, the better his chances of slipping into a coma and never waking."

"As tragic as that would be for you, you'll be gratified to know our friends say they've got him stabilized. Looks like you may be able to practice your artistry on all three of them after all."

Scaevus grinned; an expression better suited to the maximum-security cell of a psych ward than the casual elegance of their bistro. "A fitting reward, considering you insisted on haste last time. Guns are so crude."

"Indeed," Hael agreed, leaning in for a tête-a-tête with his worker drone. "And since you've redeemed yourself somewhat in light of your skillful surveillance, you can add the disposal of the mothball priest and Astronut, the carrot-haired monk, to your list. I doubt they've been able to enlighten our three stooges on anything of value, but it is cleaner that way."

A nervous tick in Scaevus' left eye betrayed him to his exemplar. "No need to lick my boots yet. The one we serve has been magnanimous. It wouldn't hurt to show our gratitude. Offering something...or someone...in return for revealing our enemies would be appropriate, don't you think? Enjoy your creativity but be quick."

A faraway gleam replaced the nervous tick. Scaevus nodded, gears already clicking away with the trying task of matching his intended victims with the fitting method of disposal. A sudden thought confused the issue. "Should I do Sinistrus as well?"

Hael made a sour face. "Undoubtedly, he's proved to be a first-class imbecile. But no, I have other plans for my wayward protégé that will ultimately further our cause and teach him a much-needed lesson. You see...Sinistrus' biggest mistake is thinking the student can surpass his master." Glaring sharply at Scaevus, Hael continued. "I trust there won't be a need to repeat that lesson down the road."

"A fortunate man is one who understands his place in the world and takes pride in his work. It is enough knowing my particular talents will always be a valuable commodity."

"Well said! Why can't the rest of humanity go about their business with the same enthusiasm? You have my blessing, but call me when you take care of Rhomer. Legends...even those circulated by fat little prelates...have to start somewhere."

"Then I have one favor. I want to move among them invisibly again. Like you. It may be to our advantage since they'll be on their guard after Sinistrus' and Canicula's attack."

Hael's eyes narrowed. "Just so you remember, the perk is temporary. By tomorrow afternoon the cloaking will have worn off. Make sure you take appropriate precautions."

A small, childish hand appeared in his own without warning, the desiccated fingers barely supple after many months. He plopped it on the table between them as if it were a limp fish and he a fishmonger plying his trade, took out a thin knife and slashed deeply into The Slayer's outstretched palm. Murmuring the required incantation, he allowed the blood to pool before pressing living tissue into dead and covered both with his own.

Scaevus threw his head back and closed his eyes, neck muscles straining with the sudden pressure as the molecular structure within him seemed to mutate. A weight bore down on him, so dense, it felt as if all oxygen had been sucked out of the atmosphere. No stranger to the side effects of his superior's *gifts*, Scaevus struggled against the smothering sensation. He gulped a ragged lungful of air, waited for his panic to subside, then opened his eyes.

Hael was gone, along with the Hand of Glory, vanishing into the ether as abruptly as they'd materialized. Excitement drowned out the nameless anxiety he usually suffered around his exemplar. As of this moment and for the next several hours, he was the unseen. Should he desire, he could walk up to his fellow diners, breathe down their necks, and feed off their heightened fear as they shivered against a sudden draft. He fought the temptation. Hael had rules about such things and he did not want to follow in Sinistrus' unfortunate footsteps. Much better to save his energy for his upcoming session with Pearce Rhomer. As the first in a long line, he'd give the priest a singular honor. Regret that he could have chosen the end of a barrel over the long, excruciating night recorded on every square inch of skin, would be followed by an even greater one: the knowledge that his friends would suffer the same fate. Hard work, but Scaevus was up to the challenge.

And to think—he reminded himself, shivering at the prospect—it all begins tonight.

THIRTY-TWO

St. Peter's Hospital

D on't mind me. I'm just here 'cause I heard the food's great," a voice interrupted, causing Logan to quiver like a mirage before fading along with the distant strains of *Rise of the Phoenix*. A spark of irrational anger flared before I noticed Pearce sitting up in bed, staring at Logan and me, pretzeled together on the couch. He moaned when I jabbed him in the ribs—as if, impossibly, he and I had shared the same dream of an embarrassingly-clichéd picnic, complete with pastoral meadow and quiet strums from my guitar.

"Ten-Hut!"

Logan's eyes snapped open at the familiar command.

"Works every time!" Pearce teased as we pried apart limbs that had hopelessly become entangled as we'd slept.

Embarrassment took a back seat to the delight of seeing him awake and sense of humor restored; hopefully, a sign everything else was in working order.

"About time, buddy," Logan quipped, tripping over me to get to him. "Your head might be made of Kevlar but don't you think you were cutting it a little close? In case you didn't get the memo, there's no future in getting bushwhacked with a tire iron."

"Is that what it was? Next time I'll make sure I give precise instructions which parts are to be avoided," he said, wincing as he fingered the bandages wrapped around his head.

A slew of doctors and nurses interrupted our reunion; the result of some monitor blaring out an alarm that Pearce's stats had changed. Logan and I waited patiently while he was prodded, injected with meds to kill his massive headache, and instructed he'd be kept under observation another twenty-four to forty-eight hours.

"Better fill me in while I'm still conscious," Pearce advised when they'd left. "Whatever they pumped into me, I'm fading fast," he said, already slurring his words. Logan and I brought him up to speed on the events leading up to Gregory and Chloe's arrests, ending with how we'd interrogated them without success. Taking Logan's threats to heart, neither had twitched a finger at us, but neither had they bared their souls. Their reaction to our questions of cosmic doom and how it related to their triads and labyrinths seemed strangely subdued; their furtive exchanges, proof that our newly-discovered knowledge base was missing large chunks.

"So the world as we know it is coming to an end, but we still don't know how they're using it to their advantage," Pearce caught on without missing a beat. "A bit presumptuous."

"In what way?"

"Their arrogance again. Believing their unholy alliances will save them. You're sure they didn't let anything slip out accidentally?"

"Not so much as a lifted eyebrow," Logan recalled. "The worst part was fighting the temptation to smack the annoying smirks off their faces. Good thing the police showed up when they did or I might be sharing a cell with Kadzik right now."

"At least they're out of the picture," I reminded. "Maybe a few nights in jail will loosen their tongues where we couldn't."

Pearce's skepticism shown clearly through his yellowing bruises. "You think they'll be in there that long? I bet they've got a veritable legal dream team on retainer for just this sort of thing."

"Even with the smoking gun complete with Chloe's prints all over it? Although technically it is a smoking tire iron."

"You'll understand if I no longer share your trust in due process. All your life, you're taught there are certain rules that govern the so-called civilized world. Then in one defining moment, you realize there's a second set of rules altogether; one that thumbs its nose at the ninety-nine percent who still think order is part of their universe.

"I learned that lesson six years ago, but somehow I ended up forgetting it and it almost cost us our lives. All I'm saying is, be careful. Our two rats might have left a vacancy, but you can be sure several more are waiting to move in. Remember, as bad as Gregory and Chloe are, at least we know what they look like."

I didn't want to ruin our reunion by airing my thoughts. Locked in some ludicrous game of survival with our enemies, ultimately, did it really matter which side won since neither would likely survive?

"Point well taken. We'll expect the unexpected," Logan agreed. "Now, seeing as how some people will do anything to get out of work, what do you want us to do while you're serving your sentence, boss?"

"Nothing that'll make you want to see me in any official capacity," Pearce smiled before becoming serious. "You may want to talk to Father Aberto again. Now that we're all on the same page, he may be willing to open up."

His eyes stuttered shut before suddenly widening again.

"And ask him about the nun in Portugal. Something McCullough said the other night struck a chord. It may be important," he murmured, finally succumbing to the drugs.

For a while, we both watched the sleeping priest in silence, his words taking root in my head. "Do you really think some nun's secret can have anything to do with me? With Gregory and his triads and labyrinths? With Mallory?"

Logan shrugged. "Sounds like a long shot, but you never know. Regardless, we already got the bad news from McCullough. Whatever the secret's about, can't get worse than a cosmic wave of doom."

THIRTY-THREE

Saturday, March 22
Rome Police Headquarters

O blivious to the clip-clopping of her heels against dirty concrete, Chloe paced the confines of her cell; the stab of lingering pain above her knee and cut to her lips, grim tokens of her disastrous encounter with Trina and that two-bit hack she suspected was her boyfriend.

With nothing better to do, she allowed her imagination to soar. If she could do it over, she would have O'Neill as the appetizer, Rhomer as the entrée, and save Trina for dessert. Still, it hadn't been a total waste. She knew the priest hadn't died from the blow she'd inflicted but hope did spring eternal.

Pressed against the back wall behind her, a line of tired faces traced her every move in curious silence though none dared approach. Just as well. That was all she needed—a bunch of strung-out Roman whores, a biologist's wet dream of communicable diseases—clamoring for her autograph while she festered in this rotting jail, abandoned by all. Served her right—going along with

Gregory's attack when her gut told her this was simply his latest moronic idea. Then again, The Council had advised her to keep an eye on things, and she couldn't very well keep her eye on things from across the Atlantic.

At least that's what she hoped they'd think considering how badly things had ended. It wasn't her only beef. When she finally got out of this shithole, it wouldn't surprise her to see her mugshot plastered around the globe with a less-than-flattering caption beneath it. Though nothing new, damage control was still such a bitch.

The possible penalties for pissing off both The Council and her adoring public gave her a migraine. Chloe switched to more immediate concerns. Grossly indifferent to how her exemplar planned on saving his ass, her first move after her arrest was to call that carefully-memorized number. The voice on the line had listened silently and then hung up without a word.

White-knuckling the bars as if she'd been in the slammer for two months rather than two days, she shook them a couple of times for effect. Her impatience elicited some quiet cackles that, in her present mood, grated. She swung around to face the women, sensing in them the same edginess. Flexing her acrylic nails arched like a raptor about to strike, she took a menacing step towards her prey, scowling when three short beeps forced her to postpone her entertainment.

"How did you manage it?" Chloe whispered after a single, silent nod from her benefactor signaled her captivity was over. Ignoring the cat calls and crude gestures accompanying her departure, she sprinted towards freedom before it was revoked and hurried after Hael, eager to make her point.

"Whatever Gregory's told you, he's lying. Once you hear my

version, I'm sure The Council will realize I was just doing my job."

An amused glint appeared in Hael's eyes. "Gregory doesn't know I'm here. The time for The Quickening is nearly over. The Summoning is imminent. We can't allow ourselves to become distracted with the petty insecurities of one lowly lieutenant. What he does at this point is irrelevant. He got himself into this mess, he can get himself out. He's not without his resources."

Powerless to wipe the huge grin off her face, Chloe hung her head and followed Hael past the other cells obediently. Neither of them spoke again until they'd climbed into the limo idling outside the back of the station house.

"It certainly took long enough for my call to get to the right channels," she accused.

"Didn't anyone bother teaching you that patience is a virtue?"

"Dear old mom and pop...another epic fail to be sure. But then there have been so many."

"Mastery over one's emotions is necessary when one is a member of The Council," Hael continued, gazing out the window absently.

She blinked in quick succession. "You mean...you mean..."

"There's been a recent vacancy. It seems you've been voted in; on a trial basis, of course," Hael added, handing her a stout drink from the fully-stocked bar.

Chloe felt a familiar blast of euphoria and forgot about her foul mood and the events that had led to it. It was the same rush as before a performance when her fans chanted her name; or during an invocation when her frenzied gyrations gave way to the raw presence of The Old One. This was better though, as it had not been drug induced. Unaware of her lopsided grin, only one question burned. "My seat at the table...Baphomet's table I mean... when do I take my rightful place?"

"When you learn not to drool like a bitch in heat. You should know by now membership comes at a price. Better to ask how you will pay for the privilege."

Chloe stared into an unseeing void until it hit her. "I need to be tested. Of course I need to be tested. Tell me. Whatever it is, it shall be done, my lord."

Hael crossed his legs comfortably, then leaned into her, snaking an arm around her bony shoulders. She shivered in delight as he whispered into her ear like a long-lost lover and tried to wrap her brain around his astonishing words. By the time she realized he expected a response, her emotions had long since spun out of control, leaving a sputtering, quivering mess in their wake.

For the first time in her life, Chloe Six had been rendered speechless.

THIRTY-FOUR

St. Peter's Hospital

*I*t all begins tonight.

The mantra grew more urgent as he crept along the corridor leading to Neurology by way of a detour. Since his cloaking and the late hour practically guaranteed him his privacy, he felt inspired to first raid a few of the more exotic tools in a surgeon's arsenal. Now possessing these instruments, Scaevus knew his creativity was bound to reach new heights.

Ignoring the nurse's station and its muted chatter, he fixated on the corner room at the opposite end and scanned the area. Satisfied, he crept on, his mind suddenly occupied by a new distraction. Lulled by the dimly-lit ward and the hum of artificially-prolonged life, would anyone hear the strained gurglings of a dying man? He doubted it. No one ever did. If he wanted, the entire floor was at his disposal—as long as he took care of business first. A quick glance at the room number proved satisfaction lay just beyond the door. He let himself in and peered through the darkness, to the hospital cot and the mound beneath the blankets.

Forced to keep the monstrous fury that never left him to an irritating whine until his exemplar saw fit, Scaevus now turned up the volume as far as it would go.

THIRTY-FIVE

Rome Police Headquarters

Anyone walking by Gregory Kadzik's cell would've been struck by his masterful control, his focused discipline. Choosing to ignore his throbbing broken nose, the burning around his neck, he sat stock still on the edge of the dirty cot with his eyes closed and in deep meditation; his chiseled, stony features more reminiscent of a Buddhist monk at prayer than a suspect in an attempted murder case.

Thankfully, it helped he was alone in his holding pen, although tuning out the clatter, chatter, and general chaos of his neighbors had proved more challenging than he'd anticipated. Still, in time the hum of voices faded as did the flushing of toilets and the metal against metal of sliding cell doors. The last things to go—the subtle shuffling of feet and whispers of electric current—he didn't even consider distractions, and were left behind as he transcended into a completely foreign and yet oh-so-familiar state. Those primitive cultures that had come and gone, leaving evidence of their interdimensional journeys on cave walls were right; the shadow world was the only one that really mattered. Everything else was a lie.

Gregory appealed to The Old One, calling upon the twelfth chakra above the crown of his head to reveal the portal. Although he was certain he could make the connection on his own, it never hurt to funnel every effort through the lord of the dark realm out of respect. He set his parameters then began dialing them in slowly. Since he was after very precise information, he would remote view only those forces having direct influence upon his destiny. The suggestion he made gradually shifted to an image; hazy and blurred gray tones that shimmered into focus with crystal clarity.

The vision flung him back into his body with such force, he suspected his guards of cattle prodding him while in an altered state. Steel bars wavered uncertainly, edging closer, then contracted like gelatinous rubber. Gregory slammed a mental door on the aberration and sprang off the cot, dimly aware of his spiking blood pressure but clueless to the foamy spittle dribbling down his chin. Could the vision be true? There was always a margin of error with these things. But no, running it over in his head, he knew his technique had been flawless.

Reluctant to vent his hatred publicly, Gregory swallowed it whole, the spastic tremors in his facial muscles absorbing the rage.

Something was happening to him. He was being ripped apart, the agony of it so excruciating, it made a mockery of his life's quest to find the delicate balance between pain and pleasure; that sublime, all-too-brief apex when both existed simultaneously without canceling each other out.

Years of self-inflicted torture were reduced to a paper cut compared to the torment taking center stage; the cruel twist of his exemplar's lips as he'd informed Chloe they were leaving him behind; her satisfied smirk; and worst of all, the shock of his indifference for his *lowly lieutenant and his petty insecurities.*

A whispering voice in his head suggested he should explore this new possibility further.

You must mix the reality with the lie.

Had he fallen for the lie?

Could it be this wasn't the first time he'd been betrayed? The only time? The whispering voice threw open the floodgates and suddenly everything became eye-rollingly simple. Chloe was on The Council's payroll. She had weaseled her way into their inner sanctum and his exemplar had not only allowed it but encouraged it.

Stupid! Stupid! Stupid!

Gregory slammed a shoulder into the metal bars and felt the impact radiate through his body, eclipsing the pain of O'Neill's attack but not the treachery of his closest confidants. Not yet. He repeated the blows several more times before losing count and giving up. Numbness set in, rendering any other self-mutilation useless, but helping him to focus.

He staggered back to the cot, ignoring the widening blood stain on his sleeve and willed himself to think rationally.

There's more—the friendly voice percolating within him insisted. Yes—there was more, he remembered. Before being expelled from that other world, he'd glimpsed other whispered words; echoes of powerful emotions, triumphant jubilation oozing out of Chloe.

He wasn't concerned yet, just intrigued. Could the roles of acolyte and exemplar been reversed? Did his protégé now possess knowledge and wisdom he didn't?

By all accounts, the session should have lasted longer and

though he could have another go at it, he knew his agitated state would never allow it.

Then again, as the voice that had been joined by another claimed, even the little he'd been allowed to see was an unexpected windfall. Hadn't it cleared the cobwebs shrouding his vision for too long, obliterating the path leading to his destiny? In a strange glitch, hadn't the knowledge that had ripped apart his carefully-constructed universe, also handed him the tools he needed to create a better one? One without the enemy?

But who is the enemy—the voices that had now multiplied to four, prompted.

The list rolled off his tongue.

Chloe and her new BFF, for their treachery.

Those members of The Council who'd paid for her get-out-of-jail pass while leaving him to rot.

O'Neill for nearly strangling him.

The priest he hoped was attending his own funeral—for being a priest.

His arresting officer—the jailers bringing him the slop they called food—his lawyers, for taking their damned-sweet time getting here.

In fact—and the thought astonished him—the enemy was simply everyone.

How did one go about exterminating the lot of them?

A chortle bubbled up from between his lips. He tempered it by biting his tongue. "Shhh!" he whispered, sniggering a little. No one must know yet. There was much to do before he set things straight. His old self, the one exuding charm and quiet sophistication had to be in place. The illusion needed to be flawless if his attorneys were to succeed in having the charges against him dropped.

You're forgetting someone...

The voices had given birth to a litter, making it impossible for him to pick out one over another.

"Who?"

The one whose betrayal bought you all the others. The first to betray, she should be first to die...

The reminder darkened his already-foul mood. "I haven't forgotten! Can't you see I've tried? By all accounts, she should be dead by now. It's obvious she's protected."

Or perhaps, you were meant to fail; sacrificing a minor success for the glory of a greater one...

"What are you saying?"

A man's dreams must be equal to his stature in life...

"She's untouchable!"

We know a way; we know a way...we know many ways...

Trust us...

Gregory hesitated, intrigued at the possibilities laid out before him, and felt a cool breeze shift the black cloud over his head a few inches off center.

Was there a way to get to Trina Langford after all, restore balance, and perhaps surpass his own earlier triumphs? If there was, he couldn't see it. Lucky for him, the cacophony of voices in his head, now too numerous to count, seemed to have an endless supply of suggestions.

Curled up with his knees against his chest, Gregory threw the blanket over his head and began to listen.

THIRTY-SIX

"Did you know Muslims have a great affinity for the Blessed Mother?" Father Aberto asked, watching us with interest. "This is true. She is even mentioned in *The Koran*. Perhaps that is the greatest miracle of Fatima; Heaven's ability to bridge the world's past, present, and future, into a single defining moment proclaiming redemption for all, if they want it."

"Maybe so," Logan said. "I still don't see how some remark allegedly made by a pope relates to the apocalypse. And he's not even the current pope."

Seated across from Father Aberto inside the small café just steps from his flat, Logan and I had already devoured the sweet, pastry-like croissants known to the locals as *Cornetti*, and were now working on refills of black coffee to make up for the lack of sleep. Silhouetted against the blaze of the morning sun, refusing our invitation to join our feeding frenzy, Aberto waited patiently for us to finish. It turned out our phone call early this morning had been a welcome distraction.

Although shocked to hear of the attack on us, he was relieved Pearce was on the road to recovery. He seemed energized this morning, as if McCullough's lecture to us on micronovas had thrown the door wide open for him to speak his mind; or maybe it was simply our query into the Portuguese nun that had given him a new lease.

Aberto pondered Logan's remark for some time before answering. "I am ashamed I didn't think of it first," he finally admitted. "Pearce was right to question this. After a century, the mystery of Fatima, Portugal continues to affect the world in a very real way."

"But what *is* Fatima?" Logan asked, beating me to the punch by a split second.

"In the beginning, not a what, Mr. O'Neill, but a who; a beautiful princess named for Mohammed's favorite daughter; one who captured the heart of a Crusader knight and was taken from him shortly after they wed. Grief stricken, her people paid their respects the only way they knew how; they named a tiny, obscure Portuguese village after her. And so it remained for the next four hundred years until 1917, when three small children, shepherds who'd never ventured farther than the outskirts of town where they tended their flock, brought Fatima to the world stage with a message for all humanity."

"Prepare to die?"

Aberto grinned. "Quite the opposite, actually. The message of Our Lady, Christ's mother, is ultimately one of hope. If we turned away from evil, we would have peace."

"And if we didn't?"

The priest's smile faded. "The apparitions of Fatima all took place within a six-month period and on the thirteenth of each month. Among the first things revealed to the children was that the two youngest, Jacinta and Francisco Marto, would be taken soon, but that their cousin, Lucia dos Santos, was to remain alive longer. As prophesied, Jacinta and Francisco died within months of each other, victims of the Spanish flu. As for Lucia, once she reached the required age, she entered a convent and is believed by most to have lived to the ripe age of ninety-seven. Some say it was because the prophecies had to be received anew by each generation. Brother McCullough was right. The children were given a secret in 1917; a secret divided into three parts.

"In the first, they were shown a vision of hell and then told that World War I would soon end...as it did the following year. The Virgin then warned that if the world ignored the warning, there would be an even greater war; one in which the good would be martyred."

"World War II."

"That's right. 'When you see a night illuminated by an unknown light, know that this is the great sign given you by God that He is about to punish the world for its crimes, by means of war, famine and persecutions,'" Aberto quoted. "It is believed that the huge blood-red beam seen throughout Europe shortly before Germany invaded Poland was that very sign.

"The next piece was more complicated since it involved Russia and international politics; topics the seers knew nothing about due to their isolation and poor schooling. The Virgin revealed that Russia would spread her errors throughout the world, promoting wars, and that various nations would be annihilated. Many believed it to be a warning against the spread of communism. She went on to ask for the consecration of Russia to her Immaculate

Heart and warned of an even greater calamity if her request was not heeded."

"But the Soviet Union did collapse," I chimed in.

"And yet others were more than happy to pick up what had been discarded."

Aberto wavered, the sadness I'd seen in his eyes days ago, returning. "The third part of the secret remained a mystery even to church officials until 1944, when Lucia, now a nun, wrote it out in a letter under the guidance of the Virgin. The instructions were precise: it was to be read by the Holy Father and revealed to the world no later than 1960 or right after Lucia's death, whichever came first. For whatever reason, this was never done, though I suspect fear played a great part. To understand how great, we must go back several decades; to the exact moment when the seal guarding the secret was finally broken..."

THIRTY-SEVEN

August, 1959
Castel Gandolfo—Italy

Angelo Giuseppe Roncalli was having a very strange dream. Seated at the enormous kitchen table at his family's farmhouse, he no longer questioned why he was back inside his childhood home, and decided to simply enjoy it.

The past, long forgotten, materialized, taking its rightful place once more in the order of things: the daily ritual of freshly-baked bread—its yeasty aroma competing only with his Nonna's other culinary miracles; the good-natured clash of brothers and sisters, aunts, uncles, and cousins around the table—their lively exchange interrupted barely long enough for the blessing; the table itself— worn and pitted but smelling faintly of olive oil.

As Angelo watched, one by one each family member faded and disappeared, until only he and one other remained. A figure sat at the far end, waiting for Angelo to speak his mind as he'd always done in the past.

A strange dream indeed.

"Great Uncle Zaverio? Is that really you?"

"And why shouldn't it be? Did I not promise to guide you if you needed help?"

"Do I look like I need help? You should see it. I have more advisors and counselors, organizing, scheduling, telling me when to get up, when to go to bed...than the weeds smothering the radicchio in our fields."

"Precisely. Which is why you are here. Do not forget that in addition to being your uncle, I am also your godfather. You have had a great shock, my boy. The only way to deal with it is to root out everything that is an obstacle. Only then will you see your dilemma for what it truly is."

"But it appears so insurmountable. What if I can do nothing? What if I am too late?"

"I am surprised at you, Angelo. How many generations has our family worked the unforgiving soil beneath our feet? Was that not insurmountable as well? There is always something that can be done. God does not offer challenges without solutions."

"You make it sound ridiculously simple."

"It usually is...in theory at least. Do not mistake simple for easy. There is not much time left and you are already dangerously behind. To remove your obstacles, you will have to be wise as a serpent and innocent as a dove."

He felt a cool breeze across his forehead; something acrid flaming his nostrils, displacing the hot, crusty loaf smell. Zaverio wavered, receding into the ether.

Frustration washed over him. He wasn't ready for the dream to be over. There were still so many questions he needed answered.

"Uncle...what if I cannot recognize the obstacle?"

He came to lying on the couch surrounded by expressions of

panic and Monsignors Tavarez and Philippe. While one fanned him madly with the edge of his cassock, the other held smelling salts under his nose as his lips moved in silent prayer.

Pope John XXIII brushed them away impatiently, propped himself up and swung his legs to the floor.

Not to be dissuaded, Philippe persisted. "In view of the circumstances, Your Holiness, I strongly suggest we call for a physician."

"Noted and declined. There will be no more fainting spells."

"With all due respect, perhaps the incident is related to your heart. Surely you realize it would be best if..."

"I'm not ready to die just yet. Hence, I will need neither the services of a physician nor an undertaker today," John XXIII insisted. "Now, where is the letter?"

Tavarez fished it out of his pocket and handed it to the pontiff.

John scanned it quickly; not because he could read its language, but because he needed more information than what the words themselves could give him. He needed to get a sense of the woman who wrote it; the urgency behind her pen—her anguish and dread.

He studied the single sheet now yellowed with the passing of years, caught the whiff of ink, still sharp and metallic after all this time. Most of all, he paid special attention to the lines. There were only twenty-four. And yet within those short stanzas, the fate of the world balanced precariously.

Was such a thing even possible? Had he missed something? Some subtle nuance in the meaning?

He handed the sheet back to Monsignor Tavarez. "Once more, if you please."

The priest took it from him, eyeing both pope and letter nervously. He read each line of the Portuguese first, followed by the Italian translation—the tremor in his voice as pronounced as during the first reading—then handed it back. John wondered if it was due to the words he'd read or the fear they would cause the pope to pass out again. He suspected it was a little of both. He looked from one face to the other, aware of their uncertainty, their speculation; a microcosm of what he would recognize in his flock worldwide if he made the contents of the letter known.

He thought of his Uncle Zaverio; that stubborn obstacle that lay hidden—most likely under his very nose—but that he had only a vague suspicion existed; like the fleeting shapes detected at odd moments on the edge of one's vision.

The world trembled on the brink and he had the sense that whatever he did now would have immeasurable ripple effects. On some far-off future date, would history be rewritten and he found guilty because he refused to discuss what he held in his hands today? More importantly and presumably sooner, would God judge him harshly because of it?

John XXIII wavered unsteadily as he made his way to an ornate desk and sat down behind it. An envelope lay flat, completely intact due to the care the three had taken in breaking its seal. He folded the thin letter back into its original quarters and placed it inside, instructing the men as he worked.

"Both of you will serve as my witnesses. Monsignor Philippe, you are aware of what must be done?"

"I will draft the document this afternoon. Are there any comments Your Holiness wishes to add before I submit it for your approval?"

"Only one. You are to write that after careful deliberation, I have found Sister Lucia dos Santos' letter, dated January 3, 1944, to be authentic and the genuine article, but that its contents, the third part of the secret of Fatima, does not pertain to the reign of this pontiff and is, therefore, not worthy of dissemination."

"And where are we to safeguard this letter then, Holiness?"

John hesitated, a hard glint appearing in his eyes. "In one of those archives which are like a very deep, dark well; to the bottom of which papers fall and no one is able to see them anymore." The hard edge lingered as he looked meaningfully at Philippe and Tavarez. "Need I remind both of you, the discretion with which you are entrusted is equal to that of the confessional."

"Of course. I will personally make the necessary provisions," Monsignor Philippe replied, lowering his eyes.

"One more thing. As you know, it has been my intention to convene a new assembly for some time. In light of recent developments, I feel a new urgency. I wish this assembly to take place as soon as possible. This year even."

"Another Council? Is this even feasible? With respect, you, more than all others, understand the difficulty with which these things come together. To convene such an assembly, it will take months if not years! If this is a result of the letter and its secret..."

"I wish never to be reminded of this letter or its damnable secret again. And you will do what you can to bring about this congress soon. Very soon. I may not have years left. Our bishops face tremendous challenges. Everything is changing too quickly. We must be ready. That, I believe is the essence of the letter and its warning."

"I beg your pardon, Holiness; but what if after all that work, the Council is not enough? What then?"

John XXIII sealed the envelope with his papal insignia and handed it to Philippe before answering. "Then we will have eternity in hell to debate how we could have saved mankind."

He dismissed the two men, eager to spend a few minutes with his own thoughts. Even here at Castel Gandolfo, away from the rigidity of the Vatican, privacy came at a premium not even he controlled.

He crossed to the windows overlooking the opulent garden below and stared at its beauty without enjoying it. "Zaverio...I need your wisdom," he murmured to the ghost in his head. "Am I doing this for the glory of God? Or is this the excuse of an old man who would like to spend whatever nights he has remaining on this earth, sleeping in peace?"

Several minutes passed before Pope John XXIII, his mind churning with the problem of obstacles, caught sight of a young priest below him and beamed. He'd seen him before; one of Monsignor Philippe's aides no doubt, taking lunch. From the blissful radiance lighting his face, the man was probably deep in prayer, and John felt a measure of peace returning to him.

Perhaps he'd read too much into it. No matter how many obstacles existed, as long as fine young men such as these endured, yearning for the sacrificial life only Christ could give, the Church would not only overcome its challenges, but flourish; a beacon for all future generations.

THIRTY-EIGHT

Saturday, March 22

So he learns about the micronova, passes out, then figures he won't be around for the show anyway, and decides to make it someone else's headache. Why am I not surprised?"

"Do not condemn him yet, Mr. O'Neill," Father Gandini said. "You see, I believe something else might have induced his reaction. A shock so great, his senses could not deal with it."

"Because the destruction of the planet isn't enough? How do you know this?"

"I don't, at least not with certainty. But I believe we may have some clues."

From the inside of his jacket, the priest produced a small, tattered book that fell open to an ear-marked page and handed it to me.

"An old friend sent this a year ago. Heinrich Weismann; a priest and scholar who made Fatima his life's work. This book is the culmination of that research. If you would be so kind..." he urged, pointing to an underlined passage.

I looked at him uncertainly, leaned in so I wouldn't have to shout, and began reading.

"*'Pointing to the earth with his right hand, the Angel cried out in a loud voice: 'Penance, Penance, Penance!'. And we saw in an immense light that is God...something similar to how people appear in a mirror when they pass in front of it...then a bishop dressed in white. We had the impression that it was the Holy Father...going up a steep mountain, at the top of which there was a big cross of rough-hewn trunks as of a cork-tree with the bark.*

"*Before reaching there, the Holy Father passed through a big city half in ruins and, half trembling with halting step, afflicted with pain and sorrow, he prayed for the souls of the corpses he met on his way.*

"*Having reached the top of the mountain, on his knees at the foot of the big cross, he was killed by a group of soldiers who fired bullets and arrows at him.*

"*Beneath the two arms of the cross there were two angels each with a crystal aspersorium in his hand, in which they gathered up the blood of the martyrs and, with it, sprinkled the souls that were making their way to God.'*"

I put the book down, my eyes reflecting the obvious question Aberto answered promptly.

"Excerpts from the alleged third secret. John Paul II was shot on May 13, 1981; the anniversary of the first apparition in Fatima. He first read Sister Lucia's letter while recovering in the hospital and soon became obsessed by it. Overwhelmed by God's mercy in allowing him to live, he finally decided to consecrate the world to the Virgin as she had requested so many years earlier. Only some say the act did not go far enough since he did not specifically name Russia and he acted on his own, without the authority of the bishops.

"More importantly, following in the footsteps of his predecessors, he still refused to reveal the third part. It wasn't until the year 2000 that the Vatican made a huge production of supposedly disclosing to the world what you just read."

"They lied?" Logan and I asked simultaneously.

"Or heavily censored," Aberto admitted.

"Like the parts about the oceans flooding the earth and millions dying?"

"To begin with. While I believe the passage is a fragment of the true secret, it in itself, raises some disturbing and unintended questions about an even greater calamity."

"I still don't see where you're going. What we just heard...the city in ruins, corpses littering the streets, the death of the pope, doesn't it point to the destruction caused by a celestial event?"

"The catalyst perhaps, but according to this account, their deaths are a result of men's actions, not just the forces of nature. Who are these men? By whose order do they kill? Do they seek to destroy out of hate? Out of fear? Remember what I said that first afternoon about the nature of evil. The passage we heard suggests a great spiritual malevolence in addition to the physical destruction. Until today, I never realized the coming nova may be the excuse used to bring this spirit of Antichrist to complete and perfect fruition."

"Antichrist...as in Revelations and the Horsemen of the Apocalypse?"

The priest shrugged. "Vatican officials quickly dismissed the idea of course. They claimed the event had already occurred and that the message was actually about Christian persecution in the twentieth century, culminating in the failed assassination attempt of the pope. Even his successor stated it would disappoint the public since no great mystery is revealed, no future events unveiled."

"Then why wait so long to release it?" Logan asked.

"Officially...to not cause confusion or wild speculation, though many believed they were hiding something. People became increasingly suspicious. My instincts tell me they had to release something in order to appease the barbarians at the gate."

"There was more to the message?"

"As my friend Weismann points out, the discrepancies are many and difficult to overlook," Aberto reasoned. "Take for instance the ordinary and dull interpretation of the letter. Why hide such vague information for decades? It seems improbable that the Virgin Mary would consider the survival of the Holy Father, no matter how miraculous, as a turning point for humanity.

"Then there are the warnings themselves. Parts one and two deal with man's damnation and a global war of unimaginable devastation; both utterly catastrophic events that attack both the physical and spiritual realms. If we are to believe the official explanation of the third part, catastrophe is now avoided, though the world is drowning faster than ever in its own evil.

"And then there's the physical proof. The text the Vatican released was handwritten on four sheets of paper, contained no words attributed to the Virgin and was not written in the form of a letter. Those present when they read Sister Lucia's letter, all attest that the text was written on a single sheet as a signed letter to the Bishop of Leiria and that it contained actual quotes from the Blessed Mother. Reportedly, she not only warned of a great cataclysm the likes of which the world has never seen, but that the

Church itself would be subverted by evil from within."

He looked down at his hands and blinked away the tears that had suddenly appeared in his eyes.

"The apostasy would reach the highest levels. Many that had once served God would now serve Satan."

"Like Cardinal Mallory?"

"He is not alone. There are others like him who, having learned from his mistakes, have hidden their allegiances with much greater care."

I shivered despite the heat of the day and inched closer to Logan. "Okay, the Church guards its secrets well. But if they were meant for mankind, why not give people a chance to save themselves?"

"I can only assume that with the Church infiltrated, those working against her would naturally wish this knowledge suppressed."

"Something else, Father," Logan said. "You said Lucia, the last seer, was believed by most to have lived to ninety-seven. The way you said it puzzles me. Do you have doubts?"

"There was a time I would have vehemently denied such duplicity on the part of my superiors," Aberto said. "But yes, I have my doubts. You will understand more when you read Weismann's book. Be careful with it as it is the only reminder I have of my friend. The poor man died in a fire only days after sending it to me."

"If it's that valuable, we can always get another copy, Father."

"You're holding the only one in existence. A few days after Heinrich's death, his publishing house also burned to the ground along with all electronic drafts and several hundred copies of the book, bound and ready for shipping.

"The point is not whether these tragedies were accidental

which clearly they were not, but that he questioned the same things you are. I decided Heinrich must have sent me his first copy out of eagerness to share his research. Perhaps once Pearce recovers completely, we can discuss together what Heinrich and I never could."

He looked down at his watch, muttered something in Italian and gathered his belongings.

"Please excuse me now. At my age, I am privileged to still offer the Sacred Mysteries. You will understand it is only fitting I not be late."

"One more question, Father."

Aberto eyed me curiously and I leaned into him again, catching a faint whiff of the same mustiness pervading his flat.

"We now know as much as you do about the coming nova and what it's going to do to us. I know as a priest you have to believe in the pot of gold at the end of the rainbow but still, I guess what I'm asking is, don't you feel a twinge of anything? Fear maybe? Doubt...regret?"

The astonished look on the priest's face quickly turned to shrewd understanding. "I have a certain advantage, young lady. Perhaps it is easier for me to accept my ultimate demise since I have come to the realization that death is not the worst that can befall a person; not even close to the worst. No, if I feel anxiety and doubt, it is because I work out my salvation in fear and trembling. What you are really asking is how you yourself can live with this knowledge, is it not? How to end the despair, the hopelessness?"

Holding me captive with his unflinching blue eyes, he grabbed my hand suddenly and pointed to my makeshift bracelet.

"Does it not occur to you that you hold the key to this already? The symbol you wear around your wrist, is it not a reminder that even the humblest vessel can hold water? Meager as you may think it is, someday you may be called to pour it out."

"I'm sorry...I don't understand."

"The phoenix is the symbol of death and rebirth," he explained. "It dies to itself in order to live again. To give life to others. The only way to end your fear is to die to it. That is your solution. Only then will you be able to look beyond yourself and use whatever has been given you to your advantage. And to theirs," he added, pointing to the crowd vying for a spot at the counter.

The priest rose quietly, reminding us our session was over, then bent his lips to my ear.

"Remember my dear, death awaits everyone, regardless of the form it chooses to take. But its sting can be surprisingly sweet if we have practiced for it well and often enough."

He turned, melting into the throng of coffee drinkers, his whispered words a haunting echo guaranteed to keep me up late into the night.

I looked down at the eagle charm draped against my skin and wondered if perhaps I wasn't seeing it for the first time.

THIRTY-NINE

Reluctant to return to a hotel still bearing traces of Pearce's blood, Logan and I spent the rest of the morning and much of the afternoon in the small diner, waiting for the hour he was to be discharged. Once we were all together again, we would decide our next move.

Rather than venture into the noon-day heat, we found a lonely nook and took our time examining what Father Aberto believed could further our quest. The volume was the size of a dime-store paperback, black, with a simple *THREE* emblazoned across the front cover and along its spine in raised gold letters. Nestled comfortably close, we opened it to the first chapter and began reading, waiting patiently for the other to catch up like an old married couple who knew each other's habits inside out. I took unexpected pleasure in that notion.

By the end of the first chapter, the author's obsession with Fatima became obvious. By the third, his obsession became ours and we devoured the pages greedily, pausing only to add our own brief comments.

Shadows replaced the mid-afternoon rays as we reached the last paragraph, reminding us it was time for the hospital to release Pearce into our care. We rose together, silent and unable to process all that we'd read just yet. This much was obvious: Heinrich Weismann's tale was no dry retelling of ancient events but an exposé of lies, intrigue and murder which, if we were to believe the author, still affected world events today.

"How much of it is true do you think?" I pondered as we made our way towards the hospital on foot; the walk helping us digest what we'd learned.

"I couldn't have done a better job in the old days," Logan said. "The thing's fully annotated and footnoted, referenced and cross-referenced. Weismann wasn't taking any chances with this. He knew his critics would call him out on it and made a point of dotting his *Is* and crossing his *Ts*. It certainly answers my question about Lucia surviving as long as she did."

"But an imposter?" I argued, remembering the author's allegations that the third seer of Fatima had been replaced by a satanic faction operating within the Church.

"Makes sense. Under heaven's inspiration, Lucia pens a letter not only describing a great cataclysm, but also warns church officials of an internal coup taking place within their ranks. Her knowledge is now deemed a threat to these plans by the very ones responsible for it. While she can't be allowed to live, her so-called presence, safely tucked away in some obscure convent, can be used to their advantage. No uncomfortable questions. Outwardly, those in power are seen as complying with the message of Fatima and the faithful remain content. But even the most meticulously-crafted lies fall apart at the seams under close scrutiny."

"Sister Lucia's before-and-after pictures," I admitted, unable to deny the dramatic differences in the images Weismann had included in his book.

"And don't forget her extended isolation beginning in September of '58."

"She *was* rumored to be seriously ill at the time."

"Maybe. But then why not allow family to see her for the last time or bar her own trusted confessor from unburdening her soul? And what about the other oddities? The abrupt change in handwriting and temperament; the way even her most personal thoughts and opinions shifted after 1958 and she no longer criticized those in power. People don't change that dramatically without good reason."

I turned Logan's words over in my head. Perhaps the old priest was right and we should've been looking for collusion rather than coincidence all along.

"You look like you're ready to pass out. Breathe, Trina."

"I'm fine. I'm just wondering why they've gone through so much trouble? What are they all waiting for?" I deliberated as we stepped into the hospital lobby and headed for the elevators. "Let's say that Gregory hasn't sold his soul merely as a way to gain more wealth and power. What other reason can he have for doing so and recruiting others? Why risk so much to come after Eddy and me unless Chloe revealed something damning that last night? And why did Mallory throw away his reputation, not to mention a chance at eternal bliss? Why all the lies, Logan? What's so important that they would kill for only a whisper of a threat and a book?"

"You jarred Pearce's memory before. Now that his head's

better, maybe he'll have an answer," Logan replied, holding his room door open for me.

The antiseptic odor of industrial-strength ammonia hit me first, followed by the priest's absence and the freshly-made bed.

"Where is he?"

"Released early maybe? It would explain why his stuff is gone."

"But not why he didn't sign the required forms," said a heavily-accented female voice behind us. "Your friend disappeared early this morning. We were hoping you knew where he is, as I must tell you he is in grave danger."

FORTY

Sunday, March 23

In a weird way, the next several hours were somehow worse than anything I'd already been through; worse than finding Pearce unconscious, the attack in El Paso, or the discovery of a doomsday cosmic wave; worse even than watching a man burn to death or my baby's murder.

Okay, maybe not worse than those but it was the final straw. Normally, any one of those events would have taken weeks, months, a lifetime to process. Circumstances demanded I adjust to them in a matter of days.

Throughout that evening and into the wee hours, Logan kept the darkness lurking at the edge of my sanity at bay with a reassuring smile or small gesture, never leaving my side for more than a few minutes and then only when necessary. Any lingering doubts I may have had about him evaporated during those hours. If anything separated us now, I wasn't coming back from it.

By the time the morning sun painted the anemic walls in cheerier hues, the mystery of Pearce's disappearance deepened, frustrating us and the hospital director who, despite her playful bob, wore her tailored power suit with a perpetual scowl that seemed to mask irrational anger. I couldn't understand why, unless it was because her hospital had been turned inside out. She refused our request to join the search for the missing priest and invited us to wait in her office; a gesture I thought was due more to her distrust of us than any largesse.

"Why would Pearce be in danger?" Logan asked, once we were seated beneath the fluorescent lights above her desk.

She wrinkled her nose as if the medicinal smell wasn't the only thing to offend. "With his type of injury, supervision for the next thirty-six to forty-eight hours is vital. His prognosis was good, but you never know with head trauma. We were under the impression that as friends, you may have persuaded him to leave before he signed the necessary forms."

"Then shouldn't we have been notified sooner?"

"If he did relapse, chances were we'd find him on the grounds merely lost and confused. There was no sense worrying you prematurely."

"And the security cameras?"

"I checked the feeds myself minutes before you arrived. There's no record of him leaving the room all night." From a desk drawer, she took out a small brochure and handed it to Logan. "This is the only item we found. It must have fallen under his bed before he left."

We studied the glossy paper. It was a schedule of upcoming events at St. Peter's Basilica during the week preceding Easter. Pearce must have planned on attending since he'd circled a couple of dates.

Wary of revealing our mounting anxiety under her watchful eye, we remained silent until security returned without the priest and local police were called in; a plain-clothes detective whose specialty was placating annoying *turisti* while raised eyebrows screamed *Americani go home!*

"At least Gregory and Chloe aren't responsible this time," I said after he'd outlined the manhunt already under way, beginning with a second, more thorough search of hospital nooks, crannies and laundry chutes.

Interest flickered across the detective's face. "The couple Mr. O'Neill attacked?"

"That was self-defense and you know it."

"Still, you should be glad neither of them filed counter charges as their injuries were not all that minor."

"Neither were Pearce Rhomer's. He almost died!"

"The distinction being that he didn't. Your friend is right. The lady and gentleman in question are no longer relevant since they each boarded separate planes back to the States hours ago. Our famous celebrity was released late last night, Mr. Kadzik, this morning."

"On what grounds?"

"Sit down, Signor O'Neill. Forensics could not identify the prints on the weapon with certainty. They were too smeared to prove who was behind the priest's attack beyond reasonable doubt."

"But the security cams..."

"Signorina Langford, The Valencia was built over a hundred years ago. Updating security..." He rubbed his thumb against his fingers in a *pay me* gesture.

"I can't believe this."

"This is not one of your Hollywood scripts. For the last time... our men followed them to the airport; they watched them board their planes; they watched the planes take off. What more do you want?"

The detective's expression softened. "I should not worry too much. All measures will be taken to find your friend. He could not have gone far."

He could not have gone far.

It was the only thing left to us.

Minutes later, the director saw us to the elevator and stuck around long enough to make sure we weren't coming back. She needn't have worried.

We headed into the cloudy morning already promising to be a scorcher, jumped into a cab, and rattled off an address. Lulled by the gentle rocking as it wound its way through the city, I promptly dozed off but soon woke, staring at a familiar dilapidated building.

"Keep your fingers crossed," Logan muttered as we took the stairs two at a time and ran down the hall to Aberto Gandini's flat.

FORTY-ONE

We pressed our ears against the wood and listened for signs of life: sleepy voices, clanging coffee mugs, shuffling feet; anything suggesting we'd interrupted a regular morning's routine. Optimism slipped with each second of silence prompting Logan to pound his fists against the peeling paint.

"Easy," I said, placing a hand over his arm. "He may have gone back to the hotel."

"I don't think so. If Pearce left under his own steam, this is the first place he'd come."

Impatient, he swore under his breath and twisted the knob. The door opened with a rusty groan, catching us off guard, and I followed him inside, peered through the shadows, and had a moment before I decided the laundry piled on top of the sofa wasn't a lifeless corpse.

"Stay close. Something's not right," Logan cautioned, though I didn't need it spelled out. The apartment was shrouded in gloom;

strange—when one considered Aberto's admitted aversion to darkness. It shifted our focus to the only strip of light anywhere; the bright rays puddling beneath a closed door we guessed was a bedroom. As we approached it, a whiff of something familiar but out of place competed with the musty smell of ancient walls and faded upholstery.

My stomach lurched in protest and I glanced at Logan, knowing he too smelled it and recognized its oddness.

"Father, it's Logan O'Neill and Trina Langford. We're coming in," he warned as he pushed the door open and allowed it to thud against the wall.

Hot lights blinded us. I had the impression I'd stepped on to a stage illuminated by dozens of beacons, all screaming for the audience to feast on the carefully-constructed scene laid out before us.

In the moment before Logan barreled into me, before I was ejected back into outer darkness, before one part of my brain could send the proper impulse to the other, I caught a glimpse of that scene from the corner of my eye. Despite the soothing coolness of the wall I was pinned against, it would live in my head rent free for the rest of my life.

Logan's hands were on my arms propping or restraining— couldn't tell which and didn't much care. He was saying something, his mouth forming words I didn't hear because I had more important things to consider.

The police had lied to us.

Gregory and Chloe hadn't left the country. They were still here; or rather, they *had* been here. What other explanation could there be for the familiar, larger-than-life inverted crucifix hung on the wall behind the bed? The thought slipped a little as soon as I had another. A memory. A vague irritation from the past. Something I had found bothersome at the time because it felt grossly out of character for a man who worshiped bloodlust. Though still a grotesque perversion, Gregory's icon was also the poster child for a generation preferring a pasteurized, homogenized Christ over One Who bore the jagged gashes and shredded skin of His sacrifice with a quiet and awful dignity.

No such politically-correct sensitivities had been taken with the crucifix around the corner. Rather, the sculptor had gone to great lengths to draw our attention to the pulverization that had taken place; a clever, sly taunting that played with the mind's insistence that no way, no how can a human body be stuffed into a meat grinder.

The tableau a few feet away offered unquestionable proof.

"Step right up ladies and gentlemen and take the challenge if you dare"—a carny yelled in a flawless, dead-ringer send up of Gregory. *"See here. Notice the play of crimson against the puckered, shriveled skin on his palms—a reminder, no doubt, of his misspent life in service to a folly, a myth, a sign of contradiction to a mind crying out for meaning in a meaningless world. Should he not die as he lived then? If two nails are good, are not many more, better? Be the first to count them all up and win the prize: a first-class, all-expense-paid, once-in-a-lifetime, one-way trip to your favorite destination and mine..."*

Logan's voice came to me garbled, as if just below the surface of a placid lake.

I screamed; one continuous, undiluted tidal wave of misery that was only beginning as I made my final descent into the abyss.

EXODUS

FORTY-TWO

Monday, March 24
Termini Station—Rome

A pleasant female voice blasted the announcement in Italian before translating for the benefit of English and Portuguese visitors: boarding for the 6:20 to Lisbon would begin in five. Travelers were required to show their passes if traveling on to other Portuguese cities.

I glanced at Logan signaling for me to wrap it up and turned back to the man whose voice shook in my ear. Not surprising considering what I had just told him.

"What do you mean *no physical evidence?*" McCullough stammered into the phone.

"It was spotless. I don't know how they managed it but when we returned with the police, there was no sign of Aberto, no blood, no nail holes in the wall. It was as if it had never happened. If Logan hadn't been with me and seen it..."

And maybe in some alternate universe, the last two years never happened. I never meet Eddy, Gregory, or Chloe. I never get pregnant only to have the baby ripped from me—and an old priest with the shape of a crucifix seared into his hand is still be alive.

I ignored a stab of unreasonable anger directed at the universe.

"Bottom line, they're not convinced it was murder. They think Aberto left town without telling a soul. They're saying we made it up; crying wolf to get them to take Pearce's disappearance seriously."

"But what about forensics? DNA? Prints? If this is the best Roman police have to offer..."

"Forget about the police. We have a different reason for calling," I said, locking eyes with Logan and recognizing the urgency behind them. "We're disappearing for a few days."

"With one priest missing and Father A..."

"It's our only lead. We'll let you know more when we get back."

"Wait! Where are you going?"

"Best you don't know but in the meantime, you need to find some place safe. If they got to Aberto, they'll get to you."

I didn't have time to give him the rest of my theory. That carefully-staged house of horrors was solely for our benefit. Was Aberto's crucifixion a scare tactic to keep us away, or a warning that we were next?

"Can I at least call you when you get there?" the friar sniffled, blowing his nose. "I found something that may help."

"We're being followed," Logan whispered, tugging at my sleeve. "Don't look. Just act normal," he added as I spun around, causing whiplash.

"It'll have to wait," I hissed into the phone. "Do you have a place to stay? Someone you can trust?" I grabbed Logan's hand, and waded through the crowds to the boarding platform.

"Actually I have the perfect..."

"Not over this line."

"Duly noted. Are you sure you can't hold on for a minute? It's about the symbol. I finally figured out where I've seen it. Remember the other night I was throwing out ideas? Turns out I was partly right. The glyph is alchemical but predates those known by...get this...at least a couple thousand years. Say, you don't think Rhomer ran into those bastards do you?"

I clicked off. Thinking about Pearce at the hands of Aberto's sadistic killers would send me spiraling anew into that abyss from which I had barely crawled out; counterproductive when we were about to embark on a fishing expedition for proof of an alleged murder at a convent in Coimbra. But after the last twenty-four hours, the promise of having something to do dangled before me like a carrot, kept me upright and at least visibly sane. Perhaps Logan had suggested it for just such a purpose.

"Didn't think they'd find us so soon," he said, dragging me in line with other passengers.

"How many?"

"Three. Two men behind; one by the vending machines. They mean business or they wouldn't have .45s tucked under their shirts."

"Is that even allowed?"

"If they're legit. I'm guessing they're working a side job."

"On whose payroll?"

"You heard the cop at the hospital. Kadzik and Chloe were released on a technicality. If I had to bet, someone on the force is taking bribes. What else are they willing to do for a few extra euros?"

"In coach...pick us off anytime they want."

"And if we decide not to board, follow us until they can. Unless...what if we don't make it easy on them? Trina, you once said you didn't know if you could trust me. Do you trust me now?"

"In theory."

"Come on then," he prompted, hustling us towards the ticket booth. A couple purchases later, we joined first-class jostling towards their private accommodations. I glanced back as we boarded, my eyes scanning each face for murderous potential and spotted them forty feet back; two thugs—Italian versions of Gregory's goons minus the black ties—clearly fixated on us. Torqued at our exodus, one spoke into a wrist mike then both bolted towards the first class carriages. The third man stood his ground at the far end of the platform.

"Logan..."

"I see 'em. Don't stop for anything."

Easier said than done. Our new compartment might have bought us a temporary oasis but the train was packed and getting there meant navigating an obstacle course. The good news—short of shooting their way to get to us, the hoods were stuck in the same mess.

Then again—applying reason only worked when dealing with the reasonable.

I looked back again and wished I hadn't. The men were gaining, craning to keep us in their line of sight from behind scores of bodies lugging suitcases. How desperate would they have to be for the .45s to come out?

Inside the restaurant wagon, Logan tugged at me unsuccessfully. "Dinner can wait, dontcha think?"

"Plan B can't," I said, pointing to the handful of seated diners engrossed in their menus, then to the floor-length linens.

"Knew you were special ops material," he chuckled, following me to a vacant table far from prying eyes. Commotion filled the air moments after we'd ducked beneath.

Through gaps in the fabric, two pairs of new trainers moved up and down. We recognized a few choice cuss words as the men finally exited, gave it a few extra seconds for good measure, then scrambled out before they had the chance to double back.

"Brilliant move, Ms. Langford. They're not on to us yet," Logan said, peering through the glass separating us from the next carriage.

"*Yet* being the operative word."

"And why we need those four walls pronto."

We barely made it into the cabin car when they reappeared from the opposite end. The taller of the two sounded the alarm and together they sprinted forward, dodging anything that moved. The race was on.

We avoided the mom navigating the tight walkway with a toddler in each arm and one pulling at her pant leg clutching a battered bear. We weren't as lucky with the jovial German— belting out a tavern ditty as a tribute to the kegs of *Peroni* in each hand—struggling with the key to his cabin while blocking egress to ours.

Logan grabbed his card, jammed it into the slot and shoved him inside as I rammed our own into the key box next door. It beeped red. I flipped it over and tried again. Burly fingers grazed my wrist. Logan swiped at the thug, missed. The man groaned and stumbled back, tripping over a velveteen bear ground into the floor, its frantic owner wailing.

The distraction worked, earning us time to slip in, slide the door shut, and flip the lock before the assassin recovered from his bout with the stuffed toy.

At once Logan went to the window overlooking the station while I perched on a sofa like a bird about to take flight and tried to calm my sudden shivers.

The compartment absorbed most of the clatter from beyond but felt cramped and reeked of stale tobacco despite the *non fumare* signs; a minor blip considering my real focus was on the persistent shadows loitering beneath our door.

"Now what? They're waiting for everyone to get settled and then that lock isn't keeping them out."

"If this works, it won't have to," Logan murmured, alternately watching the platform, studying his phone, and the map he'd bought earlier.

"If what works?"

"The plan is not to be here when they kick in the door."

"Hide again? They won't fall for that twice."

"And why we're leaving through this window."

"Window?" The word felt unreal; wispy. What could he possibly mean?

"Before we begin moving...right?"

Logan shrugged. "Wouldn't do any good with their guy by the tracks watching who comes and goes. Let's just hope if the idea crosses their minds, they dismiss it because it sounds just as crazy to them as it does to us. Shouldn't be long now," he murmured, still studying the station through slats.

A high-pitched whistle was followed by a screech of wheels. The train lurched forward, breaking through my mental fog.

"Oh hell no! You want us to jump out of a moving train?" I rose, my focus torn between the men lurking outside and the picture forming in my head.

"Unless you've got a better idea. Besides, considering what was done to Father Aberto, jumping out to meet death on our terms seems preferable to getting blindsided by maniacs getting off by torturing their victims."

"Meeting death? You mean suicide!"

"Not necessarily. I've been studying our map and the velocity charts. We can do this if we time it right, Trina."

As soon as we cleared the station, he pulled up the blinds then flipped the lever locking the glass in place and cracked it open. A freakish burst of wind, too strong for the supposed lack of speed at which we were traveling, blew me back a couple feet.

"So far, so good. We should be approaching the mouth of a tunnel in another few minutes," he explained, oblivious to the lump that had formed in my throat.

"And then what?"

"It's a pretty long tunnel. We should have a thirty-second window of opportunity to clear the tracks, pardon the pun."

"But why a tunnel? Why can't we do it like in the movies? A meadow? Soft grass?" My voice shook; terrifying proof I was actually considering doing this.

"They'll be paying us a visit long before we get to a pasture. Don't worry...the train will reduce speed as it enters the shaft."

"I can't go through with it, Logan. I don't even like roller coasters."

"Neither do I," he laughed, tossing me my rucksack then rummaging through his own. "Thick jeans, a heavy coat or leather should do if you've got them," he instructed, adding a layer of wool over his tee and then, realizing I stood paralyzed, stepping forward to take my hand.

"You won't be alone, Trina. I'll be right there with you," he reassured.

"You're sure there's no other way?"

"It's the lesser of two evils. Look...I won't force you but neither will I leave you alone. Either we go together or not at all and we both face what's on the other side of that door. It's your call but you need to make it fast."

I needed assurance everything he said was true and looked at him squarely. What I saw in his eyes temporarily erased the last twenty-four hours. Behind a ferocious determination to keep me safe, I recognized an abiding love I'd only known once, before a drunk driver ripped it from me.

I threw my arms about his neck. "Logan, in case I don't make it, I just want to let you know I meant what I said the other night."

"Shhh..." he whispered, silencing me with his lips. The kiss conveyed what words never could but, as usual, ended too soon. "You can tell me tonight over room service," he insisted, setting me back gently.

Unwilling to say more, I added the necessary layers of clothing, swung my rucksack over my shoulder and pressed my forehead against the glass, watching the tunnel fill my vision at an alarming rate.

Swallowed by darkness, Logan slammed the window open the rest of the way, unleashing a tornado. He launched himself over the table directly below it, grabbed my arm and lifted me up, motioning I should follow his lead.

I brought my knees up to my chest, twisted towards the blurry darkness whinging past us and swung my legs up and over the six-inch gap separating table from window, pressing them against the metal. Fighting an unnerving sense, I leaned back on my elbows, gripped the narrow sill above us for leverage, then dragged myself towards the precipice below.

With my weight balanced over a ledge no more than an inch thick, leaning too far forward would propel me into the tunnel before the narrow walls widened enough to clear the tracks. Sandwiched between steel and a dynamited shaft, what was left would be smeared across hundreds of feet of jagged rock.

Then again, leaning too far back wouldn't give me the necessary thrust and I'd simply plummet. Either way, the effect would be the same.

To survive, I'd have seconds to perfect something that took acrobats years and yet, staring into the vortex, I realized no amount of training would ever be enough. If Logan's spur-of-the-moment calculations were off even by a few seconds...

Out in the corridor someone took a battling ram to our door. Surrendering my death grip on the upper sill, I moved my hands to the ledge and closed my eyes. Since my leap of faith required hurling myself into an unseeing void, it seemed silly to keep them open.

"Jump!" Logan yelled, his command and the sound of tortured metal exploding into the cabin lost in the roar of the engines grinding their way through the shaft.

"Trina! Now!

Muscles screaming for release, I sprang forward, hoping I really was flying rather than falling. The sensation was unexpected, liberating.

Freed from the solid and material for the first time, fear evaporated for one euphoric moment; then returned with vengeance as gravity slammed me into what could only be a bed of spiky nails.

It only lasted an instant; until mercifully, my brain decided it could no longer deal with the agony and complexities of a shattered body.

FORTY-THREE

Apparently mercy is overrated. I came around after only mere seconds; my back and head nestled comfortably against Logan, while my chest, arms, and legs screamed in protest to my invisible stoning.

"Can you move?" Logan panted. His breath fluttered against my hair, the vibration reaching deep into the roots, somehow making it hurt.

I nodded, or at least thought I did, then tried sitting up, nearly succumbing to a wave of nausea held in check only by fear of adding to my misery.

"You made it." Impossibly, his voice carried a hint of pride. "You're first jump out of a moving train."

"You mean there'll be more?" I poked and prodded gingerly, trying to determine the extent of my damage.

"Already checked," he said, waving his phone's flashlight over my body. "Other than some bruises, it probably feels worse than it actually is, though we'll know more when we get out of here. Important thing is...imagine the stories we'll tell our kids."

Despite my knowledge of certain upcoming events, the words restored some of my depleted energy and I suddenly became aware of other things besides my pain; the sharp gravel beneath our bodies, the faint echo of the train rambling farther away, the tang of ozone and hot iron, carrying the scent of scorched steel. All good sensations proving that, all in all, things still worked as they should.

"What about you? No broken bones? No cracked vertebrae? Next you'll be telling me you were bored out of your mind."

He laughed in the near-perfect darkness, broken only by our flare and a chink of lingering dusk whose distance eluded me. "Impossible. Not with you around to keep things hopping."

Given Logan's warning of coming face to face with another train, hobbling out of the tunnel didn't take long. Breathing a little easier once we'd cleared the tracks, we paused long enough to give each other a quick once over, gratified his earlier diagnosis was on the mark. Though shredded, our rugged jeans and thick, fleece-lined jackets had absorbed most of the impact. Apart from cuts to our hands, a scrape to my chin, and one to his forehead, other bruises remained hidden beneath our clothes for now.

We slid down the small ravine to the main highway paralleling the tracks and paused to study the map. We were only twenty-five kilometers from Rome and though we'd escaped the men on the train, the ruse was over. Since others would likely take their place, striking as we limped along the busy autostrada back to the city, we headed away from it, grabbed a taxi in the next village, and ignored the cabbie's persistent stares. The message was clear: Portugal was a bust with travel venues in their sights. It was time to rethink plans and by the time we hit packed Roman traffic, one already began taking nebulous form.

Rather than turning on to the familiar street leading to our old hotel, we drove southeast, eventually leaving behind the trendy shops, cafés, and tourist traps for a lesser-known part of Rome not found in guidebooks. Here, even the Valencia would have been a stretch. We pulled up before a crack house posing as a hotel, the name Amalfi lit up in blinking neon.

The cabbie turned to us, ignoring the two women who drifted closer in the hopes of appearing enticing. "This not good neighborhood," he insisted nervously. "You stay in proper hotel. If too expensive...I take you somewhere cheap but good...uhh... safe."

"Safer than you think," Logan retorted, paying the fare. The driver shrugged and barreled down the street while we hurried into the building, ignored the clerk's smarmy winks, and beat it up to the third-floor room as fast as our battered bodies allowed.

Behind our locked door, Logan studied the street below as I pulled the chain on the one, dull, overhead light. The walls and ceiling were dingy and yellow, with large exposed sections of plaster; the carpet, mostly threadbare but for the odd stain I wasn't about to study too closely. The king-sized bed with its firm mattress and clean linens, on the other hand, was a testament to its overriding importance in such a place.

I decided trading our fear of being massacred for the roach motel had been a genius call and took a deep breath, not caring in the least that I had just inhaled a life-time's worth of second-hand smoke. Any relief I felt at our temporary safety was doused by a wave of panic at what we were doing here in the first place.

"You're such a natural at this, I forgot about your bruises,"

Logan said, hurrying to my side. "Where do you hurt?" he asked, folding me in his arms like a china doll.

"Everywhere...nowhere. It's no use, Logan. Not without Pearce. Coming to Rome was his idea. He was supposed to figure all this out and he couldn't even protect Aberto or himself."

Logan shook his head. "I refuse to believe he wouldn't have seen another attack coming. Before he ever thought of becoming a priest, he was a soldier and a damned good one. If there was a way out, you can be sure he took it."

I thought of McCullough's last words to me. "But if whoever killed Aberto..."

"We've been over this. If we can't get to Coimbra, we'll make Coimbra come to us. Under the circumstances, I think he'd approve of us going to the source. Whatever the hell the third secret's about, it's tied to what's happening. If there was an easier way, don't you think we'd have figured it out by now?"

He released me, stepping back to gain some needed perspective. "It's our last shot, Trina. We need to take it before whoever is causing all this, destroys it. Who knows? It may be Pearce's last shot too."

He was half way out the room before pausing to look back at me. "What we did tonight...I think we bought ourselves some time. Just the same, lock the door and jam that chair under it. I'll be back in ten. There's a small market across the street. I'll get us some aspirin and something to eat." I recognized his familiar lopsided grin. "You didn't think I'd forget my promise of room service, did you?"

I followed his instructions, sat on the edge of the bed to wait, then bolted again, pacing restlessly. My eyes drifted from the door to the cheap clock mounted over the bed and back again—

obsessing. In a room that rented by the hour and where time was money, I was sure my use of it would be considered a monumental waste. Then again, given my choice of material to obsess about, I could do worse. My mistake was to think jumping out of a train was the worst that could happen to me. Now, with fingers and toes intact, our next suicide mission had already turned today's into a wistful joy ride.

Logan was right. We had gone over it again and again and desperate times did require desperate measures. But rather than making it clear, my brain felt muddled as if it knew what we were about to attempt went beyond the craziest definition of insanity.

Yeah, we were definitely *going to the source*, as Logan insisted. And yet the question remained—just how were we going to get close enough to the pope to confront him, convince him to spill the beans about this mysterious third secret of Fatima, and still live long enough to make good use of the information?

The answer eluded me long after we'd finished our deli subs and the bottle of Chianti. Despite his earlier promise, exhaustion and our tasteless surroundings made it clear this was no time for declarations of love. Instead, huddled beside him with his arm secured protectively around my waist, I fell asleep shortly before dawn, wishing I'd had a second bottle to drown out the exaggerated moans of passion next door.

FORTY-FOUR

Friday, March 28
New Mexico

Alone as it wound its way through the high desert, the limo stood out too stark and black against the monotonous gray ribbon of road.

Seated in the back, insulated from the world's vulgarities, the senator known as Hael in certain circles, scowled. Membership in The Council had its privileges; meeting with The Caretaker was not one of them since he never knew what to expect from the man. His moods were as volatile as the tectonic plates around the Rim of Fire—and quite often, just as deadly. Hael's own coven, the most influential, powerful individuals on the planet, suffered anxiety at the mere mention of his name, even as they followed with the determination of chicks chirping after their mother hen.

He nearly laughed before admitting the man did inspire a smidgen of concern. No small thing, but he'd chalk it up to flying blind.

The Caretaker had not elaborated why he'd whisked him out

of Rome at moment's notice. Inconvenient since he still had unfinished business—but not all that unusual considering he expected his minions to come running from half way around the world if he so much as sneezed.

Could he be questioning Hael's performance in containing certain loose ends? Admittedly, Scaevus had suffered some minor setbacks, but his last report was promising. The Slayer was back on schedule.

Mulling over the possible reasons for the directive, he paid little attention as the car slowed and veered off the main drag on to a narrow dirt strip.

Despite the state-of-the-art suspension beneath him, he bounced up, down, and side to side, the erratic motion jarring things back into perspective. Better focus as he'd need his wits.

Before him, the mountainside opened as if a swarm of forty thieves had uttered the secret command, swallowing the car and its occupants whole.

The limo idled while Hael and his driver were instantly blanketed in darkness giving the impression they alone were the last remnants of the human race. It was a deception like everything else in this sophisticated complex that had never been built officially. They remained still while invisible cameras scanned and rescanned their DNA down to the last molecule in an array of electromagnetic wavelengths.

The whole process took less than a minute. Their identities established, overhead lights flickered on one at a time revealing an endless tunnel wide enough to stack a dozen semis side by side. Today the limo did a solo run, its reflection mirrored in the highly-polished metal walls. Eventually, Hael felt a gradual shift as the ground sloped down at a five-degree angle. Out of necessity, they slowed to a tedious crawl. The next phase of the journey was simply a series of switchbacks leading progressively deeper into the bowels of the earth, the polished walls giving way to subterranean rock oozing moisture.

The driver paused before a flashing overhead sign announcing they'd reached Platform One. Despite Hael's insistence that most things on this round world were depressingly flat, he leaned over, peering out the window with interest. The limo was moving; a descent so slow and effortless, it rivaled earth's daily 360-degree orbit.

Reality shifted once again as the elevator transport halted on the third level. The scene transformed into a marvel of high-tech engineering that boasted shamelessly of what could be done with an unlimited black budget.

Someone opened his door and he stood, keeping his eyes focused on anything but the quartz floor that appeared oddly liquefied and played with his equilibrium. Guards in light gray uniforms, armed to the teeth, approached, ready to escort him past technicians in lab coats, none of whom paid him heed.

The Caretaker stood out immediately among the sea of white. Dressed entirely in black but for the small square at his throat, he kept his back to him and nodded, intently focused on his discussion with one of his senior-level drones. He dismissed the man several minutes later with a reassuring pat to the arm and, still treating Hael as a non-entity, busied himself with the files on his desk.

"It was encouraging to hear about the exorcist and his assistant. How are we progressing on our other loose ends?" The Caretaker asked at length.

"We've intercepted a transmission between them and McCullough."

"The traitor among the ranks. He's shown remarkable skill, hiding his secret talents all these years."

"Not too remarkable. We're tracing the GPS now. It shouldn't take long. They seem to be woefully lacking in certain survival skills now that Rhomer is out of the picture."

"There's no doubt he's dead?" The question seemed to elicit some interest, bringing a spark into the lifeless eyes.

"Scaevus is nothing if not thorough."

"Excellent. We don't want anything marring the triumphant opening of the gateway," the man answered lightly.

Hael caught his breath. "I knew we were close but is it really ready, after all those decades?"

"You mean centuries, don't you? Why so little faith, Hael? Did you imagine our labors would be in vain? Gather the elect and instruct them to report at the appointed hour. You will see that all requirements are satisfied beforehand. Is the Tribute ready?"

"Nearly, my lord...but still..." he quickly ran through some dates in his head..."two weeks doesn't leave much time for preparations. Some may have trouble getting away."

The Caretaker shrugged. "There can be only one hour, chosen before history was recorded. What could they possibly have on their agendas that's more important? Please convey my apologies at the short notice and assure them that their presence will not go unnoticed. As, of course, neither will their absence."

Father Luca Bertolucci awarded Hael with a genuinely-warm and sincere smile; albeit one that failed to dissolve the veil over the priest's eyes or offer an inkling of what lurked behind them.

Had Hael known, he would've been stunned to learn that The Caretaker's peaceful countenance had less to do with the culmination of their long-awaited goals, than with the memory of their conception; how on a balmy summer day in his distant past, he'd played a hand that not only shaped his own destiny, but that of every human on the planet.

FORTY-FIVE

August, 1959
Castel Gandolfo—Italy

Z *averio...I need your wisdom. Am I doing this for the glory of God? Or is this the excuse of an old man who would like to spend whatever nights he has remaining on this earth, sleeping in peace?"*

Sequestered three stories below the pontiff, Father Luca Bertolucci sat before an elaborate recording unit in a room no bigger than a broom closet. He took off his headphones and wondered—who was this Zaverio—and why did he not hear him enter the room earlier? He would have to make some discreet inquiries before submitting a full report. Meanwhile, it was useless sitting here any longer. He'd gotten it all—every single bit—and his head was still spinning. If even half of it was true, his superiors would be celebrating in grand style. He would have liked to give them his own interpretation on the matter, of course, but didn't think it would sit well. Ridiculous—since his willingness to do their dirty work had been vetted time and again. What were they waiting for? An encore to the wet work he'd performed on the cloistered seer in Coimbra? Clearly, he was not paid to think.

At least not yet—he amended on a high note.

He spooled the tape onto a single reel, placed it in its case and concealed the fruit of his labor under his cassock in a special sewed-in pouch. Locking his *office* carefully, he made his way up the many flights of stairs, a spring in his step, his enthusiasm boundless. He headed towards the gardens, smiling generously to those who passed him and exchanging small talk.

Outside, the afternoon sky had turned a deep azure. He was young, handsome, and smart. His future in the Church was limited only by his ambition. He paused before a cluster of roses, breathing deeply of their fragrance, unaware that the tables had turned; unaware of being watched...

FORTY-SIX

Saturday, March 29

The voices were adamant and since they also happened to be Gregory's best and only friends at this time, he thought it reasonable to do as they say and not piss them off. They were much easier to understand since they'd stopped screaming over one another. With the instruments fine-tuned, the symphony could begin.

Had begun, truthfully—if he were to count that sweet prelude in the back alley behind the Valencia in the early morning hours. Though the tramp wasn't a trophy by any means, he'd used him the way musicians used scales to warm up. He looked forward to scheduling a few more practice sessions in between his other prep work for the main performance.

Right now, however, the voices clamored for him to pay attention.

Gregory tuned out everything but the taxi driver yammering on endlessly. Getting him to cut to the chase in broken English had taken all his patience and a few hundred Euros but looked as if it might pay off.

"*Pazzo* I tell you. Looks can be deceiving, ehh? They seemed like nice couple but torn and dirty, like maybe they had been digging in coal mine and uh...how you say...*ansioso*...uh...anxious. The woman, she holds on to man like so."

Gregory moved out of the man's grasp before he could demonstrate.

Still, the picture he painted slowly came into focus and coincided with his previous intel. He had to admit, it had been well thought out, though dicey. From what he'd learned about O'Neill, the move wasn't much of a stretch though Trina's secret abilities infuriated. Regret came to him unbidden before the voices told him to move on.

"And the hotel you dropped them at...you're sure that's where they're staying?"

"*Sì...Sì.* It was safe, the man said." Still in denial, the cabbie shook his head. "You want I drive you there?" he asked frowning as if Gregory might just take him up on his offer.

"No, that will be all. *Grazie,*" he murmured, slipping the driver another few bills before leaving the station in favor of a rented Fiat he drove back to the city. He parked in the Testaccio district—Rome's inner neighborhood—ditched the car, donned the tourist gear he'd forced himself to wear on the advice of the voices, and set off on foot.

The address wasn't difficult to find. He made his way into the Amalfi without pause, knowing even Langford and O'Neill wouldn't give him a second look if they happened to peer out of the wrong window at the right time and gave credit where it was due. Just like their attempt to lose themselves in the Italian countryside by jumping out of a train, the rundown inn was a brilliant move.

He didn't bother with small talk but plunked down a wad of bills on the front desk and watched the clerk eye it greedily.

"A man and woman came in a few nights ago. Americans. Not your usual customers. What room are they in?"

The clerk pocketed the cash before answering. "Three-eighteen, Signore."

"And would that be east or west facing?"

"West."

"Counting left to right, how many windows over?"

The clerk thought for a moment. "Six. But they not here now."

"When will they return?"

The man shrugged. "I cannot say for sure. What our guests do is their own busy-ness. But for last several days, they leave around nine in morning and come back after dark. Always with packages. You want to leave name and number for them?"

"I want you to forget you ever saw me," Gregory replied, bringing his face within an inch of the man's, the stench of garlic nearly overpowering him. He tempered the words with more money before making his last request.

"The grocery across the street...do they rent rooms upstairs as well?"

"*Sì, certo!* That would be my cousin, Edouardo," the clerk enthused, wariness replaced by oily speculation. "I call him for you. Perhaps you want room for a couple of weeks, just like friends?"

His last sentence fell on deaf ears as Gregory was half way there already, his mind churning with the concept of smoke and mirrors. That's all it was, of course. That's all it had ever been—

but then, that's all it could ever be.

Reminded of Chloe and The Council, he choked back a mad chortle. Clearly, they were not the only ones capable of deception.

Once his attorneys had paid for his freedom, palming his jailers with the obligatory pieces of silver, he'd taken a page out of his former protégé's play book, bought himself an airline ticket, allowed the authorities to think he was out of the picture, then rang up the names endorsed by those same jailers and made them offers they couldn't refuse. His instructions were clear:

"Do whatever you want to the man but bring the woman to me."

Their failure to produce the desired results was his failure. No longer would he pay others to do his bidding.

A half hour after he'd shelled out triple the going rate to cousin Edouardo for his silence, Gregory waited patiently for the occupants of three-eighteen across the street to return.

From his lookout behind the window, he'd watch their comings and goings, study their routine. When they went out again, he would follow. Sooner or later he'd learn their agenda, devise a way to weave it into his own, then strike.

Had anyone caught on to either side's deception yet? Not important.

Had the priest recovered from Chloe's attack? Didn't know, didn't care. Nor did he care if The Council took out half the population of Rome to get to the reporter, as long as they left the woman to him.

Gregory jerked up at the sudden ruckus. Applause roared inside his skull, nearly masking the whispered promises of a thousand voices.

Yes...kill her first...we won't let you down...then we'll help you find the others...they insisted repeatedly.

He settled back into his chair for the long haul. Good to know his new friends approved his bold decision.

CONFESSION

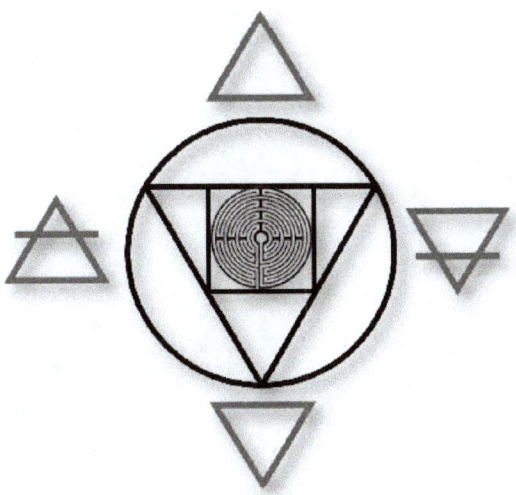

FORTY-SEVEN

Friday, April 18

Stuffed inside a non-air-conditioned cab piled with equipment we'd collected over a couple weeks was bad but not my primary focus. I watched the body being loaded into a coroner's van steps from us. Had one of the hotel regulars overdosed? I would likely never know but felt grateful that despite what the day offered, I wouldn't have to set foot in the Amalfi again—even if its dingy walls had worked as a cloaking device these many days.

"What can possibly be *good* about a man's torture and crucifixion?" I murmured.

"Pearce explained it once. Originally, I think *good* meant holy. You can ask him yourself when he gets back," Logan said.

Unwilling to discuss Pearce as we baked, I changed the subject.

"So what are the odds we'll make it through the day without getting shish-kabobed by guys in over-inflated striped pajamas?"

"Don't let the uniform fool you. The Swiss Guard is a highly-trained special forces unit but our luck's held so far. Considering our options, Pearce would say it'll have to do."

"And what would he say about committing cardinal sin on such a good and holy day?"

"You know it has to be today or never. You're not having doubts, are you?" he asked, flashing me a concerned frown.

"Only when I think of the Swiss Guard as a merciless special forces unit. If you don't mind, I think I'll go on imagining them in their PJs."

"Whatever floats your boat!"

Trying to lighten the mood suddenly felt too demanding. With nothing left to say, we both fell silent.

A couple blocks shy of the main entrance to Vatican City, the cabbie pulled into a gas station and drove to the back, idling alongside a door marked *Bagno* while we paid the fare and unloaded our gear. We watched him merge into heavy traffic before dragging it all into the single unisex stall behind us and locked the door.

Given our cramped quarters, it took nearly a half hour to complete the metamorphoses, but in the end, the transformations were both stunning and terrifying. I studied Logan's reflection. The man who'd walked in radiating strength was gone; the one staring back sunken and shriveled in his wheelchair—only days from certain death.

"Not bad," Logan said, locking eyes with me and whistling approvingly.

"Yeah...okay. Maybe there is another career out there for me after all, seeing as how the whole singing bit isn't going so well."

"As long as I have the woman I love back at the end of the day. How about a last kiss for good luck?"

"You sure you're up to it? It might just kill you," I teased, bending to give his newly-withered lips a quick smack. The enormity of our plan swept over me. I followed the first kiss with a deeper, more desperate one before he broke off abruptly.

"Showtime!" he whispered as I wheeled him into the heat, and I could've sworn I heard a smile in his voice.

FORTY-EIGHT

The Vatican

I scooted Logan across the Via della Conciliazione towards the city state and resisted the urge to stare into the cameras tracking our approach.

We fell in step with other visitors moving steadily towards St. Peter's, broke left before reaching the main steps and rounded the corner. The first of many Guards, all in full regalia, stood ready to check tourists at the west entrance, retrofitted with ramps for wheelchair access. He smiled sympathetically at Logan, hunched over, barely able to lift his head.

"Welcome to the basilica. Please follow me," he said, ushering us into the cool interior turned into a security checkpoint. I handed him our passports hoping the *credentials expert*—highly recommended by the Amalfi's own night manager—was worth the time and exorbitant price tag and then, needing a distraction, tucked the blanket around Logan's legs and waited. Sweat rolled down one side of my face and dripped on to Logan's fingers folded across his lap, smearing a couple of painted-on liver spots.

"Thank you, Signora," the soldier said, pressing the documents back into my hands. "I know it is most inconvenient for you and your husband since he is clearly in a great deal of pain. But you understand...the rules must be followed for the Holy Father's protection."

"Of course," I mumbled, sagging against the wheelchair as he led us through a metal detector. He handed us off to a modestly-dressed young woman who avoided the crowds and directed us towards the north end of the papal altar lined with a series of ornate booths serving as confessionals. One additional structure, both larger and more elaborate than the others, dominated the area temporarily erected for today's private audience.

Along with Logan, only a dozen others were privileged for the face to face with the pope this morning; two amputees in wheelchairs, one on a hospital gurney, and a handful of others who apparently wore their human suffering invisibly since I couldn't tell what special circumstances had bought them favor.

We joined them behind the rope barrier and at precisely one, a side door opened, ushering in the pope and an entourage of priests. Those who could, stood to receive his blessing while I resisted the urge to squeeze Logan's hand for fear of smearing anything else.

When we'd conceived our plan, the odds of getting close enough to the Bishop of Rome for even a glimpse seemed like a lousy bet. Our luck shifted when we'd gone over the dates on the brochure Pearce had left behind in the hospital.

Once a year on Good Friday, the pope would hear the confessions of the general public. To be selected for this honor, complimentary tickets were given out on a first-come-first-serve basis but months in advance. To finagle an extra pass, all we had to do was convince Vatican aides Logan wouldn't last the week and his dying wish was to have the pope grant him absolution. The condition made it easier to spin our elaborate lies.

The priests soon disappeared inside their respective booths to prepare for Good Friday's rush, while the pope vanished within the larger confessional, and his security detail surrounded the building.

I nudged Logan.

"I know. Not like we didn't expect it though."

"Too many of them. You'll never get the chance."

"Then I'll have to talk faster."

From the beginning, we both agreed the heightened security around the pontiff was our greatest threat. Although we'd ruled out the existence of a da Vinci-like, built-in trap door connected to an underground roller coaster that could whisk the pope out of harm's way in case a penitent went postal, other options seemed far more likely. Chief among them, a panic button sounding a silent alarm through a subtle flex of the knee, a tap of the toe; a simple, convenient solution and one that still protected the privacy of the sacrament. Our success or failure hinged on that one assumption.

Last to arrive, Logan was also last to be summoned. I moved automatically, wheeling my *dying husband* up the ramp to the make-shift confessional and handed him off to a guard, allowing him to slide in before me.

I imagined Logan's unspoken appeal to get away as quickly as I could; that above all, I can never allow myself to be taken since it would be my death sentence; that he trusted me to come out okay; that he loved me. Hugging these thoughts, I made my way out of the church against the flow of human feet and pushed through the heavy doors without looking back, a strange sense of foreboding settling into my bones.

Though I should have been grateful for these few moments—most likely my last as a free woman without a price on her head—I braced myself for what was coming next and what I knew to be the most dangerous part of our plan.

FORTY-NINE

U pon entering a confessional, Catholics are sometimes faced with a decision: use the privacy screen separating priest from penitent; or, if you happen to be a martyr soul, opt for face to face and prepare to take your lumps. Though it had been a while since he'd seen the inside of a confessional, Logan now chose option number two.

Since he was sure what he was about to confess was a first, it was essential he look the pontiff in the eye and gauge his reaction. It was equally essential that the pontiff recognize the truth in his. If the supreme leader of more than one billion Catholics decided he wasn't speaking to a raving lunatic, it might just buy him time to make his point.

The confessional didn't resemble any he'd seen. A single room divided by a makeshift half wall with the familiar privacy grate cut into it, it was large and airy with ample space for a wheelchair or gurney. But for its thick, wall-to-wall carpeting, it reminded him of a mobile medical clinic.

The guard wheeled him around the barrier, left discreetly and suddenly, Logan was eye level with a frail-looking old man he suspected would need a wheelchair of his own before too long.

Dressed in a white cassock, the traditional *zucchetto* on his nearly-bald head, the Holy Father smiled broadly and greeted him in a thick accent.

"May our Lord Jesus Christ help you to make a good and complete confession."

"Thank you, Your Holiness. My name is Logan O'Neill."

"Names are not necessary."

"I know. It just feels right to tell you."

"As you wish."

"Bless me Father, for I have sinned. It has been way too damned long since my last confession."

The old man's eyes shot up. "But never too late for repentance. What are your sins, my son?"

"I have a problem, Your Holiness. A huge problem. And a very dangerous one. I didn't know who else to turn to."

"Of course. Sin is very dangerous indeed. Its stain on our souls is certainly not worth the risk as sooner or later, we are all destined to face our Redeemer. You were correct to come here now. Remember, despite outward appearances, it is God who forgives your sins."

"Yeah...well...I'm not sure either one of you have heard what I'm about to say."

"I can assure you, both of us are intimately acquainted with temptation and human frailty at its worst, and have survived."

"Then you wouldn't be shocked to learn that this has to do with a woman?"

"It has been my experience that most things do."

"Not in the way you think though. She's wonderful...the woman I mean. But now, someone's trying to kill her and maybe my friend is...maybe my friend and I as well because we got involved."

"If this is a criminal matter, perhaps you need the police rather than a priest."

"We've tried that route but it didn't get us anywhere. In fact, you might say all the roads we've taken keep leading us back here to Rome. How's that for irony?"

"I fail to understand."

"You will. What does the name Fatima mean to you?"

"You refer to the apparitions of the Blessed Virgin to three shepherd children in 1917."

"And her subsequent messages revealed to the world by the oldest seer, Lucia dos Santos."

"Yes...a great miracle to be sure. But what does this have to do with you being here now, with the woman and your friend?"

"That's just it, Your Holiness. We don't know. We were kind of hoping you could fill in the gaps for us."

Though the pontiff had shown only mild confusion at the bizarre line of questioning, his demeanor now shifted subtly to one of irritation and caution.

"Signor O'Neill, if this is a joke, I assure you it is a very bad one. Receiving the Sacrament under false pretenses is, in itself, a grievous sin. You, of all people, should realize this as I was under the impression you are seriously ill."

"Please...you already know I've been checked out. I'm not armed and I'm not crazy. I only ask you to hear me out for another minute. After that, you can push that buzzer under your foot till kingdom come, or your guard; whichever gets here first."

The pope raised an eyebrow. "And I should believe you... why?"

"Because it's the only thing that's going to help you save mankind from that galactic wave hurtling through space towards us. That is what you do, isn't it? Save souls?"

"Who has told you of such things?"

"Does it matter? Are you denying it?"

"What is written must come to pass. One cannot go against the will of God."

"Is that what you tell yourself when you deny the world the truth of the third secret?"

"You speak of saving souls and mercy. I have seen much in my long life. There are things you do not know; that should never be known or spoken of. If you were blind, you would have no sin, but since you say you see, your sin remains. Sometimes ignorance is the greater mercy."

"How can you be so sure? Isn't that what the secret was all about? Giving people a choice to decide whether to accept mercy or not?"

"What is it you want of me, Signor O'Neill, if that is what you really call yourself?"

"I want to know the true message of the third secret as dictated by the Virgin Mary to Lucia dos Santos; the real Lucia."

"You do not understand what you are asking. The burden you and your friends share now is nothing to the one that would be unleashed. It would crush you."

"I don't think so. The little we already know...the floods, the earthquakes, the pole shift...I'm not going to deny it was easy to wrap our minds around these things, but we're adapting. We're coming to terms. Help us to understand the rest, Your Holiness.

Help us learn why we're being hunted by the enemies of Christ you once took a vow to protect us against."

A shadow flickered across the pontiff's face. Forgetting his supposed weakness, Logan leaned forward.

"That's right. While you've kept ninety-nine percent of the world ignorant out of some misguided sense of compassion, the remaining one percent already know and they're getting ready. Unless you tell me why, it won't just be the woman I love or my friend who'll die, it'll be the ninety-nine."

"It is too late. Nothing I tell you now can reverse the events about to take place."

"Because they were foretold? Was Father Aberto Gandini's death foretold? Surely you've heard of him. Retired exorcist... living less than two kilometers away from the papal palace?

"At least he did until someone literally crucified him to the wall behind his bed two weeks ago."

The old man inhaled sharply and Logan pressed his advantage. "His death didn't have to happen and maybe ours doesn't either."

"Americans always think knowledge can buy them everything. If it were that easy, my predecessors in the Chair of Peter and I would have already done it!"

"Your Holiness," Logan said, half rising out of his chair. "How many more have to die before you're convinced? Isn't saving some better than losing all?"

Perhaps the movement was perceived as a threat because the pope's next words came out agitated. "You should leave now. You were mistaken to come here."

"Only because I thought you might give a damn!"

"May God have mercy on you, Signor O'Neill."

"Wait...please!"

Too late, the pope shifted his weight. The move was nearly imperceptible but Logan was watching for it and understood.

He got to the count of two before a camouflaged door behind the pontiff burst open, ushering in guards whose plain clothes and holstered Glocks didn't appear comical in the least.

What happened next occurred with utter precision.

There was a quick foreign exchange between the soldiers and their charge.

Correctly surmising he had no need of a wheelchair, two of them hoisted Logan to his feet while another two hovered protectively over their boss.

Though no weapons had been drawn, he knew resistance would be met with force. Logan followed his escorts out of the confessional obediently.

The opulence of the church felt too impersonal after the intimacy he'd left behind.

He shifted his thoughts to Trina, glad she'd been spared this humiliation and wondered how she was faring on her own.

As usual, he felt a familiar swelling of pride. She was a trooper. Going along with his stunts, memorizing the intricate plan he'd laid out before them like a pro.

When—if ever—all this was over, he planned on telling her how proud he was as well as many other things.

The simple dream faded with the certainty of being watched— not by the faithful, but a malevolence that drew Logan to it like a magnet.

Weakness stole over him as he recognized the familiar mouth misshapen with hate.

Cloaked in false piety at the end of a pew only an arm's length away, Gregory Kadzik could have easily reached out, grabbed one of the guards' holstered nine millimeter, shot him, and still had plenty of rounds to spare before anyone blinked.

Trina...

FIFTY

Reciting the layout of the Vatican in my sleep hadn't been a waste after all. I headed towards the east side of the basilica on auto pilot and walked into the women's restroom.

As expected, a full-time attendant sat in one corner, monitoring the flow of traffic in the crowded, noisy facility. I used the chaos to my advantage, barricaded myself in the stall farthest from her, and peeled off my clothes.

The striped bell bottoms came off first; reminders from another age that trendy doesn't necessarily equate good taste. Although the fashion police would've hurled, tackiness wasn't a crime yet, or Chloe Six would've been thrown into solitary ages ago. Hopefully, what it had done was create a powerful illusion.

The denim jacket was next, followed by the foam padding around my middle, a small knapsack, and the belt holding them in place.

Freed from restraints, black slacks I'd rolled up against my waist slipped down around my hips and legs, while I adjusted the long-sleeved navy blouse hidden beneath my jacket, over the top. A brisk scouring of my flat-heeled pumps with a wadded-up seat cover turned them black again and completed my quick change.

I looked at my watch, realized I'd already flushed two minutes down the toilet, and whipped off the short, gray wig and elastic cap hiding my own shoulder-length hair, combing it out the best I could with my fingers. Stuffing everything but a few necessary items into the knapsack, I focused on the trickiest part of my makeover.

Since I didn't have a mirror, I'd have to remove thirty years of aging, sagging jowls, dentures, contact lenses, and an olive complexion solely by touch.

I got to work plucking and scrubbing, hoping what eventually reappeared beneath the layers was my own again, then swung the sack over my shoulder and stepped out of the stall to wash my hands.

The attendant rewarded me with a brief smile and nodded. I smiled back, hoping I conveyed the proper amount of polite indifference, dropped a few coins into the basket at her feet and exited before she had time to overthink certain discrepancies.

The ten pounds I'd shed made the heat tolerable. I hung a left behind the basilica where only a handful of visitors braved the mid-day sun then paused, pushed the sack through a boxwood hedge and joined the other tourists.

Where was Logan?

Whether or not his confession fell on deaf ears, he'd reasoned he'd be taken to the Palazzo, the building directly behind the basilica housing the admin and security personnel running the city-state.

Was he already in the custody of the pope's men? Were they turning the city-state upside down looking for his accomplice—a stricken, aging wife, stubbornly clinging to an age of flower power and free love? Or were they looking for me?

I rounded the northeast corner of the basilica and realized I'd come full circle. Like it or not, I'd soon have my answer.

FIFTY-ONE

H e's...come...to...kill...her."
The officer's eyebrows rose then settled back in annoyance. "So you've said. Though considering the fraudulent name on your passport, you'll understand why we may not believe you."

"He's here I tell you!"

"Where exactly?"

"Fourth pew from the back, second man in. He's..."

"Yes...?"

Logan scanned each row. The faces were curious but friendly. None leered.

"He couldn't have gone far. He's wearing tan Dockers, a cream-colored shirt and a light jacket with a zipper in the front. There's a camera around his neck."

"Finally! Something we can believe. Particularly since you've described ninety percent of the male population on the premises.

One problem at a time, Signore. After we have assured ourselves you are no longer a threat to anyone including the Holy Father, we will see about this man you say is dangerous. Who knows? Maybe he is simply your third partner along with the woman claiming to be your wife."

"It'll be too late by then. She'll be dead."

No sooner had he uttered the words, Logan sensed their prophetic nature and knew he needed to act decisively and with force—thirty seconds ago.

He saw the gap amid the men, recognized the bad odds, but took them anyway, and struck out at the two closest guards, hoping to stun them into temporary inertia. Hands tightened around the back of his neck and arms, proving he should've listened to his gut.

The commander shook his head. "Foolish and foolhardy. Enough of this! Cuff him before he gets any other ideas. And from now on, no more stops!"

The papal guard wasn't nearly as cordial the second time around. He swallowed a groan as the zip tie binding his wrists behind his back bit into his skin and he was shoveled towards a side door to the ominous strains of an organ.

Within the basilica, a choir launched into a mournful rendition of *Christus Factus Est*. Though their voices echoed through the resplendent halls, the harmony was ruined by a single, dissonant tone he recognized immediately.

It was the voice of a man, and he was laughing.

A little rusty as to how one went about begging for divine intervention, Logan hoped his silent petition reached heaven before Kadzik reached the woman he loved.

FIFTY-TWO

Within Gregory, voices of a different kind clamored for attention. He shook his head and the words fell into place on his own mental Scrabble board.

It won't be long now. Go and make the necessary arrangements and she will come to you...

In good time.

Curious Trina hadn't sensed his presence as she'd walked within feet of him earlier. He, of course, had seen right through her disguise. As much as he would've liked to have grabbed her there and then, the voices had a better plan—leaving him, for the moment, to his own devices.

Careful not to arouse suspicion, he followed O'Neill out of the basilica and studied the faces of the faithful fools about the square. He had no trouble finding one dark with misery, pressed against the window of a white van pulling away from the curb. Kadzik drank of his fear greedily, then offered him his brightest smile, watching as the van turned onto the cobbled pavement and disappeared behind the basilica.

Pleased at the stimulation he'd drawn from the exchange, he headed back into the church's cool interior, fingers closing around the ancient blade in his pocket, and realized the voices had been right all along. He had been on a journey of the soul for the past month. His earlier failures were not meant to humiliate or shame, but to prepare him for something far greater.

How fitting that despite all of Trina's arguments and betrayals, despite all her irritating protests, today she would give herself to The Old One after all.

Kadzik looked down at his watch.

Now it was time.

FIFTY-THREE

Logan scanned the inside of the Palazzo. The layout matched the blueprints he'd studied all week; a two-floor marble atrium surrounded by cramped bureaucratic offices upstairs, probably stuffed with cheap desks and metal filing cabinets. They might come in handy now that his options were reduced to one. Question was, would his armed guards take the bait?

"You know, I might be a tad more cooperative if I had the use of all my digits," Logan reminded.

The guards hesitated, assessing the risk.

"Come on guys...you and I both know I'm not goin' anywhere," he coaxed, wiggling his fingers.

More relaxed now that they were on their own turf, the men looked to their commander for the go ahead, then approached warily. Logan kept his eyes neutral as they sliced the tie from his wrists. He willed himself to remain still while core muscles churned and twisted, coiling in anticipation of the violence he was about to unleash. Trina's survival depended on it.

He breathed deeply then exhaled, letting go of anything that might weaken him or result in failure, and sensed a familiar energy driving him; a shift back to the Marine he'd been once.

The old ways were taking over again—with one difference. Years ago, he'd fought a regime he'd been told to hate because it was a threat to liberty and freedom. Now, by some weird, fateful quirk in the cosmos, he was forced to do battle with an unlikely enemy; one with which he would have felt kinship under different circumstances, since providence and Kadzik called the shots.

A new thought clamped the seal on his transformation. He'd always wondered what it would be like taking on an elite force such as this.

Well now—he managed to rationalize before instinct took over—this ought to be fun.

FIFTY-FOUR

There were only three ways to get into the Vatican Grottoes—the mausoleum directly beneath the current basilica housing the remains of the popes since Christianity began. The first could only be accessed from inside the church, beneath its main altar. The other two, from the streets above. Logan and I had purposely settled on the northeast entrance, nestled beside a small courtyard, since its proximity to other Vatican venues meant most tourists were likely to come here first; an advantage if one hoped to look like one.

I joined the line, bringing up the rear, and tried not to imagine what might be happening to Logan. Had he had the chance to tell our story? Had the Guard taken him into custody?

My thoughts shifted along with the protective shade shielding us against the heat. I was thankful when a guide herded two dozen of us through the familiar security measures and the face and name on my real passport remained off their most-wanted lists.

If everything went according to plan, it would stay that way until after I'd exited the city-state along with the crowds tonight and made it back to our old gas station to wait for Logan.

And if it didn't...

Determined to ignore my doubts, I followed our guide down a steep stairwell whose simple, overhead fixture wasn't nearly bright enough to dispel the increasing gloom.

FIFTY-FIVE

Among fighting forces, protocol when handling detainees and persons of interest didn't differ much. When possible, their protection—usually behind bars—would always be of vital concern; not out of any overriding sense of charity, but due their potential as intelligence sources or trading collateral. Logan sensed this objective in his captors even before they marched him towards his holding cell. He couldn't allow it to happen.

First order of business—get rid of the guards flanking him in such a way they wouldn't use deadly force. He calibrated his angle of attack to allow for the slight differences in height and jabbed his elbows into their throats, his goal to disable; too hard a blow, and the guardsmen would choke to death as their esophagi swelled shut. The move had the desired effect. Both soldiers staggered back, gripping their throats rather than their weapons, and Logan turned to their replacements, already crowding in.

He took the unit commander rushing at him from behind next,

his fists connecting to a jaw, then to a washboard ab, and grunted, reminded he was dealing with a professional several years younger. Still, he was gratified when the man fell hard against the door and crumpled in pain.

A twinge of guilt didn't last long as the screech of a siren shifted his focus to more immediate matters. He hadn't expected them to respond this quickly. At this rate, the city-state would be crawling in minutes with every security force Rome had to offer. Tipped off they were no longer dealing with an amateur, Logan suspected it would be with guns blazing—at least that's the way he'd play it. He'd have to step it up.

Caught up in these new details, his response time lagged by a few seconds. The fourth sentry came at him from his blind spot, stepped forward, grabbed him by the scruff of his neck and ground him into the floor. He sprawled across the travertine and felt a new cut forming across his forehead. Figures loomed over him, blurry and hazy, then cleared. Now that he'd disturbed the nest, the hornets were swarming.

Nowhere near sufficiently recovered, he twisted to his feet before they could grab anything else and ducked between them. Hunched low, he spun around, barreling his shoulder into the closest sentry. The man fell as his partner struck back with a boot to the gut, the blow radiating up into his chest; a clear sign his own abs had grown a mite soft. Ignoring the burn, he rolled out of aim before the soldier could add insult to injury.

He staggered to his feet a little slower this time, sucking air with a rusty wheeze, and eyeballed the next four rushing at him from his left.

It was time to get the hell out of Dodge!

VIGIL

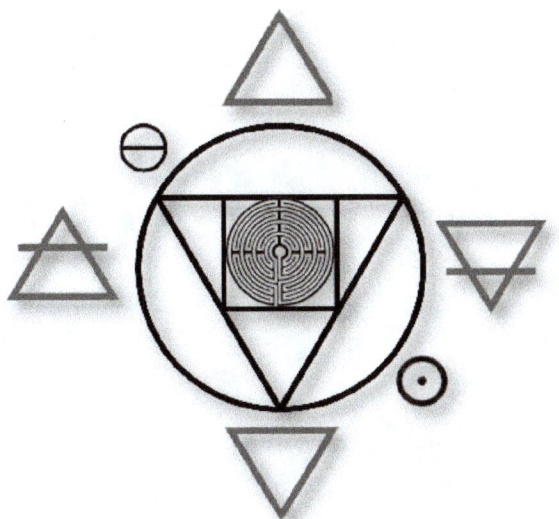

FIFTY-SIX

The guide funneled us to the end of a long, narrow corridor. She paused beneath the marbleized, doleful expression of the Madonna surrounded by key Church figures casting reproachful looks our way.

From within the mausoleum, a stagnant breeze picked up a strand of my hair, played with it a moment, and let it fall over my left cheek. I shook my head to break free of it, and felt my core temperature plunge to the same level as the cavern.

Gregory's mouth brushed against my ear lobe, his breath hot and sour, infecting the tiny, hair-like receptor cells controlling my equilibrium. I jumped as if tasered.

"Shhh...don't move or the blade pressed against your spine will sever it, causing instant paralysis."

He wasn't lying. I felt something sharp poking into my back, knew he'd enjoy every thrust and wondered how he got the knife past security.

The others were rapt, engrossed in the guide's tale. No one had heard a word. If I sounded the alarm, could I make it past Gregory before he sliced into me? Didn't like the odds as I'd probably be dead or paralyzed before my head hit the ground. The insight gave way to another. He'd changed, and it hadn't been for the better. His newly-minted, brazen decision to kill me in full view of a group of tourists proved it. Even if he couldn't hack away at me, he had his pick of potential victims on which to take out his anger issues, and it wouldn't take much provocation. The irony of adding a few extra bodies to the mausoleum housing the remains of the popes would not be lost on Gregory. As long as I was around, no one was safe.

"I'm glad you believe me," he continued. "Your cooperation will only add to our fun and games."

He nipped my lobe playfully to prove it, sending spasms of revulsion rippling through me.

"You may be insane but you're not stupid. You're not going to gut me in front of all these witnesses."

"Is that a challenge? I've had quite a bit of practice with this sort of thing lately. Do you know what I've learned? As a species, you're all too dim-witted to see what's under your very own noses. Take last night's escapade below a certain open window at the Amalfi. Tell me...was that you sawing logs so blissfully or Mr. O'Neill? Either way, I must thank you since it masked some of the more unavoidable noises made when one is having her throat ripped out."

This morning—the body loaded into the van.

He'd known where to find me because he'd known about the Amalfi; and if he'd found me, he'd found Logan. The scream caught in my throat emerged as a whimper and the blade at my back twisted a fraction. I felt a sting as something hot trickled down the curve of my spine beneath my clothes.

"So Trina Langford likes to take risks after all. Surprise, surprise. You almost had me convinced otherwise that last night."

"What did you do to Logan?"

"Safely tucked away...for now. Make a fuss, these folks don't make it out and his story ends before you get the chance to say goodbye. You'll never find him without me and I'll never tell."

Tucked away where? Why would I never find him?

I pressed pause on my thoughts as he dragged the point of the blade down my back, corkscrewed it into my flesh a quarter turn, drew it up, then repeated the process across, completing his design—and got it. He was branding me with the inverted mark of his master.

I hoped Gregory's obsessive desire to remake me into a human pin cushion was distraction enough, bent my leg and flexed my right foot, aiming my shoe just below his knee. Now all I had to do was wait for the guide to motion us towards the next exhibit.

Upon her signal, the group stirred, came alive. I leaned forward, raked my heel over his bony shin and gave him points for self-control. His yelp was barely audible as I darted away from the crowd and behind a granite partition.

I'd bought them some time, but there was only one option if I was to avoid signing innocent peoples' death warrants and finding Logan. Since Gregory stood between me and the main exit, I'd have to find another way out; I'd have to do the unthinkable and allow him to see me.

The guide steered the tour west, inching towards the area directly below the main altar. I lingered long enough to ensure I'd caught Gregory's eye, then veered off to the left, weaving towards a secluded alcove crammed with stone coffins, thankful Logan had insisted I memorize the complicated layout. Once he appeared, all I had to do was keep heading south. Another thirty paces, and I'd be staring at a short flight of stairs leading to the Piazzetta Braschi above and daylight.

I waited for the guide's reassuring drone before darting deeper between the tombs. Not bothering to read the inscriptions, I knelt behind the largest, and waited for Gregory to round the corner. He materialized from the second one over, blocking my escape; a supernatural creature able to teleport at will. Not possible! The only way he could have beaten me here was to have *known* this was the path I'd choose.

He's got a natural gift; only it's grown because he's tapped into something more. Something not human...

I shrugged off the suggestion and turned on my heels as he lunged, closing the three-foot span between us in a single stride. He missed—lunged again—grabbed a fistful of fabric and used it as leverage to slam his knee into the small of my back, directly into the patchwork quilt he'd carved moments ago. Was this how he'd prolonged Father Aberto's agony? The sheer brutality of the assault brought me to my knees. I doubled over, unable to breathe, but his fingers were already digging painfully into my ribs, hauling me to my feet like a marionette whose strings he alone controlled.

Outside the alcove, voices carried, echoed. The guide made a joke and the gathered crowd laughed, muffling the dance of death played out just steps away. I was pinned to a raving lunatic, unable to resist, but struggling just the same.

"Not this time, Trina," he murmured, peppering me with spit. His fingers moved up and down my body, lingering over my breasts. "When you denied me, you also denied The Old One. I won't allow either to happen again."

Pressed against him, his heart pounded with the force of a sledgehammer, excited at the prospect he'd laid out. Without overthinking it, I slammed the back of my skull into his face. My head exploded in pain—though not nearly as much as I had dreaded. The response was instantaneous. Gregory released me with a strangled curse. I leapt out of his reach before he regained his senses and sprinted between the tombs, tripping into the main colonnade. By now the tour had moved beyond it, to an alcove similar to the one I'd left behind but on the opposite north end of the Grottoes. Rejoining them wasn't an option with Gregory in the way. I fled deeper into the gallery, turning when the squeak of a shoe sounded the alarm.

He was closing in on me, the damage to his shin clearly not enough to slow him down, though the dents in his face showed promise. I assessed my handiwork with satisfaction. He was bleeding generously from his mouth, nose and left eye, already turned a lively shade of eggplant. My blow had dislocated his jaw bone connecting those perfect teeth to the orbit of his eye.

The dance continued as we circled one another like tributes in the Coliseum; lion tracking his prey; prey widening the arc, listening as the sound of shoes shuffling across the floor faded. The tour had disappeared deeper into the alcove but the guide's words grew more animated, assuring our privacy. Gregory smiled, his newly-lopsided grin macabre as he edged me closer to the stone wall hoping to pin me. I slid past him and dashed towards the long corridor leading to the main stairs. Not having to circumvent the stone coffins had its advantage. He got there first.

Giving up on the dance, I ran east along the wall towards the Peribolos, the rounded court housing the Clementine Chapel, under whose altar lay the bones of St. Peter himself, stepped into the tiny, opulent sanctuary, and screeched to a halt. It was the end of the line. There was no way out—only down—into the very heart and history of the Church; the Scavi—the catacombs of the ancients.

South of the chapel entrance I saw the dim outline of a door and launched towards it, ignoring the sign posted in three languages reminding visitors Scavi tours were not given on holy days. With its simple lock and wooden cross-beams, the entrance to the ancient city was unexpectedly modest and ajar. I winced as it squeaked shut behind me, my new nightmare mixing with an old, taking on the familiar trappings of Gregory's basement. It faded in and out of my vision as I descended crude wooden planks, centuries flying by like the pages off a calendar until, finally, my feet touched the cobbled streets of first-century Rome.

I turned a corner, letting my eyes adjust to the dim bulbs hung every few feet above the narrow, maze-like pathways. The prospect of finding my bearings died as the door above creaked open, casting its beam of light all the way down to the tips of my shoes. I shuffled into the shadows, held my breath, and waited for the familiar click. It came too soon, abandoning me once again to the gloom and a moment of stale silence before the first drag thump of a slow, arrogant footfall. It was followed by a wet *squoosh*, making it likely that my first attack had done enough damage for the blood dripping off his shin to soak into his athletic shoes.

"Ask and ye shall receive," a voice suddenly pontificated. "Seek and ye shall find. Knock and it shall be answered unto you."

Drag...thump...squoosh...

"For all who ask, receive...those who seek, find...and those who knock, will surely be answered...sayeth The Old One."

I was damn sure The Old One never said anything even remotely similar, but wasn't about to argue.

"You have no idea how special you are or how long I've wanted you, Trina. You will when you feast your eyes on the spectacle waiting for you. How fitting. The woman who denies me in my own paltry grotto, now given to The Old One in the magnificent temple of the dead; the most exalted monument to the true bearer of light. No longer an ancient, rotting mausoleum, but a pulsating womb, ready to burst forth with new life as fresh blood mingles with the bones of antiquity surrounding it. A new covenant for the ages. History remade as it was intended!"

Drag...thump...squoosh...

"But then as I've said, it always has been about the sacrifice, hasn't it?"

I ran—no longer certain of anything but one, single truth. From the onset, this was Gregory's end game. He had lured me here and I had played into it thinking I was eluding him. Everything that had led up to this had simply been a ploy; physical and mental manipulation to get me where he wanted. To get me alone. If security cameras existed, he'd somehow disconnected them. If the door leading to the Scavi had once been locked—he'd made sure I would find it open. Words I'd spoken to Eddy a lifetime ago, rose up out of the ashes in a way he never would again. *He is evil... using every psychological trick ever written to control you.*

That was the part that consumed me. I'd known. *I'd known!* And still I'd fallen for it!

I ran—heels slipping over smooth stones worn by countless sandaled feet and heated by the blaze of a normal sun. On either side, dilapidated structures eaten by time, melded into an unrecognizable mass of brick and mortar. Once the refuge of the living and the dead, they now became my prison; leading me increasingly deeper through that labyrinth Chloe claimed existed; to a slab of cold marble that I just knew had my name on it.

FIFTY-SEVEN

The main door was out of the question as the soldier Logan decked was getting his bearings. He opted for the broad, winding staircase, using the iron railing as momentum to skim his way to the second floor.

A lunge away, the one who'd put a dent in his obliques followed as he'd expected. Shorter than his comrades, he was also quicker, built like a brick shithouse, and closing in faster than anticipated.

Logan redoubled his efforts.

He bought seconds by ignoring the last two steps, crouching low, and vaulting over the hip-level railing when the alarm suddenly went silent. The ensuing quiet was just as shattering, distracting him when he could least afford it. The layout he'd memorized refused to materialize in his head, but with the closest hunter now at arm's length, there was no time to bring it up.

Fists swung at him. Logan jumped back and sprinted around the corridor. Empty offices blurred past, their occupants long gone at the first sign of trouble. He thanked them silently and ducked inside the first, grateful no one had thought to lock it.

Rows of computers presented few places to hide. He looked past them to the only other exit, bounded towards the framed wooden door with its frosted panes and eased it shut as someone steamrolled into the adjacent office.

The room was arranged in a maze of cubicles with three doors dotting its perimeter. He guessed the one facing east led back to the atrium corridor crawling with security, while the one straight south connected this office to its twin.

Ignoring the first two, he approached the door tucked into a corner, an idea taking root. He took a moment to prove he'd found the supply closet, left it ajar and took refuge behind the nearest partition.

No sooner had he flattened himself along the modular wall, company arrived. He bent his knees so the top of his head didn't stick out and listened, picking out a single pair of feet moving across the floor.

The man was alone. He hoped it was the short, stubborn one who'd refused to give up the hunt. There was something about the soldier's face; a certain sincerity that had drawn Logan into thinking he might be open to what he was about to do. He shook his head to get a grip. That was a lot of ifs—ands—and buts and yet his instincts were spot on as the guard approached said closet.

He chanced a quick peek and recognized the man's familiar form as well as the tension that went along with facing an unknown threat. He could relate. The soldier's attention was focused on the darkness beyond the open closet.

Logan eased out from behind the partition and approached his target. Though he knew his measured steps were silent, something gave him away—the soldier's well-honed intuition, or maybe the psychic awareness of another's presence, not unheard of on the battlefield, zoning in on him like a tuning fork. Whatever it was, the man turned a fraction too soon, the muzzle of his Heckler & Koch MP5 nearly fully trained on him before he had time to react.

Counter to what the guardsman expected, Logan moved in and to the side, thrusting his knee up into the steel with a violent jerk. He dislodged the weapon from the soldier's grip and seized it. The man's eyes bulged at having been bested, then drooped—not in defeat, but humiliation. Logan quickly backed him up against the wall noting his name along with his rank.

"Do you speak English, Captain Forrester?" He berated himself. Of course the man spoke English. He was sure it was one of the requirements of his post. Nonetheless, the soldier nodded, his wary gaze switching between him, the pointed gun and the door—no doubt counting the seconds to when his buddies burst through. Logan hurried to press his point.

"Then listen. I'm not going to hurt you," he continued. "I'll prove it to you, just promise to hear me out."

"Why should I promise you anything?" he asked in perfect English, with more annoyance than accent.

"You're my last chance to be heard. Apparently, something of a stretch even for the pope these days."

"Then it's true what they say. You sought out *Il Papa* under false pretenses. You threatened him."

"No! Well...yes...I did pretend to be someone I'm not, but I never threatened him. That was the only way we could tell him our story."

"We...?

"The woman who risked her life with me in order to expose the truth. She's here right now, hiding on the grounds of your precious Vatican."

"Not possible. Our security is state of the art. No one gets in or out without our knowing it."

"We did. Quite easily I might add. But dammit! That's not the point. Bottom line, I don't have time to argue."

Logan flipped the weapon over. He wrapped his fingers around the top of the rifle and held it away from him, urging the younger man to take it. "As a sign of good faith. I wouldn't be doing this if I wanted to harm you."

The guardsman eyed him dubiously and shrugged. "Who knows? Maybe they're right. Maybe you are just crazy," he said, taking his gun before the offer was rescinded.

Logan scowled, expecting to have the muzzle shoved in his face again. The soldier merely set it before him, his position alert but nonthreatening.

"My men will be here any moment. You have less than that to make your point."

"I'll have to reach into my breast pocket," Logan warned, waiting for the nod of approval before proceeding. He took out a thick, sealed envelope and passed it to the soldier, whose surprise shown clearly on his doughy face. "I would've handed this over earlier if I'd had a chance. It's all in there. Names, dates, every bit of research my friends and I have acquired during the last few weeks. There's even a video. I only have two requests."

"You're not exactly in the position to request anything."

"Maybe not but I got you listening and that must mean something I said rang true." He sensed the man's indecision and jumped when the sound of boots thundered by; a sign the cavalry was close. He turned back to the Captain, noting the beads of sweat dotting the man's forehead.

"You see it, don't you? Or maybe you just feel it."

"Feel what?"

"That things just don't add up anymore. That something is horribly wrong and that it's going to get worse. Much worse. Part of the answer is in your hands now. The other, the part we don't know, is why we're here. The thing is, there isn't much time left."

Wood splintered next door, giving a whole new meaning to his words.

"Help us. Help us now."

Forrester sighed. "What do you want?"

"I need everyone to know what's inside the envelope. Get it into the hands of the media and make sure it goes viral. Then make copies before you hand over the originals to the Holy Father."

"You don't ask much, do you? Anything else?"

"Give me a five minute start before following me down to the Grottos."

"To do what?"

"To save a woman from being butchered by a mad man. I may already be too late."

"I can't allow it," he said, holding up a hand as Logan began to protest.

"But let's say that when I was in pursuit of this American fugitive, he managed to overpower me. In such a scenario, I can't see how I could have stopped him from going through the door to your left. It leads to the back of the building and the Chapel of Santa Marta. They'll think you're still here. You'll have a few minutes before they widen their search."

Logan stared at him blankly.

"Go on. You won't get a second chance."

Could he trust this man? He didn't exactly have a choice. Half expecting he'd been duped, Logan dashed between the cubicles.

The layout was coming back to him now that the Captain had tweaked his memory. He maneuvered the winding corridors and reached the empty chapel without resistance. Ignoring his throbbing knuckles, he walked into the sunshine as casually as patience permitted and headed for the basilica suspecting what he'd left behind paled in comparison with what lay before him.

Without realizing it, his measured strides turned to a jog and then to a full-fledged sprint.

FIFTY-EIGHT

Long on shadow, dim lights transformed into a surreal, gray painting by Escher; the ramps, dead ends and false burrows reminiscent of the artist's impossible architecture. Niches that once held the ashes of wealthy, first-century Romans lay bare; while larger, arched recesses serving as graves for the ancients, remained shrouded in darkness, still impenetrable despite the technology of twenty-first century man. With my entire being concentrated on all-things Gregory, I was either unwilling or unable to give them more than a passing nod, and felt only an infuriating familiarity.

In short, I was going in circles.

I ground to a halt and listened. His drag—thump—squoosh was gone, replaced by a happy hum, muffled by the low ceilings and hard to pinpoint given the erratic twists and turns of the narrow streets. I recognized the tune; one of Chloe's old hits about love slaves begging for orgiastic annihilation on the altar of sexual excess. Given its simplistic phrasing and repetitive lyrics, chanted in a husky, syrupy tone more suitable to an opium den, it had accomplished the unthinkable, remaining on top of the charts forever. Apparently, Gregory meant it to be my swan song. I tuned out its trance-like rhythm and focused.

Although I'd studied the Grottoes in detail, I'd been less enthusiastic about the Scavi, arguing with Logan that it was a waste of time. Now, without him beside me, making me eat my words, I still had enough sense to know I was beneath the dome of St. Peter's and the general vicinity of the Clementine Chapel above. There had to be at least one other exit, most likely at the end of a long, obscure corridor. The trick was finding it.

Mid-step, a prickle of suspicion warned me to keep moving.

I passed a series of small tombs I knew I'd passed before, my eyes searching for a hidden niche in the brick, an opening I could have easily missed. Now on the lookout, I saw it at once. The feeble light had blurred the edges of the exit, its repetitive geometry fooling my brain into thinking it didn't exist.

I squeezed through the narrow slit, struggling to free the back of my belt as it scraped across jagged clay and something unexpected; icy skin flexed over taut knuckles. From inside a crude, windowed opening, Gregory's fists clenched around my waist, tightening. Too late, I realized his strategy. Rather than barreling after me, he'd simply waited for me to round the bend. I gave up trying to pry him off and grasped the corner of the wall instead.

Sensing I'd changed tactics, he did too. I felt my feet lifted into the air, then a moment of weightlessness before the tug of war began.

I gained an inch, but lost four when Gregory jerked me back, ancient brick peeling back my nails like a cheese grater; the pain, a mere shadow of things to come as he stuffed my legs through the gap in the tomb wall.

Despite the fabric over my legs, the rough ledge shredded both shins, paying me back with interest for my earlier attack on him. Thighs and hips followed, my scream insufficient to either wake the dead or alert the living.

Gregory gave one more mighty tug and I lost my grip altogether.

Head, shoulders, and arms sagged as the bloodied tips of my fingers grazed then scooped the fine dust littering the street. He grabbed a fistful of hair and dragged me over the threshold, slamming my back against a wall before I could gulp air.

As is so often the case with the insane, his demeanor shifted without warning. No longer in a frenzy to secure his conquest, he took his time circling me, his movements as deliberate and sensuous as any male fashion model, but marred by his broken mouth and shattered teeth; the blood that had run down his face, now dried and cracked in weird, worm-like shoots.

I followed his movements carefully, buying time, looking for a chance to strike.

"Killing me won't help. It's too late. There are others who know about the cycle and the magnetic excursion. Whatever it is you're planning, you're not getting away with it."

"You know nothing. And you're quite wrong, my dear. The sublime pleasure I will take in resculpting you into a masterpiece suitable for the master can only be eclipsed by the favors he bestows upon me through the sacrifice."

"So that's it? You torture and murder your own clients to get a merit badge from the devil? How many others have you killed? How many innocent old men have you crucified?"

He raised a misshapen eyebrow. "Interesting. As appealing as that sounds, I can't take credit for everything...although I do consider the work I did on that pathetic piece of flambéed flesh to be some of my best."

"Monster! I should've let Logan finish you off when he had the chance! Nobody deserves to die like that. Not even Eddy. Your mother never gave birth to you. She just kept the egg toasty warm waiting for it to hatch."

"Edward Pindar was never my primary target. You were. And you know what they say...practice makes perfect. Should have taken my first offer as it won't be repeated, but then, I'm not surprised that you would prefer burning alive to worshipping the prince of the world. "

Prompted by the threat, I threw the dirt clenched in my fists, aiming for his eyes. A high-pitched wail masked my own grunts of pain as I bolted for the window and pulled myself up over the frame.

He knocked me off my perch before I swung a leg, hurled me into the corner then followed up with a hard blow across my temple.

The shock wave sent me reeling. I fell to the stone floor, fighting the sudden nausea and double vision—both made worse the moment he began humming that annoying tune again. Or was he merely talking to himself?

I tried moving, failed, and continued to bait.

"Is this where I'm supposed to die? An empty tomb? A little anti-climactic after your own gothic palace. Where's its pull? Its power and essence? Why here when you can rip my throat out before the splendor of all that priceless art!"

"On the contrary. Take a look around you, Trina. This is exactly where you need to die," he said calmly, his voice taking on a sing-song quality. "By the way, it's just perspective, really, since it won't be empty for long."

Thinking his words to be the ravings of a madman, I followed his gaze to the strange depression in the floor inches from my head. Tiles had been removed, replaced with press board before further excavation could be done. I turned a fraction, saw the original tiles stacked neatly against a wall and looked to Gregory for answers.

"What? Still can't connect the dots? Or are you just unwilling to make that leap?"

He closed the distance between us and I shuddered, expecting his foot to connect with a part of my anatomy again. He crouched instead, sitting back on his haunches, hands pressed against the stone like a gargoyle delivered up from hell.

"Shall I enlighten you then?"

He hesitated, tilting his head to one side as if he were receiving locutions from an invisible entity.

"Another history lesson? Your last one didn't make much of an impression."

"If I recall, you bolted before the really interesting part. Rest assured that won't be happening again. In fact, think of this as an opportunity to finish what we started that night. Now then, what were we discussing that made you so skittish...ahh, yes! The power of sacrifice."

"To the true bearer of light. So where is this monument?"

"You're lying in it."

"There's nothing here."

"Only because it has remained undefiled, waiting to be given life. Waiting for you. But no! The better question is...who is this monument honoring?"

He pointed to the wall above and to the left, where I'd missed the small fresco of a figure mounted on a stallion; its colors still vivid after two millennia.

"What do you see, my dear?"

"Some guy on a horse?" I ventured, squinting to see past the blurriness still clouding my vision.

"Lucifer. The Bearer of Light. The angel of music. Once the most exalted in the heavenly realm for his strength and ferocious intellect."

"The Old One..." I muttered, sufficiently stunned to forget my fear. I thought of Pearce and his own history lesson, now seemingly a lifetime ago. "But this is the Vatican. How..."

"Long before it became a tribute to your God, this hallowed ground honored the true prince of the world. And see here..." The gargoyle leaned into me, growing more animated. He grabbed the edge of the makeshift lid and dragged it off, exposing a deep, gaping hole in the floor, five feet long by less than three-feet wide. "I'm afraid your history lesson will have to continue a while longer. Any idea what you're looking at, my dear?"

"The pit to hell?"

"Clever and not completely off the mark. But technically, it's a libation hole designed by those pagans of old, who followed the ancient ways. Much like the Egyptians, they made sure their dearly departed had sufficient food and drink for their final journey."

"You said no one ever used this place as a tomb."

"What an apt pupil you are. But in this case, the offerings were poured out not to appease the bones of the dead, but the one waiting patiently since the beginning of time for the end of it. Until a true sacrifice could be made. As you can see, I've taken the liberty of enlarging it to suit our needs."

"You're not that insane! Even Chloe isn't anorexic enough to fit down there."

"Glad we're on the same page as alterations will most certainly be necessary."

His sleight of hand was too quick. I blinked and a round metal can appeared, the fluid inside sloshing about. I felt something corrosive burning my eyes and nostrils, liquid drenching my skin and hair—and held my breath, transfixed.

"What a waste. Those long, lovely limbs I imagined so often, wrapped around me. That should've been your future, Trina! And what did you choose instead? Arms and legs, charred to nubby sticks." He sighed, his face a mask of dejection both real and mocking.

"Sadly though, circumstances dictate we'll have to do it the old-fashioned way."

A small, gold square suddenly gleamed through his fingers. He waved the lighter in my face and flicked it on, the flame, first hypnotic, then too hot as it licked and teased the invisible hairs along my cheek. I swatted it away, avoiding that initial touch with the liquid that would ignite my body into a raging inferno, intimate insight of how I was about to die, strangling my scream.

"Now...now. No more of your attitude or I'll have to sever what I just nicked upstairs," he warned, once again conjuring up the familiar-looking blade that still bore traces of my blood.

"You can burn while writhing in agony. Or you can burn wishing you could writhe in agony. Your choice, doesn't matter to me," he finished too brightly.

I twisted sideways, scrabbling to my feet as he sprang to his. The sudden movement only made my vertigo worse, slowing me down.

Gregory pounced, nailing my chest to the floor with his knee and ripped the blouse off my back in a single sweep. I felt the tip of his knife hovering over the base of my spine, waiting for some invisible signal from The Old One to drive it through, paralyzing me.

"Your faithful servant is here, my lord. I've brought her to you as promised! No longer will you be made to suffer the indignities of the ancient offerings. Take what is yours. Quench your thirst. Gorge yourself on the blood of the living."

A faint but unmistakable whisper, like someone sweeping a broom over the dusty bricks, wrenched my focus from the blade now probing just below my skin. "Wait! Did you hear that?"

Gregory paused, listening to the scurrying of feet moving closer. He swore under his breath, the steel at my spine quivering uncertainly before he whisked it away, sheathing it in his back pocket.

"Probably just your boyfriend, come to save the day," he muttered, pulling me to my feet by my hair.

"But you said..."

"I say many things."

"You lied to me!"

"One must mix the reality with the lie."

"Logan, it's a trap! Don't come any nearer!"

My forehead slammed against the wall ending any other attempts to warn him. Blood dripped down into my eyes as he dragged me back across the floor to the pit.

"In you go," he announced, throwing my knees out from under me.

Dizzy, unable to fight the momentum, I toppled into the narrow cavity head first, my shoulders, hips and arms pinched between the narrow ledges.

"Oh! This will never do. You may not be the living, breathing

skeleton Chloe is, but you're no fatty either. Come on now.
Behave! Get in there!"

A jolt crushed my back; Gregory jack hammering the full
weight of his leg into my spine, unleashing new spikes of pain.

My body budged an inch, then another. Jammed half way
between the bottom of the hole and the surface, his voice above
me sounded unreal.

"Just temporary, you understand, until your boyfriend arrives.
And won't it be nice to have an audience for our fine symphony?"

"Please! Don't do this!" Compressed between the walls of the
narrow tomb, the cry came out as a useless wheeze; my mistake,
as lungs strained for whatever stale air remained. How long did
I have before they collapsed altogether? How long before Logan
found us, and did it even matter since he was walking into an
ambush?

All was silent for several seconds. Unable to twist, I blinked
away the murky specters beneath me before the next wave of
panic hit full on.

A muffled clunk at the opposite end of the libation hole
proclaimed my short but immediate future with devastating
clarity. Darkness deepened as Gregory replaced the tiles one by
one, disguising once more what had remained hidden for so long.

True to his word, Gregory Kadzik was feeding the beast; only
this time, he not only offered it human flesh and blood, but the
strangled cry in my throat that reached perfect silence as the last
square fell into place, squeezing out all remaining light.

FIFTY-NINE

The challenge of lugging the last brick to the pit and dropping it in place without pinching his fingers proved harder than expected. He was glad when the final satisfying thud erased all traces of Trina Langford then ordered the voices to shut the hell up. Gregory quieted his breathing and listened. Not a squeak emanated from beneath the thick tiles. Outwardly, the tomb was as empty as when he'd come upon it and wouldn't be giving up its secrets any time soon. Or would it?

He sensed motion behind him, then slow, measured applause shattering the brief silence and turned, unprepared for the nearly-perfect blob of black perched across the windowed opening, dangling her legs.

"You! How did you find me?"

"A little birdy whispered in my ear. And just in time too, from the looks of things. Poor, pathetic little Trina. Guess neither her star nor anything else will be rising out of the ashes like a phoenix after all. She always was a one-song wonder. By the way, thanks for handling her for me. Nice to know if I can't double my pleasure, I can still halve my work."

An unfamiliar sense of menace sizzled within Gregory. Before he could react to it, Chloe eased herself inside, approaching her exemplar in custom-leathered athletic shoes tinted in neon fuchsia. In the unlikely event they were unable to halt traffic on Hollywood and Vine, rhinestone laces shimmied, throwing prisms around the room. Then again, knowing Chloe, she might have paid extra for the real thing.

The thought took a back seat to the semi-auto she removed from her waistband, its muzzle masked by the more efficient one on the silencer.

The hum in his head was back. A cacophony of gibberish all going off at once.

"What exactly do you think you're going to do with that?" Hard to take the whore seriously when she stole admiring peeks at her feet every few seconds.

"I'm going to kill you..." she glanced at her watch "...in exactly seven-and-a-half minutes."

"So the acolyte thinks she can usurp her exemplar."

"I don't think. I know."

"Damn right you don't think! You don't have the brains for anything this elaborate. Smuggling a gun into the holy of holies? How did you manage it?"

"The same way you did the knife, though in my case I still have friends everywhere."

Keeping the pistol trained, she sauntered over to the nearly-invisible libation hole and stomped on it a few times, the prisms on the wall responding wildly.

Gregory licked the sweat above his lip and worked to keep up with this new development. In addition to being shown Chloe's betrayal that fateful night in his cell, he'd also sensed an aura of victory. Before learning more, the vision had petered out and now he understood why: he couldn't be allowed to see more. Hael would have known Gregory would try to remote view his future. With his talents, it would've been child's play to block any knowledge of their murderous schemes.

"Hael must be dredging the bottom of the pond, or has he run out of lackeys to do his bidding? Don't you think this is a little over the top considering you've had ample opportunities to pull the trigger before this?"

"Have you forgotten what you taught me?"

"Okay so he's testing you. Must you keep looking at your damned watch! It's annoying!"

"Actually...yes. You see, you were right. Sacrifice does buy you everything. Only this time, you're the sacrifice. The witching hour...it's almost here."

"What are you talking about?"

"Three o'clock on a Friday afternoon ring a bell? The Deceiver, nailed to His cross, breathing His last? A sacrifice was required then. A sacrifice is required now. Seeing as how you were already in the dog house, Hael thought you'd fit the bill. Cheer up. At least you'll be going out with a bang, pardon the pun."

Gregory stared until the loudest of the voices screamed, setting off an instant migraine. "Explain yourself!"

"The Quickening is over. The Summoning is about to begin. Or at least, it will be once I take care of business."

A mock expression of surprise shown in her eyes. "What? Didn't Hael send you the memo? Oh, that's right, you're out of the loop these days."

"And your prize for taking care of business? Let me guess. A seat at Baphomet's table. You're more of a mental defective than I would have guessed."

"Because I was chosen over you!? Perhaps The Council sees in me what you never could. Or were you just afraid of how far I'd get on my own?"

She moved sideways, forcing him to do the same to keep his distance. "Oh, don't get me wrong. You were one of the great ones. Once. Only now it's time for forward thinking, bold action."

"And you're the one to do it, are you?"

He reached casually into his back pocket, fingers closing around the handle of his blade for when her attention slipped.

"Why not? Hael said The Council needs fresh blood and he's right. I'm the future. I don't follow trends, I create them. With my influence, the rats won't just be trampling over one another to see who witnesses The Summoning first, they'll be exposing their tender necks. Even at your peak, your influence could never match mine. Hael was right. You are old."

"I wasn't too old when you craved knowing the ancient ways."

"For which I paid my dues. Just so you know, grunting in the throes of ecstasy while some dried up old prune on Viagra goes at it whenever the hell he gets the urge..." She paused, stuck out her tongue, jammed a finger down her throat, and gagged.

"Too bad Trina's appetites were as dull as her taste in clothes. I could've used a night off. She rejected your advances, if I recall. Oh, well...look where it's got her now," she murmured, checking the time again."

The duo had circled one another like the hands of an invisible dial. It stopped ticking the moment Chloe halted.

"But just to show you it's nothing personal, I do have a parting gift for my exalted master. Remember wondering how it would feel to have Trina beneath you, her body squirming under your touch? You're about to find out. Well...part ways at least. Under the circumstances, it's the best I can do."

Her words made no sense until he realized she'd led him directly over the tiles he'd replaced a short while ago. He jerked his head towards her and felt three sharp pricks to the middle of his chest, an uncomfortable numbness spreading too quickly. Surprise that she'd actually gone through with it and shot him kept other sensations at bay for now.

He didn't notice he'd fallen to his knees, couldn't comprehend why the voices he'd relied on over the last several weeks seemed to dim then grow quiet, or why his ears felt like they were stuffed with cotton. Acute fury at his acolyte's betrayal took center stage, but even his rage couldn't hold out against the damage wrought by .38 slugs tearing into heart tissue. Eventually, walls blurred, then shifted to a static gray like a channel going off air at midnight.

Unaware that his organs were shutting down one by one, that he lay sprawled and bleeding over one woman's grave while the one who put him there loomed over him with only mild interest, his world was reduced to a single, blissful sea of white that held him captive. Immersed within it, Gregory Kadzik, for one blindingly-clear and insightful moment, perhaps the first and only in his sixty-eight years, enjoyed an instant of pure, undiluted joy. Somehow, he understood why.

He was seeing a blank canvas, uncorrupted and incorruptible, full of promises waiting to be fulfilled. A future of what-ifs, never realized because he'd allowed the master strokes to be created by one using the point of a blade for a brush, ripping into his masterpiece in anger. Always in anger.

The thought brought fear and ruined the moment.

His sea was broken by an unexpected splotch of black, then another, raining down in an oily deluge that blanketed the canvas and finally consumed him in a weightless, noiseless, colorless void his mind insisted couldn't be real and had to end and oh— suspicious how it resembled that damp, dark tomb of childhood; that little chamber of horrors tailor fit for him that would forever make devotees of deprivation tanks crave the din of a never-ending carnival.

From out of the void, a whisper gathered force. One voice coalescing into two, then three, then legion, attempting in vain, to reform into his familiar symphony but falling short.

His old friends were back, bringing with them someone familiar yet monstrous and suddenly, Gregory would have given anything, everything for that oppressive silence to return. Just as he knew who it was tagging along and that he was no longer hearing the voices physically, he also knew it was the beginning of the end; an unlimited end, cycling around in ever-tighter spirals, chipping away at him until only raw consciousness remained.

Until even the hole into which he'd crammed Trina Langford beneath him, seemed luxuriously spacious by comparison.

SIXTY

*I*n...feeling...something...

Logan?

No...Something sticky and cold soaking uncomfortably through my ripped blouse, bringing me back from the dead. Not dead. Not yet anyway. Just temporarily unconscious—regrettably. Didn't want to think about Logan being slaughtered above me. Didn't want to remember him that way though soon I would no longer remember anything.

Pain threatened then backed off. Oxygen deprivation did have its perks.

Slipped back into the shadow world gratefully...rippled through something wet and amorphous. Unsubstantial.

Out...and...*In*...

I was back. Hopefully, for the last time since it hurt to breathe; my ragged lungs, the only sound beside the tick of my watch keeping up with my heart and probably hard-wired to quit with its last syncopated beat. I remembered it had an illuminated dial feature and struggled to turn it on with the deadened tips of my fingers. An eerie glow bathed the earthen walls and eagle charm I'd never bothered to take off—a reminder from the other side that I'd soon be joining Eddy—and I quickly turned it off again. Won't be but a moment now...

Out...and...

Damn!

Chest constricted—struggling. Now nearly impossible to take a full breath...

Now a half...

Now—nothing.

I was sure I'd made peace with death. My body proved otherwise as panic spiked, shooting an urgent message through my muddled brain.

Breathe! Breathe!

I didn't care that it was fetid and stale, or more carbon-dioxide than oxygen. It was time.

It was one...

Last chance...

To live.

A new sound competed with the doomsday clock fastened to my wrist. Soft sobs ricocheted off the compacted walls grieving my imminent death.

The heart-rending cry that had saved me from slicing my wrists only a few weeks ago was back, marking this new tragedy in the making with its sad song. I didn't know why since this time it was too late to save anything. *Out*...

Something swam beside me in the cool darkness. It flashed,

illuminating a scene, silent but too bright, too confusing. I turned back to the soothing gloom, drifting—only to be jarred again.

Another flash. This one with sound. Not deafening, but cocooned and muffled as if my ears had breached water.

"How long did he have her down there?" It was a voice I knew, followed by others I didn't.

"We'll never know unless we get her heart pumping again. Then perhaps she can tell us herself."

"Do it. When I think, all those minutes wasted because his body was in the way. I should've followed the signs. If I hadn't heard her weeping..." The voice shuddered and I felt wispy breath over my face.

Two more bursts in rapid succession. A photographer obsessed with capturing a single moment for eternity. Don't you get it? There's nothing to see here. Move on and let me be. Let me die...

"You did well. Don't blame yourself. Leave it to us now."

"I almost walked away!"

"But you didn't."

Light was coming in fast and furious now, a blitz of faces and uniforms, scurrying about with no rhyme or reason, followed by sudden pressure to my chest.

Gregory doing a death dance on my grave?

Rather than causing new agony, the heaviness suddenly lifted, as if something wicked and foreign had been expelled from my body. It was my only reprieve. Mostly dead, my lungs rebelled in an explosion of raw pain. I was inhaling shards of broken glass and chasing them with battery acid.

I ignored the assault and gulped greedily, deciding there and then, I would gladly go through this agony every day for the rest of my life since it was undeniable proof I was still alive.

REVELATION

SIXTY-ONE

Saturday, April 19
The Vatican

The lights of St. Peter's reflected the night in flattering, other-worldly hues. In the square below, thousands flocked with lighted candles to receive the papal blessing; their beacons, a gigantic wave in a sea of darkness, their voices lost to the bells rising from the basilica, proclaiming The Resurrection.

I turned from the window, the chimes a closer reminder of the hell hundreds of feet below than any salvation.

More than twenty-four hours had come and gone since I'd been found, but we still didn't know why Logan and I were housed in adjoining apartments as guests of the Vatican, rather than thrown behind bars.

We were treated by the pope's own private physician, who insisted I was lucky to have made it out of my make-shift grave with only a mild concussion, a couple of cracked ribs and the ugly wound in the small of my back. His strange comment that I'd survive to fight another day rattled me, adding to my already overloaded list of questions, but neither he nor the silent nun bringing us our meals were talking.

As soon as I could focus on something other than pain, Logan filled me in on Gregory's strange death, reporting that neither he nor Eddy had been tagged by the media yet, then showed me the tiny pink rhinestone he'd swiped off the tomb floor. Since it seemed unlikely the bauble had fallen off the rags of a first-century Christian or the team of archaeologists charged with digging one up, it raised some disturbing issues. I knew if Chloe's predator-like instincts sensed opportunity, she wouldn't think twice about destroying her own mentor.

Who was bankrolling her murderous ambitions and why were they hell bent on destroying anyone standing in the way of their mysterious triangles and labyrinths? Next to them, Gregory came off looking like a boy scout, and given his reluctant denial of Aberto's death, it now seemed likely that even he'd fallen prey to them. Had Pearce?

That was as much as Logan and I were willing to discuss about either priests at this point. Some things were still too raw to think about and we spent as much time as we could consoling one another that, at the very least, we hadn't lost each other.

Fearful this was about to change, I slid into his waiting arms, my own tightening around his waist as if I'd glimpsed a tornado gunning for us.

"Marry me," he whispered, his lips skimming the vivid bruises around my left eye and cheekbone like a cool breeze. I untangled myself long enough to prove he was joking.

"Must've suffered more oxygen deprivation in that tomb than I thought. I don't think I heard you right."

"Marry me, Trina," he repeated without any trace of humor.

"Before or after the Vatican convicts us as terrorists? Before, I guess, if we want to outrun the earthquakes and pole shift. Oh...and let's not forget Chloe and her newest business partners. You're dreaming!"

"Agreed. But it's a good dream. The best I've ever had."

"It's too late!"

"Too late would've been not hearing you call out to me; not finding you in time. I may not be able to change what's about to happen to the world or to us. But I can damn-well guarantee it'll go down easier with you beside me."

"How can you guarantee anything? A month ago you didn't even know me."

"You said you loved me once."

"I still do."

"Enough to finally bury Eddy?" he asked, gingerly touching the charm still bound to my wrist.

"It's not like that," I explained. "It's true, for a time I wore it to remind me of my mistakes. But after what Aberto said that last morning, it's also a reminder that those mistakes might have bought me one or two unintended benefits. Bottom line, I still don't know whether I'm looking at an eagle or a phoenix."

"Why not both? Your past and our present and future all rolled into one."

"You don't give up, do you?"

"Not by a long shot. Together we've seen and done more in one month than most married couples have in fifty years. We're alike, you and I."

"Because I let you talk me into jumping out of a moving train? A lot of good it did us anyway...and while we're on the subject, I never called out to you. I couldn't. I barely had enough air to keep me alive as it was."

"How's that possible? I heard you loud and clear. You were crying. It was the loneliest, most wretched sound I've ever heard in my life."

"I know, I've heard it before too, but it wasn't me. Listen, there's something I haven't told you yet; something that's only happened once before. I don't know how it works but the first time was the night I came home from the clinic when I almost sliced my wrists. I think I would've gone through with it if it hadn't been for this..."

A soft rap indicated my confession would have to wait. Our poker-faced nun peered through the door, the terse nod of her veiled head, grim reminder the vacation was over. Doubt gnawed at me as we followed her down a sumptuously-appointed corridor that could have been a museum unto itself.

Would we be given a chance for later? Or was our time together ticking down with every step?

Grabbing Logan by the arm, I brought my lips up to his ear and began whispering furiously.

SIXTY-TWO

The drawing room surprised me, its warm glow a foil for the darkness beyond its walls. I'd expected opulence, over-the-top antiques, priceless works of art. We were met with comfortable and surprisingly modest, given it was the home of the supreme pontiff.

I welcomed the shift in thought since it made me forget the possible reason for our summons. Anyway I looked at it, I couldn't come up with anything reassuring.

An invisible door opened, ushering in a lone figure dressed in familiar garb. The pope smiled broadly, taking me off guard and extended his hands as he walked towards us.

Mistaking the gesture, Logan stooped to kiss his ring.

"Please, Mr. O'Neill," the pope admonished gently, grasping his hand instead.

He turned to me next, his eyes searching my own for signs of distress. "It is a pleasure to finally meet you, Miss Langford.

A blessing I found necessary to postpone due to my obligations leading up to the Easter Vigil tonight. I trust the inadequate rest you have received will be the beginning of a complete physical recovery. For all else, I can only pray your ordeal might fade over time like a deplorable nightmare one wishes to forget."

"Kind words, Your Holiness, but it's obvious my...our... nightmare is just beginning."

"How do you mean, my dear?"

"What's about to happen. Our arrest. Are we to stand trial at some Vatican tribunal or just deported?"

"Is this what you were both led to believe?" he asked, inviting us to sit on a well-worn sofa while settling in the one across from us. "That you were allowed to recover merely to survive your journey to a prison cell?"

His eyes glinted in mischief. He was enjoying himself and I reddened, embarrassed he'd seen through me.

"Let me dispel your doubts. Nothing could be further from the truth. In fact, I had hoped to give you more time."

"But if you're not pressing charges, why are we here then? Time to do what?"

"To rebuild your strength. I fear you will need it in the coming days."

"So we've been told," Logan interjected. "Have you read the contents of the envelope I gave your guardsman?"

"Captain Forrester delivered it to me promptly. Although it was helpful in confirming certain facts, I must tell you, it did nothing to promote the argument you so assiduously defended in the confessional."

"How can you say that? Are you so far removed from reality locked up in your ivory tower you can't recognize truth when you hear it?"

"Your report could not sway me because I had already come to a decision. No sooner did I hear of these dreadful events, I knew I could no longer turn a blind eye to what is coming. To what is here. It was my wake-up call, as you Yanks say. What this young woman endured, her nearly tragic death, this is what now compels me to reveal what you seek."

"The last secret of Fatima. Then we were right. There is more for the world to know."

"That has never been the question but rather, what you will do with this knowledge once you have it."

"If you're gonna ask us to sign some kind of non-disclosure, forget it! What's the point of all this if we can't warn anyone?"

"I pray your impatience may be a stepping stone rather than a stumbling block, Mr. O'Neill. On the contrary. I do not seek your discretion, but your dedication and courage. Within my inner circle is a small group of like-minded individuals; each of them hand-picked by my predecessors and I, unique in their qualifications and gifts, and dedicated to serving humanity at this time. We need people like you. Both of you. Miss Langford is somewhat of a celebrity, I am told. And of course you, Mr. O'Neill, are no stranger to the press, especially in regard to your expertise in the sciences. Despite our histories, or perhaps because of them, there is always something we can offer others. Do not underestimate your worth."

His words resonated, uncanny in how closely they resembled those spoken by Father Aberto before his death.

"You're asking us to work for you. To be part of this organization."

"In a manner of speaking. I have invited another member of

our team as he can explain the details. I believe you have already met."

He looked past us into an alcove harboring a small dining area. From behind a high-backed chair rose a familiar form I'd have known anywhere. He ambled towards us, his tousled carrot locks swaying despite the lack of breeze.

"Guess we're not through with the cloak and dagger stuff yet," McCullough beamed, greeting us cheerfully. "As you can see, I took your warning to heart, Trina. Figured this place was as safe as any."

SIXTY-THREE

W hat is this?" Logan murmured. "Exactly what are we getting ourselves into here?"

"Brother McCullough is merely inviting you both into the SIV. *Il Servizio Informazioni del Vaticano.*"

Despite my meager knowledge of Italian, I got the drift and turned to the scientist for corroboration. "The Vatican Intelligence Service? You're a spy?"

It seemed logical and a good way to break the silence since Logan was busy scraping his jaw off the floor.

"We prefer the term watchman," the monk admitted. "The other makes people think of 007 and martinis. Like I said last time, I just try to get the word out when I can...which is what you'll be doing...if you accept of course."

"I remember reading something once. How you guys were just a myth. A made-up story that never gained traction."

"Anonymity has its virtues," the Holy Father explained. "The safety of our members is of prime importance."

"How many of you are there?"

"Need to know, Mr. O'Neill. Let me be clear. The Church has always had its enemies; waiting, plotting, exploiting whatever means to twist truth and serve their own misguided beliefs...to the point they would even use an ancient pagan tomb built before the church above it ever existed, to murder the innocent.

"Yet for the last seventy years or so, my predecessors and I have seen something more. An insidious and diabolical force gradually but systematically seeping into the cracks that grow larger each day."

"Sounds just like what a murdered exorcist said to us once."

"Perhaps because it was a subject he and I discussed often since he was a member of the SIV. He was a good priest and my close friend for more than thirty years."

"You led me to believe you'd never heard of him."

"It was necessary. Indeed, the ivory tower you spoke of exists, but it is designed to keep the wolves at bay."

"One of the most powerful men on the planet doesn't know who his enemies are?"

"Power is reduced to dust when the wolves resemble sheep but hide their sharp teeth behind silver tongues. I believe both Cardinal Mallory and the imposter calling herself Sister Lucia in later years are proof. This is why the information you brought me is of tremendous importance at this time. Feigning ignorance has had its tactical advantages in the past, but it is time to act. You could be of vital help with this, if we're not too late. Given their brazenness during these recent days, it is obvious we are getting perilously close to The Summoning."

"Summoning what? Rats, cockroaches?"

"The similarities are striking," the pontiff answered, motioning for McCullough to take over.

"It's the code name for D-Day; call it The Apocalypse, the day of reckoning. They've been waiting for it for over two millennia."

"The arrival of the galactic super wave?"

"In part. Do you remember what I said to you the last time we spoke?" he asked, turning to me.

I peeled back the layers of the past few weeks and recalled snippets of a rushed phone call in a crowded rail terminal. The urgency of what we were about to do had eclipsed all other thought until now.

"You'd discovered the origins of Mallory's symbol. You called it al...al..."

"Alchemical."

"What does it mean?"

"I'll get to that. Point is, I didn't realize that what I'd found had anything to do with the third secret until His Holiness showed me Sister Lucia's original letter. Trina, you were right," he said, dropping his voice an octave. "Mallory's message isn't just the scribbling of a madman. It's a calendar of sorts; one that gives us the precise day and time of The Summoning. Now. During the Easter Triduum, the three most important days in all of Christendom commemorating Christ's suffering, death, and resurrection.

"What His Holiness said about the pagan tomb was right. Once Christianity had taken root by the end of the first century, the early Fathers decided the best way to eradicate the worship of idols and false gods was to build on top of them, so to speak. They adopted the pagan festivals, kept the dates, but transformed them into Christian celebrations. Before Easter ever became Easter, it was a season of renewal culminating in The High Feast of Ostara, a ritual that ushered in spring and the Vernal Equinox and included human sacrifice, sexual magic, and something else; something that was allowed to occur only on that specific date. The creation of a Magnum Opus. A Great Work of renewal and transformation."

"We know. You and Aberto already said as much."

"But what you don't know is that Magnum Opus isn't only limited to the spiritual. It can also refer to the transmutation of matter through the age-old practice of alchemy, ancient civilization's answer to modern science. Most have forgotten these archaic ties. Some haven't."

From his pocket, McCullough produced the paper depicting Mallory's artwork and laid it out before us.

"You might have already guessed the middle spiral represents a labyrinth within a triad. The alchemical symbol above the labyrinth signifies the Vernal Equinox; the one on the bottom right, sulfur and the last represents the sun. This is the true meaning of Mallory's doodles and...it complicates things."

"So you're saying alchemists are after us?" Logan murmured, looking as clueless as I felt. "Even if they can convert base metals into gold and silver...and that's a big *if*...why would they need to? They're probably already richer than Midas."

"Take it to the next level. What if by some unimaginable technology, they've learned to transmute pure energy into a real, physical, and material substance?"

"Are we talking electric...kinetic...mechanical?"

"You're over-thinking it," McCullough argued. "Start with the basics. What is energy by its simplest definition?"

"The ability to make things happen. A force that creates motion or causes a reaction. But I fail to see how any of this has..."

"And would you agree that this force flows through every living thing including us?"

"Yesss...but if you're expecting me to have an epiphany, I wouldn't hold my breath," he warned, taking in the monk's obvious frustration.

"What Brother McCullough is referring to in his roundabout way is the spirit, Mr. O'Neill," the pope explained. "In addition to being indivisible and indestructible, it also has the power to bend the will, to create ideas."

"Silly me. I thought that's what the brain was for."

"The brain is simply an organ. It's part of our physical body," McCullough corrected. "The body can't know, love or hate anything. It can't decide. It can only react physically to the information sent to it by the spirit."

I realized where I'd heard all this before. "Pearce did say everything begins with thought."

"That's right. Only we're not just dealing with the spiritual realm, but a fusion of the spiritual with the material. The natural with the supernatural. It's why these folks are so dangerous. They've taken the general principles of alchemy to a whole other scale. Something twisted and deviant."

"In order to usher in this Summoning."

McCullough nodded. "That's where the superwave comes in. We believe the cyclical event is meant to correspond with their agenda, or at least arrive on its heels."

"Makes sense. Once we can no longer ignore the effects of the coming micronova, we'll be too busy to deal with this thing."

"An unintended benefit but not the primary one. Can you think why it's an absolute necessity if they're to pull off the transmutation?"

Logan thought for a moment. "Of course...the magnetic reversal already in progress and gaining strength. They want to harness its electro-magnetic energy. Why would they need that kind of power?"

"They wouldn't...unless what they're creating is so massive in scale, it's never been attempted," I said, wiping my suddenly sweaty palms. "What are they hoping to achieve by all this?"

The monk smiled crookedly. "I thought it was obvious. The elixir of life. Immortality. That's always been the true goal of the Magnum Opus. The only thing keeping them from achieving their goal up to now has been their inferior methods. Bottom line, they've had to wait for science to catch up."

"This is what killed Pearce and Aberto? What Gregory and Chloe risked everything for? The fountain of youth? Some potion designed to make you live forever?"

"You're only half right, Trina," McCullough said. Shifting to Logan, he asked, "What do you know about CERN?"

SIXTY-FOUR

The question left him scrambling.

"The multi-billion-dollar facility outside of Geneva, Switzerland, experimenting with particle physics? It's home to the world's largest hadron collider; the one designed to recreate the Big Bang, when energy was first transformed into..."

"Mass. That's right," McCullough said. "You kick-started the whole thing, Trina. After we spoke last, I constructed an algorithm using all our known data and tested it against other probable factors: geography, size, facility, necessary expertise. AI did the rest, eliminating the criteria that didn't fit. Bottom line, CERN hit all the markers. Aerial maps show it as a circle sitting within a triangle or triad; a larger-than-life replica of Mallory's image symbolizing the completion of the Great Work."

Logan sank back against the cushions. "One of the world's most prestigious scientific organizations tampering with the occult?"

"Any scientist worth his mettle knows there's a tipping point; mathematics transcending into the realm of the esoteric. But in truth, most of those on the payroll probably don't have a clue to what's really going on. I'd be willing to bet only a handful have been initiated into the darker agenda. It's safer that way, as you well know."

"All because of a single geographic anomaly?"

McCullough smiled. "Remember all those broken globes? The one in the United Nations? Turns out the U.N. provided much of the financial backing for CERN in the 1950s. Then there's the company logo: a clever juxtaposition of three sixes stacked one on top of another and the biblical sign of the beast; the statue of Shiva, Hindu god of destruction, welcoming visitors and of course, most importantly, their choice of CERN as an acronym.

"CERN stands for the *Conceil Européen Pour la Recherche Nucleaire*; the European Council for Nuclear Research. Remember what I said about the dual nature of alchemy mating science with the occult. Traditionally, Magnum Opus can only be completed upon the summoning of an ancient, supernatural deity; *CERNunnos*...the Celtic god of the underworld, who holds the power of necromancy, the ability to raise the dead, in his hands."

He looked away, and I sensed he was still hedging, trying to get us to come up with the answer on our own when he finally gave up. "Your Holiness, I think that's your cue."

Sirens blared in my head as the pope rose. To quiet them, I focused on the envelope he held in his hand. It crackled like an autumn leaf about to disintegrate, its musty scent reaching across the years to assail our senses. A name, too faded to read, penned in neat, precise cursive, competed with darker smudges, as if those that had held it in the past, had also wept over its contents.

Too late, I decided I didn't want to know anything of Fatima after all.

Logan held out his hand but the pontiff merely smiled and shook his head. "Unless you read Portuguese, it wouldn't do you any good, Mr. O'Neill. I am afraid you will have to make do with my translation."

"The one read publicly years back?"

"A partial truth I won't repeat. In any case, my predecessor did what he believed had to be done at the time. Do not judge too harshly. The words you are about to hear, dictated to Sister Lucia dos Santos by the Blessed Virgin are genuine, confirmed through the expertise of those who make it their business to know such things. I am afraid the only other proof of their authenticity is my admission that they have been seared into my soul and impossible to forget. After you have heard them, I think maybe we will have something in common."

The old man began to speak, his words reduced to a series of emotionless syllables memorized over time, delivered with the ease of someone who recited them even in his sleep; and I knew that just as he'd promised, they were true.

SIXTY-FIVE

Geneva, Switzerland

The faces peering from beneath the cowls were an eclectic mix of old and new, strangers and colleagues. Some, like Chloe Six, convening for the first time as a member of The Council, Hael recognized due to the odd flash off her feet. Others, such as the newly-released former cardinal, was known to him only by reputation and that strange scar embedded in the palm of his hand. Still, despite differences in age, talent, and rank, he agreed they all shared the same expression; a fusion of fear and dumbfounded awe that reduced these astute, ruthless followers of The Old One to the level of idiot sheep.

Even The Slayer, newly-returned from his victory kills, seemed uncharacteristically subdued and avoided his exemplar's questioning gaze. He supposed it was a combination of their alien environment with its irritating, low-frequency hum, the promise of The Summoning, now moments away, and being in the presence of the Almighty Oz.

Hael hid his smirk beneath his own cowl and only half listened as Bertolucci pontificated. The habit must have been hard to break since he'd spent most of his life behind a pulpit, even if it had been a lie. Perhaps the elect were wrong to fear the rusted figurehead they'd elevated to the status of the boogie man. With The Summoning in place, he didn't see why there couldn't be a changing of the guard—after an appropriate amount of time, of course.

Mustn't be impatient. All in all, things were falling into place nicely. Suggesting Chloe for a seat at The Council had been a master stroke. She'd proved more than capable in procuring the required sacrifice when she'd slain her exemplar. Kadzik, himself, had conveniently taken care of Langford, and The Slayer had wielded his blades on Gandini and Pearce Rhomer with his usual happy abandon. Hael shivered in delight. So much for legend. Obviously, being a paragon of virtue and integrity had its limits.

That left only two loose ends: McCullough, who'd taken an unexpected leave of absence more than two weeks ago, and whose whereabouts, despite his best intel, still remained unknown, and O'Neill, who'd disappeared after his girlfriend's demise and was probably drowning in a bottle of whiskey this very hour. Annoying but nearly over. Before long, both men would reappear, Scaevus would complete his mission despite Kadzik's meddling, and Bertolucci would be off his back for a while.

Speaking of which...

The spotlight on the old man shifted, shrouding him in darkness while illuminating an enormous bronze behind him. Half man, it sat cross legged, a snake in one hand, a torc symbolizing mastery over its minions, in the other. Half beast, the horns sprouting from its misshapen head branched out in a lavish display of power and dominance.

"Many of you recognize our mascot," The Caretaker's disembodied voice rose above the vibrating whine. "Some know him as Cernunnos, others Baphomet, Lucifer, Shiva, and Horus. It matters not for he has been known by many names throughout the untold centuries. What is important is that you recognize him as our master builder; the very reason we gather here tonight, joining our colleagues throughout the world. Tonight, my brethren, our transformation is fulfilled with the arrival of our long-awaited redeemer."

SIXTY-SIX

F ifty years ago we would not be here," Bertolucci intoned
from atop a platform looking down on his subterranean
kingdom.

"In the old days, we gathered in churches whose rotting
timbers were a tribute to the rotting corpses surrounding them.
Thanks in part to those selfless men and women whose names
can never be uttered but will never be forgotten, this has changed
forever. Behold your new church; one that will never decay and
bears witness to mankind's true destiny through his own genius;
its rare metals, not merely a foundation for its walls, but a portal
by which we are guaranteed eternal life. Not one of servitude and
indignity promised by the Great Deceiver, but the life of a god
who is meant to rule, to subjugate the weak and feeble who beg
for our direction. Kneel brethren and prepare to welcome your
liberator."

Though Bertolucci knew the elect clung to his words, he wondered if they truly understood their significance, their raw reality. But for a few old timers like himself, he didn't think so. They would've had to be there at the beginning, crawled out of the slime alongside him to appreciate the scope of their success. What did they know of the dangers, the constant threat of discovery. What did they know about the tactics of The Enemy; the barriers littering their path, sometimes in the most unexpected of ways.

The incident rose out of the past in the usual manner; without warning, like a tropical fever rearing its ugly head at the oddest of times. He'd only been a neophyte then, hiding behind those rotting timbers; an underling whose task was to symbolically torch the old age in order to usher in the new. While that one, single event had pitched his world upside down, it had also given him purpose and a goal. Tonight, at long last, the goal was realized.

Had he been capable of shedding tears, Bertolucci would've sobbed.

SIXTY-SEVEN

June, 1963
The Vatican Grottoes

He bit his lip to hide his helpless grin.

Nothing, absolutely nothing, could be allowed to ruin the solemnity of this great event. In his never-to-be-humble opinion, the Clementine Chapel, known in earlier centuries as the chapel of St. Peter, as it was squeezed directly between the public basilica above and the saint's tomb in the ruins of the ancient Roman streets below, had never looked more impressive.

Following the instructions that no electric lights were to be used, a dim glow from dozens of long, black wax tapers encircled the altar and illuminated the priceless graffiti along the walls and ceiling; the frescoed images of man mingling with the divine, coming alive as the flames quivered to the constant draft and rhythmic hum of those gathered.

On this most auspicious night, the small alcove had been modified in other ways as well. Required items had been brought in; others, removed, all under the veil of secrecy. As tiresome as that had been considering the great care with which this had to be accomplished, it was necessary since the location had never before been used for this esteemed purpose and, of course, the location was prime.

More than just a bridge between the old world order and the new, it was also a symbol of the countless years of meticulous planning and sacrifice; a testament to those who had labored invisibly just beneath the mask of public approval, paying lip service to One while bowing to another.

The presiding high priest—masquerading as a prince of the Church in his other life—had likened it to a book whose middle pages were stuck together altering the essence of the story, changing its meaning as the reader read on, perfectly oblivious.

Right here, right now, he and his brethren were changing everything; writing a new chapter that might not be completed in their lifetimes, but essential to the outcome nonetheless.

Gratified, he felt a painful swelling of pride in his chest and steeled himself for what was coming, since it would either render tonight an absolute success or an abysmal failure.

His eyes narrowed to the single, white consecrated Host resting on the black linens before the high priest and resisted the overwhelming urge to spit on it. This was what they labored against, he and his brethren. This ridiculous wafer; a symbol for a God that was as dead as his vows and any misplaced emotion he may have harbored for Him once.

While he joined the shrouded figures flanking the steps of the altar, their chanting rising to a crescendo, his real focus was on the voices emanating from the crude speaker connecting them by a simple telephone line to the other side of the globe.

In a small, out-of-the-way chapel in the wilds of the American

South, another thirteen had gathered without whom it would have been impossible to complete the ritual.

On command, the high priest in that other world began his last appeal; in this, the city of the dead, The Necropolis, his twin did the same, synchronizing his words across the miles, the endless hours of practice making it a simple thing to keep pace with the other.

As much as he would have liked for them to complete the entire ritual under the dome of St. Peter, there were certain acts even his high-ranking exemplars considered too risky. Faced with how to overcome this dilemma, they had devised a new plan. That faraway chapel would employ a doppelganger; a physical representation that would link them forever with the spiritual sacrifice they offered here tonight. Not quite as satisfying, maybe, but still potent and effective as they were about to prove.

The climax was upon them. Voices rose in hypnotic frenzy on both sides of the Atlantic.

The speaker cracked and hissed with static, but neither man nor machine could completely obliterate another sound in the background; the sob of a child—young enough to possess the virtue of innocence, old enough to understand the honor and prestige of being selected as the perfect victim.

The prelate's mouth twisted into a gaping maw, aping the hunger gnawing at his own gut.

Connected through their unholy alliance, time and distance merged through the long centuries into this single moment. Moving deliberately, the prelate's fingers closed around the handle of a relic, while on another continent, his twin mirrored each of his movements with laser precision. He gripped the dagger firmly, drawing it up over his head and plunged the tip of the ancient blade of the Roman, Longinus, through the center of the Host.

Recognizing himself in both this high priest and the other, Bertolucci's eyes darkened into wondrous pools of black. More himself than ever, he felt the actions of the high priest as if they were his own.

A piercing cry of abject pain broke through the satisfied sighs and groans of the witnesses and Bertolucci watched the prelate shudder in one endless spasm of relief.

Lost in his own euphoria, it was a few moments before he realized the gasps of ecstasy around him had turned to shock. Drawn by the others' fixed stares, he turned to look and felt a nameless horror creeping through his veins.

Directly below him, the union of white Host upon black fabric was marred by a burst of crimson. Not the cheerful red of a valentine or a bouquet of exquisite roses—but the dark, nearly black plum to which cardiovascular surgeons were subjected each time they penetrated a patient's chest cavity.

"Complete the incantation!" the prelate snapped, quickly ending the growing murmurs with a single glare.

"What's wrong? What's happened?" a voice crackled through the lines.

"Nothing of consequence. Has the sacrifice been offered?"

"It has been accomplished." The satisfied tone, impossible to miss, was followed by a small pause. "And yours?"

"Ye...yes. Of course. The One who sat upon the throne has been vanquished. The world is Rome; Rome is the world. The dawning of a new power shall rule Rome, brother."

"Then it has begun and only one thing remains," the voice advised.

Well versed in what needed to be done to seal the dark covenant,

Bertolucci followed the prelate's movements as the man picked up the bleeding Host by two fingers and dropped it into a small bowl. Sharing the high priest's revulsion, he swallowed bile, knowing that if it were him, he would have rather plunged his hands into a mess of squirming maggots, and nearly missed his exemplar's signal.

While the others watched, eyes large as saucers, Bertolucci approached the altar carrying a lighted taper, appalled when his fingers trembled. He hesitated for a moment, then dipped the flame towards the Host and ignited it, gratified when it sputtered like any other ordinary wafer, then watched until every last speck had been consumed and reduced to ash.

A measure of calm returned to him, aided by the spitting roar of the inferno taking place in the Carolinas. He conjured up the proper visuals to match the sound effects.

Regardless of the unexpected, distasteful glitch, there was no doubt they had succeeded tonight. The Roman Church had been infiltrated; its cell walls injected with a cancer that would spread through its body eventually killing it. It was the beginning of a new era. The era of The Quickening which, though long and laborious, would give rise to The Summoning, when humanity would learn to accept its true savior.

Yet in some indefinable way that beaded his forehead with sweat and resisted his attempts to leave the scene of the ritual some two hours after the coven had stolen away—something had been ruined for him.

"You're dead...You hear me! You're dead!"

Though the echo of his rant lasted only a moment, falling on ears that had long since lost the ability to hear anything, he now suspected something terrible. For as long as he lived, not a day would go by where he wouldn't repeat those words over and over in his head, trying to convince himself they were true. Whatever the cost, he would make it his life's mission.

SIXTY-EIGHT

The Vatican

My daughter,
Humanity has now entered its final hour of Divine Mercy. Draw near and immerse yourself within it. The war about to unfold is merely a shadow of worse conflicts to come, each one multiplied endlessly by unimaginable atrocity. And yet these things are but a prelude to the grave deception that will be set before you. The smoke of Satan has wormed its way into my Son's Church, perverting the hearts of the very men entrusted with its truths. The result will be souls too weakened to resist the lies of the Evil One and his disciples, sowing the rebellion of nature itself. The energumens will use the power of your star to usher in an insidious force: one that draws ever nearer to you, called through the blasphemous technology prepared to open a portal between worlds. Take care it remains sealed, for once the abomination is loosed, it becomes the door to my Son's wrath. Though heaven weeps, God is allowing this as justice for a world bursting with

the fruit of its own corruption. If you do not enter through the door of His Mercy, you will enter through the door of His Justice, for in the end, they are one and the same."

A hush enveloped the pope's chambers as he uttered the final words in a weak voice. My own strength ebbed as something close to grief poured over me.

I thought of the broken globe outside the pope's window, advertising to the masses what must have been known to science and religion for at least a couple of generations, the extent of the lie perpetrated on humanity.

I thought of Pearce speculating on the possible meanings of the labyrinth and triangle—and then to Aberto, theorizing about the genetic composition of evil, unwittingly giving us our answer with his lecture about ancient monsters, the esoteric meaning of shapes and numbers—and took it a step further; to where McCullough had been leading us all along with his talk of alchemy, sulfuric symbols, transmutations, and finally figured it out.

The elixir of life wasn't a potion—it was a being.

"Then Pearce was wrong," I said, rising slowly. "This was never about a *spiritual* awakening. Why don't you call The Summoning by its real name? Incarnation! A physical incarnation or birth, and together, the labyrinth and triad form the birth canal ushering in this entity."

I felt Logan's hand sliding around my waist and shrugged it away. I didn't want to be comforted—just contradicted.

"Is this true?" he asked, eyes shifting frantically between the two men.

Seconds ticked by as we waited for a nod of the head, a dismissal. Anything. After the first few, confirmation was no longer necessary.

I sat back down and waited for the onslaught, curious as to how it might manifest, slightly disappointed when it didn't. The pontiff's apartment remained intact, clumps of hair didn't litter the floor, and there were no dents in the walls. Last month had conditioned me well.

"So this Cernunnos or whatever-the-hell it calls itself..." Logan murmured. "What is this creature supposed to be?"

McCullough exhaled heavily. "I believe you just answered your own question."

It took a moment for it to sink in.

"That's impossible."

But I knew better. Those on the path no longer had to rely on their secret rituals to link them with hell because hell was coming to us. And the triad and labyrinth were the highway to and from hell, designed to give once-spiritual beings substance and physical form.

The devil was coming to town and the chosen ones were lining up to receive his ultimate offering.

Immortality.

I understood why McCullough had qualified his statement on the elixir of life. This one would be bought and paid for with the blood of humanity.

SIXTY-NINE

April 20
Geneva, Switzerland

In a matter of minutes, the discordant hum reached fevered pitch. A collective sigh emanated from the elect as the lights dimmed, illuminating a quartz floor undulating in milky opalescence. Growing in both size and intensity, the liquid-like beam crept towards the triangular walls and continued its upward sweep, eventually engulfing even the ceiling.

While the others gazed upon this modern miracle in rapt wonder, Hael averted his eyes to the only possible safe haven; the still form of The Caretaker, still perched silent and nearly invisible upon his pedestal; his eyes, a paradox of shrewd watchfulness and boredom within the gloom.

Given his exceptional psychic abilities, Hael felt the subtle drop in pressure before glimpsing the shift through his peripheral vision. He knew the initial phase was complete and sensed the strange energy pulsing forward to the center of the chamber; a push and pull that tested its environment as it advanced on the miles of coiled, transparent tubing rising into the air, dwarfing the elect gathered below.

At first glance, the three-dimensional mass of tight loops and twists appeared chaotic, random; a creation befitting any museum of modern art. A closer look revealed a vertical labyrinth, its engineered swirls and eddies geometrically perfect but dead, waiting for the encroaching beam of energy to give it blood.

Hael staggered, fighting both vertigo and the sudden need to retch. Focusing on The Caretaker was proving difficult with the transformation taking place out of the corner of his eye.

The structure was changing, its skeletal guts blurring into a gelatinous form that defied even the genius that had borne it.

Something primordial reared up through the muck before sinking back into it. Something huge and grossly misshapen that poked fun at the term humanoid and only hinted of its bronze likeness.

Hael recognized it, was intimately acquainted with it, and filled his lungs with its putrescence, even as he resisted the urge to look. He didn't have to *see* to know it had crossed untold distances and dimensions to get here, that it was the first of its kind and that many more would soon follow on its heels, hungering for delicacies only hinted at by the Jeffrey Dahmers of the world.

Staunchly focused on The Caretaker, Hael blinked, then blinked again, wondering why the darkness had chosen this moment to deceive him and then decided perhaps it wasn't the darkness that was to blame but the man cocooned within it. The weathered face of Father Luca Bertolucci—priest, spokesman for the sciences, and warden of the The Summoning—slipped a little, revealing his best and truest self and Hael trembled.

The Caretaker's head twitched, convulsing as he consumed his share of the energy coming off the labyrinth. Hael decided it was only right since he belonged to it somehow.

Flaccid, sagging skin boiled and bubbled as the entity clawing its way to the surface raged for dominion. It paved the way for what appeared serpentine and vaguely phosphorescent, its lifeless gaze the one remaining feature making it recognizable as The Caretaker. If the eyes were windows into the soul, his were proof he'd never had one.

Oblivious to the frenzied screams of the elect, Hael wanted to look away but understood the futility of such a thing. There was nowhere left to look and—the thought took him by surprise— nowhere to hide. None. Not a single point of refuge on a planet bearing the scars of its past invaders in suffering silence but that would not, could not survive the raping that was coming. That was here.

The last to fall to his knees, Hael did so now, the cry in his throat lost among all the other cries of supplication, and worshipped.

SEVENTY

April 20—Easter Sunday
The Vatican

Take as long as you need," the Holy Father assured as Logan and I made our way out of the pope's apartments towards the gardens.

Take as long you need?

When time was a dwindling commodity and the threat of cosmic Armageddon the least of our worries? What would hell unleashed look like in a world already wading waist-deep through a different type of fire?

Without the noise and bustle of tourists, the fragrance of spring blooms arranged in neat beds rode easily on the early morning stillness. Rather than calming, I found them sickeningly sweet, overpowering, forcing something hard and raw to the surface. Having existed so long in a state of constant fear and danger, I'd buried it deep within where it had simply lain dormant until now.

Anger swelled inside; a rush of loathing for what had been done to me, to my life and those around me. To my baby. The supreme injustice of it all. The waste.

Logan heard the moan escape my lips. He turned, questioning me silently. Unable to speak, I merely shook my head and walked away, his disappointment and hurt sticking to me like sweat. Alone at last, I allowed my thoughts free rein.

Fury was here to stay, I decided; the most recent addition to my already-overstuffed emotional baggage. And once more I'd have to adopt it, make peace with it; take off the old man and put on the new. But how? Maddeningly, awareness of what I was supposed to do didn't provide the means.

Defeated, I beat it back to the papal apartments as the sun made its slow crawl over the city and joined Logan, already waiting stiffly beside the pontiff.

The Holy Father slumped, staring at the floor as if he couldn't bear to witness the desolation written across my face.

"Perhaps you will say I ask too much. Yet I pray that as you shoulder the burden of this knowledge throughout your days, you will not think too unkindly of me for placing it there. It is, after all, only upon your request that I have done so. And now, I must be even bolder and ask if you have an answer to my invitation. Have you chosen your path?"

He looked up suddenly, startling me with his clear gaze. Though I caught fleeting glimpses of doubt and weariness, I also recognized curiosity and a certain acceptance mingled with deep-seated peace.

Whatever legacy history and the world finally prescribed to this man, he'd already come to terms with it. I suspected that having practiced for it over a lifetime, death, when it came for him, had at least a fair chance of being sweet and envied him.

Could I do the same in light of mankind's imminent

annihilation? I didn't possess the magic formula for coming to terms with anyone's destruction let alone my own or Logan's. Didn't bother adding Pearce to the growing list of casualties dropping like flies in my wake. Didn't have the slightest illusion that accepting the pontiff's invitation meant I'd be offering up my head on the chopping block again.

My answer came unexpectedly as Logan's fingers curled around mine, silencing the tremors that had begun with the first of McCullough's revelations.

Could either of us go back to our old lives, pretending the world was normal and the last month never happened? Pretending we never happened? Logan's earlier question to me nagged with increasing persistence.

What did it matter if we had a single day together or an entire lifetime? Ten lifetimes wouldn't be enough but I'd take what was offered; all of it, and gladly pay the price later, for I finally understood what Pearce and Aberto both had been telling me.

It was an all or nothing deal.

The good with the bad, the painful with the sublime. Life in the midst of death. Nothing more, nothing less, that nonetheless held the chance of sweetness at the end—if you worked it right.

That elusive notion of possibilities I'd glimpsed a lifetime ago stood out stark in its simplicity and this time it didn't run from me.

Or perhaps, it had been there all along and I was finally ready to face it. Now it offered an invitation to join; to hitch a ride into a different type of abyss that was neither empty nor finite but teemed with everything there ever was and ever could be.

I squeezed Logan's hand and turned, gazing unflinchingly into his eyes.

"The answer is yes, Your Holiness. Yes. To everything."

When I managed to tear myself away from Logan's shining face, the expression in the old man's eyes had changed once again. And this time—I saw hope.

RESURRECTION

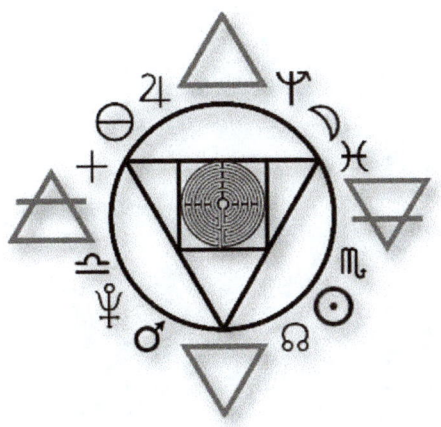

APRIL 21

Outside El Paso, Texas

The church and its adjacent buildings appeared to have been snuffed out of existence. Aided by a cloudy night and the shattered, motion-activated security lights in the compound and along its perimeter, the walls loomed deep and heavy against the paler black of the horizon.

As oppressive as it felt, the atmosphere indoors was worse. With the sanctuary candle beside the tabernacle extinguished, perfect darkness competed with a stale, sour humidity that lingered like rotten meat buzzing with insects.

Kneeling by the foot of the altar, Pearce Rhomer understood why and grieved even before the clouds dissipated and moonlight filtering through stained glass illuminated the ragged mass stretched out before him.

Unable to speak in his eagerness to right the unspeakable wrong, he automatically reached for one of the crude railroad spikes defiling the matted, sticky fur absent its tag, and felt a restraining hand on his shoulder.

"Don't."

The voice was firm but compassionate.

"I can't leave him like this."

"You must."

"I have to bury him. It's the least I can do."

"Courage, Father. Take those nails out, disturb this scene in any way and all our efforts will have been wasted. They'll know you're alive."

"Is that supposed to mean something?"

"It does to me and one day it will to you too. Or have you forgotten the risk I and others in the SIV took dragging you out of that hospital before those vipers could finish you off? Contrary to what you believe, you're not just a pawn to be sacrificed early in the game."

Pearce stood and turned towards Heinrich Weismann, whose long, thin face appeared almost gaunt in the silvery beams. "So you've said. But what of those who risked everything and died as a result?"

The older priest and scholar gazed at the impaled form before them with watery eyes.

"What we've both lost is not in question. Aberto was my friend as well. The only one I trusted with my work before it was destroyed, and now even that solace has been taken from me. Yet be assured, it's just the start. Much more will be required of all of us in the coming days. In the meantime, take comfort in knowing that at least some of your friends are safe."

"I've wondered about that. Was it really a kindness or a curse, slipping away without a word, allowing Logan and Trina to think the worst? They may be safe now, but for how long? I've never been afraid to die, but losing my friends like this, one at a time, at the hands of this unspeakable evil...that's something else and intolerable."

"All the more reason to retrieve what we came for before whoever did this comes back. And so we're clear, you would do well to neither underestimate the skill and courage of your friends, nor the importance of staying alive in order to fight another day."

Seconds ticked by as Pearce considered Weismann's words. Then abruptly, he motioned for the priest to follow him out of the desecrated church, towards the muted structures behind it.

Keeping to the shadows, they went around the back of the modest building Pearce had called home up until a month ago. Moments later, they paused, eyes adjusting to the darkened kitchen, and headed for the stone hearth in the living area.

Working only by the natural light streaming through the windows, Pearce counted off the river rock left to right, grasped the seventh by its smooth edge, and tugged. Different from the others as it had never been cemented, it popped out easily and he reached into the hollow hidden behind it and pulled out a small bundle wrapped in cloth.

"It's still there," Weismann whispered, watching as Pearce unfolded the fabric in his palm, exposing the article in question.

"Why shouldn't it be? I told you, after Mallory was locked up and the tribunal was deliberating our fates, Aberto and I decided to keep a couple things to ourselves. While he held on to the actual video testimony of the exorcism, I kept the one item that made it so remarkable. I placed it here almost six years ago and never once looked at it. To be honest, I was hoping I'd never have to."

Pearce stared at the silver crucifix gleaming brightly in the filtered moonlight, felt the low-level, electrically-charged vibration through the cloth, and nearly threw it back into the cavity.

"You're sure we need to bring it with us?"

"I wouldn't have risked returning here if I didn't. May I hold it?"

"Better not. Even now it feels alive somehow. No need exposing you until we're ready," Pearce mumbled, folding the fabric over the crucifix once more and cramming the parcel into a pocket of his leather jacket. "With its history, never know what might happen."

"And yet, this is precisely why we must have it," Weismann explained, watching as Pearce fitted the rock back into the fireplace. He hurried to keep up with him as he retraced their steps out of the house.

"Whether you like it or not, what happened to all of you in that flat so long ago was a turning point. This thing you possess is no longer just a symbol. It's a weapon in the war that lies ahead of us. A very powerful one, I suspect."

"I hope you're right Father, because neither Aberto nor Teufel deserved any of this," Pearce said, pausing to look at the darkened church one last time.

"The truth is, I really don't care whether it's a crucifix or my bare hands that destroys this monster. As long as at the end of the day, the monster is dead."

The quiet words hung in the air long after the two men vanished into the night towards the Rio Grande; the promise they carried, waiting to be fulfilled like the point of a knife balanced precariously on edge.

The Beginning

Writing may be a solitary endeavor but research and editing are not. I owe the following individuals a huge debt of gratitude for their generosity, kindness and immense knowledge.

Author Larry Fowler

Author Ben Davidson

Father Malachi Martin

Exorcist Father Chad Ripperger

Although *Dominion* is a work of fiction, precaution has been taken to ensure the accuracy of the historical, scientific and theological information contained herein. The author, publisher and those individuals listed above assume no responsibility for any errors or omissions. No liability is assumed for damages that may result from the use of information contained within.

Ad Majorem Dei Gloriam

Go to
tjfalco.com

for a special sneak peek of

DOMINION SONG

THE ENERGUMEN CHRONICLES II

Thank you for joining us on this journey through the
shadows and mysteries of *Dominion -- ECI.*
If you enjoyed your adventure with Trina and the dark
forces she contends with, please consider leaving a review.
Your feedback not only supports the author but also helps
other readers discover some real-world enigmas woven into
the narrative. Share your thoughts on Amazon, Goodreads,
or your favorite book review site. Thank you for your
support and keep the pages turning!